Foothold

Book Two of Reaching out of the Shadows
by Mannah Pierce

1

Rae scampered along the service duct. He had three thoughts: track Jax; stay hidden; be on Scar's ship when it left.

The three men in the corridor above him were walking too fast to be carrying two pods. Rae was pretty sure that one of them, probably Scar, had Jax slung over his shoulder. Being unconscious, on his belly and with his head hanging down would explain the way Jax's breathing sounded.

It was easy at first. The ducts followed the corridors. Then the duct came to a dead end. There was a grille. Rae peered through. It was a shaft with a ladder.

Boots appeared and he pulled back. It was the man carrying Jax. Rae inhaled deeply; imprinting the man's scent into his consciousness. Another man followed, carrying Noe. After him came a third.

Rae breathed more shallowly as the second and third man passed. He wanted to follow the first one, not the second or third. The first man was carrying Jax.

Once they had gone he crept forward and investigated the grille. It was unlocked and hinged. Rae shut his eyes: concentrating on listening; making himself wait until the men left the ladder before opening it.

A glance up and down; the shaft was empty. Rae moved: out of the duct and onto the ladder; down at a steady speed; holding his breath each time he passed an opening; stopping at the first rung that did not smell of the man's sweat.

This had to be the corridor they had taken. Rae pricked his ears and took a lungful of air. Yes, this was the way they had gone.

There was a grille from the shaft into a duct under the corridor, just like the level above. Rae scampered along it, closing the gap between him and Jax.

This level was a lot noisier and, as they continued along the corridor, busier. Rae's confidence started to evaporate. The ship they were on was much bigger than he had thought; more like a small spacestation than a ship like the Willow.

It might have a docking bay. If it did, that was where Scar's ship would be. Trouble was, a docking bay would be completely separate from the big ship, because they were depressurised before the smaller ship was launched.

How was he going to get into the docking bay and then onto the ship?

He risked catching up; with all the noise purebreds should not hear him. Someone else had joined the group; there were four men rather than three.

"Is the Talon ready to go?" the first man asked.

Having heard him speak, Rae was sure that the man carrying Jax was Scar.

"Yes, Captain Scar," the new person answered, confirming Rae's deduction. "Fully fuelled and provisioned."

"And the crew?"

"Most of them. There are a few stragglers."

"Anyone we can't lift without?"

There was a short pause. "Medico Kem has yet to arrive. He has reported in and is on his way."

Scar growled. "If he wasn't so good at his job…" He trailed off, leaving Rae wondering what Scar did to people who disobeyed him. "We launch as soon as he is aboard. I want everyone at their stations and I want the docking bay evacuated so we're ready to go. Kem'll have to come aboard suited, along with any others who make it in time. Make sure someone is ready to give them suits and instructions."

"Will do, captain."

That sounded hopeful, which was good because that was when his luck with the duct ran out. There was a junction and no duct going the way Jax went; Rae guessed Scar and the other men had crossed the threshold of the docking bay.

Then there was a siren and a booming voice. *"Docking bay prepare for depressurisation. Depressurisation will begin in three minutes. Leave the docking bay or suit up."*

He was wearing a suit.

Rae went back along the duct to the last junction, listened and followed the duct under the quietest corridor. Then he was out through the next hatch cover and walking back along the corridor towards the docking bay at a purebred's pace, raising his helmet to hide his ears and fur.

"Docking bay prepare for depressurisation. Depressurisation will begin in one minute. Doors are closing. If you are not in a suit, leave the docking bay."

Rae had not allowed for the doors closing before depressurisation started. He closed the access points on his suit, shut his faceplate and started to run.

He made it just as the doors started to close.

The docking bay was deserted; Rae guessed that everyone was on the ship, which looked about the size of the Willow. He ducked behind what could be a crane and waited, listening to his suit adapting as the air pressure dropped.

At least he was on the right side of the door; Jax's side. If it came to it, he could cling to the outside of the ship.

Then a light over a much smaller door next to the big doors started flashing; it was an airlock and it was cycling. The light went blue and the door opened. Out stepped one...two... three...people in suits.

Rae had to decide if he should join them and bluff his way onto the ship. It was risky but it had to be better than trying to cling to the hull.

The first two men sprinted towards the open airlock. The third was trying to do the same but he was carrying three large cases and making a hash of it, first dropping one and then another.

Rae was moving before realising that he had made the decision. He picked up the case that was currently on the floor and walked towards the ship.

The third man followed.

The airlock was the same size as the smaller one on the Willow. Getting four people and three large cases in was tight and the cases had to be piled one on top of the other. Being crammed together gave Rae an excuse to be between the cases and the wall where eye contact with the others was impossible. No one prodded him, touched helmets or tried to plug a communication cable into his suit. He could sense the other people's agitation; they were shifting from foot to foot. Rae imagined them thinking about Scar and how cross he was going to be that they had delayed launch.

He needed a diversion, so the men would not see where he went. The latches for the top case's lid were less than a hand's span from his nose. Reaching up, he flipped them open.

The light went from red to blue, the inner door of the airlock opened and the first two men jumped out, ran to a ladder and started climbing upwards. The third man went to pull the top case from the pile and, as Rae had hoped, the lid fell open scattering the contents across the floor.

The man crouched down to pick them up and Rae took his chance. He shot out of the airlock towards the shaft, opening his faceplate on the way. Jumping onto the ladder, he slid down; if the ship was anything like the Willow, there would be fewer people at the tail end.

Three levels down he took his first deep breath. The level that was hydroponics on the Willow smelt like a badly kept, over-crowded crewroom. He could no longer smell Jax and there were only faint, stale traces of Scar's scent.

He scrambled back up the ladder, deciding to hide on the second level down from the airlock. On the Willow, all parts of that level were well over one gee; patches were as high as five. In Rae's experience, purebreds avoided places where the gravitational field was high.

Sure enough, it was a storage hold. Like on the Willow, the storage crates were piled floor to ceiling and wedged tight. Rae looked about for a hiding place. At the moment all that mattered was being out of sight but that would change once the Talon undocked and switched on her gravitational field generators. Then there would be places that were five gee, maybe higher.

To his relief someone had painted parts of the floor red; Rae guessed they were the dangerous bits.

Then the ship started moving. Rae was momentarily weightless and then there was an ominous rumble. It sounded a bit like the Willow's lateral rockets only much, much louder. Then it was as if the floor was pushing up on the soles of his feet. He just managed to lie down before it felt like six men were sitting on his chest. It was all he could do to breathe.

Scar was using rockets to accelerate the Talon.

Rae told himself that it would have to stop soon; no ship carried that much rocket fuel. The floor was hard; it felt like his bones were bending. At least his suit gave his neck and spine some support.

Then, thankfully, it no longer felt like six big men were sitting on his chest and a small push sent him floating away from the floor; they were in free fall.

A siren, three short bursts, and he was upside down and being slammed into what had been the ceiling. A twist and he managed to turn his landing into a roll. Then he crawled to a place between stacks where the gravitational field was lower; less than two gee.

They had activated the ship's gravitational field generators.

He curled up for a while, recovering.

After a while he took a few sips of water and began searching his suit for food, finding a high energy bar in a thigh pocket. Breaking the wrapper, he gave an exploratory sniff. It wasn't as bad as those he used to steal in Carrefour. He bit in, regretting leaving his backpack with Kip, but then he shook himself; Kip would look after his stuff and Rae was better at finding food than Kip would be.

What next? The Talon was like the Willow; there was no network of service ducts large enough for him to crawl through. No, he would have to wait for ship's night. He checked the chronometer built into his suit and tried to remember how to set an alarm. A few false starts and he worked it out.

He would sleep now and look for Jax later.

Kip lay in the duct, staring at the place Rae had been. Questions cascaded through his mind, each generating a multitude of possible answers, all of them terrifying. Soon every part of his mind was yammering with fear.

Then he remembered Tre's lesson. This was like getting into his suit. Kip grabbed the panic, thrust it into a corner of his mind and slammed down a partition, creating some space to think.

Rae was doing what he did best. Kip would do the same; he would find a way to hack the ship's systems.

Usually the outer edges of any ship were less busy than the core. Kip decided to crawl in a straight line until he came to a dead end. It would be safer there than here, which would be one of the first places they started looking if Rae was discovered.

There wasn't much space. It would be easier without his suit but there wasn't enough room to get out of it.

He backed up to where they had entered the duct; there was enough room there to turn around.

The backpacks were where they had left them. He tied the straps to his left ankle and set off, slow but steady, trying to make as little noise as possible.

The layout appeared logical, which was promising. The main ducts, the ones big enough for him to crawl through, were set out as a grid. They were lit; the light level was similar to ship's night. At regular intervals there were smaller ducts, too narrow for him, that carried services to individual rooms.

Kip could see pipes and cables. He wanted to stop and investigate but was determined to reach a dead end first.

There wasn't one. Instead he found himself at a T junction rather than a crossroad. Having decided that this was as far as he was going to go, Kip settled down to begin work.

The cables were of types he recognised. They were even colour-coded, which was nice. He could see a data cable, suggesting that they used a hardwired network, or at least had one. There was a junction box right there, which meant that he didn't have to cut a wire, which was good because interrupting the data flow might draw attention.

Within five minutes he was wearing his goggles and studying a plan of the ship, the Maul, overlaid with a map of the data network. He risked a tiny ping and located his position; at the outer edge of level C+3.

The ship was a five layer 175-hex-eight-6, so she had five separate gravitational field arrays spaced nine levels apart. She was five times longer than the Willow and about four times as wide; big. Kip was three levels above the third gravitational field generator array.

Further investigation confirmed that this was not a busy level, which was good. It was a 'mission level' rather than an 'operational level', a 'supplies level' or a 'residential level'. From what Kip could glean within a few minutes, 'a mission level' was kept empty so that it could be used for the purpose of the current 'mission'.

Kip guessed the current mission was getting Jax, delivering him to the client and making sure there weren't any witnesses. That didn't require a whole level. It appeared to only need a room for the pods and some guards, especially now that Scar had taken Jax.

That left a lot of empty rooms; maybe he could use one.

Not yet though; it would be far too risky and there were more urgent matters. Top of his list was finding out what was happening and second was getting a message out there in case someone, probably Tre, was in a position to respond to it.

It turned out that the crew of the Maul weren't into data collection. They had sensors but they mainly used the live feeds; they didn't record much so there wasn't a lot for Kip to review. All he managed to establish was that Scar's ship, the Talon, was on its way to Verdant and that the Willow had been destroyed.

They had recorded the Willow's destruction, perhaps to provide the client with proof that they had done as instructed. Kip watched. It made him angry. How dare these strangers, these mercenaries, these pirates, destroy the home Ean had built for them?

After that he gave up on looking for information and switched to working out how to send a message to Tre. The best starting point had to be whatever signal the beacons in the pods were giving out.

A quick check confirmed that the pods didn't seem to have beacons or to be broadcasting any signals. Kip expected that. They were loaded with stealth technology so that no one but Tre could find them. Unfortunately no amount of stealth technology had stopped someone watching them being ejected and picking them up.

Kip kept looking; there was no way Tre didn't have a way of tracking Jax's pod.

By the time he had found it and worked out a way to mimic it, Kip was stiff, tired, thirsty, hungry and desperate for a pee. Peeing outside his suit didn't seem like a good idea when he was trying to hide. The only sensible option was to connect his penis to the tube that led to a reservoir in his suit.

It was even trickier when stuck in a service duct; Kip silently thanked Ean for insisting he practised.

Resealing his suit, he looked for a meal bar. There were plenty in Rae's pack. He ate half of one and had a few mouthfuls of water from the bottle built into his suit.

Then he pushed on, modulating the signal to carry data and sending his message. He did not bother to encode it. If anyone was skilled enough to find the pods' signal hidden in the background radiation, they wouldn't be slowed down by any code simple enough for Tre to decipher.

Tre had watched the Willow explode, partly because the death of such a fine ship should have a witness but mostly to make sure that there was no potentially lethal shrapnel heading in his direction.

Then he activated and boosted his suit's receiver. Once his inbuilt processor had filtered the pods' signals out of the background radiation he would be able to track Jax's pod.

Instead of an immediate result, a percentage appeared in the lower left corner of his field of view. It was increasing but far too slowly. For a moment he wondered if the suit was malfunctioning.

Then he realised that he was comparing it with the Willow's receiver and processors. The technology in his body and his suit had been cutting edge twenty standards ago. Now it was old fashioned; second rate.

He dared not activate the suit's scanners; that would overload his processor even more.

Instead he used his eyes. He could see three ships, one large and two small, and a sea of debris; wreckage from the Willow and the remains of the small fighters. One of them was arcing across his field of view, split open, with the body of a small hybrid still strapped into the pilot's chair.

Disposable; that was how most people thought of hybrids, particularly ones with fewer human genes like these ones. Maybe, if he was honest, Tre had thought the same way before Rae.

Then he spotted them; the swarm of small, dark, space-suited figures who may have left the Willow to avoid the explosion but who were now on their way back to continue scavenging.

Tre had a bizarre image of them crawling all over him, disassembling his suit.

He selected a trajectory that would take him away from the wreckage but towards the ships. He accelerated slowly and changed direction gradually; if the hybrids' vision was like Rae's they would be hypersensitive to sudden changes in movement.

Even that simple manoeuvre slowed the upward crawl of the numbers towards one hundred.

Watching it wasn't going to speed it up. Tre allowed his mind to wander for a moment only to stop himself; he could not afford to think about Ean. Instead he concentrated on the tactics behind the attack.

He had never heard of pirates who masqueraded as rescuers and had a battalion of undersized hybrids. Given that he went out of his way to research the different types of attack, especially at gates, Tre wondered if they had been imported from another sector specifically for this job.

It was possible, particularly if a mother ship had been sent to fetch them; it had been over two standards since Jax had gone into hiding.

How had they identified the Willow as Jax's hiding place? Noe? Art? Klennethon Darrent? No, not Klennethon Darrent. Klennethon Darrent was going to be annoyed if anything had happened to Kip.

Tre smiled; people who annoyed Klennethon Darrent suffered.

Who was behind the attack? Gil? The Edgers? Another clan? He had no way of knowing.

The numerals were making a sudden push towards the finishing line: ninety-six, ninety-seven, ninety-eight, ninety-nine… The results of the analysis appeared and Tre scanned it eagerly.

Five occupied pods, two unoccupied, all clustered together on the largest ship. None of them contained Jax. Worse, Jax was no longer within one hundred paces of the pod he had been in, because if he had been the beacon would be broadcasting that fact.

The urge to roar, to charge, to destroy, was overwhelming. Tre recognised it for what it was; a surge of adrenaline. He held himself rigid, riding it out; refusing to react until the worst of it had passed.

He decided that there were three possibilities. Firstly, Jax could still be on the ship but there could be shielding between him and the pod, preventing the transponder in his brain operating. Second, he could be in this system but more than one hundred paces away from the pod.

The third possibility was based on the fact that two of the pods had vanished. There had been nine, now there were seven.

The receiver built into his suit was more than adequate. Pods' beacons were activated when they were occupied. Either the pods had been destroyed or they were no longer in this system.

Tre looked in the direction of the gate; Jax and his pod could already be through it.

He speeded up, no longer caring if one of the hybrids spotted him. Either Jax was still on that ship or someone on that ship knew where he had gone.

Halfway between where the Willow had been and the large ship, an extra pod appeared on the display in the lower left of his field of view. It was flashing.

Flashing? His processor had started translating the message from long-short to text before his brain had caught up.

Jax is prisoner on a 14-hex-eight-6 called the Talon, heading for Verdant, to be delivered by a man called Scar to whoever paid the pirates. Noe is with him to be kept not delivered.

A string of numbers followed and then the text message repeated.

It had to be Kip. Tre was confident no one else could have sent him a message that way.

Jax and Noe being on a different ship from their pods explained the empty pods if not the vanishing ones. Noe being with Jax was suspicious, particularly if he was to be kept. It suggested that Noe might have history with the pirates.

Tre had not seen the Talon leave, which was puzzling.

He turned his attention to the numbers Kip had sent and quickly worked out that it was information about the Talon's trajectory and progress. Further analysis revealed that it had undocked from the large ship while he had been hiding in the cupboard.

The thought of it made him irrationally angry. He wanted to hunt down the little hybrids one by one and break every bone in their bodies.

A few deep breaths got the worst of it under control. He didn't remember the suit affecting him so badly. He had to focus on following Jax, which was not going to be easy. The Talon was unusually quick. It must have used its rockets; a drive could not accelerate a 14-hex-eight-6 like that, even if the ship's mass was stripped down to a minimum.

A few basic calculations confirmed what Tre had feared. He could not catch up with the Talon. Worse, his suit, despite being designed for travel as well as survival, did not have the range to get to the planet. He could make it to one of the spacestations but it would take ten days and he would have to put himself into stasis for most of the journey to conserve oxygen.

No, he needed a ship, the quicker the better.

By the time he was closing on the smallest of the three ships, Tre had decided that the time for discretion and subtlety was over. So far the sensible approach had only led to a gap between him and Jax that was growing minute by minute.

The ship was ideal. She was small, sleek and she looked fast; more like a yacht than a ship people lived on. He considered the possibility that she was not part of the pirates' flotilla but dismissed it; she was far too near the large ship not to be associated with it.

About one hundred paces distant, he launched a jammer. If detected, which was unlikely given its shielding, it would look like debris. At worst it would be used as target practice.

The occupants appeared oblivious to its approach. Once the jammer was within three paces of the hull it began broadcasting.

Tre waited until it was attached to the hull to begin sniping. The small calibre, high velocity, ultra-hard rounds pierced the hull in places that should ensure multiple holes in each cabin but minimal damage.

What occurred next would depend on who was aboard. Most spacers would react to multiple breaches in the hull by abandoning ship. They would not even wait long enough to work out what was happening. Spacers who hesitated died.

A few might be more interested in defending the ship. An exceptional tactician, and the pirates obviously had at least one of those among them, might sacrifice the ship in order to eliminate a potential threat.

That was why Tre had risked using the jammer; he did not want someone activating a self-destruct from one of the other two ships.

He saw one, two, three pods leave as he landed near the airlock. Two shaped charges, one larger, one smaller, dealt with the inner and outer doors of the airlock.

They had not even shut the inner blast doors while they evacuated ship.

Five seconds and he was in the control room. The systems were not locked and appeared to be standard. He closed blast doors and deactivated the data network in case there was anyone left on the ship.

Then he set course, activated the drive and fired the rockets.

Once Kip had the message for Tre broadcasting, he went back to collecting data. The ship's live feeds, all forty-two of them, were connected via his interfaces to a dedicated section in his data crystal array. That done, he sorted out a three-by-three, four-deep display for his goggles.

The other five live feeds were sound; a microphone he had managed to activate in the control room, the main intercom and their four most used radio channels.

He connected the control room microphone one of his earpieces, the intercom to the other and the radio channels to his suit radio.

There was a burst of static from one of the speakers in his suit. Kip stopped what he was doing and began analysing that radio signal.

It was from a jammer. It had to be Tre. Kip brought up the live feeds, wishing that the people controlling the detectors were more efficient.

What would Tre do? The answer was obvious. He would steal a ship to follow the Talon. Not this one, it was far too slow.

Only how would the pirates react? Not well; Kip knew that much. At worst they would destroy the stolen ship. At best they would radio the Talon and tell Scar to destroy it.

He had to do something. Problem was, all his efforts so far had been focused on staying hidden and collecting data. He hadn't even considered trying to control the ship.

There wouldn't be time for anything subtle.

There was a panicked voice in his left ear; the earpiece that was connected to the microphone in the control room.

"The commander's yacht is moving away. I can see escape pods. It must have been boarded."

"Calm down!" a steadier voice ordered. *"Open a channel to the Dagger."*

Then there was more of the static, this time via the microphone in the control room.

"Mulligan's teats." The voice sounded less steady now. *"Get me the commander on his private channel. Get the attack rats back into their fighters and on standby."*

Kip didn't know what attack rats were but they sounded bad. Fighters had to be launched. He hacked into system control only to find that only key systems like power and life support were controlled centrally; orders might be given from the control room but they must be implemented locally.

One of the other speakers in his suit activated. *"This is the commander."*

"This is Kurt, commander. Someone has taken control of the Dagger." The voice was steady again.

"Transmit the self-destruct command," the commander ordered. *"The code is eight-five-alpha-two-zeta-nine."*

Kip hadn't thought of that. He should have concentrated on taking out the transmitter. Tre was going to die.

"Radio communications to and from the Dagger have been jammed, commander," Kurt admitted.

Relief washed over him. Tre had thought of it, even if he hadn't. Kip made himself concentrate, exploring different options with the separate layers of his brain. He had to find a way to stop the commander.

"*Get the attack rats into their ships,*" the commander ordered. "*And man the guns.*"

Then Kip thought of it. Nothing on a ship worked without power. Even the drive went into maintenance mode when its electricity supply was interrupted.

"*The first wave of rats will be ready to launch in two minutes,*" Kurt replied. "*Gunners are powering up turret one and five.*"

Kip checked. Yes, he could do it. Only there wasn't time to be selective. He took down all the batteries or none. Everything would be switched off, even life support.

Once the power was down, he would not have the means to reinstate it. People could, probably would, die.

He was in a suit. So was Rae if he was still on board. The others were still in their pods. Kip smashed through the security settings and deactivated all batteries.

The lights went out. The live feeds were cut off one by one. All the vibrations and hums he could feel or hear ceased.

He had killed the ship.

Kip lay there, staring at the inside surface of his goggles.

What had he done?

2

Jax was thrust into consciousness. He recognised the signs; he had been given a wake-up shot. His suit was gone. He was lying on what felt like an examination couch with the head end raised. There was something across his neck, which he refused to admit was frightening.

He made himself stay still, his eyes closed, like his trainers and Tre had taught him.

"Why isn't he waking up?" a deep, rough voice demanded. It was no one he recognised.

"He's awake," a softer, more conciliatory, but equally unfamiliar, voice replied. "He's just being cautious."

He was in the hands of strangers.

He opened his eyes slowly. It was a small infirmary with two examination couches including the one on which Jax was lying. A tall, muscular man with a scar across his throat was sitting on a chair between the two couches. Lurking close to the door, as far away from the scarred man as possible and looking as if he wanted to run, was a smaller man with sandy hair and eyeglasses. On the second couch, the other side of the scarred man, lay Noe; still unconscious.

Jax wished it were Rae on the other couch, not Noe. Belatedly, he realised that he could not move his hands or his feet. He checked. There were wide, leather cuffs attaching his wrists and ankles to the couch. Thinking about it, the strap across his neck felt like leather as well.

The scarred man leaned forward. Jax had to stop himself cowering away. He refused to admit his fear, never mind show it.

"So you are Joaquin Oro Sebastiano Socorro of the Navaja's son," the scarred man stated.

Jax's mind filled with everything he had learnt about the way his father operated. Did this man admire his father or loathe him? He decided to say nothing.

The scarred man's hand came towards him. Jax tried not to tense. A finger traced the line of his chin.

"So pretty," he commented.

Jax managed to stop himself freezing. He heard Tre's voice in his head: stay relaxed; never allow your enemy to read you. Did this man want him? Was he going to poke him? Where was Tre?

"The commander says I cannot have you," the scarred man continued. "You have to be delivered untouched to the client."

It was a relief but Jax tried not to show it. Who was the commander? More importantly, who was the client?

"So he gave me a substitute," the scarred man continued, gesturing towards Noe. He leaned forward and whispered into Jax's ear. "Everything I do to him is something I want to do to you." He leaned back and turned to the other man. "Wake him up. Then get out."

The man with the eyeglasses sidled around the edge of the room and pressed a hypospray to Noe's neck. Then he scuttled out the door.

There was a delay before Noe's eyes opened. Jax could feel the man watching him rather than Noe. He remembered one of his trainers, not Tre, talking about using loved ones in torture situations. Looking away was bad, because it made the torturer do worse things to make you react.

He no longer wished it was Rae on the couch rather than Noe.

Then Noe's eyes fluttered open and Jax felt the man's attention leave him.

"Who are you?" Noe asked in a whisper with huge eyes and a quiver in his voice.

"You can call me Captain Scar," the man answered. He leaned towards Noe. "You are mine now."

Noe gave a tiny whimper and drew back but at the same time his lips parted and his knees moved a little apart.

The man, Scar, groaned slightly and shifted in his chair. His eyes momentarily went back to Jax but Noe made another whimper, this time a little more breathy, and Scar's gaze was drawn back.

It was a standoff. Jax watched; fascinated. Scar was battling to cling to his original plan; the one where he used Noe to get to Jax. Noe was determined that Scar would forget about Jax and only be interested in him. Every time that Scar remembered that Jax was there, Noe would shift his position or make a sound or use those amazing eyelashes.

Then, suddenly, Noe had won. Scar moved. He gathered Noe up, slung him over his shoulder and headed for the door.

As soon as he was over Scar's shoulder, Noe's gaze locked with Jax's. His eyes said, "I have done my part, now it's up to you."

Jax hoped his gratitude showed.

Once the door had shut Jax assessed his surroundings. It looked and felt like a ship or a spacestation. He listened more carefully. He was on a ship. It did not sound very different from the Willow. He searched the room with his eyes. On the wall was a small chronometer; it was evening. Jax focused on the smaller figures displaying the date, intent on finding out how long he had been in stasis. To his surprise it was still the same day; this morning they had all been together on the Willow.

He tried moving his arms. It was hopeless. He shut his eyes to help him think. Maybe he could work on the man with eyeglasses when he returned. Perhaps Noe would find out some useful information.

Given what Scar had said, the ship was on its way somewhere to deliver Jax to someone. He took a few deep breaths. The transfer from Scar to the client would probably be his best chance of escape or, more likely, Tre's best chance to rescue him.

Then the door slid open only there was no one there. For a moment Jax hoped to see Rae's whiskered face peering around the doorjamb but instead it was the man with the eyeglasses.

"Captain Scar left," Jax informed him in what he hoped was a warm and confident voice. "He took Noe with him."

The man slipped into the room and closed the door behind him. He looked at Jax as if he could not quite believe what he was seeing. "Is that the other boy's name? Noe?" he asked cautiously.

"Yes," Jax answered. "I'm Jax."

"Emanuel Rafael Jax Esteban of the Navaja," the man specified, as if reminding himself this wasn't just any lad of thirteen standards. "My name is Kem. Do you need a drink? Or food? Please inform me if you have the urge to urinate or defecate."

Jax wondered how old Kem was; probably in the first half of his fourth decade. His eyeglasses and his choice of language, combined with him being in an infirmary, suggested some medical training. "And how did you come to join the Talon's crew, Medico Kem?" he asked.

The man was motionless for a moment. Then he blinked. "Wrong place, wrong time," he admitted.

Jax tried not to show his delight. Kem was terrified of Scar and it sounded like he had been captured rather than recruited. If Jax could build a relationship, perhaps the medico would help him; as little as looking the other way for a split second could be crucial. "I am thirsty," he said.

Kem was gentle and caring. He lifted the head of the couch higher, so that Jax could drink more easily, and tilted the cup carefully. Jax did not ask for the restraints to be unfastened. Under the circumstances it was an unreasonable request that was more likely to alienate Kem than be successful.

"Do you know what happened to the rest of my crew?" Jax asked.

Kem glanced at the closed door. "I treated one of them on the Maul; a big man who had been knocked senseless and had a cut to his scalp." He pointed to the hairline above his right eye.

It sounded like Vic. Jax remembered Tre ordering Vic out of the engine room. It was good to know that he had made it.

"He was doing fine by the time I left," Kem assured him. "And I think there were others, brought onto the Maul in pods."

Jax guessed that 'Maul' was the name of the other ship. He tried a big-eyed look, like Noe had used but less extreme. "Thank you," he replied. "It helps to know at least some of them survived."

Kem flushed slightly, as if no one had said anything so nice to him in a long time.

By the time ship's night was approaching Jax had made considerable progress. The ship, the Talon, had not jumped and they were headed for a planet, so that had to be Verdant. They would be there within three days because when Jax had asked how long he would be stuck on the couch, Kem had answered two nights and two more days. From what Jax remembered about the Verdant system that was remarkably quick. The Talon's crew was large, over thirty, but was divided into what Kem called officers, crew and servants. There were about two dozen crew, who were mostly muscle and did little other than squabble and fuck while they were travelling; they lived in the tail end of the ship. There were six officers other than Scar. They lived in the head end of the ship with Kem and three servants.

Jax noticed that Kem did not think of himself as officer, servant or crew.

It was like the officers and the servants made up the actual crew while the 'crew' were what Jax's tutors would have called marines. Jax would have liked to know more but he knew better than to press. Kem was lonely. He wanted to talk. Asking specific questions risked drying up the flow. However, he decided it would be safe to ask one.

"Do you think Noe will be coming back?"

Kem hesitated. "I don't know." He bit his lip. "He looked very young. Is he experienced? With men?"

Jax was careful how he answered; Noe had been playing a role. "He's a cat," he replied.

The medico looked relieved. "Then he'll probably stay in Captain Scar's rooms. Nero, the captain's orderly, will see to him."

Jax realised that Kem had been worried that Noe would require treatment beyond what 'Nero' could provide. He tried not to think what might be happening to Noe. Instead he made a note that if Nero was Scar's personal servant, he must be someone Scar trusted.

Kem's gaze had gone to the chronometer. "It will be night soon. I will be sleeping next door. You are safe. Apparently the commander himself said that no one must touch you."

Jax hadn't thought of that until Kem mentioned it. He imagined someone coming in when he was strapped down.

"You will be fine," Kem assured him, picking up on Jax's reaction. "The blast door this side of the crewroom is locked while we are underway. Some of the crew sniff stuff when they are bored. Captain Scar does not trust them to behave when they are high. They have been known to raid the supplies and even…" Kem stopped himself. "You will be fine," he repeated.

Kem lowered the head end of Jax's couch until it was only slightly raised and draped a cover over him. Jax found himself wondering if the man had children. If he did, he might be willing to take some risks in order to return to them.

The ship's lights dimmed as the chronometer reached midnight. Jax lay back and shut his eyes. It would be sensible to sleep. Sleeping would conserve his reserves and mean that he was ready for action should an opportunity present itself.

Only he couldn't. His mind was too busy. He wondered where Rae was. Jax hoped he was safe. As for Tre, an unwelcome little thought had started to grow. Was he dead? Was there any other explanation for Jax ending up in the hands of strangers?

He had just started to drift away when he heard the door open. For one awful moment he thought it might be Scar or, worse, some of the crew high on stuff.

Rae's whiskered face appeared.

Jax had never been so pleased to see anyone. When Rae's eyes lit up and his whiskers arched, Jax wanted to run to him and hug him so he was fine with Rae jumping onto the couch, butting Jax's shoulder with his head and uttering small yips of pleasure.

It was only for a moment. Then Rae pulled himself together and began working on the strap holding Jax's right wrist.

"Stop," Jax ordered.

Rae obeyed but pulled back a bit and gave a 'why not' whisker-twitch.

"You might not get it done up in time if someone comes," Jax reminded him. "First of all you need to find a hiding place in here in case you hear someone coming along the corridor."

They spotted a hatch cover under a trolley. Jax watched Rae making a careful note of where and how the trolley was positioned before moving it to investigate. Under the cover was a void that, surprisingly, was empty.

On the Willow Ean used all such cubbyholes for storage.

Rae practised jumping into the hole, repositioning the trolley and then sliding the cover into place. It was reassuringly quick. Rae re-emerged and came over to the couch.

Jax imagined Scar pulling the trolley away and yanking off the cover to reveal Rae crouched in the hole beneath. "Maybe you should still hide somewhere else during the ship's day," he suggested. "Somewhere with more exits."

Rae looked at him and twitched his whiskers, which Jax interpreted as agreement.

Rae already knew where he was going to hide. As soon as the ship's lights had dimmed, he had gone scouting. Creeping up the shaft, he had quickly picked up Scar and Jax's trail. It had led to the level in the same place as the crewroom level on the Willow. Rae had resisted the urge to go straight to him. Instead he had investigated the level below.

Hiding there was a bit more risky. Nose-end levels were used more because the direction of the gravitational field was always the same. On the other hand, the field was still high and it hadn't looked like anyone lived there. Rae had found storage rooms, a gym and room with some unused hydroponics equipment.

He'd decided he'd be fine as long as he avoided the gym and had picked out a new place amongst the hydroponics equipment. Then he had gone to find Jax and found him in an infirmary.

Despite being in the infirmary Jax didn't look injured, which was a relief. Rae wanted to curl up next to him, like they did in Jax's bunk on the Willow, but there wasn't enough room on the narrow couch. Instead Rae sat at Jax's feet where there was space because Jax wasn't as tall as an adult.

Just being close to him made Rae happier.

Jax told Rae what he had found out about the Talon and the other people on it, all of which was useful. Rae then told Jax everything that had happened to him, some of which made Jax smell very anxious and unhappy. Rae realised that Jax didn't like it when Rae took big risks, like bluffing his way onto the ship.

So Rae decided not to tell Jax about his plan. Rae had thought of it as soon as Jax told him that the blast door to the tail-end crewroom was locked. Rae intended to kill everyone this side of the locked door and hope that he and Jax could work out how to operate the ship.

Then Jax suggested that they wait another day before doing anything so that they could collect more information. According to Medico Kem, they had tomorrow, tomorrow night and the next day before they reached Verdant. Rae thought about it and agreed. He would be able to listen to the crew from his new hiding place and Jax could get more information out of Medico Kem.

Also it would give Rae more time to decide about Noe. Was Noe still part of the Willow's crew, so should live, or had he joined the Talon's crew, so should be killed? Jax might think that Noe had gone with Scar to protect him but when Noe used his eyelashes it affected Jax's judgement.

After that Jax fell asleep. Rae couldn't because he had to listen in case anyone came. It was still good to be so close to Jax, even if he was asleep.

It was difficult when the chronometer showed a hundred minutes to ship's dawn. Rae didn't want to leave but he must. Ean was often up by ship's dawn. The same might be the same for some of the people who lived on the Talon.

He didn't wake Jax. Jax looked pale and tired; he needed to sleep. Rae made sure that the hatch cover and trolley were perfectly placed and then listened at the door.

He could hear Jax asleep behind him and adult purebreds in the two cabins either side. Slipping out into the corridor, he went past doors to three cabins with one person sleeping in each; the mature purebred male he had been able to hear from inside the infirmary, a younger purebred male and an older purebred male who wouldn't be able to run fast or far.

Next was the galley, the smell of which was nowhere near as good as Ean's galley but still enough to make Rae's stomach rumble. He made himself walk by; it was much safer to check the storage hold for food.

He paused at the junction with the main corridor that ran the width of the ship from one shaft to the other. Did he scout out the whole level or should he go straight down the nearest shaft?

He decided that a few minutes' scouting might pay off in the long run, so he turned left rather than right. Reaching a door he sniffed the edges. They smelt of Scar and another man. Rae listened carefully, concentrating on each sound in turn. There were two sleeping men, one of whom Rae was pretty sure was Scar.

The other man was probably the one Jax had called Nero, Scar's personal servant.

There was a third, more familiar sound; Noe. He was separate from Scar and Nero. Most importantly, he was not asleep.

This was the moment. Should he trust Noe? Did he need to? Could he really kill ten adult purebreds before one of them put a hole in him with a laser pistol? Pirates used guns; everyone knew that.

Jax trusted Noe, even if Rae didn't.

He crept further along the corridor, pressing his ear against the wall at intervals, but the sound of Noe faded so he turned and worked his way back, past the mouth of the corridor that led to the infirmary.

There was another narrow corridor on the other side, just before the shaft. Rae had one last check for any new sounds and turned down it. He pressed his ear against the wall to his left; Noe was louder here while the noises that Scar and Nero were making were fainter.

Rae found one of the struts that held the wall panels, took a deep breath and tapped. There was no change to the way Noe sounded. He tapped harder.

Noe was suddenly very quiet. Rae tapped again and there were sounds of Noe moving about followed by a soft clunk. Rae recognised the sound of the open end of a cup being pressed against the wall panel; one of the tricks purebreds used to hear properly.

Rae tapped until the sound of the cup being slid about stopped. Now they should be on opposite sides of the strut.

Noe tapped out a message in long-short. "*Jax?*"

Rae hesitated but then replied. "*Rae.*"

"*Stowaway?*"

"*Yes.*"

"*Access to infirmary?*"

"*Ship's night.*" Rae thought about it and added, "*Next. Hide now.*"

"*Get lots sleepdrug next night. Tap after. Hide now. Go.*"

It was a good idea; Rae didn't know how and when they could drug the Talon's crew but having the sleepdrug opened up more options. "*Gone*," he tapped.

Then it was down the shaft to look for food among the storage crates before settling into his hidey-hole for the day.

When Jax woke up he discovered that Rae had left. He told himself that was good, because it was long past ship's dawn, but Jax could not help but miss him. Jax hoped that Rae was well hidden and that he wouldn't take it on himself to do anything rash.

He really wanted to pee. He tried to think of something, anything, else but quickly all that mattered was not wetting the bed, which would be shameful. Luckily Medico Kem arrived before Jax lost the battle.

Kem had a bottle around Jax's rod within seconds; Jax guessed he had looked pretty desperate. Then he fed Jax a meal bar broken into small pieces and some water.

Jax hated being cared for as if he was a baby but Kem made it as easy as possible, distracting him with conversation.

About halfway through the morning Kem tensed up. Instead of doing small tasks and talking about nothing in particular, he was rereading the same screen on his tablet and glancing towards the door.

He had to be expecting someone and, from how uncomfortable Kem was, it was probably Scar.

So Jax was ready when the door slid open and Scar strode in. What he wasn't expecting was for Scar to look back over his shoulder and speak to someone behind him in the corridor.

"Now!" he ordered.

For one horrific moment Jax thought it might be Rae but it was Noe. Noe looked different, far more like the Saber's cat than the Noe who had lived on the Willow. His clothes were too tight and too skimpy; his eyes heavily painted and his lips bright pink.

Scar had sexy clothes that were small enough to be tight on Noe. It was not a good thought. Whatever the 'client' intended to do to him, Jax was grateful that he had specified that Jax should be 'untouched'. Otherwise it might be him in those clothes with that paint on his face.

He stopped short of imagining what else Scar had done to Noe. Instead he thought about what Noe would do to stay alive. Given his history, the answer was absolutely anything.

Scar ordered Kem out and then pointed to a chair. Noe sat down with one ankle on the other knee and a hand strategically placed to display a wrist and draw attention to his crotch.

"Be good," Scar growled.

Noe put both feet flat on the floor, held his hands in his lap and looked up at Scar through his eyelashes.

Then Scar drew his knife. The edge looked wickedly sharp. Jax watched it coming closer.

"What would you do if I cut him?" Scar challenged.

Jax realised that the question was directed at Noe and the knife at him. He braced himself for Noe's answer.

Noe's chin came up and he sniffed. "You won't," he replied.

Jax wondered if Noe had a death wish.

The knife stopped. "I won't?" Scar queried, his tone dangerous.

"You will follow the commander's orders," Noe told him with confidence. "It is your code and you will honour it."

Jax wondered again who the commander was and why Scar obeyed him.

Scar snorted. "I shouldn't have left you with Nero," he acknowledged. "How do you feel about him?" he demanded, gesturing towards Jax.

Noe glanced briefly in Jax's direction and shrugged. "Not much," he replied as if uninterested by the question. "We were members of the same crew. Now we aren't. A cat belongs to the crew strong enough to take him. I ended up on the Willow because my crew challenged for Jax and our enforcer lost. The Willow was too Trad for me but they did their duty by me. They fed me and clothed me." He fixed Scar's gaze. "It was boring. I cleaned and sewed and did laundry."

It was utterly convincing; Jax had no idea if Noe believed what he was saying or not. All Jax knew was that Noe was telling Scar what he thought Scar would like and, based on Scar's slight smile, it seemed to be working.

Then Scar scowled. His arm shot out and he grabbed Noe by the neck. Scar's hand was huge; the fingers and thumb wrapped around the sides of Noe's neck, almost touching at the back.

Noe's eyes widened briefly in shock and his hands started upwards by reflex. Jax saw him control his reaction: drop his hands to his lap; close his eyes; relax his mouth.

For the first time Jax realised that Noe was, in his way, amazing.

Scar turned on Jax. "What about you? Should I snap his neck for his disloyalty to you?"

He refused to panic. Instead Jax emptied himself of emotion, as he had been trained to do in crisis situations. "He is your cat now. It is up to you what you do with him," he replied.

Scar's grasp loosened and somehow, Jax did not know how, Noe smiled. Every part of his body broadcast the message that he was Scar's and that Scar could do whatever he wished.

"You will do," Scar stated and, again, it was directed at Noe rather than Jax.

Noe pouted, making it clear that he wished to be considered more than sufficient; there was no hint that he resented Scar for threatening to snap his neck. Scar responded with a less than convincing scowl and signalled that Noe should leave. Noe headed towards the door and, to Jax's relief, Scar followed.

Neither of them acknowledged Jax's existence as they left.

Jax just lay there for a moment, fighting a sudden surge to struggle against his bonds. He shut his eyes and forced himself to relax. Staying calm conserved resources and kept your enemy guessing. Also, if it came to it, it was a Navaja's duty to die with his dignity intact.

A question crept into his mind. What would Noe do when he and Rae tried to take the ship? The truth was, Jax didn't know.

It was difficult waiting for ship's night. He tried talking to Kem but the medico was less forthcoming than the day before and was called away mid afternoon. There had been a fight amongst the men who lived in the tail end of the ship. Kem had vanished with his medical kit and returned much later looking weary.

Jax watched as he replenished the supplies in his kit. The combination for the coolbox where the drugs were kept was 270321; Jax wondered if it was the date Kem had met the love of his life or even the day his child had been born.

"Do you want me to bring you some food from the galley?" Kem asked him as he closed his kit, placed it in a locker and locked the door.

"No thank you," Jax replied. You never ate an enemy's food unless there was no other option. "Strange food might disrupt my gut," he added.

Kem nodded and took out another meal bar from a drawer. "Only two more nights and a day," he pointed out.

"Two more nights?" Jax queried. The day before Kem had said two nights, not three.

Kem looked apologetic as he unwrapped the bar. "I was going on the landing slot, which is booked for tomorrow evening, but apparently we are keeping you until the following morning." He cut the brown, sticky block into small pieces. "Captain Scar will have built some slack into the schedule. The commander would not be pleased if the rendezvous had to be postponed."

Jax decided to push for more information. "Isn't he worried that the client will attack the ship as soon as it is on the ground, pretending to be someone else, so he doesn't have to pay?"

Kem's hand paused briefly halfway to Jax's mouth. "Beck and Cage were complaining that the captain was paying out for a secure berth. Maybe that is why."

Jax moved his head to take the food between his teeth. As he chewed, he considered what Kem had said and how it might affect them. A secure berth was usually a silo that could be sealed; the planetary equivalent of a private dock in a space-station.

Getting out of a private dock was easy; all the security was focused on others not getting in. Was a secure berth the same?

He realised that Kem was holding another piece of food two finger-widths from his lips. Jax decided to concentrate on eating; the last thing he wanted was Kem questioning what he was thinking.

Once he had finished, he shut his eyes as if he was tired so that Kem would leave him alone and he could think.

"I could give you something to help you sleep tonight," Kem offered.

Jax's eyes snapped open; that was the last thing he wanted.

"No, I am fine."

It felt like ship's night would never come but finally it did. Jax was determined not to fall asleep but next thing he knew he was being woken by Rae shaking his arm.

"I'm awake," he insisted.

Rae twitched his whiskers in disbelief. "I talked to Noe using long-short. He suggests stealing sleepdrug."

Jax took a moment or two to catch up. Rae had been in contact with Noe?

Working out a plan was hampered by Noe being locked up in one room and Jax strapped down in another but Rae went between them until they had it. Jax told Rae the combination for the coolbox and Rae took the sleepdrug from the back of the supply, filling the vials with water on the off chance that Kem would check them.

They discussed taking other drugs but decided against it.

Then Rae hid the sleepdrug where Noe said he would be able to find it and put it into the evening meal. If Noe didn't have a chance to do that, they would have the whole of the next night to come up with something else. If they tried it and Noe was caught...

Jax didn't want to think about that.

The next day crawled by minute by minute. Jax had to force himself to relax every time Kem walked in the direction of the coolbox but he did not even open it, never mind check the contents.

Jax tried not to think about everything that might go wrong. What if Noe was caught putting the sleepdrug into the food? Jax suppressed a shudder at the thought of what Scar would do if he realised that Noe had been lying to him.

Then an unpleasant thought crept into Jax's mind. What if Noe hadn't been lying to Scar but to him and Rae? What if Noe was going to expose Rae as a demonstration of his loyalty to his new crew?

He dismissed it. If Noe was going to do such a thing it would have happened by now. Jax would have heard something. Kem would have gone to the coolbox and checked the vials of sleep-drug.

Or maybe not; maybe Rae was already dead, spaced through one of the airlocks. The thought of it made Jax feel so ill that he could not eat the meal bar Kem offered him at noon.

Luckily Kem put it down to him being nervous about being delivered to the client next day.

The ship was due to land during the second half of the afternoon. Kem put Jax's examination couch flat, fastened a strap around Jax's waist and assured Jax that it would be fine. Jax wasn't convinced but Kem was using the other couch, the one Noe had been on, so it was obviously the way they did it on the Talon.

There were very few announcements; just a hundred minute warning to get everything secure and a ten minute warning for everyone to strap down. The pilot used the rockets more than Captain Mel had done and although it was a rough ride the gee force was never so high that it was painful. Jax hoped that Rae was all right. The examination couch might be nowhere near as comfortable as one of the acceleration chairs on the Willow but it was a great deal better than the floor.

Then it was back to waiting. Jax checked the chronometer. Another forty minutes until ship's dusk. Kem offered him a meal bar, which he declined, and a chance to pee into a bottle, which he accepted.

Ship's dusk, which was suppertime on the Talon, finally arrived. Kem left. Another thirty minutes passed.

Jax strained to hear something, anything, but it was impossible. Forty minutes, fifty, sixty: on the other two evenings Kem had returned to check on him by now.

The door began to open. Jax braced himself. Was it Kem? Or Scar? Could it be Rae?

It was Noe. He dumped the bag he was carrying on the floor and walked towards Jax.

"We have to go," he announced. "Now."

3

Kip lay in the duct and listened to the silence; hoping to hear any sounds that suggested that someone realised that each individual bank of batteries needed to be switched back on manually.

He waited for what seemed a long, long time. Nothing happened. The other layers of his mind began offering other options, ones he had already discarded; some of them were beginning to look more appealing. He thought about crawling back along the duct towards the pods to check if the guards were still there. He considered getting out of the duct and reactivating the battery bank on this level; that way he would have enough power to monitor what was going on.

No, he had to wait. He set two alarms. One would be triggered if the air quality dropped and the other if there was any sign of the power being restored.

Then he went to sleep.

The sound of the alarm in his earpiece woke him. After checking the air quality, which was fine, he consulted the chronometer in his suit. He had been asleep for over four hundred minutes, four hundred and seventeen to be exact, and his alarm had been activated by the power coming on for this level.

Kip activated his goggles so that he could check which of the live feeds were up and running. Not many, which was good. Best of all, they hadn't got the transmitters or receivers working yet, so he could prevent that happening. He really didn't want the commander communicating with Scar.

It was only a few minutes' work to make sure that neither transmitters nor receivers would respond to any of the standard commands.

Once that was done, Kip rewarded himself with a meal bar and a few mouthfuls of water. Then he watched power being restored to the rest of the ship; each time the batteries on a level were reactivated, more of the live feeds came online.

One of the last was the microphone in the control room. Over the next fifteen minutes there were a few snatches of conversation, but nothing particularly interesting. Then one of them said, *"He's on his way."*

Kip guessed that 'he' was the commander.

"Calm down." That was Kurt; Kip recognised his voice. *"Any luck with the transmitter yet?"*

"No. Nor the receiver. Nor the backup of either. Kurt, he's going...."

"Shut up. Here he comes." There was a pause. *"Commander."*

"Kurt. Update please."

"Only nine battery banks left to reactivate, Commander. Unfortunately some key systems appear to have been adversely affected by the power outage, the most important of which appears to be communications. However, using the telescopes

we have confirmed that that Talon is still on route and on schedule."

"What about the Dagger?"

Kip heard Kurt's sharp intake of breath. *"We have lost track of her. As you know, her beacon was extinguished almost immediately. We are trying to find her using the telescopes."*

There was a short, ominous silence before the commander spoke again. *"She can't overtake the Talon,"* he conceded. *"What about the Blackjack?"*

"She turned back once Captain Ort realised we were in trouble, Commander. She is alongside."

"Flash a signal telling Ort to warn Scar that we've lost the Dagger and that he may have someone on his tail. Then tell Ort to get over here for a meeting."

"Yes, Commander."

"What are Mutt and his rats up to?"

"Still scavenging. There was a lot of high spec kit on that ship, Commander. Even the scrap is worth having."

"No ideas as to the cause of the power outage?"

"No, Commander."

"What about the delay getting the power back?" There was no immediate reply. *"Kurt?"*

"No one knew what to do," Kurt admitted. *"We are very short on engineers."*

"And?" the commander insisted.

Kurt's voice was thin with fear. "*The engineer from the Willow was in the infirmary. Medico Kem had patched him up before leaving on the Talon. He said he knew what to do and he did.*"

Kip's heart skipped a beat. Vic was alive?

"*On balance…*" The commander's tone was dangerous. "*On balance, that was the right decision. Well done, Kurt. You show potential.*"

"*Thank you, Commander,*" Kurt replied and Kip could hear his relief.

"*I shall be in my cabin, Kurt. Don't let that engineer go anywhere unaccompanied. When he's finished activating the batteries, get him to sort out communications. If he begins to have second thoughts, come and tell me.*"

"*Yes, Commander.*"

There were the sounds of people standing up, moving and then sitting down.

"*Thanks, Kurt.*" It was the one who had sounded scared.

Kurt sighed. "*You should have taken the credit yourself, Owen. You let the Willow's engineer loose on the battery banks.*"

Owen laughed; to Kip he sounded a bit hysterical. "*No way. He'd have killed me. You know that. You can get away with stuff no one else can. He likes you.*" He took two ragged breaths. "*When he offers you a captaincy, promise you will ask for me.*"

"*You know I will,*" Kurt assured him.

Kip shut his eyes for a moment, while his mind integrated the information he had gleaned. One thought was particularly worrying; he liked Kurt and Owen. He told himself that they were pirates and members of the crew that had destroyed the Willow but it didn't change what he felt. He decided not to think about it. He had more important things to do, like trying to talk to Vic.

If Vic was going to be running diagnostics on the transmitters and the receivers, Kip should be able to make contact.

To Tre's astonishment only the smaller of the pirate's ships had pursued him and she was much too slow to catch him. There had been none of the small fighters manned by the hybrids and no missiles. The big ship, the Maul, had done nothing.

He had used as much fuel as he dared to accelerate the ship. Then, once she was travelling at a steady speed, he had found the self-destruct and disassembled it. Next he had patched the holes he had made with the small calibre rounds. There was nothing he could about the damage to the airlock; he had settled for making the top two levels of the ship, the control room and the cabins below it, airtight.

Then he had stripped off his suit; the adrenaline surges it caused made it difficult to think.

The ship was small; an eleven metre wide 4-eight-hex-6 arranged on eight levels around a central shaft; only twice as tall as she was wide. Luckily she was capable of dropping to Verdant with the fuel he had left her.

He started working through the details. Taking the attack on the Willow as day one, the Talon could be on the surface by nightfall of day three.

Tre could make it just before dawn of day four. Possibly that could be soon enough. Maybe, just maybe, the rendezvous to hand Jax over would be scheduled for the morning.

By the dawn of day two, Tre had done everything that needed to be done. Firstly he had reset the ship's beacon, changing the ship's identity and constructing a false history in the ship's log that would be nigh on impossible to check. Second he had switched off the jammer so that he could transmit and receive. That allowed him to book a secure berth in each of the five spaceports on Verdant; provided he could keep track of the Talon, he would be able to land close by. Third he had worked out how to feed the output of the ship's sensors through to his processor via a modified tablet.

Having done that he had been liberated to leave the control room and investigate the rest of the ship. There was little to be found. The lower levels, which he had to wear a suit to search, included accommodation that had been occupied but not lived in; the only personal effects were the type you took with you on a short trip.

The level below the control room was different. The main cabin was luxuriously fitted out to a single person's taste. The small cabin looked like it might be for a valet or other personal servant.

Tre returned to the control room to check on the Maul and the smaller pirate ship that had been pursuing him. To his surprise, the Maul was still inert and the other ship had turned back, presumably to give assistance.

Tre suspected that Kip had done something.

The next day crawled by. Other than checking on the Maul and the Talon, Tre had little to do. He went through the ship's log and found little of interest; other than occasional trips to spacestations and planets the yacht had spent most of its time in the Maul's docking bay. He searched the main cabin but discovered nothing; the same person might stay there each time but he had taken all his personal effects with him when he left.

Tre forced himself to sleep and eat; he had to be at peak performance when he reached the planet. There were no more coded messages from Kip, presumably because the Maul's transmitter was still down.

The main cabin was more than comfortable. Tre lay on the bed, thinking how much Ean would have liked staying there, even though he would have complained it was not 'homely'.

Would he every see Ean again? Tre doubted it. The pirates would have been instructed not to leave any witnesses. Even so, Tre could not help but hope. Maybe the pirates would be keeping him in stasis; organ harvesters paid more for living bodies.

Not that Tre was in any position to rescue him. First he had to retrieve Jax or die trying. Even if he survived, protecting Jax was not compatible with boarding a pirate ship to search for Ean.

No, he should accept that Ean was gone from his life forever. Only he couldn't; he kept hoping. He found himself thinking about Kip, the wildest of wild cards. If Ean was still alive, perhaps Kip would save him.

❋ ❋ ❋

Rae waited in his hidey-hole for Noe's signal. He had made sure he was well fed and fully rested. When ship's dusk had arrived, he had checked through the items he had scavenged from the storage chests, including meal bars, an assortment of clothes and a large duffle bag.

The clothes were worrying. They had been in bags in a half-filled chest. From what Rae could smell the clothes in each bag had belonged to a different person. Each bag only contained clothes of one size and they were all too small to fit an adult. Rae imagined Scar's servant packing up the clothes when they were no longer needed.

Rae's fur stood on end and he shuddered. There had been nine bags in the chest; Scar had got through a lot of boys.

Going on shoe size, Rae had picked out bags of clothes that should fit him, Jax and Noe. He had added them to his duffle bag, along with his suit and the meal bars.

Then he had waited, trying not to think too much about what they would do if the sleepdrug plan did not work.

Finally he heard the signal; Noe calling down the shaft. Rae slung the duffle bag across his back and set off.

He smelt blood and vomit as soon as he reached the shaft and the smell of both was stronger as he climbed the ladder. An overdose of sleepdrug might make people sick but it didn't make them bleed. Noe must have decided that dead people didn't wake up and decide to hunt you down.

Rae wondered how many of them Noe had killed.

Jax was already unstrapped and sitting on the edge of the couch. Noe was painting his face and Jax was not happy about it.

"Stay still!" he ordered as Jax turned his head towards the door. Then he glanced in Rae's direction. "Rae. Good. Did you find some clothes?"

Rae nodded, got the three bags out of the duffle and emptied each onto the floor in a small heap.

"Good work," Noe acknowledged.

"I do not see…" Jax began.

Noe glared at him. "Shut up. This is not something you know anything about. This is stuff that Rae and I know about. Rae, I need you to dress tough. Think prize fighter or a bouncer."

Rae had been thinking that Jax looked really pretty with his eyes and lips painted. He pulled his gaze away and began looking for leather or denim.

"There's some harnesses and belts over there," Noe told him, waving a brush towards a bag on the other couch.

Rae found boots, leather pants, a belt and some studded cuffs. After a few moments' hesitation he added a black sleeveless top and a studded collar.

Noe had finished painting Jax's face. He quickly picked out

some clothes and thrust them into Jax's arms. "Get into these."

Jax opened his mouth as if to object and then closed it again. He hopped off the couch and began undressing.

"No underpants," Noe insisted. "No whore wears underpants like those. You can wear a thong if you want."

Jax froze as if he could not decide which was the less unpleasant of the two options.

"Up here," Noe told Rae.

Rae sat on the edge of the couch and relaxed his face so that Noe could paint it.

"I am making you look older," Noe told him. "We need you to behave like an adult. Some hybrids are small." A few smudged lines and he was done. "Smile but make it threatening," he instructed.

Rae imagined Scar treating Jax as he had those other boys.

Noe paled and smelt scared. "Exactly like that," he confirmed, recovering quickly. "Now let's get packed up and on our way." He glanced over to Jax. "Aren't you dressed yet?" he demanded.

Jax finished buttoning his shirt and stood tall. He was wearing a skintight pair of green iridescent pants, a lacy white shirt and a pair of cute ankle boots. Rae thought he looked amazing.

Noe sighed. "No one is ever going to mistake you for a cheap whore," he complained.

Jax scowled slightly as if trying to decide if Noe had paid him a compliment or not.

"At least looking so good explains why men put up with your sulky attitude," Noe added. He picked up a cloak and threw it at Jax. "Cloak on, hood up. Never display the goods unless they have agreed to pay." He turned away and began sorting stuff into two piles. "Any idea where we can hide the stuff we aren't taking?" he asked.

Rae showed Noe the cubbyhole under the floor. Rae dropped in the unwanted stuff and replaced the cover while Noe put the rest into the duffle. Rae saw him pack three knives, a garrotte and four laser pistols as well as clothes, medical supplies and meal bars.

"Did you manage to scavenge any funds?" Jax asked.

Noe shook a small pouch. It chinked. "A handful of gold credits and some jewellery. I couldn't find much. It'll have to do."

Then it was down the shaft, out the small airlock and down the ladder. The air in the shaft was still hot from the rockets. It smelt complex, like the air had on Janine, but not as nice. Rae could smell fuel and oil as well as unfamiliar, harsh chemicals. They headed for the door at the base of the silo.

Like on the Willow, all the security was focused on stopping others getting in, not the crew who had rented the berth getting out.

"We need to contact Tre," Jax said as they closed the door to the berth and reset the lock.

"No, we need to find somewhere to stay," Noe corrected him. "Then we can decide what to do next. Rae, you'll have to do the talking."

Rae wasn't sure if he could manage that. Smiling threateningly was easy; he had teeth. Acting was completely different.

"What's our story?" Jax asked.

"Been working our passage," Noe told them. "Looking to have some downtime before finding another ship. Not taking clients until we've had some rest." He looked towards Rae. "Any other questions, smile at them. If they persist; growl."

A short passage took them to the bottom of a stairway. They started up towards the surface. Rae felt the breeze; they were definitely on a planet. He looked up. The sky was dark but the surface was illuminated by harsh electric lights. There was a lot of concrete. Close by there was a circular railing around the mouth of what Rae guessed was a closed silo; probably the one the Talon was in. Similar circles of railings repeated as far as Rae would see.

"This way," Noe announced. Rae checked that Jax agreed and they set off across the concrete towards a fence. After a short distance Rae realised that they were heading for a gate. He sniffed the air. It was manned.

There were three male purebreds wearing matching jackets with badges. Rae thought about looking to Noe for instructions but decided against it. He was meant to be the adult.

"Officers," he acknowledged in as scratchy a voice as he could manage. Then he tried the smile. Based on the way the way they smelt, it was remarkably successful.

"New in?" one of them asked.

Rae looked directly at him. They weren't spacers, so asking

their business was not an insult, but it was still rude. He smiled again, showing even more teeth, and the man paled like Noe had done. "Minding our own business," he replied in the scratchy voice.

"And what business is that?" another asked, ducking down and trying to see under Jax's hood.

Rae had growled before he even realised it. Luckily it wasn't very loud; maybe the men had not heard it.

"You promised to find somewhere we could sleep," Noe complained in a whiney voice that put Rae's teeth on edge. "I'm tired."

The man who had spoken first opened the gate and the others stepped to the side to let them through.

"Best avoid the local girls and lads," he told Rae as they passed by. "They won't appreciate the competition."

Rae settled for a nod and kept walking.

Jax loathed Noe's plan but he did not have anything better to offer. Noe was correct; the heir to the Navaja clan would never choose to dress as a whore, not even to save his own life. That alone made it an excellent disguise.

Rae had done really well with the three security guards. The scratchy voice was a good idea because Rae's normal voice was too high pitched to be anything but young. As for the smile, even Jax found it a bit scary.

He wished he had asked more questions before they left the Talon. What would happen when Scar woke up? What would the commander do? How would the client react when Scar didn't bring Jax to the rendezvous?

Beyond the gate was a road with warehouses on either side. At the end of the road Jax could see a junction with people walking by.

"We go into the first bar unless it looks really bad," Noe stated. "We'll check the notice board first, look for somewhere to stay."

Jax didn't agree. "No. If anyone is following us they will do the same thing. Let's walk down the street. We can always try a bar further along."

Noe looked over at him. "Fine," he conceded.

The street was busy. Jax stuck close to Rae, telling himself that it was part of staying in character. He couldn't see that much with his hood up but he spotted spacers, alone and in crews, and other men who were probably stevedores. There were bars, shops and a street vendor at every corner. It was noisy.

Perhaps Noe was right and they should go into one of the bars.

Suddenly they were surrounded by brightly painted faces and colourful clothes. Noe's hood was pulled down from the back and Jax felt the same happening to him. He could see more, which was good, but he felt horribly exposed.

Rae snarled and gave a warning growl.

Most of the people surrounding them drew back leaving only one to face Rae. She, or he, Jax wasn't entirely sure, was old. Her face paint had clumped and collected into her wrinkles. Her hands were gnarled by arthritis, like some of the old women who lived on the high plains.

"You are not welcome here," she stated.

Jax did not believe her. The way she was studying him and Noe reminded Jax of the queens in Carrefour. Looking about, Noe was far prettier than any of the whores who had surrounded them.

"Off one ship, will leave on another," Rae replied in his false, scratchy voice. "Looking for some downtime." He twitched his whiskers. "Can you recommend a place to stay? My girlies are tired."

Jax could not believe that Rae had just called him a girlyboy.

The woman smiled showing teeth that had served well but were giving in. "You could stay with me."

Rae's smile displayed teeth that could rip flesh from bone. "It would be an imposition. Perhaps a suitable hostelry?"

Jax was surprised that Rae knew words like 'imposition' and 'hostelry'.

The woman nodded. "Second left. The Golden Moon. Ask for Carl. He has rooms." She looked from Noe to Jax and then back at Rae. "Better put those hoods back up. Hoods just promise something good."

Noe reached over and raised Jax's hood before doing the same to his own.

The whores faded away as quickly as they had appeared.

"That was a bit of luck," Noe suggested in a low voice.

Jax could see that. The old woman had appeared to accept them and whores were unlikely to give up any of their own to outsiders. "Golden Moon it is then," he agreed.

They walked quickly down the street to the specified junction. The Golden Moon was marked by a neon sign. It didn't look like much, just a door between two shops.

They went through the door and up a flight of stairs. At the top was a room with a counter. Rae rang a bell and a man appeared.

He was Carl. Noe negotiated what they would get for a gold credit and left a small piece of jewellery with Carl as security.

Jax didn't understand how that worked. Wasn't giving Carl the jewellery to hold the same as paying in advance?

Their room was at the top of the building, up two more flights of stairs. It was small but not tiny. Jax was relieved to see bolts on the inside of the door and the window. There was a single, large bed but Jax could live with that, especially as there was a shower and a lavatory.

Noe undid Jax's cloak and drew it away. Jax thought about objecting about being undressed but decided it was not worth it.

"You go have a shower," Noe suggested. "Then we'll talk and after that you can sleep."

It was tempting; Jax considered arguing but agreed.

The bathroom was shabby but moderately clean and the water was warm if not hot. Jax scrubbed the paint off his face and then washed the rest of his body. The soap was harsh compared with the bodywash they used on the Willow.

There was only one thin towel, so Jax rubbed all the excess water away with his hands before using it. That way it would dry quicker so that Rae or Noe could use it.

Noe had picked out some looser, more comfortable, clothes for him. Jax pulled on the pants and top before sitting down on the bed. He wanted nothing more than to lie down and sleep.

"Let's start by assuming Tre made it," Noe began. "How are you meant to contact him?"

"Leave a message at the Stellar Exchange," Jax answered promptly.

"I'll be doing that then," Noe stated. "Rae will stay here with you."

Jax hesitated. He didn't want to share Navaja secrets with Noe. "I'll need to code it."

"You do that here and then I will take it," Noe insisted.

Jax looked towards Rae but Rae only looked determined and nodded his agreement.

They decided that Jax should sort out the message before going to sleep. Jax ate a meal bar to keep himself awake and worked on the message while Noe was in the shower.

They had no tablet or writing implements, so Jax used one of Noe's eyeliners and a mirror on the wall to work out the coding. Once he was done he carefully transposed the message to the plain side of an unfolded box from one of the hyposprays Noe had taken from the Talon's infirmary. After reassembling the box Jax wrote the name that would attract Tre's attention on a lid torn from another container.

Noe came out of the shower. He was naked, wet and looking about for something to dry himself on.

To Jax's horror, his skin was covered in bruises; the marks Scar's hands had left on his body. They were still vivid; purple with hints of crimson where more blood had pooled under the skin.

Then they were gone, hidden from Jax's sight by a strange assortment of garments chosen for their absorbency rather than their style or fit.

"You done?" Noe asked, nodding towards the mirror that Jax had still to clean.

Jax explained how Noe should hire a tape locker in the name Tre would expect, put the box in it and then set the lock to a combination that Tre would try. Noe repeated back the instructions.

"I'll go first thing in the morning," he added. "I'll do some shopping at the same time. Is there anything you want?"

Jax asked for a notebook, a pencil, some bodywash that wouldn't be too stinky for Rae and maybe another towel. Rae didn't ask for anything. Noe began laying stuff out for the morning. Jax noticed that the clothes he was picking out were plain and would fit loosely.

"What if Tre doesn't come?" he asked and then wished he hadn't. Hearing the words was much worse than thinking the thought.

Noe sniffed. "We aren't going to talk about that yet," he stated. "You are going to sleep now." He pulled back the bedcovers. "In you get."

"I need to clean the mirror," Jax insisted, even though all he wanted to do was curl up and go to sleep.

"Rae will do that, won't you, Rae?" Noe checked.

Rae gave an affirmative whisker twitch.

Jax crawled to the centre of the bed and did not object as Noe covered him up. He shut his eyes. He could hear the slight squeak as Rae rubbed a cloth over the mirror whilst talking quietly with Noe. Noe was admitting that there was no more hot water and Rae was saying that he would wait until the next morning to shower.

Then there were the sounds of Rae undressing and Rae climbed in beside him. Back on the Willow, Rae always stayed on top of the covers, wrapped in the blanket Ean had made for him. It was the first time they had shared a bed and Jax discovered that he was fine with it. He didn't mind that Rae was a bit ripe, because smelling Rae was much better than being too aware of his surroundings; a shabby room on a strange planet.

With Rae beside him Jax felt safe. They had each other and, to Jax's surprise, they had Noe. Even if Tre didn't come they would be fine.

4

Kip wasn't sure how much longer he could stay in the ducts. Every joint ached and he stank so much that he was sure it wouldn't take a hybrid to smell him.

At least he had made contact with Vic, piggybacking messages to and fro on the diagnostic programme. Between them they had worked out a believable reason for the power outage and communications failure. The same peak in voltage that had tripped the circuit breakers on the battery banks could have blown a fragile component common to transmitters and receivers.

Needless to say, Vic had ensured that the identified components were now thoroughly fried.

Vic had been told to replace the damaged components with parts found amongst the Maul's salvage. With this in mind, a workshop had been established on the mission level and an apartment opened up in which Vic was expected to eat and sleep.

Kip was waiting in the ducts under the corridor between the workshop and the apartment. Even if Vic was locked in, Kip intended to wait until the guards had gone and exit the ducts. He was pretty sure that he and Vic could make short work of any lock.

Instead there were footsteps and one of the inspection covers in the floor was lifted away. Kip scrabbled backwards and cowered.

"You there, Kip?" It was Vic.

Kip wriggled forward. He managed to get onto his knees but even that hurt. He was grateful when Vic lifted him out of the duct and onto the floor.

"Owen decided that locking this section of the level was enough," Vic explained. "I think it was because that was easier than ordering the guards about." He smiled. "Let's get you out of that suit and into a shower."

"My stuff," Kip pointed out and moved back towards the opening.

Vic reached down and snagged his and Rae's packs.

Kip insisted on hardwiring his monitoring system into the ship's systems before yielding to the temptation of a hot shower. Vic helped Kip remove a panel in the sleeping room of the apartment and watched him connecting his data array and interfaces. Kip set the system to record before installing two sockets, one for his goggles and another for his earpieces, where they would be difficult to see but could be accessed from the upper of the two bunks.

Then he replaced the panel. "I'll just need to pull the cables to the earpieces and goggles free if anyone searches," Kip explained.

Vic shook his head. "I'm more worried about hiding you than your kit," he pointed out. "You go clean up," he suggested pointing towards the shower. "I'll look for a place."

By the time Kip had finished in the shower, he felt considerably better. He wrapped himself in a surprisingly luxurious towelling robe and went to investigate what Vic was up to. Kip knew he had been making or altering something; he had been able to hear the sounds of tools over that of the shower.

There had been a bunk-width deep locker between the head ends of the bunks and the wall. It was now only half that depth and Kip could drop into the space behind from the top bunk.

"Will I be able to get out again?" Kip asked.

"You can climb up what remains of the shelf supports," Vic assured him. "All you have to remember is to pull the top cover into place, like with the service ducts." He packed away the tools and began cleaning up all traces of the alteration. "What did you do with your suit and the clothes you were wearing?"

Kip felt himself flush; they were on the floor of the shower room.

"I'll sort it out," Vic assured him. "You get some sleep."

Tre was closing on Verdant by midnight of the third day. The Talon had landed in Verdant's largest city, Nova Urbo. Tre recalculated the remainder of the journey; he could be on the ground thirty minutes before planetary dawn.

Maybe that would be soon enough.

Every second could count, so he dressed and laid out his kit in advance. By fluke, he was the same size as the luxury cabin's previous occupant. Even the boots fitted. Tre checked his appearance in the mirror and discovered that the close-fitting pants and short tailored jacket made him looked uncharacteristically smart.

Looking unlike himself was not such a bad idea. Tre combed his hair back from his face and secured it with one of the clasps from a jar next to the mirror.

Then it was back to the control room for the tricky transition into the planet's atmosphere and to land the ship.

He depressurised the ship as he descended and only paused once, as he hovered tail-down above his assigned silo. From above it would be possible to see which silos were occupied and which were not. He used the ship's cameras to take a range of images and transferred them via the tablet to his implanted data crystal array.

As soon as the ship settled, he was out of the acceleration chair and down to the cabin. Weapons went into their various holsters and the bag of equipment was slung across his back. Then it was through the ruined airlock and a controlled drop to the ground. He exited the berth, sealing the door behind him. Running up the stairs to the surface, he finished processing the images he had taken. The infra-red camera had confirmed that only one of the occupied silos was still warm; that had to be the Talon.

Tre risked sprinting across the illuminated concrete towards the Talon. The sky above confirmed that planetary dawn was only minutes away. The silos were arranged in hexagons; each stairway down accessed six. Tre used his processor to zoom in on the image he had taken from above. The Talon was in silo eight-four and he was heading for stairway seven. He changed direction towards stairway eight.

There was someone coming up. Could it be Scar with Jax? Tre listened. No, it was a single individual carrying something heavy. Tre slowed to a pace that could be considered normal. Did he question the person on his way up? He might not be off the Talon; four of the six silos were occupied.

He decided against it. The man, who was skinny and sickly-looking with eyeglasses, pressed himself against the balustrade as Tre passed him.

At the bottom of the stairs Tre took the passage leading to silo eight-four. He did not bother wasting time on the lock; small shaped charges on the hinges and the door yielded to a carefully placed blow.

Even from the ground he could tell that the smaller of the two airlocks was open. That was odd; no spacers, not even pirates, left their airlock open. He climbed the ladder quickly; being slow only increased the chances of being spotted and targeted.

As soon as he was through the airlock he smelt the vomit.

A few minutes later he was sure that Jax was not in the nose-end of the ship. There were ten men; eight unconscious and two dead. One of the two dead men was in the best cabin and had an old scar below the fresh, gaping wound across his throat. Tre guessed he was the Scar to whom Kip had referred.

The blast doors to the tail end of the ship were sealed and

locked from this side. Tre hesitated. He thought about the skinny man on the stairs. Did he run after him or check what was behind the blast doors?

On balance, it was unlikely that Jax was still on the ship. The most likely scenario was that Scar had been betrayed by one or more of his crew, who had taken Jax.

If the skinny man knew anything, Tre had to know.

So it was out of the ship, down the ladder and up the stairs at top cyborg speed. Luckily silo eight-four was some distance from the gate. Tre spotted the man, weighed down by his big bag.

Was the bag big enough to hold Jax? Was the skinny man Scar's killer? Tre sprinted across the concrete, drawing a laser pistol. He dared not call out; it might alert the guards at the gate. He settled for a warning shot a couple of paces ahead of his quarry.

The man froze, staring at the small, smoking pit in the concrete ahead of him. Then he turned and what little colour had been in his face drained away. Tre thought he might faint.

At least he had the sense not to flee.

Tre slowed, laser pistol still in hand. The bag did not look like it contained a body but Tre decided he had better check.

"Put the bag down and step away from it," he instructed.

The man did as he was told.

Tre walked up to the bag and felt it with the toe of his boot. "What's in it?"

"Personal items and medical supplies," the man answered, his voice shaking with fear.

"Are you off the Talon?" Tre demanded. The man hesitated, unwilling to answer, so Tre aimed the laser pistol at his knee.

"Yes!" the man squeaked. "Please don't shoot me. Are you looking for Jax? When I woke up he had gone. So had Noe. Scar and Nero were dead."

The man's answer opened up another possibility. Perhaps Jax and Noe had escaped. Tre refused to be distracted by thoughts of two youngsters in a city like Nova Urbo without a protector. "Was there anyone else missing?"

"No." The man considered. "I suppose someone could have come on board and taken them, but there wasn't any sign of it. I don't know how he did it but I think Noe took all the sleep-drug from the infirmary and put it in the stew."

It sounded like something Noe might do. "So why are you conscious?" Tre demanded.

"I don't know," the man admitted. "I ate a full portion and I fell asleep like the others. All I can think of is that one of them gave me some antidote."

It was a clever twist. By the time the others woke up, this man and the two boys would be gone. They would blame the man, not Jax and Noe. They would look for him, not two youngsters on their own.

Tre wondered who had thought of it, Jax or Noe.

"What is the earliest they could have left?" Tre asked.

"Yesterday evening," the man replied. "We eat at ship's dusk."

68

It was depressingly long ago. Tre wanted to grab the man and shake every scrap of useful information out of him but his instincts told him that reason would work better than threats. "My name is Tre. I am Jax's protector. My aim is to find him."

The man nodded. "My name is Kem. I am a medico. I want to get away from those…" he trailed off.

"Pirates," Tre supplied. He had to decide what to do with the man, Kem. There were four choices: kill him, let him go, put him somewhere where he could be retrieved or keep him close. For now the fourth option was best. He picked up Kem's bag. "You are coming with me."

Kem did not argue; Tre guessed that he had become accustomed to others controlling his life. As they walked to the gate, Tre began revising his plan. Jax knew what to do; leave a message at the Stellar Exchange. Unless someone interfered, that was what would happen.

The sooner Tre found them the better. He found a map of Nova Urbo in his data crystal array; they could walk to the Stellar Exchange within fifteen minutes. If they went directly there, they should be there by the time it opened.

The guards at the gate just nodded them through.

"Where are we going?" Kem asked once they were walking through the docks towards the commercial centre.

Tre decided to glare at him; he did not want to converse. He did not want to do anything other than find Jax.

"You aren't scary next to Scar," Kem informed him. "You protect youngsters like Jax." He shivered. "Scar did unspeakable things to them. That's why the commander gave him Noe, so he wouldn't be tempted to damage Jax before the rendezvous."

Tre remembered Scar lying there with his throat cut. In Noe, Scar had finally met a youngster who knew how to fight back. "Do you know anything about the rendezvous?"

"No, just that it was this morning. I doubt that Scar knew much himself. The commander keeps any important information to himself."

"The commander?"

"The man who leads the......pirates. For a moment, at the spaceport, I thought you were him. He's your size and you dress like him."

It made sense; the Dagger must have been the commander's yacht. "How many of the commander's men would die for him?" Tre asked.

Kem did not answer immediately, which Tre thought was promising.

"Die for him because they are loyal, not because they were too terrified of what he would do to them if they said no?" Kem checked.

"Yes," Tre confirmed.

"Scar, but he's gone now. Probably Ort, he captains the Black-jack. Maybe one or two of the young men who would prefer to believe their fantasies over reality. Most of them don't live past their first few interactions with him; he values skill and efficiency, not imagination."

That explained why Kem was alive; skilled medicos were few and far between. "Describe how he recruits," Tre demanded.

"Mostly during missions. That's what he calls it when he attacks a ship. Long ago, before the commander, the Maul was a salvage ship. It was Mutt's family business. Then the commander took control. He started attacking ships, making it look like an accident, so that there would be more salvage opportunities. Then he began offering to take out specific ships for a fee.

"Anyway, when he started attacking ships there couldn't be witnesses. Apparently they used to just kill everyone but then the commander decided to sell the people to organ harvesters. Now anyone who survives the attack is podded, so they can be delivered fresh. Usually the commander picks out the best looking young man to interrogate. Sometimes he'll find out about someone useful, like me, and unpod him. Very occasionally, the young man impresses so much that he is allowed to join the crew."

Cas was more than good looking, he was beautiful. "Will he do that this time?" Tre asked.

"I doubt it," Kem replied. "We were brought a long way for this one. The fee must have been huge. This time no witnesses will mean no witnesses. He'll kill them or at least blast their memories with an overdose of forgetting pills before handing them over to the organ harvesters."

Tre tried to ignore the way his gut twisted at the thought of Ean dying or his memories being destroyed. One thing at a time: retrieve Jax; collect as much information about the situation as possible; try to make contact with Kip on the Maul. He reviewed what Kem had told him.

"Mutt?"

"The Maul and the hybrids belonged to Mutt's family. They are all dead now other than Mutt; the commander picked them off one by one."

"And Mutt isn't loyal to the commander?" Tre checked.

"He's terrified of him," Kem confirmed.

The situation was looking better moment by moment; a number of people would like to see the back of the commander.

They were past the warehouses and cutting through the spacer quarter with all its bars, stalls and brothels. It was eerily quiet this time in the morning; just a few stall holders cleaning up and a solitary open bar offering breakfast.

Kem had fallen silent. From his breathing Tre could tell it was all he could do to keep up, even though the pace was steady. Tre retrieved the map of the areas around the Stellar Exchange from his data crystal array and zoomed in; there was an eatery from which he should have line of sight to the entrance.

Down one street, turn left and up another; shops and offices replaced the brothels and bars. Kem was beginning to wheeze but Tre maintained his pace; it was critical that they arrived before the Stellar Exchange opened.

There were eight minutes to spare. Tre checked that no one was waiting outside the Stellar Exchange and then headed for the eatery he had identified. None of the tables in the window were occupied, so he chose the one with the best view. Kem sank gratefully into the indicated chair. Tre put Kem's bag well out of his reach and sat down.

"We have to go up to the counter to order," Kem pointed out once they have been sitting there for five minutes.

Tre did not take his eyes off the entrance to the Stellar Exchange. "Someone will come over," he predicted. Sure enough, a rather surly looking woman approached their table. Tre placed a quarter gold credit piece on the table and her attitude immediately improved.

"What can I get you?" she asked.

"Real coffee for one and whatever he wants," Tre replied.

"Tea and…" Kem studied the board. "Tea and a breakfast special please. Thank you."

The Stellar Exchange opened. Tre did not take his eyes off the doors. The woman delivered his coffee and Kem's breakfast. Self-doubts were creeping out of Tre's subconscious. He began imagining all the things that could be happening to Jax while he was sitting here drinking coffee.

Someone was approaching the table. He risked looking away from the doors for a split second, expecting to see the woman.

It was Noe. Jax was not with him.

Tre gestured him over. "Where is he?"

"Asleep," Noe replied, bringing up a third chair and sitting down.

"You left him alone?"

Noe looked hurt. "Of course not. Rae's with him." He smiled at Kem. "Good morning, Medico Kem. I did not expect to see you."

Kem smiled back at Noe, apparently oblivious that he had been set up to take the blame for their escape.

"Rae?" Tre queried.

"Long story," Noe replied, glancing at Kem.

"Time to go," Tre stated, draining his cup.

"Wait," Noe suggested. He pointed across the square. "Look there."

Tre looked and stiffened. He would have known that the men were Edgers even if he had not recognised the one in the middle. It had been many standards since they had last met, the boy was now a man, but there was no mistaking that it was Nevin Edger; the youngest brother of the clan leader.

Nevin was the most unpredictable of the four surviving siblings; the one who had reacted worst to his nephew's death and his older sister's humiliation. Aaden, his elder brother, would not have hired pirates. Aaden Edger was an honourable man. However, it would appear that Nevin valued vengeance over honour.

How long would Nevin Edger wait before investigating why the rendezvous had not been kept? The answer was obvious; half a morning at the most.

Tre picked up the gold coin and flipped it to the woman. Then he slung his own bag across his back and picked up Kem's. "Back entrance," he muttered and pointed at the door behind the counter. "Lead the way, Noe."

✳ ✳ ✳

Jax felt strangely content when he woke. He could feel Rae's whiskers against the back of his neck and his breath against his skin. Rae's arm was around his waist, holding him tight. Jax couldn't remember ever being so intimate with anyone and yet, weirdly, it felt right.

He wriggled free, waking Rae, and headed for the lavatory. Noe was nowhere to be seen and the clothes he had laid out the day before had gone, so Jax guessed he had left for the Stellar Exchange.

Rae was dressed by the time Jax emerged from the lavatory, which was good because Jax didn't know what he would say if Rae mentioned the snuggling.

Jax looked at the iridescent pants and the lacy shirt hanging on the back of a chair and stayed in the more comfortable clothes he had slept in.

"Do you think Scar will come after us?" he asked, handing Rae four energy bars and unwrapping one for himself.

Rae twitched his whiskers. "No," he replied.

Jax scowled at him. "Why not?"

Rae was about to answer but was distracted. He was suddenly very still with pricked ears and arched whiskers. Jax knew what that meant; he had heard something.

"It's Noe and Tre and a stranger," Rae told him, pulling him off the bed and pushing him into the bathroom. Jax was still thinking about objecting when the door slammed between them.

He was considering peering through the keyhole when the

door opened again. It was Tre. Behind him, close to the door to the hallway, Jax spotted Medico Kem, which was unexpected.

"We're leaving," Tre announced before Jax could even greet him. "You need to dress like you did when you arrived here."

Noe ducked under Tre's arm and thrust the iridescent pants and lacy shirt at him. Jax hesitated, he really didn't want Tre seeing him dressed like that, but decided to comply; they were in too much of a hurry to waste time arguing.

Sure enough, Tre radiated disapproval.

"You walked though Nova Urbo looking like that?"

Noe pushed a chair into the back of Jax's knees and started painting his face as soon as he sat down. "He was wearing a cloak," Noe replied. "And we had Rae to protect us. Show Tre your smile, Rae."

Rae obliged.

"That I approve of," Tre admitted. He shook himself. "It is an effective disguise," he admitted.

Jax wanted to ask Tre about their plan but Noe was painting his lips and by the time that was finished Jax had decided that he wasn't sure how much he should say in front of Kem.

Then Noe and Rae had loaded everything they weren't wearing into Rae's duffle bag and they were off.

There was a dicey moment when they stopped at the counter so that Noe could settle their account. Carl made a comment about them finding clients so quickly. Jax thought that Tre would kill him. So did Carl; Jax could tell from the way all the blood drained from his face.

Luckily Tre pulled himself together. "We'll wait for you outside," he told Noe, who was paying the bill, and guided Jax towards the stairs. "Keep your hood up," he added.

As if Jax needed reminding. "Are we keeping Medico Kem with us?" he asked in a low voice.

"For now," Tre replied. "He may have information that we need. I haven't had time to find out."

Jax would have asked more but the other three joined them and they started towards the docks.

There weren't many people about, just a few stallholders and bar owners opening up in the hope of some early business. Jax guessed that most of them would make the same assumption that Carl had; they were with their new clients, heading for the docks to ship out.

He glanced towards Tre. Would anyone recognise him as the enforcer off the Willow? Or even as one of Jax's father's men? Probably not; Jax had never seen him dressed so formally and he looked different with his hair pulled back.

The guards at the gate had changed. Tre gave them the code that confirmed that he had a secure berth booked and checked that the ship had been refuelled. Then they were off across the concrete.

It looked very different in daylight.

The ruined airlock confirmed Jax's suspicion that Tre had

stolen a ship.

"We will only be pressurising the top two levels," Tre told him. "Up you go, Rae."

Medico Kem was standing looking up at the ship. He turned horrified eyes to Tre. "You stole the commander's yacht?"

"Small compensation for what he did to our ship," Tre replied.

Jax wondered what had happened to the Willow. Has she been destroyed? Did Tre know what had happened to the rest of the crew?

"Give your cloak to Noe and go to the control room," Tre told him, pointing to the ladder that ran up the central axis of the ship. "Noe, can you make sure everything in the cabin is secure, including what we are bringing on board, and look after Medico Kem?"

Noe smiled brightly at Kem. "No problem, Enforcer Tre."

The control room was small but there were three acceleration chairs. By the time Jax arrived, Rae had adjusted one to its smallest setting and was moving on to the second.

They were still a little large but they would have to do. Jax took his place, strapped in and began looking over the controls.

Tre stepped off the ladder and took the captain's chair. He flipped the switch for the intercom.

"This is Tre in command of the Briar Rose. Be aware that only the control room level and the level below are pressurised at this time. Until further notice we will be using the level below those two as an airlock. Lift in two minutes. Noe?"

"This is Noe. I am with Medico Kem in the cabin. We are ready for lift."

Tre looked at Jax.

"This is Jax. Ready," Jax replied.

"This is Rae. Ready," Rae added.

The acceleration chair was much more comfortable than the couch in the Talon's infirmary.

Once they were in orbit, Tre activated the gravitational field generators before pressurising the gun turret above the control room and suggesting that Rae investigate. Rae looked at Jax and twitched his whiskers, which was odd because usually Rae obeyed Tre without question. Jax nodded and Rae vanished up the ladder.

Jax unfastened the safety straps holding him to the chair and tested the gravitational field. It was low, about half, which wasn't surprising because getting a smooth gravitational field for such a small ship would need custom made generators. They probably had the field optimised for the level below, where the living quarters were.

"Nevin Edger was waiting for Scar in the square outside the Stellar Exchange," Tre informed him. "I doubt that his brother knows anything about it." Tre studied him. "You don't seem surprised."

"I know about…" Jax hesitated. "…my brothers. Kip gave me full access to all parts of the Navaja archive, even my father's private files." He took a few deep breaths. "I haven't looked through all of it but I've seen enough to know…" He trailed off. He could not bring himself to say it.

"That your father put clan interests above all other considerations," Tre supplied.

Jax guessed that was one way of putting it. "Fill me in," he ordered.

Tre stuck to the bare facts: the Willow was destroyed; the crew captured; Kip had freed himself and hacked into the Maul's systems.

Jax made himself concentrate on the positives. "So we have no confirmation that any of the crew have died," he pointed out. "And as soon as the Maul starts transmitting again, we should be able to make contact with Kip."

"Jax…" Tre began.

Abandoning his crew led to a place where a father killed his sons. Jax looked Tre directly in the eyes. "It isn't just about preserving my life. It is about a better future; a future in which a leader stands by his people and does his best for them."

Tre tried again. "Jax, they blast their captives' memories with the drug you get in forgetting pills. Then they sell them, podded, to organ harvesters."

Jax felt sick; becoming a mindless living corpse was worse than dying. Even so, he did not change his mind. "We get our people back," he insisted. "We don't stop until we have them, whatever state they are in; alive, mindless or dead."

Tre was studying him. Jax looked back. He was determined. He was willing to be defiant. Finally Tre nodded and spoke.

"I agree."

5

When Kip woke there was a note from Vic pinned to his pillow. It explained that he was in the workshop and that the apartment was locked from the outside. If anyone started opening the door before knocking, Kip was to hide.

Kip wasn't sure he would have woken up.

Vic had cleaned and dried his pants and underpants; Kip found them folded up in the modified locker beside the bunks, along with some clothes that would be a much better fit on Vic than him. He pulled on the smallest top he could find, rolled up the sleeves and told himself it didn't look like a dress.

After looking for a bit, he discovered his stuff and Rae's hung inside the hiding place. He had a meal bar and then spent some time rigging an alarm that would sound in his earpiece if someone touched the lock on the apartment door.

That done he settled down to review what had been happening.

The answer appeared to be not much. The Blackjack was still alongside. It looked like it would remain so until the Maul had a working transmitter and receiver. According to a message flashed from the Blackjack to the Maul, the Talon had landed on Verdant and was on schedule to make the rendezvous.

They had lost track of the commander's yacht, which was a relief. Kip hoped that Tre was on his way to Verdant to rescue Jax.

Kip checked the chronometer. In his note, Vic had said that he would check on Kip about noon, which was still over a hundred minutes away. He decided to occupy himself by finding out everything he could about the pirates. Given their dislike of electronic records and lack of centralised systems, it was not easy. However, Kip liked a challenge.

He had quickly discovered that the Maul wasn't really the Maul at all. It was a salvage ship called the Petunia Mae, which had been run by a single family, the Tuckers, for generations that spanned centuries.

What made the Tuckers interesting was that they worked with hybrids. Living in the tail end of the ship was a colony of mink–human hybrids that bred naturally and bore live young.

Kip had heard about hybrids like that. They had been designed and produced millennia ago by the Central Colonial Service to provide self-sustaining labour forces for planets with a less than welcoming environment; places where the standard ecology had not taken or had been modified by local factors.

The Central Colonial Service no longer existed; modern Centre was all about trying to isolate itself from the Fringe rather than developing it. It had also resolved its ambivalent attitude to genetic engineering. Ten millennia ago Centre had banned all forms of genetic engineering, non-human as well as human. The Central Civil Service had been tasked with eliminating all hybrid engineers, wherever they were located.

They had only been ninety-nine per cent successful. Some hybrid engineers had hidden out in the Far Fringe; others had continued to operate in systems far from the gated shipping lanes. The current hybrid engineering industry had grown from those remains.

Knowing even a little of the Maul's, or rather the Petunia Mae's, history explained a great deal. She was an ancient vessel, modified again and again over the centuries. To the Tuckers she had been home; Kip imagined that she had been lovingly maintained and the mink–human hybrids carefully managed. To the commander the ship and her unique colony of hybrids were just tools. Hybrids were bred to be no more than cannon fodder and the ship was falling apart.

It explained why the commander hadn't been surprised by the power outage.

From what Kip could discover about the commander he was a loathsome excuse for a person. Everything he touched was either corrupted, like the Petunia Mae, or destroyed, like the Willow.

At first Kip had been interested in what motivated him. That had been before he discovered that the commander sold the people he captured to organ harvesters. Worse, he sold them podded so that they could be vivisected.

Now all Kip cared about was stopping him before he could do that to his crew; before he could do it to Ean.

At noon the alarm Kip had installed went off in his earpiece.

He jumped down from the top bunk, anticipating Vic's arrival. Vic had a tray of food with him but it didn't smell very appetising; Kip decided to have another of Ean's meal bars instead of sharing it.

Vic hadn't been able to find an excuse to delay mending the backup transmitter and receiver. The malfunctioning parts had been delivered to the workshop along with a box containing over twenty of the required component.

No one was going to believe that all twenty-six were faulty.

"The minkies are installing the repaired parts in the transmitter and receiver now," Vic explained. "They should work. They did when I tested them. Kip, they are going to realise that something else is up if they don't."

Kip didn't want Vic blamed if they did not function and, anyway, the lower layers of his mind were supplying a stream of reasons why it was better to have the transmitter and receiver working. "I'll make sure they do," he promised. Vic had used a word he didn't know. "Minkies?" he queried.

"The mink–human hybrids," Vic clarified. "The others call them rats, but they prefer minkies. Cute little things. Clever in their way. Good with their hands. Some of them understand the ship really well, but none of the purebreds other than Mutt listen to them."

"Mutt Tucker," Kip guessed.

Vic frowned. "I don't know. Everyone refers to him as Mutt. I'm expected to mend the main transmitter and receiver this afternoon. After that I expect they'll stick me back in a pod."

"You could offer to join the crew," Kip suggested. "They are desperate for an engineer."

Vic sighed and shook his head slowly. "No. If I say I want to join the crew I have to be willing to do it and I am not."

If Vic went back into a pod the commander would sell him to organ harvesters for vivisection. Kip opened his mouth to argue but stopped himself. That was what the commander offered; corruption or destruction. Vic would prefer to die because Vic was a good and honourable man.

"Someone should kill the commander," Kip complained.

"I expect lots of people have tried," Vic replied. He rested a hand on Kip's shoulder. "You must promise me that you won't do anything foolish."

Kip had no intention of being foolish; rash perhaps but not foolish. "I won't."

Vic hesitated, as if having second thoughts about what he was considering saying. "I do not think Tre will come back once he has Jax. His oath to protect Jax will outweigh his loyalty to us, even his feelings for Ean."

As soon as he heard the words Kip knew they were true. He discovered that he was not angry or even disappointed. Tre would be doing what he believed to be right.

Kip hoped that Rae had made it and was with Jax when Tre reached him; Noe too.

"Then it's up to me," Kip pointed out.

Vic opened his mouth, closed it again and then had another go. "You will only be effective if they do not realise you exist."

It was an excellent point. Kip resolved to be careful.

Food eaten, Vic decided to go back to the workshop. That way it would be less likely that anyone would come to the cabin. Kip went back to sitting cross-legged on the upper bunk, which was incredibly comfortable after lying in the service ducts. He had just put on his goggles and earpieces when there was a message from Vic.

It didn't look like they were going to put him in a pod. Waiting for him had been four trolley loads of equipment that needed mending.

Kip went back to digging out information about the pirates with an eye on the transmitter and receiver. As soon as the minkies had installed the mended components, Kip reprogrammed them so that they would work. Not too well; he made sure there was lots of background noise and interference so that he could hide a constant trickle of incoming and outgoing data.

Then he hacked the light speed data relays and checked the Stellar Exchanges on Verdant and on the spacestations. It was reassuring to be reconnected to the data streams. There was nothing about an incident at one of the gates in the Verdant system. Kip wasn't surprised. It had only been three and a half days and the Willow was just a small ship whose drive had overloaded.

At the same time he put together a message for Tre. Even if Tre wasn't coming to the rescue, they could still exchange information.

✳ ✳ ✳

Having established that they were going to rescue Kip, Ean and the others, there was the question of how. Jax insisted that he, Tre and Rae talk about it in the control room while Noe looked after Medico Kem and sorted out the best way for five people to live in such a tiny space.

"It will depend on the situation on the Maul," Tre pointed out. "Her beacon has come back on, so I am assuming they have power again."

"They didn't?" Jax queried.

"Kip disabled the ship completely," Tre admitted. "Lady knows how."

Jax was reminded of what Tre had said about Kip being the second most dangerous person he had ever met. "But no sign of a message from Kip?"

"Not yet." Tre gestured towards one of the consoles. "I have set up an alarm to warn us if anything comes through."

"Other than this ship, what other resources do we have?" Jax asked.

He had never asked that question before and, as soon as he had, Jax realised that it was long overdue. What resources did Tre have? Enough to fit out the Willow so that it bristled with up-to-date technology, but the Willow was gone now.

"We have Medico Kem," Rae answered. "He knows a lot about the Maul and its crew."

"Good point, Rae," Tre acknowledged but offered nothing.

Jax cast about for something. "What about the person who asked you to take Kip?" he asked. "Would he help?"

Tre's nostrils flared slightly. "He is not someone you would wish to be beholden to," he warned.

"You have already rescued me," Jax pointed out. "You are only asking for his help rescuing Kip. How will he react if you don't ask and Kip dies?"

Tre considered and then nodded. "I will send a light speed message. However, he may not be able to do anything constructive soon enough to make a difference."

Jax could not see that it could make matters worse. He went through the different groups in his mind. There were the pirates, Kip, them and the Edgers.

"What will Nevin Edger do when the pirates do not keep the rendezvous?" he asked.

"It depends on how keen he is to hide what he had been doing from his brother," Tre replied. "The sensible reaction would be to walk away. Unfortunately Nevin Edger was being driven by vengeance rather than reason, so his actions are difficult to predict."

"And the pirates?" Jax queried.

"Their leader, the man they call the commander, appears to be tactically astute. The most likely outcome was that they will forgo the balance of the fee and maintain the illusion that they are a simple salvage ship cleaning up after a tragic accident. They'll jump out of the system and go on their way."

"Where do you think they will take Ean and the others?" Rae asked.

Jax glanced at Tre and then squared up to the task of telling Rae about the forgetting juice and the organ harvesters. He was just about to start when there was a squawk from the console.

"Kip," Tre confirmed. "He has this system for sending information. It comes in three streams and the three streams decode each other." He paused and shook his head. "I confess I don't fully understand it. Why don't you and Rae respond to what he has sent while I go below to speak with Medico Kem? Remember to record everything."

Jax nodded, Tre redirected the feed. There was a message in long-short.

Captain's tray?

Jax guessed he had to input the correct response in long-short and send it over the same channel. They had always used the same tray to carry stuff to and from the captain's cabin.

Black.

Things started happening. Indicator lights flashed; systems briefly hummed before falling silent again.

"Programmes he has sent are installing," Tre reassured him. "His stuff goes through any security systems as if they aren't there. The prefix you will need is 25-pi-lambda-8."

Text began appearing on one of the small screens embedded in the console. Jax reached for the button to turn on the record function only to find it was already activated. Then he angled the screen so that it was easier for Rae to see.

This is Kip. Unexpected result! They don't have an engineer and they had to get Vic to restart the battery banks and mend the transmitter and receiver. I am out of the service ducts and hiding in Vic's cabin.

Kip had to be one hundred per cent certain no one could decode his messages; he hadn't been careful about what he had sent. Jax glanced over at Rae, whose whisker twitch said, "He closed down the battery banks?"

Jax agreed; no one but Kip would think of taking a risk like that.

More text was appearing on the screen.

I have set up a trickle feed of information about the Maul. By the time you read this it will be installing in your ship's databanks.

Jax checked. Sure enough a database had been established and was filling up.

Which ship are you on? Any news of Jax? Or Rae? Or Noe? Use the usual prefix. After that you can use text. The system is secure.

Jax was glad Vic was alive and still Vic. It was good that Kip wasn't alone. He put in the prefix and started inputting text.

This is Jax. I am with Tre, Rae and Noe on the Briar Rose that used to be the commander's yacht. Medico Kem is with us. He was on the Talon and the Maul before that. His status is uncertain but he might know stuff. Do you have any questions for him? We

have to work out a way to get you and the others off the Maul and to safety. I have persuaded Tre to send a message to the person looking out for you. Maybe he will help. Can you do the type of stuff you did on the Willow? The pirates' client is Nevin Edger. Tre saw him in Nova Urbo. Can you identify his ship? Or tell me how to do it?

Jax paused. Did they know anything that Kip didn't?

"Tell him what we did on the Talon," Rae encouraged. "Tell him that Scar and his servant, Nero, are dead."

"They are?" he queried.

Rae nodded. "Noe slit their throats." He twitched his whiskers. "And tell him that they blast the captives with forgetting juice."

Jax guessed Rae had been able to hear his conversation with Tre from the gun turret; so much for him not knowing. "You sure?" he queried; it would upset Kip a lot.

"He can't stop it if he doesn't know about it," Rae pointed out.

It was a valid point so Jax reluctantly included the information as something Medico Kem had told them. Thinking about it, perhaps Kem was the person who gave the captives the forgetting juice, which would be good because he was on the Briar Rose rather than the Maul.

Did doing bad things because you were terrified of the person telling you to do them make those things less bad?

Scar had been a pirate. Did that mean it was fine for Noe to slit his throat while he was unconscious? What about Nero?

"Scar did sex-stuff with boys until they died," Rae told him as if he had been reading Jax's mind.

Jax wondered how Rae knew. "And Nero?" he queried.

Rae shrugged.

Kip felt like he had been kicked in the stomach. The pirates blasted their captives' memories with forgetting juice? He had been sure that Ean and the others were safe in their pods.

Instead they may have been murdered; their personalities and memories gone forever.

He had to check. Pushing up his goggles, he pulled out the jack from its socket and jumped down from his bunk. Then he was out into the corridor with the intention of re-entering the service ducts.

Strong arms were around him from behind before he could lift the hatch cover. Kip began panicking and wriggling before recognising the arms wrapped around his waist.

"Vic," he acknowledged and stopped squirming.

Vic yanked one of the cables leading to Kip's earpieces, pulling the left one out. "What in Known Space are you doing? You have to stay in the cabin." He hustled Kip back into the cabin and shut the door. "Owen was here only fifteen minutes ago." He looked Kip up and down. "What's wrong?"

Kip looked at the wall and bit his lip. He didn't know if he could say it without crying and he did not want to do that in front of Vic.

"Have you heard from Tre?" Vic encouraged.

"Yes. He's got Jax, Rae and Noe with him," Kip replied.

"And they are all right?" Vic checked.

Kip nodded. He had to do it, Vic would keep asking. "They've found out…" He trailed off but made himself try again. "They've found out that they destroy the captives' memories with forgetting juice." He felt tears trickling down his cheeks and swiped them away with the back of a hand.

Vic paled. "Are you sure? No one mentioned it to me." He took a deep breath and let it out slowly. "Not that they would," he admitted. "When do they do it? Maybe it's just before delivery to the organ harvesters."

Kip had not thought of that. There would be advantages of doing it that way. It would mean that they could still use the person during a crisis, like they were using Vic, or that they could return the person if their loved ones came up with a big enough payment.

"Can you check?" Vic asked. "Without wandering around the ship," he added quickly.

Kip could ask Jax to talk to Medico Kem. "They have this medico with them. Someone off this ship. He was on the Talon."

Vic's eyebrows went up. "Skinny, sandy-haired with eye-glasses?"

Kip did not know. He shrugged.

"Could be him. He was in a rush to get to a ship," Vic recalled.

"His name is Kem," Kip supplied.

"That's him," Vic agreed. "He patched me up." He pointed to the healing wound on his temple.

"I'll get Jax to ask him," Kip suggested.

"Good idea," Vic acknowledged. "You must promise me that you will stay in the cabin, Kip." He rested a hand on Kip's shoulder. "Remember, you can only help the others if the commander doesn't realise you exist."

Back up on the top bunk Kip sent another message to Jax, asking him to press the medico for details. Now he had to wait at least eighteen minutes, nine out and nine back, for a reply. It would probably be longer than that; Jax would need time to speak to Kem.

What would he do if Medico Kem's answer was that it had already been done? Vic might have been an exception; he had not been brought onto the ship in a pod but as a captive in a suit.

Kip thought back to those minutes in the room with the pods. There had been time to throw all the lids open and hit all the wake-up buttons. Maybe more of them would have made it into the service ducts. Perhaps if Ean and the others had been walking, talking captives they would have been treated like Vic rather than having their memories wiped.

He checked the chronometer. Only two minutes had passed since he had sent the message to Jax.

❈ ❈ ❈

Jax had finished sending information and moved on to the kind of questions that Kip had been able to answer when they were on the Willow, like the name of Nevin Edger's ship and where it was going.

There hadn't been anything from Kip himself in a while, just the continuing trickle of information into the database. Jax checked the chronometer. His gut twisted. Kip had stopped sending when he had received the message about the forgetting juice.

"I said it would upset him," Jax complained.

Rae's whiskers drooped. "He needed to know."

Jax imagined Kip's reaction. It would be worse than his; much worse than Rae's. They came from backgrounds where terrible things happened to people. Kip didn't. "I hope he doesn't do anything stupid."

Rae was about to reply when a new message appeared on the screen.

Just got your message about the forgetting juice. Scary. Please get more information from Medico Kem. Is there a way of changing the records or marking the pods so that it looks like it has already been done?

It was a huge relief. If Kip was inputting text he wasn't running around the Maul checking if Ean still remembered them. Jax grabbed a tablet and stood up.

"You keep sending him stuff," he told Rae. "Anything to distract him. I'm going to talk to Medico Kem."

Rae twitched his whiskers but nodded.

He headed for the ladder and climbed down. He hadn't paid much attention on the way up; on the level below there was a landing around the ladder and five doors, three of which were open. One led to a small galley, where Noe was making an inventory and probably eavesdropping on Tre and Kem's conversation.

Noe stopped what he was doing and looked at Jax.

"We've made contact with Kip," Jax told him. "Rae's trying to think of stuff to send him. He could probably do with some help."

Noe nodded, wiped his hands on a cloth and headed past Jax and up the ladder.

Through another of the open doors, Jax could see Tre and Kem in a much larger room. It was luxurious without any hint of femininity; Jax guessed it was the commander's cabin.

They had stopped talking. "Jax," Tre acknowledged.

"There are some urgent questions for Medico Kem," Jax explained being careful not to mention Kip.

Tre nodded, giving permission for Jax to proceed.

"We need information about how the captives are treated and kept," Jax began. "If we are going to rescue them, the smallest detail may be useful. We are particularly interested in what you told us about them being treated with the drug in forgetting pills. If possible, we very much want to avoid this happening."

To his surprise Kem flushed a deep red.

"Medico Kem?" Tre queried.

"I got rid of it all," Kem admitted. "I replaced it all with saline and sugar pills." He frowned as if reconsidering. "Well, maybe not all but as much as I could find." He flushed again. "Memories are important. They make a person who he is and keep him going through the bad times. Also, staying who they were until the moment the organ harvesters cut them up gave them a chance, however slim."

Jax wondered how long Kem had been clinging to his memories of home and loved ones.

"Wasn't that a huge risk?" Tre asked.

"Not really," Kem replied. "The dose was massive, so there was no point unpodding anyone who had been treated; at best they would be a drooling idiot and at worst they would be a violent maniac. If a captive was found to have his memories intact, there were lots of points in the process where someone could have mucked up. Even if the commander got as far as checking the vials, he would probably think he had been ripped off by the apothecary who supplied them." He shuddered, as if imagining what the commander would do to him if he realised who was to blame. "It was worth the risk," he insisted. Then his chin came up. "I am a medico. When I took my oath to do no harm I meant it."

There was something painfully noble about this fearful little man reaching a line he would not cross. Jax searched for the best words; ones that would make Kem feel good about what he had done without being condescending.

"Hopefully we have reached a point when your decision will make a difference, Medico Kem. If we can liberate those in pods on the Maul, they can be returned to their loved ones with their memories and personalities intact."

Kem's eyes filled with tears and he turned away to hide them. "That would be good," he admitted.

Jax felt Tre's hand on his shoulder; a slight squeeze confirmed his approval. "Why don't you take Medico Kem into the galley and make tea," he suggested. "He can tell you about where and how the captives are kept." As Jax turned his head to reply, Tre dropped his voice so low that Jax was reading lips rather than hearing words. "I'll make sure Kip knows that the forgetting juice has been switched, so he isn't tempted to do anything rash."

The galley was tiny when compared with the one on the Willow but it had a small table that folded out from the wall and around which three or four people could sit. Jax propped up the table and lifted down two folding chairs from where they were stored on the wall.

Then he started investigating what pirates kept in their cupboards; hopefully it included tea.

The surface of the cupboard door was reflective; Jax caught sight of smoky green eye sockets and glistening purple lips. He had forgotten that Noe had painted his face. He grabbed a cloth, thankfully it was clean, and rinsed it through with hot water. Squeezing the majority of the water away, he rubbed the cloth over his face, hoping that the heat would melt the paint and make it easier to remove.

Repeated attempts, refolding the cloth each time so that he was using a clean surface, left his face unusually pink but relatively paint-free.

A glance confirmed that Kem was pretending not to watch him. Jax dropped the cloth into the sink and went back to searching the cupboards. Assuming this was indeed the commander's yacht, the man had excellent taste. Jax found coffee beans, a brand of whisky he recognised and some good-quality tea.

The teapot left much to be desired but Jax did his best.

"This is nice, thank you," Kem acknowledged. "I would not expect the heir to the Navaja clan to be making me tea."

"I am a cabin boy," Jax replied. "Cabin boys make tea."

Kem shook his head. "I know little about spacers."

"The Willow was a Traditional ship," Jax told him. It hurt to be talking about the Willow as if she had no future. "A Traditional crew is like a family. It takes on boys, often from difficult backgrounds, and turns out men who are skilled and honourable spacers."

"Boys like Rae and Noe," Kem suggested.

"And me," Jax insisted. He hadn't really thought about it before but maybe guiding Joaquin Oro Sebastiano Socorro's son through adolescence was even more difficult than raising a feral hybrid or a child whore.

Or a genius; Jax was determined not to forget Kip.

Tre had selected the Willow. He had chosen Ean to queen the crew. Jax needed to think more about that but not now. Collecting information for Kip was more urgent. He used the tablet to open the database Kip had created about the Maul.

"So, Medico Kem, what can you tell us about where and how they keep the captives?"

Once Kem had told Jax everything he could remember, Jax went back to the control room and took over from Noe, who was still sending messages to Kip. Noe went down to the galley, to try to squeeze a meal out of the meagre supplies in the cupboards. Tre was looking through the information about the Maul. He was wearing earpieces, facing the opposite way and had his eyes fixed on a display.

Rae looked distinctly flustered. His eyes were wide and his face was flushed.

"What's been happening?" Jax whispered.

Rae shook his head. "Nothing important," he insisted.

Jax was sure he had missed something but decided not to push. Instead he started telling Kip what Medico Kem had told him.

"You washed the face paint off," Rae observed.

Jax felt himself flush. "Yes."

"It looked good," Rae assured him.

Jax was about to say that only whores wore that much paint but he stopped himself. Rae was being nice, trying to make him feel better about being dressed up like that.

"You are much prettier than Noe," Rae added.

For a moment Jax didn't know how to respond. From his father or one of his father's men it would have been an insult but Rae obviously meant it as a compliment. Jax decided to ignore the negative connotations. "Thank you, Rae."

Rae's smile lit up his face and, for a moment, the irises of his eyes were pure gold.

Jax could not help but smile in return.

6

Kip had stopped doing anything other than watching the chronometer and trying to keep all the layers of his mind absolutely still. Thinking just generated questions that led to explosions of possibilities; most of which were too terrible to contemplate.

Once he had Jax's reply he would be able to formulate a problem and work on it.

If the reply was that Ean and the others were gone, their personalities destroyed, the problem would be how to kill the commander, preferably after shooting him full of forgetting juice.

Words began appearing, scrolling across his field of view. Kip held his breath, only to release it when he read the first few sentences.

This is Noe. Rae is with me. Jax is talking to Medico Kem as you asked. I hope you are looking after yourself and Vic. After all, that's part of a cat's job.

Despite himself, Kip smiled. He had a shrewd idea that Noe wasn't referring to cooking and cleaning.

When we escaped from the Talon we disguised our-

selves by dressing up as a pimp and his girlyboys.

Rae was the pimp. Having teeth made up for being small. Jax made a very convincing girlyboy. Rae wasn't the only one who thought he was really pretty. Now Rae is blushing.

Kip could imagine.

Do you want to try sex by text? The time delay might make it tricky but we could try.

He was about to reply that 'sex by text' wasn't a priority when more words appeared.

This is Tre. Medico Kem assures us that he has substituted all the memory-disrupting drugs on the Maul with saline or sugar pills, so even if the captives have been treated the treatment will be ineffective. I will now hand you back to Noe for your sex by text session.

Relief washed over Kip, leaving him dizzy, followed by embarrassment, which made him hot and bothered. He decided to try to stop Noe even though he knew it was pointless; Noe would be nine minutes into it by now.

Thank you for offering, Noe, but there are other matters on which I need to concentrate.

As Kip had expected, his message did not faze Noe in the slightest. Instead he merely paused for a moment and suggested that Kip keep the text for later when he was less busy.

That meant there was a stream of teasing, suggestive and occasionally blatant suggestions from Noe scrolling across the bottom of Kip's field of view while he worked. Despite being sure that he wasn't in the mood, the occasional one caught his attention and made his rod twitch.

Kip knew it was Noe's way of showing that he cared.

First on Kip's list was reassuring Vic about Ean and the others. He sent a coded message to the tablet Vic was using at his bench. Back came a reply. Vic was not surprised; apparently Medico Kem had impressed him as a good man in a bad situation.

The comment gave Kip the energy he needed to work on his plan to subvert the commander's hold on the Maul's crew. Based on what Kip had heard when eavesdropping, what Vic had said of Medico Kem was also true of Owen and Kurt and probably Mutt Tucker.

A soft ping announced incoming information that Kip's monitoring algorithms had identified as important. Kurt was opening a channel to the harbourmaster's office for the commander to send a message.

"This is the captain of the Maul and the owner of Interstellar Salvage. I am sending you a copy of my electronic credentials. You have one of our ships, the Talon, in secure silo eight-four. I am sending you a copy of the receipt for the booking. We are having issues communicating with the Talon. Please could you send one of your security personnel to check on the ship and ask the captain to make contact? I am transferring twenty credits as recompense for this additional service." There was a click as the microphone linked to the transmitter was deactivated.

He had sounded so reasonable; not in the least like a murdering pirate. Kip built and sent a worm that would burrow into the systems of the company that owned the secure berths in the Nova Urbo spaceport. If they investigated the Talon, he would know.

"How soon can we expect a reply, Kurt?"

"Just over nine minutes there, same back, commander." Kurt replied. *"Are we thinking of moving closer to Verdant?"*

"No, we stay at the gate," the commander replied. *"What's the earliest jump slot that is available?"*

Kip did not like the sound of that at all.

"I'll check, commander," Kurt replied.

What could he do if the Maul went to jump away from the system? Another power outage? Fiddle with the gate? Kip had worked out how to deactivate a gate standards ago but it really didn't seem a good idea. The Gaters might take an interest and, although Gaters were fascinating, Kip didn't want them looking for him.

No, it was much easier to book all the jump slots. He set to work. It was a challenge to create enough virtual ships quickly enough but Kip soon had a system going; every time he generated a ship it booked the next available slot.

Radio traffic between the Maul and the harbourmaster's office confirmed that the guards at the secure berths had been contacted. Kip checked, he could see the request in the security company's system.

This could be the perfect moment to begin sending messages to the crew. Kip was certain that such messages would not be traced back to him. If the commander was capable of tracking them, which Kip doubted, he would discover that they originated on the Blackjack

It was true that they were bounced through the Blackjack's systems.

Kip sent his first message; it would scroll once across every display on the Maul to which he had managed to make a link, with the exception of the ones in the control room or the commander's cabin.

Scar is dead.

Five minutes later he sent the second.

Finally someone did the right thing and slit his throat.

Just after he sent the second message he received a copy of the report the guards had made about what they had found on the Talon. As Kip had hoped, they had included images of the dead bodies. Kip stripped out the image he needed, processed it so that it could not be identified as the picture the security guards had taken and integrated it into his third message.

It was done properly this time.

Then he set the three messages cycling, one every five minutes, and sat back to monitor the fallout.

No one rushed to tell the commander or even Kurt. Interestingly, more displays were turned on than off, suggesting that rumours of what had happened were circulating. Kip took that as a good sign.

When the response from the harbourmaster's office came through Kip listened carefully, more interested in the commander's response than what the harbourmaster said.

"As in all such cases, the security company took images to provide evidence of what occurred," the harbourmaster stated.

Kip began flipping through the images. Interestingly, there was no sign of the hinges that Tre had destroyed with the shaped charges; the door to the silo had been replaced so that there could be no suggestion that the security company was to blame for the incident.

It was an unexpected bonus; there was now no sign of Tre's involvement.

"In the nose end of the ship there were two bodies and eight unconscious men," the harbourmaster continued. *"A medico was summoned and the unconscious men responded to a wake up shot. The tail end of the ship was still sealed and was not opened. Attached is an invoice for the medico's services. Doubtless your men will have been in contact before this message reaches you."*

They had not been and Kip could not see the commander being too happy about that.

The commander sent a brief confirmation and transferred credit to cover the medico's fee. Once he had closed the channel there was hardly a sound from the microphone in the control room. Kip knew Kurt and Owen were both there. He imagined them being too terrified to even breathe deeply, especially Owen.

"*Open a private channel to Captain Ort,*" the commander ordered after another few minutes of tense silence.

"*Yes, commander,*" Owen squeaked.

"*There is a message coming in from the Talon, commander,*" Kurt announced in his usual, calm voice.

"*Belay opening the channel to the Blackjack,*" the commander decided. "Who sent it, Kurt?"

"*It is Cage, commander,*" Kurt replied. "*Visual as well as audio.*"

"*Put it through,*" the commander told him.

Kip put the live feed directly through to his goggles. It showed a young, square-jawed man with what would have been brown skin if he hadn't been so pale. Instead it was an interesting sallow colour.

"*This is Cage, commander. There has been an incident. Captain Scar is dead. So is Nero. Medico Kem is missing, as are the two captives.*"

The commander paused the video. Over the microphone Kip heard him swear under his breath. "*Owen, start monitoring a ship called the Orca. Kurt, are you sure there isn't a jump slot? If not, begin contacting the ships with slots booked and finding out what they want for a swap. Owen, forget the private channel to Captain Ort. Tell him to get the Blackjack over here and into the docking bay. Then tell Mutt to get all his rats aboard without delay.*"

So the commander knew that the client was Nevin Edger and intended to get a head start on any pursuing Edger ships. The video was restarting.

"*The rendezvous has not been kept, commander,*" Cage admitted. "*What do you want us to do? We could go looking for Kem.*"

The commander stopped the video again. "*Idiots,*" he complained. "*Open me a channel to the Talon, Owen.*"

"*It is open, commander,*" Kurt replied.

"*This is your commander. Refuel and then lift immediately. Proceed as quickly as possible to gate four and jump out of the system. I will contact you again with further instructions.*" He closed the channel.

There was a short silence and then Kurt spoke. "*Do you wish me to book them a jump slot at gate four?*"

"*I very much doubt that will be necessary,*" the commander replied and restarted the video to view the rest of Cage's message. "*Concentrate on finding us that jump slot.*"

It took a moment for Kip to realise that the Talon was being sacrificed; a target for Nevin Edger to focus on and, most likely, destroy.

"*I usually make my rounds at this time, commander,*" Kurt replied. "*Owen could look for the jump slot now that he has finished speaking to Captain Ort.*"

"*Very well. I shall be in my cabin. Owen, contact me as soon as you confirm we have a slot.*"

"*Yes, commander,*" Owen replied in a more normal voice than before.

There was a lengthy silence from the control room; Kip imagined Kurt and Owen waiting double the usual time after the commander's departure before speaking.

"*Mulligan's teat,*" Kurt muttered. "*You had better find us that slot, Owen.*"

"*Scar's dead?*" Owen queried.

There were the sounds of someone standing up. "*Catch up, Owen. Kem grew a backbone. Now we have a pissed-off client after some recompense. The commander is willing to throw anything to the wolves to get away.*"

"*Kem?*" Owen queried.

Kurt laughed. "*Yes, Kem. Incredible, isn't it? Kem drugs the rest of the crew, slits Scar and Nero's throats and runs off with the Navaja clan heir.*"

"*Yes, that is incredible,*" Owen stated. "*He would never have slit anyone's throat, not even Scar's.*"

"*Someone slit Scar and Nero's throats and ran off with the boys,*" Kurt insisted. "*Or the boys slit Scar and Nero's throats and ran off with Medico Kem. Whichever, the whole mission is so badly screwed up that the commander is only focusing on survival. Just be thankful you are on this ship and not the Talon. I am off on my rounds. Concentrate on getting that jump slot.*"

Kip was deciding what he would do if Owen managed to contact a real ship with an actual jump slot when Owen's voice came over the live feed from the microphone in the control room.

"*You're back soon.*"

There was no response, only the sound of someone sitting down.

"*Kurt?*"

"*There are messages about Scar coming up on every display on the ship. It's been happening since early afternoon and no one told us or the commander. What do I do? Tell him?*"

"*You can't risk not telling him,*" Owen pointed out.

This was the moment; Kip was sure. The men on the Talon had been cut off. Captain Ort and the Blackjack were not yet in the docking bay. If he hesitated he would miss his chance. He made sure that he could control any communications into or out of the commander's cabin and then sent a message to the main display in the control room.

Kem made it. You can too.

"*Did you see that?*" Owen asked.

"*Of course I saw it,*" Kurt replied. "*I am going to get the commander.*"

"*No, Kurt, don't!*" Owen insisted.

Kip wished he had not sent the message but there was no way back; he was committed. He had Owen. Now he had to convince Kurt.

You will never get another chance. Seal the commander in his cabin. Tell Ort that the plan has changed and that he is to jump through the gate. A slot will become available. Make a list of anyone you do not

trust and work out a way to isolate them on one of the levels.

"The commander is testing us," Kurt insisted.

"No," Owen replied. *"He doesn't think like this."*

"Ort will never believe the order is from the commander," Kurt complained.

"Yes he will," Owen insisted. *"If he queries it, tell him that the commander is busy trying to placate the client. Tell him about Scar and the Talon. That'll make him want to run."*

There was silence. Kip's mind began generating possibilities. Too many of them led to undesirable outcomes, some of which were very bad indeed. On balance, the risk had been too great. He should have waited.

"We do nothing until we know the commander is contained," Kurt insisted.

Kip brought up the plans of that level of the ship. As far as he could see, the door was the only way out of the commander's cabin. The ducts running to the cabin were too small for a person and the walls were reinforced for security, so it would be as difficult for the commander to cut his way out as for an enemy to cut his way in. Kip doubted he had the necessary tools.

Then he saw it; the airlock. He began thinking as quickly as he could, using the layers of his mind in parallel, and hastily composed another message.

All communication channels from the commander's cabin have been interrupted. Get Vic to seal the door.

Get Mutt's minkies to pick up the commander as he comes out the airlock.

"*Who is it?*" Kurt queried.

"*I don't care,*" Owen declared. "*Whoever it is, he's right. This is our chance. No Scar. No Ort. The worst of the heavies are on the Talon. Unless you stop me now, I'm going to get Vic to seal the commander's cabin door.*"

"*What if he opens it when you are there?*" Kurt asked.

"*I'll shoot him,*" Owen replied. "*Are you going to stop me?*"

"*No,*" Kurt admitted. "*I'm going to send the message to Ort and then talk to Mutt.*"

Kip did not want Kurt leaving the control room.

All communications channels to the commander's cabin have been interrupted. That includes the intercom.

There was a short silence before Owen spoke. "He can hear us," he whispered.

"*Who are you?*" Kurt asked.

Kip could not believe he had given himself away. He thought quickly.

A friend of Kem's. Please act quickly before the opportunity is lost.

"*I am on my way,*" Owen announced.

There was a lot to do. Kip sent a coded message to Vic that

had him arriving in the cabin rather than the result Kip had wanted, which was for him to get his tools ready and wait for Owen.

"What in Known Space have you been up to, Kip?" he demanded.

Kip could not afford to raise his goggles or take out his earpieces. "I'm sorry not to have discussed it, Vic, but a chance presented itself. Owen is on his way. I need you to interrupt the power supply to the commandant's cabin door and then seal it so it can't be jimmied open."

"Does Owen know about you?" Vic asked.

"No. Please, Vic. It's like trying to juggle ten balls at once."

There was no immediate answer. Kip wondered if he should risk making his goggles translucent but if he did he might miss something in one of the live streams.

"I'll go get ready," Vic replied. Kip felt Vic's large hand pat his shoulder. "Good luck."

"Thanks," Kip acknowledged.

Kurt had opened a channel to the Blackjack.

"This is Kurt. The commander wishes you to belay that last order. Please do not dock with the Maul."

Kip was impressed. Kurt sounded completely normal. The Blackjack was replying.

"This is Ort. Put me through to the commander."

"This is Kurt. Switching to private channel two and requesting

you do the same."

"*This is Ort on channel two. What is going on, Kurt?*"

"*The commander is in private conference with the client. The mission has gone belly-up. We lost the merchandise before we could deliver it. Scar's dead. The Talon's running for gate four. Given how slow the Maul is, the commander has decided that it might be better for you to jump ahead and scout out the situation in the next system.*"

Kip had confirmation of a swap between one of his virtual ships and the Blackjack. He put the details up on the display in the control room.

"*Your slot is today at nine hundred minutes,*" Kurt continued. "*I am transmitting the code and the electronic confirmation.*"

"*Got it,*" Ort confirmed. "*We'll have to shift to make it. The situation must be bad if the commander is willing to pay for three jump slots rather than one,*" he added.

"*I am sure the commander has it under control,*" Kurt replied.

Kip hoped he hadn't picked too early a time but having Captain Ort worrying about making the jump slot rather than speaking to the commander had seemed a good idea.

"*You can control jump slots?*" Kurt queried.

Kip realised that Kurt was speaking to him. He did not want to begin a conversation; he would give too much away. Instead he reminded Kurt of the next urgent task.

Mutt.

Summoning Mutt Tucker to the control room proved impossible. Even demanding his presence via the intercom did not work. The minutes clocked by: five; ten; fifteen; twenty. In the end, Owen was back before Kurt had accomplished it.

"*I'll go down there,*" Owen suggested. "*I'll wear a radio so you and our mystery helper can follow what I am doing.*"

Kip was beginning to panic.

Be quick. Once the commander realises he is locked in, he will be out that airlock as soon as he can get into a suit.

"*On my way,*" Owen replied. He seemed remarkably cheerful for someone taking such horrendous risks.

"*Be careful,*" Kurt warned.

There was a sound that might have been a kiss. "*I'll be fine. Mutt and the minkies like me.*"

Even if he ran, Owen could not be there in less than five minutes. Kip watched the data he was gleaning from the commander's cabin. He couldn't stop the commander opening the escape airlock, they were designed to operate whatever the circumstances, but Kip was pretty sure he would be able to tell if it happened.

He began investigating what he could do to track the commander if he escaped. The answer was not a lot; neither the telescopes nor the guns were designed to work close to the ship's hull.

"*Almost there,*" Owen informed them. "*I'll leave the channel open so you can follow what is happening.*" The sounds of sliding down a ladder were replaced by those of walking quickly along a corridor. *"Hi, paps, can you point me in the direction of Mister Mutt?"*

There was a high-pitched barked reply that might have been, *"Mister Mutt not about."*

"Look, paps, it's urgent. If Mister Mutt isn't about can I speak to one of the grandpaps or even a grand-grandpaps?"

"Owen, it has to be Mutt," Kurt complained.

"Kurt, just shut up," Owen hissed. *"You haven't got a clue about the minkies. I'll wait here,"* he added in a normal voice, obviously speaking to the mink–human hybrid.

Then Kip saw it. The commander was opening the hardwired channel between his cabin and the control room. Kip diverted the message; he did not want Kurt swayed by his fear or the commander's rhetoric.

Kip sent a message to Kurt. The commander is beginning to realise that there is something wrong.

"You need to speed up," Kurt told Owen.

"Rushing them won't work," Owen whispered. *"Here comes one of the really old ones."*

Kip had hoped that the commander would leave a microphone activated but he hadn't. He could be trying the door or already getting into his suit. Kip had no way of knowing.

"Grand-grand-grandpaps," Owen acknowledged respectfully.

There was a wheezy, high-pitched, barking reply. *"Mister Owen."*

"*Scar is dead,*" Owen began. "*Medico Kem has got away. Captain Ort and his crew are on the Blackjack heading for the gate. Scar's crew is on the Talon far away. We have this one chance. I can save Mister Kurt. You can save Mister Mutt. Mister Vic and I have locked the commander in his cabin and stopped him contacting anyone. When he realises he will come out of the escape lock of his cabin.*"

There was silence. Kip held his breath.

When it came, the mink–human hybrid's answer was surprisingly clear. "*Leave the commander to us, Mister Owen.*"

All that Kip could hear over Owen's radio channel were footsteps.

"*That's it?*" Kurt queried. "*Shouldn't you talk to Mutt? And what was that about you saving me?*"

"*Mutt will hesitate,*" Owen answered. "*They won't. As for saving you, Kurt, you've been sacrificing who you are bit by bit. I know you've been doing it to protect me but I want my Kurt, not one of the commander's captains.*"

Kip flushed, embarrassed to be eavesdropping on such an intimate moment.

He was so distracted by that he almost missed the ping from the programme monitoring the Maul's radio receiver. Someone was transmitting but it wasn't via the ship's transmitter. Kip broke out in a cold sweat. It had to be the commander; probably using the radio transmitter in his suit. Why hadn't he anticipated that?

The signal was already on its way. There was one person who must not receive it; Captain Ort on the Blackjack. Kip accessed the Maul's transmitter and blasted interference across that channel and all the others a suit radio could use.

How much of the signal had been transmitted? Kip was trembling as he accessed the recording.

"*This is the commander for Captain Ort. Kurt is leading a mutiny. Turn your guns on the Maul and issue an ultimatum. I am suited and on my way over. This is the commander for Captain Ort. Kurt...*" The repeat of the message was lost in a burst of static.

The whole message had been sent. Kip felt sick. What did he do? Should he tell Kurt?

It would be best to find out what was happening first. Kip brought up the live feeds from the telescopes. The Blackjack was not slowing; she was still accelerating towards the gate.

Maybe Ort had not received the commander's orders. Or perhaps he had but had decided to keep going. The Maul had more guns and she had the minkies.

Kip lay back on his bunk. His shirt was drenched with sweat and he felt worse than after Tre had put him through a training session.

He promised himself he would never act on impulse again. Instead he would think each possibility through and plan every detail. Nothing would be left to Lady Luck.

7

It had been six days since Kurt and Owen had taken control of the ship. The Blackjack and the Talon were long gone. Kip had purchased the Talon a jump slot at gate four. As predicted, the Orca had chased it through the gate, presumably with Nevin Edger aboard.

No one had suggested that the minkies take the commander alive so he was very, very dead.

Kip looked out across the room. In piles was stuff from the Willow that the minkies had retrieved. The small bits of ship were in another, equally large, room. Some medium pieces were in the Maul's, now the Petunia Mae's, holds. The larger pieces of wreckage was still out there, moving at different velocities through the Verdant system. The minkies were still working on some of the closer ones.

Everyone who Owen was not sure they could trust, which had turned out to be all the purebreds other than Mutt, had been podded. Vic had been working full out stopping the Petunia Mae from falling apart. He had a team of minkies helping him. Captain Mel was advising Kurt. Cas and Obe had made friends with Owen.

There was no sign of Loy or Ean.

Cas and Obe, with Owen helping them, had opened every pod on the ship. They had found the nine individuals that the Willow had been transporting to Mercy Station. They had even found two Tuckers who Mutt had thought were dead but the commander had kept back in case he needed leverage to control Mutt and the minkies.

They had not found Loy or Ean.

Mutt had asked the minkies to search among the wreckage for more pods but Kip knew they weren't out there. All nine of the escape pods that had left the Willow were on the Petunia Mae. Kip had examined them. One of them had contained Ean and another Loy. He was sure of it.

So where were they now? The obvious answer was in other pods on the Blackjack; through the gate and halfway across the next system.

Kip had let them be taken.

Today the others arrived. Kip would have to look Tre and Rae and Jax in the eyes and admit that he had failed.

Rae was excited. Today they got to see Kip and the others. True, they hadn't found Ean or Loy yet, but Rae was sure they were somewhere on the Petunia Mae, which was what Kip called the Maul. It was a big ship and Vic complained every time they talked to him about how disorganised it was. Ean and Loy were in pods in some corner; maybe on a trolley or in the wrong storage hold. Once they were aboard, Rae intended to help look for them.

"Sit down, Rae," Noe complained. "Watching you bob up and down is making me dizzy."

"Leave him alone," Jax snapped.

Five people in such a small space for six days had been difficult. Noe was bored. Jax was crabby. Medico Kem hid in the small cabin. Tre only left the control room to use the head; he even ate and slept there. Rae himself was desperate for exercise. He missed his treadmill. The Petunia Mae was a big ship. Maybe he would be able to run around it.

Tre was still really cross with Kip. Rae didn't understand why. He and Noe had rescued Jax. Kip and Vic had dealt with the pirates. Or rather they had teamed up with the good pirates, the ones like Medico Kem, and turned on the bad pirates.

Rae decided to mention it again, because discussing that was better than listening to Jax and Noe sniping at each other. It was different between them than it had been on the Willow. Noe no longer used his eyelashes on Jax and Jax rose more easily when Noe baited him.

"Do you think Tre will tell Kip off when he sees him?" Rae asked.

"Yes," Noe replied.

Rae looked to Jax.

"Tre thinks Kip took too many risks," Jax explained. "He was lucky. Like you were when you managed to get onto the Talon."

Rae twitched his whiskers. It hadn't been about luck. It had been about seeing an opportunity and going for it.

"I am worried about Kip," Noe admitted. He sounded and even looked anxious. "I have asked Obe and Vic but they just say that he is tired."

"He is probably fretting about Ean," Jax replied.

Rae agreed; they were all fretting about Ean.

Leaving the doors open made the space less claustrophobic but it meant Tre could hear every word of the youngsters' conversation, even without his augmented hearing.

They were driving him insane. Rae was like a wind-up toy that never ran down while Jax and Noe could not exchange more than a few words without squabbling.

At least Medico Kem had the sense to hide.

He shut his eyes. Rae was right. If Kip had not taken his chance their situation would be much worse. Nine of the crew were safe. Now they could concentrate on investigating Ean and Loy's whereabouts.

Tre had a plan for that. The first step was to find out who among the Maul's crew might know something and make them talk. Given that the commander was dead, the best candidate appeared to be a man called Doctor Alexander. Kem said he was more a scientist than a medico but that he had an unusually good grasp of physiology and psychology. Tre was pleased about that. In his experience people who understood pain caved in much more quickly than those who did not.

If Ean and Loy were on the Blackjack, as they suspected, Tre would refuel the Briar Rose from the tanks on the Maul and jump into the next system before the Blackjack could jump out of it. Then he would negotiate Ean and Loy's return.

Based on the distance between the two holes in the next system and the Blackjack's likely top speed, he had at least another three days.

Raised voices; Noe and Jax had found something else to bicker about. Tre shuddered. His eyes drifted to the chronometer. Another two hundred and twenty minutes; only one hundred until he could reasonably suggest that Jax man the telescopes and watch for debris.

Rae's head poked up the shaft. Gold flecked brown eyes gazed hopefully in Tre's direction.

"Come on then," Tre agreed, nodding to one of the other chairs.

Rae was off the ladder and sitting down almost before the words were out of Tre's mouth.

"Are they driving you crazy too?" Tre whispered.

Rae twitched his whiskers and looked guilty but nodded.

Less than five minutes later Tre was regretting his generosity. Now he had Rae's twists, wriggles and twitches distracting him from his efforts to tune out the voices from down below.

"Why don't you go up to the gun turret?" he suggested. "You could test the guns."

Rae was out of the chair and halfway up the ladder in the blink of an eye.

"Be careful," Tre warned. Then he walked over to the shaft and called down. "If you two don't stop, I'll spin a coin and stick one of you in a pod. Or maybe even both of you."

There was immediate and blissful silence.

Jax flushed deep red at Tre's threat. Noe's smirk did not help. Both confirmed that he had been behaving badly, not at all like the heir to the Navaja clan leadership.

"Let's sort out something to eat," Noe suggested. "And then we can pack up ready to dock. After that we could tempt Medico Kem out of his cabin and feed him tea while he tells us about the other reformed pirates."

"Kurt, Owen and Mutt," Jax listed. Knowing people's names was important. It meant it was much easier to make a good first impression. "Owen is tall with dark hair, Kurt is middling everything and Mutt is short but broad."

Noe raised an eyebrow. "So you can listen."

Jax opened his mouth to retort but closed it again. Noe was

goading him and he had to learn not to rise to it. "Let's make a meal for everyone and then pack up, like you suggested."

Noe smiled. "Lead the way."

Making the meal, packing up, eating the meal and talking to Medico Kem filled a good portion of the remaining time. Then Tre asked Jax to watch for debris using the telescopes while Rae manned the guns so he could destroy anything big enough to be a threat.

The debris was probably wreckage from the Willow. The thought made Jax homesick.

Having something to do made the time pass quickly. Next thing Jax knew they were docking, the bay was pressurising and they were ready to disembark.

Kip looked awful. Jax had not known that someone could change so much in ten days. Skinny had become gaunt. His usually pale complexion was almost grey. Jax did not know what to do or what to say. Even Noe was stunned.

Then Tre stepped forward, anticipated Kip's attempt to dodge and hugged him close.

"It will be fine," Tre said quietly. "You and I will find him. I have a plan."

The two of them parted. It was almost as if the hug had never happened only Kip looked a hundred times better. He was standing much straighter and the unhealthy pallor had gone. He looked like Kip.

"You do?" Kip checked.

"Yes," Tre assured him. "It builds on what you have already done. Is there a place where you and I can work together?"

"We can use the room next to Vic's workshop," Kip replied. "I'll have to connect some displays and speakers. They'll only be two-dimensional displays but I'll make it work."

"You go and get that set up," Captain Mel suggested. "We'll introduce Tre to the Petunia Mae's crew and then he'll join you."

Jax watched Kip vanish through the doorway and along the corridor beyond. He couldn't be offended that Kip hadn't even greeted him or Rae. It was as if the veneer of sociability Kip used to interact with others had been stripped away. Underneath was the Kip that was usually hidden; strange, gauche and horribly vulnerable.

"He's being even weirder than usual," Obe complained.

"He got you out of that pod before they could fry your brain and sell your body to organ harvesters," Noe retorted before Jax or anyone else could say anything.

Obe flushed.

"That's enough," Captain Mel ordered. "It is tough. We are all worried about Ean and Loy." He took a step towards Medico Kem. "My name is Mel. I was captain of the Willow. This is Vic, our engineer, and Cas, our pilot. Obe is one of our cats, like Noe, although both of them appear to have forgotten how cats are meant to behave when the crew is visiting another ship."

Kem nodded. Then they all went through to the corridor where two young men were waiting. One was tall and thin, with sticky-out ears and spiky black hair; Owen. The other was medium height and build with intense, hazel eyes; Kurt.

Neither of them could keep their eyes off him, even though Captain Mel introduced him as Jax the cabin boy rather than Emanuel Rafael Jax Esteban. Jax had almost forgotten what it was like to be heir to the Navaja clan.

Almost but not quite; being who he was had led to the Willow's destruction.

Vic and Tre went ahead so that Tre could talk to Kip. The rest of them made their way more slowly with Owen telling them about the ship. Jax walked next to Rae and kept quiet, as Captain Mel expected. Behind them he could hear Medico Kem speaking quietly with Kurt.

"Their enforcer, Tre, is determined to find out about the whereabouts of the missing members of their crew," Kem explained.

"As I told Vic and then Captain Mel, I know nothing about the deal with the client," Kurt replied. "The commander trusted me to run the ship but no more. I was surprised as they were when we found out that your queen and your medico were not aboard."

"I thought Doctor Alexander might know something," Kem suggested. "That's if he's here and not on the Blackjack."

Medico Kem had never mentioned that possibility while on the Briar Rose. What if no one aboard knew what had happened?

"He's here, in a pod like everyone else," Kurt replied. "It turns out that a squad of rats, sorry minkies, can be pretty intimidating when they are armed with laser rifles." He shuddered. "Luckily they like Owen. Otherwise I would have probably ended up like the commander. They brought him inside, took him out of his suit and then killed him slowly using their teeth and claws. Even the old ladies were offered a go."

"The grand-grand-grandmams," Kem corrected him. "He deserved every scratch and every bite. However many pure-breds he killed, he killed a far greater number of their sons and grandsons."

"I guess so," Kurt answered. "You'll be fine. They love you. They've been asking when you were coming back."

"The trick is to value each one of them as much as a purebred," Kem told him.

"I'll have to work on that," Kurt admitted. "I'll get Doctor Alexander's pod delivered to the mission level."

He might have heard more but they had reached the shaft and began climbing up to what Owen called the 'mission level', which was where they would be staying.

When they stepped off the ladder there were people there to meet them; a short, powerfully-built man who was presumably Mutt Tucker and three tiny, ancient individuals with snowy-white head fur, pointy ears and whiskers.

"Mutt told them that someone important was coming aboard," Owen whispered.

Captain Mel frowned and Jax realised that Owen was refer-ring to him.

"May I, captain?" he asked.

Captain Mel hesitated. Jax understood; in a Trad crew a cabin boy was a cabin boy whatever his origins. However, the minkies weren't spacers and this situation was entirely a result of Jax being his father's son. "This once," he agreed.

Jax stepped forward and waited.

"This is Mutt Tucker," Owen began. "His family own the Petunia Mae. Mutt, this is Emanuel Rafael Jax Esteban, heir to the Navaja spacer clan."

"Jax," Jax insisted.

Owen cleared his throat. "And this is the Grand-grand-grand-grandmam and her two old oldest surviving sons."

Jax did not hesitate. He bowed to the individual in the middle, whom Owen had identified as the leader. "It is an honour to meet you, ma'am." Then he straightened up before adding, "Sirs." He followed up by introducing the others. "These are members of the crew of the Willow, some of whom have been on the Petunia Mae for a number of days." He pointed to each in turn. "Captain Mel, Cas, Obe and Noe. Perhaps you have already met Vic, Kip and Tre, who are not present at this time." Then he took Rae's arm and urged him forward. "This is Rae. He is my closest and best friend."

The Grand-grand-grand-grandmam looked at Rae and then back at him and nodded. "Jax," she acknowledged in a breathy bark. "Rae," she added. Then she smiled, showing small, sharp teeth. "Medico Kem."

"Grand-grand-grand-grandmam," Kem replied. "It is wonderful to see you looking so well."

They walked on, leaving Medico Kem talking to the minkies.

Rae was looking at him, his whiskers arched.

"What's wrong?" Jax asked.

"Why did you pick me out?" Rae queried. "Was it to show that you weren't anti-hybrid?"

Jax was shocked and a little hurt. "No. The Grand-grand-grand-grandmam chose to have her two sons with her. I chose you. You are my best friend, Rae. I would have also made a point of introducing Tre if he had been there, because he is the man my father chose as my protector."

Rae's whiskers drooped momentarily in apology and then twitched. "I can smell our stuff," he announced.

Obe grinned. "Come see."

They went into a large room. On numerous tables there were piles of stuff from the Willow. There was even Rae's treadmill. Jax wondered if it had survived the explosion intact or whether Kip had rebuilt it.

Cas pointed to a specific table. Jax recognised some of his clothes and, better still, the backpack he had taken into the pod with him. He hurried over and, with trembling hands, pulled out his lockbox.

He no longer had the key. Presumably it was on the Talon.

Then Rae was there with a hairgrip. He bent it to make a straight piece of wire and inserted it into the lock. A few wiggles and the lock turned.

Rae went back to the adjacent table where his stuff was. Jax watched him burying his hands in the blanket Ean had made for him. Then Jax's attention returned to his lockbox. He opened the lid.

Inside, on the top tray, were the ear studs that Tre had given him and the little wooden bird. Underneath, deep within the box, nestled in its protective leather pouch, was his father's ring.

❋ ❋ ❋

Tre listened carefully to Vic as the two of them made their way from the level with the entrance to the docking bay to the 'mission level'. There was nothing new until he began talking about the Petunia Rae's crew.

"Kurt has leadership qualities but he's crossed too many lines," Vic explained. "That is how the commander operated; he blackmailed people into doing immoral acts and then used their guilt to hold them until they became one of his tools. I think Kurt will make it back and find himself because he has Owen. Owen is one of those people, you know."

Tre did. Owen was like Ean; someone who brought out the best in people.

"Between them and the Tuckers they could get the Petunia Mae back to what it was before the commander. Especially if Medico Kem stays with them."

Tre was not sure about that; he had a feeling that Kem might have family somewhere.

Vic sighed. "Some feedback would be appreciated," he hinted.

Tre was not in the mood. He was thinking about how he would handle Doctor Alexander when Kurt had the pod delivered. "What about Kip?" he asked.

"If we don't find Ean, I think we should return him to his parents," Vic replied.

"That bad?" Tre queried. Jax needed Kip. Tre would have to find a way of stabilising him. Maybe Noe; if Noe cared about anyone it was Kip.

"Worse. I think most of what we saw when he was on the Willow was an act. He is scarily clever. Genius does not describe half of it. Trouble is, that does not leave much room for normality." Vic's usual laid-back tone changed; his voice developing an unfamiliar edge. "Only you knew all that, didn't you?"

Vic halted, forcing Tre to stop, turn and pay attention.

"I was planning on punching you," Vic admitted. "Even though I know the punch would never land. 'A boy from a prominent spacer clan.' Talk about an understatement. Now we've lost everything."

Tre did feel a twinge of guilt.

"Did Ean know who he is? Or Mel?"

"No," Tre admitted. "Kip worked it out and Jax told Rae." He could not resist asking. "Why didn't you punch me?"

Vic sighed. "Because you hugged Kip. You always do something like that. It's why Ean loves you so much."

Tre appreciated that Vic had said 'loves' and not 'loved'.

"I didn't think you would come back for us," Vic added. "You must have taken one of those pain-of-death oaths to protect Jax. I didn't think you would take the risk."

Vic deserved to know. "He was put into my arms on the day he was born," Tre admitted. "And, no, I wouldn't have taken the risk. Jax insisted."

"Good," Vic replied and began walking again. "At least I haven't sacrificed everything for a man like his father. From what I know about Joaquin Oro Sebastiano Socorro, he made the commander look like a do-gooder."

Tre was not sure about that. It was merely a matter of scale.

Kip was waiting for him in the room next to the workshop Vic had set up. As usual, he had found out everything Tre had hoped he would and far more.

"Only I can't monitor what is happening on the Blackjack," he admitted miserably. "The two gates in that system do not have data relays and I haven't got around that yet."

Tre did not miss the 'yet'. "Once I have spoken to selected members of the commander's team, I shall take the Briar Rose and jump through the gate."

Kip lit up. "I could come with you. That way I can hack the Blackjack's systems."

"I was thinking of just paying them to hand over the pods," Tre admitted.

"What if they don't agree?" Kip asked. "The Briar Rose's guns are tiny next to the Blackjack's. If I am with you, we can react if bribing them doesn't work."

"I'll think about it," Tre decided. "After I have spoken to some people who might be able to tell us what happened."

Kip was suddenly very still. "Are you going to torture them?"

"Effective interrogation very rarely benefits from torture," Tre informed him. He cast about for a change in subject. What would Ean say? "Have you contacted your parents?"

Kip looked lost in his thoughts for a moment and then nodded. "I sent a light speed message via the Stellar Exchange as soon as I stopped hiding. I didn't want them hearing about the Willow before they heard from me. Ma would worry."

"Good," Tre acknowledged. "Now go and spend some time with Jax, Rae and Noe. It will do you good and they need reassurance that you are all right." He saw Kip's hesitation. "You are not telling me you haven't got a wireless system set up by now."

"No, I have," Kip admitted. "I'll set up some alerts in case something important comes in. There is this long shot. A ship jumped out through the gate early yesterday. I piggybacked a worm on it. It should get transmitted to the Blackjack, do an audit and then get the Blackjack's transmitter to broadcast the results at intervals. If a ship jumps from that system into this one, it should bring back the results."

Tre had followed some of that; Kip had worked out a way of finding out what the Blackjack was doing but they would only get the results if a ship came through the gate. "Sounds good," he agreed. "Go socialise with Jax, Rae and Noe."

Rae had packed up his stuff and moved it to the cabin he was going to be sharing with Jax. There were bunks, a shower and a head. It was like their den on the Willow but much bigger.

It would be a lot better than sharing with Noe, like they had done on the Briar Rose.

Then he went back to the big room to have a go on his tread-mill while Jax made sure everything in their den was arranged just so, like he always did.

He had been running for a bit when he realised that someone was watching him. It was Mutt Tucker, the purebred who had been with the mink–human hybrids. Rae did another two cycles of speeding up and then slowing down but when he finished Mutt was still there.

Rae slowed to, for him, a moderate pace. "What do you want?" he asked.

"You're amazing," Mutt replied. "The minkies are old hybrids. That's why they work so well. I didn't think anyone made hybrids that good these days."

Kip had mentioned the mink–human hybrids in one of their text exchanges. Apparently they were a breeding population from ages ago, probably from a planet on the edges of the Far Fringe.

"You're amazing," Mutt repeated. "Who designed you?"

Rae thought about growling to make it clear that he didn't like discussing such things, especially with strangers. Then he remembered that the Tuckers had been associated with the mink–human hybrids for centuries. "Don't know," he admitted.

"Do you have a marker's mark?" Mutt asked.

Rae slowed down and came to a stop. Maybe Mutt would know why he had a counterfeit mark.

"It's a false mark," Rae told him. "An imitation mark so that someone would pay more for me than I am worth."

Mutt scowled. "You're a work of art. Why ruin it by putting a false mark on you? Whose mark did they imitate?"

"Bara's," Rae admitted.

Mutt's eyes widened until they were circular. "You are kidding," he whispered. "Can I see it? Please?"

Rae almost said no but thought better of it. "I'll think about it." Then he remembered that his tablet had been among the stuff on the table. "I've got a picture. Wait here."

He ran to their new den, grabbed the tablet and ran back. Jax didn't even notice; he was too busy scrubbing the shower. Rae found the image and thrust the tablet at Mutt.

Mutt took it. Then he pored over the image, magnifying each part in turn. Finally he handed the tablet back.

"Doesn't look false to me. Wow. A Bara hybrid. I never thought I'd see one, never mind meet one."

Rae blinked. "I can't be. Bara died..." He tried to remember what Kip had said but he couldn't. "Thousands of standards ago."

Mutt shrugged. "So did the hybrid engineer who designed the

minkies. There must be a breeding population somewhere, like with the minkies. Maybe you were stolen as a baby." He smiled. "A Bara hybrid. Thank you, Rae. I have to go tell my aunt and my cousin."

Rae watched him go. A breeding population of hybrids like him? That didn't fit with what Loy had told him. Loy had said that Rae's breeding bits didn't work.

No, Kip was more likely to be right than Mutt. It was a false mark, put on a hybrid that had, by chance, turned out much better than the others. Probably the buyer had found out and Rae had been chucked away.

He jumped back onto the treadmill and ran and ran and ran.

As Kip walked along the corridor he could hear Rae running on the treadmill. It made him glad that he had spent time mending it. He went into the room. Rae's table had been cleared. So had Jax's.

Rae was running faster than ever. Kip hoped that the treadmill could take it.

He wondered where Jax was.

Rae slowed a little so that he could talk and run. "He's scrubbing the shower in our new den."

Kip was always intrigued that Rae could guess the questions in people's heads. "You did it. You rescued him."

"Noe helped," Rae admitted. "There is more to Noe than eyelashes."

It was a nice way of putting it. Kip wondered what to say next.

"You rescued everyone else," Rae pointed out.

Except Ean and Loy; they could still be with the pirates on their way to an organ harvester. There had to be more that Kip could do, but try as he did, he could not think of it.

"We'll get Ean back," Rae insisted. "Loy too."

Rae's words sparked trains of thought on various levels of Kip's mind. Something didn't fit. Kip couldn't work it out. He wasn't exhausted any more or under pressure to make decisions minute by minute. Everything should feel right and it didn't. Perhaps he needed to sort out his head. He had not done it properly in a while.

"Kip."

It was Jax. Kip wondered how long he had been lost in his thoughts. It could have been some time. Unlike other people, Rae was content to leave him to it.

"Jax," Kip acknowledged.

"Did Tre tell you what he intends to do?" Jax asked.

Kip nodded. "He's going to start by talking to some of the commander's men."

"Doctor Alexander," Rae supplied.

Kip guessed that Rae must have overheard Tre talking with someone.

"Do you know anything about him?" Jax asked.

Kip had to think. He had collected all manner of information about the crew.

"There was a man they called 'doctor' here when our pods were opened," Rae volunteered. He turned to Jax. "It was him who identified you. He said your bones were right."

Kip remembered the man if not the comment. He probably hadn't heard it.

"That could be him," he agreed. "He was more an associate of the commander's than a crew member. He had a laboratory on one of the levels." Kip frowned, trying to recall some of the details he had dug up. "I think it was him who had the contacts with the organ harvesters."

Jax scowled. "I hope Tre pulls his fingernails out. Or cooks his balls with an electric prod."

Kip could have done without such details. He was about to say that Tre didn't think torture was an effective tool for interrogation when there was a double ping in the earpiece he was wearing. It was the alert he had set for when a ship came through the gate.

"I have to go," he told them. "Information is coming in that might be useful."

"What?" Jax demanded, following him across the room. Behind them Rae leapt off the treadmill.

Kip had been going to put on his goggles but he guessed he could use the displays and speakers he had set up for Tre. He headed for the room next to Vic's workshop, explaining about the worm.

"So it's a programme," Jax checked after Kip had explained twice. "Like the one you sent to the Briar Rose that installed itself."

"Yes," Kip agreed. "Only more than one of them and more carefully hidden."

"Ship takes programme through gate, transmits to the Blackjack," Rae stated. "Programme installs on Blackjack, does its thing, transmits results and another ship brings them back through the gate."

"Exactly," Kip replied, grateful for Rae's straightforward explanation. With any luck it might stop Jax asking any more questions.

"What does it say?" Jax asked.

Kip wished he had used his goggles; it would have been much quicker.

Forty minutes later Kip gave up. There was zero evidence that the Blackjack was carrying any occupied pods or any prisoners. There was no suggestion that any pods had been transferred to the Blackjack from the Maul. Oxygen consumption, carbon dioxide generation and the level of activity of the heat exchange system suggested that there were twelve people on board.

Kip had identities for all twelve; they were the regular members of the Blackjack's crew.

"Could they be carrying two occupied pods?" Jax demanded.

"We can't completely rule it out," Kip admitted. "The data is incomplete."

Rae twitched his whiskers. "Why do we think they are on the Blackjack?" he asked.

Kip thought about it. There was only one reason. "Because they are no longer on the Petunia Mae."

Jax scowled. "Where else can they be?"

8

Ean tried raising the cup to his lips but the tremor in his arm threatened to send the tea over the rim. He brought up his other hand, intending to steady it, but Loy was there first, guiding the cup to his lips.

"I can do it," Ean insisted but the words came out horribly weak.

"I want to help," Loy assured him. His voice was warm, like a blanket.

Ean felt a tear wend its way down his cheek and then another. The cup was rescued and placed back on the table. Then strong arms, the wrong arms, were around him, holding him as he wept.

He wished he could remember what had happened. Loy said that memory loss was common with head injuries. He also hinted that Ean was lucky, that it was better to have only happy memories, like them all gathered around the table for supper.

Ean did not feel lucky. He often wished he had died but, like Loy said, there had to be part of him that had wanted to live. Ean had met other survivors. Every spacer had. Slowly he would get over his grief. He had Loy to help him. Maybe he could seek out Ben.

By the Lady he wished Ben was with him now.

It was a fluke that he and Loy had survived. According to Loy there had been very little warning. Some of the crew had made it into suits, some had not. Being in a suit had not saved those hit by wreckage that had been accelerated by the explosion.

There was a salvage ship there now, picking over the remains. Loy had given instructions and paid a hefty fee to ensure they were followed. Personal effects would be collected up, packed and sent on to them. Loy himself had disposed of the bodies.

Ean would have preferred to have been there but it had been done during the two days he was tanked.

Now they were on their way to Mercy Station as passengers on a liner. Loy had insisted. He was worried about Ean's health. Apparently brain injuries could be tricky. He wanted Ean to be scanned.

"You needed more days tanked," Loy suggested.

Ean could not see how being in a tank would help him deal with his grief.

"There is no doubt?" he whispered. He could not stop himself, even though he had asked so many times that Loy could no longer disguise a fleeting look of annoyance.

"None," Loy stated. "Nine bodies," he added this time. He picked up Ean's tea, wrapped Ean's hand around it and guided it to Ean's lips.

Next time Ean woke Loy wasn't there. He pulled himself out of bed, through the shower and into clothes. The clothes were neither his nor what he would have chosen but they were too small for Loy so obviously meant for him. He caught his reflection in a long mirror. The jacket and pants fitted him perfectly, hugging the contours of his body, while the contrast piping emphasised his shape.

It did not look like him.

He wondered what a suite of rooms on a liner cost. The answer was so much that Ean could not really complain that there was only one bedroom with one, large bed.

Loy had been apologetic about it.

After some searching, Ean found the contents of his backpack in a drawer. He lifted out the box and carried it through to the tiny sitting room. Sitting on the couch with the box on the table, he opened the lid.

Inside were his memory dodecahedrons and the projector that Ben had given him.

He picked out the dodec with the images of their vacation on Janine. Touching face after face to the projector, he studied the images: Jax swimming; Obe standing on the pier; Cas lazing on the grass; Noe putting a daisy chain around Kip's ankle; Rae running; Tre.

The sound of the door opening and then Loy was there, clucking with disapproval.

"It helps," Ean insisted. This time his voice sounded more normal.

"It does not help me," Loy replied.

Ean was engulfed by a wave of guilt. It was not only him who had lost people. He switched off the projector, put away the dodec and replaced the lid. He even managed to swallow his objection when Loy picked up the box and carried it through to the bedroom.

He listened to the drawer open and shut. Then Loy was back.

"I am glad the clothes fit," he observed. "Cerise suits you."

To Ean pink was pink; at least it was dark rather than pale. "I thought we could have supper in the dining room," he suggested.

Loy frowned. "Are you sure you are up to it?"

"No," Ean admitted, "but I want to try. We can always come back here if I discover I cannot cope."

Loy looked unconvinced.

"Please, Loy," Ean pleaded. "I need a change of scenery."

They settled on a walk along the viewing gallery. Ean would have definitely preferred the dining room: there would have been more people to watch and fewer stars to remind him of how cruel space could be.

There weren't any families. It wasn't that type of liner. Most of the passengers were rich individuals with entourages. There were some couples, of which only a few were male–male.

Wearier than he wished to admit, Ean looked about for somewhere to sit. The only option was a bench. He sat at one end and, inevitably, Loy sat beside him. He was too close. Ean wished he had sat in the middle of the bench so that he could slide away.

It wasn't Loy's fault, Ean knew that. Some people wanted physical comfort when they were hurting and others didn't. Loy was in the first group. Ean had discovered that he was in the second.

They only had each other; Ean would have to make allowances.

His mind wandered to the list of tasks he would have undertaken if he had been conscious at the spacestation in Verdant.

"You sent a message to Kip's parents?" he checked.

Loy sighed. "Yes. Also Vic's sister and the captain's cousin. We can contact the insurance provider once we reach Mercy Station. I couldn't do that before we left. It was too soon."

"I don't care about the credit," Ean snapped. Only he did because if their insurance provider rejected the claim he would be totally reliant on Loy. All his assets had been tied up in the ship.

"I know you don't," Loy replied in his most soothing voice.

Ean pulled himself together. He had been queen of the Willow. Even if the insurance did not pay out, he would be fine. Crews would fall over themselves to recruit him.

Merely thinking about being with another crew made him nauseous.

Loy had supper delivered to their suite. Ean picked at the food, even though he was sure it was delicious.

He preferred simpler food than the fancy dishes the liner's chief chef created.

There were thirty days of this ahead of him; thirty-two to be precise. Lady knew how much the two passages from Verdant to Mercy Station had cost Loy; far more than Ean would ever have been willing to pay.

"Are there any ports of call on the way?" Ean asked.

Loy froze; his fork halfway between his plate and his mouth. "Three," he admitted.

"So we will be able to visit planets or spacestations while the liner traverses those systems?" Ean checked. He was pretty sure that was how liners like this one operated.

"Yes," Loy replied.

Ean wondered why Loy was so hesitant. Maybe extra trips added a lot to the cost. Ean would have to find out.

Loy cleared the dishes and pushed the trolley into the corridor for the steward to collect. Ean went over to the small alcove where the ridiculously fancy kettle was located, intending to make tea.

Next thing he knew, Loy was behind him. His hands rested momentarily on Ean's hips. "Let me do that," Loy whispered.

Ean decided that giving in was preferable to being trapped between Loy and the counter.

Somehow the tea Loy made was always slightly bitter. Ean shut his eyes and recalled Jax stubbornly refusing to use the cheap teapot. There was a moment of pleasure at the memory before the grief crashed in.

It left him helpless and needy. Loy had to help him undress and into bed. Again Ean found himself insisting on wearing sleep pants and a top, even though both of them knew that Ean usually slept naked.

"In case I have to get up in the night," Ean lied.

Loy did not argue.

Ean's dreams were strange. There were two distinct types. The first was about when the Willow had been destroyed. Loy said it was Ean's imagination trying to fill in the missing memories.

Weirdly, what his mind came up with did not fit the facts. He was putting the youngsters into pods and pushing the pods out the escape locks. Then the dream veered off into the bizarre. There were distorted images of small, whiskered faces. The dream always ended the same way; Loy coming at him with a hypodermic needle and Ean failing to fight him off.

It would make more sense to Ean if he was more imaginative and the dream varied more. It didn't; it was always the same.

The second type of dream happened after the first. It was sexual, which would have been fine if his partner in the dream had been Tre. Only he wasn't. Ean was not sure who he was. Not a stranger; Ean was almost certain of that.

In his dream it was as if Ean was wrapped in fog: senses were dulled; sensations attenuated.

Next morning Loy was absent again. Ean guessed that he tried to get all the away-from-the-cabin stuff done while Ean was sleeping. In truth it was a relief to be alone for a bit.

This time, instead of heading straight for the shower, Ean went looking for information about the liner. There was a display frame on the wall, set to show a tasteful landscape. Ean fiddled with it, only to have a message flash up saying it had been childproofed.

For some reason it annoyed him. He went to the intercom and examined it. There was a button labelled 'steward'. He pressed it. A voice answered immediately.

"Can I help you?"

"Yes," Ean answered. "The interface for the display frame is stuck on childproofed."

There was a pause. "Sir, that is the setting that was requested for your suite."

"Well there has to be a mistake," Ean insisted. "There aren't any children staying in this suite or even visiting. How do I change the setting?"

The steward hesitated again. "I am sorry, sir, but only Medico Loy can request changes to the settings."

Ean sighed. He would have to speak to Loy. "I was trying to find out about the services that were available on the ship."

"I can help you with that, sir," the steward informed him. "I will arrange for delivery of a tablet to your suite. The information on the tablet describes all the services available."

Ean found a robe to wear for when he opened the door. The steward, a good looking young man in uniform with a silly little hat, handed him a tablet.

"You and Medico Loy have the gold star passage," the young man told hm.

Ean read the name on the hat. "Thank you, Steward Lyn."

The young man flushed. "You are welcome Spacer Ean."

Many of the ship's services were included in the gold star passage. Some of them were obvious, like meals in the dining room or delivered to their suite. Others were not, or at least not to Ean. He could visit a spa or the ship's psychologist. He could have one session every three days with a personal fitness trainer or there were group sessions every morning. There were two excursions included at each of the ports of call.

There were various images of gold star suites. One showed two single beds in the bedroom and one had bunks with the caption that some passengers appreciated having the extra floor space.

On impulse, he went over to the intercom and pressed the button.

"Yes, sir?"

"Is that Steward Lyn?" Ean asked.

"It is not Assistant Steward Lyn's responsibility to respond to the intercom, sir," the voice replied. "How may I help you?"

"Would it be possible to have the double bed in our suite changed for bunks?" Ean asked. "Now that we are here, we are finding the bedroom a bit cramped."

The person on the other end hesitated. "Yes, sir, it would be possible but a double bed was specifically requested for that suite."

Ean could not resist checking. "By Medico Loy?"

"Yes, by Medico Loy. It was specified in the booking and Medico Loy checked that particular when he boarded."

"Thank you," Ean murmured and released the button.

Maybe Loy had felt Ean would need the physical comfort of someone sleeping next to him. Or, more likely, Loy needed it himself but had not wanted to ask.

By the time Loy arrived, Ean was well into investigating the activities offered. Loy looked at the scraps of plasticard scattered over the table and then back at Ean.

"I've decided that I need to keep busy," Ean told him. "There are lots of activities. I am signing up for a group fitness session every morning and an art class each afternoon."

Loy opened his mouth as if he was going to object.

"You could always come with me," Ean added.

Loy considered and nodded.

"I am still trying to decide about the personal sessions with the trainer," Ean told him, picking up the tablet and finding the relevant information.

The tablet was plucked from his hands. "Personal trainer is probably their euphemism for high-class whore," Loy complained.

"I'll skip that then," Ean agreed. "The psychologists offer grief counselling, so I am definitely going to see one of them."

"Psychologists?" Loy queried. "What are their qualifications?" He began looking through the information on the tablet.

Ean frowned. He wasn't going to back down. He wanted to talk to someone about the dreams.

Loy studied his expression and went back to the tablet. "Psychologist Mary Bernard looks the better of the two," he suggested.

"Fine," Ean agreed. "Then there are the concerts and the poetry readings. I also have the itineraries for the six excursions."

By noon Ean had every day of the remaining thirty-one mapped out. He had asked the stewards for a large sheet of plasticard, a ruler and a pen. Then he had constructed an eight by four grid and filled in each square.

Loy's expression was suspiciously sulky. "You are trying to do too much," he complained.

"If it is too much I can come back here to rest," Ean pointed out. "And apparently it is acceptable to pull out of the excursions right up to the time they are leaving. I checked."

Loy studied the chart. "I won't be able to go on the first excursion. I have arranged to meet an ex-colleague. Given the circumstances, I thought it was a good idea to feel out possible opportunities."

It was the first Ean had heard of it, but they didn't jump into that system for another ten days. "Do you want me to come with you?"

"No," Loy replied. "It's business not pleasure. You go on the excursion."

Taking a shuttle to see some moons wasn't exactly exciting for a spacer but Ean was determined to make the most of every opportunity.

It was difficult to make himself do things when all he wanted to do was cry. Given how exhausted he was by the evening, attending the concerts would definitely have to wait, and he only made the morning fitness session through sheer will. By afternoon he felt better, so he had scheduled his appointment with Psychologist Mary directly after his art class.

"I was surprised you selected me," she admitted. "Mason Quail has much more experience counselling the bereaved and he understands spacer culture. His expertise and experience were set out in the information provided," she added apologetically, using the display frame on the wall to bring up the relevant section of the brochure.

Two images appeared. One was Psychologist Mary and the other was an extremely handsome man; Mason Quail. A short description of their experience and areas of expertise came up when one pointed at the image.

Ean had not read the resumes; Loy had recommended Psychologist Mary and he had gone with it. "I am sure it will be fine," he assured her.

It was more than fine, it was good. Mary, as she insisted he call her, was an excellent listener. Having to explain spacer life helped; it was easier than only talking about relationships and emotions.

"Did it go well?" Loy asked once Ean had returned to the suite and they were getting ready to go eat in the dining room.

Ean was scrubbing some particularly stubborn paint off the skin of his hand. "She recommended that I move to Psychologist Mason Quail," he mentioned, watching Loy out of the corner of his eye.

Loy definitely stiffened. "And?"

"I decided to stay with Mary," Ean admitted and watched Loy relax. "She suits me very well. I was brought up in a household full of women. It is nice to have female company again. I am going to see her again tomorrow."

The next day started badly. Ean's first dream had changed. As well as chasing him with the needle, the dream version of Loy had told him that Tre was a cyborg who was just a machine and incapable of loving him.

Ean wished his imagination would stop torturing him.

"How are you feeling?" Mary asked.

When Loy asked him that, Ean wanted to punch him. He wondered why it felt so different when Mary did it. "Not my best day," he admitted. He wondered about talking about the uncontrollable waves of emotion that would surge up from nowhere but decided on the dream instead.

"So you have no memories of the......accident," Mary checked once he had finished.

"No. I hit my head and have amnesia," Ean replied.

"And none of the images from the dream fit with what happened?"

"No. We never got as far as the pods." Ean sighed and blinked back tears. "I guess I dream about the pods because I want to turn back time and save them."

"Your children," Mary said gently.

Ean was about to explain about cabin boys and cats again but realised that Mary was making a point. "Yes," he agreed. "My children."

"And the whiskered faces?"

"That could be something to do with Rae," he admitted, although the faces had not looked like Rae's. "Rae is…" He corrected himself. "Rae was a hybrid."

"In the dream, Loy chases you with a needle?"

Ean thought about it. There was no actual chasing. "He attacks me and gives me an injection through one of the access points of my suit." Ean's hand went to the upper part of his left arm. It was if he remembered the pain of the needle entering his flesh.

"And tells you that Tre was a cyborg," Mary queried.

"Yes. That was the new part in last night's dream," Ean admitted. He shuddered. It had seemed so real: trying to crawl away; being dragged by the ankle; the painful words about Tre not loving him.

Mary was quiet for a bit. She made some notes. Then she looked at him.

"Was there tension between Loy and Tre?" she asked.

"No," Ean replied immediately. "They were old friends." Then he reconsidered. "Well, maybe a little. Loy sees himself as dominant and Tre, well, Tre just was dominant. He didn't have to try." He cast about for an analogy. "Tre was like a panther. Loy is like a domesticated cat that likes to hunt the odd bird."

Mary smiled even though she was obviously trying to stop herself. "Do you want to talk about Tre?"

Ean thought about it. Was he ready? "No," he decided.

"What about Loy?" Mary asked.

That was easy. Loy had backed off a little but he was still driving Ean crazy.

"I know it's natural," he concluded after what had developed into a lengthy rant. "He's lost his crew too. He's over-compensating." He sighed. "I just wish he would give me room to breathe. It is better since I started attending the activities. The other people dilute him out and being away from the suite means he doesn't have to be so physically close to me." He wondered about mentioning the double bed and decided against it.

"Do you think he is hoping you will be sexually intimate with him?" Mary asked.

The answer was obvious but Ean discovered he was reluctant to voice it. "Yes," he whispered. "I am far from ready for that," he added quickly. "Loy realises that."

"But, as a long-term outcome, it is likely," Mary pressed.

Ean considered. "I do not think it would work in the long term," he admitted. "Maybe for a while, as a stepping stone away from our grief."

"But not in the long term?" Mary queried again.

Ean thought about it. Loy was attractive enough. He was good looking and his voice was like rich honey. He was attentive and caring. There was just something brittle about him. If he were a knife he would break rather than bend. If he were a porcelain bowl he would not ring clear when struck.

He was not Tre.

"Spacer Ean?" Mary inquired gently.

"I'm fine," Ean lied.

"May I tell you some information that you may choose to apply to your situation and interpret as advice?" she asked.

Ean nodded.

"When two people are considering entering a sexually intimate relationship, it is important to know if their aims are at least compatible," she told him.

Ean was confused for a moment before realising what she meant. "You think Loy might want a long-term relationship."

"The point is that you believe that is a possibility or you would not have interrupted what I said in that way." Mary sighed. "It is impossible to see the two of you together and not realise that he is besotted with you."

Ean stared at her.

She flushed. "I apologise for making an observation that you have interpreted as inappropriate."

"No, thank you," Ean replied and meant it.

Mary was correct and now that Ean had a clearer view of the situation he could act accordingly. He realised he had been unwittingly encouraging Loy. It was not fair and it would quickly lead to the situation where their friendship was threatened.

As a first step in the right direction the double bed had to go.

Loy did not argue as much as Ean had thought he would. Ean showed him the brochure and explained that he had made enquires. He made it clear that he was pleased at having come up with a solution.

Perhaps Loy was worried that Ean would mention that he had ordered the double bed rather than there being no alternative.

Ean didn't; his objective was to end up with bunks, not chastise Loy about his behaviour.

Next on Ean's list was having the childproofing on the display frame removed. They agreed that Ean should be able to use the interface and that it was up to Loy to do something about it. Ean decided to give him a day before bringing up the subject again. No one liked being nagged.

The following day was the worst since his first out of the tank.

Ean was beyond weary; unable to hold back his emotions. Loy was incredibly sweet and supportive; the perfect friend. Ean felt guilty about having doubted him; perhaps Mary was wrong.

Next morning Ean slept late and woke to find that the worst of it had passed. As he sat eating the breakfast Loy had ordered for him, his gaze went to the display frame and he decided to give up on changing the settings. Lady knew what was going on in Loy's head.

Anyway, as one of the old ladies in his art class had told him, he could use the Library.

The Library was a small adult-only area set aside for silent study. As well as an impressive data bank of books, it had non-childproofed interfaces and access to Stellar Exchange services.

Ean checked the price list and swallowed. Sending even the cheapest, most compressed light-speed message would make a significant dent in his meagre resources. Even so, he was determined to do it.

He owed Kip's parents and grandfather that much in exchange for the privilege of having spent the last eighteen divs of Kip's life with him.

It was hard finding the right words but he managed it. He included a promise to send all the images he had of Kip by tape as soon as he could. Then he loaded the necessary credit via the credit token reader. It used up over half his reserve from his lockbox.

He left the Library feeling better than he had since waking up from the tank.

Ean decided to capitalise on feeling better. The ladies in his art class were delighted to see him. He apologised for missing the previous session and they clucked understandingly.

"Isn't Medico Loy with you?" one of them asked.

Ean smiled. Loy had decided not to attend again after realising that the class was full of middle aged and older women. The tutor herself was ancient; Ean guessed she was pushing ninety. "Not today, Bev. You will have to put up with me."

She chuckled. "You'll do, Spacer Ean."

Ean took the clay sculpture he had started the previous session out of the humidifier and set to work; he had discovered that moulding something with his hands was more restful than painting.

Today the ladies were indulging in one-upmanship about how little they had managed to pay for their suites. Apparently the company had all manner of tricks for ensuring that the liner was full, including offering a plethora of deals.

Three of them were not in the running. Ean suspected that one was so rich that it had not occurred to her to ask for a discount. The other two did not know what had been paid because someone else had made the booking, just as Ean had no idea what Loy had paid.

Ean had lost track of the conversation but his attention was caught when he heard Bev mention Loy's name.

"Medico Loy must have paid a fortune."

"What's that, Bev?" he queried.

"To have booked a suite so late. Only a day or two before departure," she clarified.

"Yes," a woman called Su confirmed. She was an expert on the company's deals. "They keep three suites for very last moment bookings. They are only available at the premier rate."

"No, we're on the gold star package," Ean told them.

There was silence. "You can't be," Su insisted.

"We are," Ean replied. "The stewards told me."

"Gold star package bookings have to be made a minimum of two divs in advance," another lady, Geraldine, pointed out.

"Yes, they might flex that a bit but not that much," Su confirmed. "How long before departure did Medico Loy book?"

Ean thought about it. "Two days at the absolute maximum."

There was another silence.

"Maybe he arranged a swap," Ean suggested. That was what a crew did when they needed a jump slot and none were available.

There was a blizzard of objections; apparently the company had very strict rules about transferring bookings.

"They must have made an exception," Bev suggested, her tone emphasising her lack of conviction.

"Or maybe Medico Loy knows someone high up in the shipping company," Geraldine added.

They decided that was the most likely explanation and moved

on. Ean worked and reworked the same small piece of clay. Loy had not suggested that there was anything unusual about the booking and the stewards definitely did not treat them as if Loy had a connection high up in the company.

Did he ask Loy about it? He was still deciding on his way back to their suite and encountered Assistant Steward Lyn walking in the opposite direction.

"Spacer Ean," Lyn acknowledged.

"Steward Lyn," Ean replied. The next words were out of his mouth before he had properly considered them. "Steward Lyn, could I ask you for a favour?"

Lyn stopped and smiled. "Of course, Spacer Ean."

"It may not be possible," Ean admitted. "I was wondering if you could find out who booked our suite and when."

Lyn looked puzzled for a moment and then nodded. "I understand, Spacer Ean."

Ean wished that he could say the same.

"I can do that for you and I will make sure I give you the information when Medico Loy is not about," Lyn assured him.

Ean felt his cheeks flush. "Thank you, Steward Lyn. Your discretion is greatly appreciated."

Lyn smiled. "You are welcome."

Next morning, on Ean's way back to the suite from his fitness session, Lyn handed him a folded piece of plasticard. Ean smiled his thanks and pocketed the note.

Once in the suite he locked himself in the head. He unfolded the note. He could barely bear to look at the date but he forced himself. It was 100140; almost three divs ago. Heart thumping, he read on. The next words were 'Company booking - Prospicient Prosthetics'.

It was a huge relief. The suite must have been booked by Prospicient Prosthetics and Loy must have pulled in favours to get them aboard rather than the company representatives. It made sense; Ean remembered Loy saying that his specialist area had been prosthetics.

Ean went to the sink and washed the plasticard clean. Yes, that had to be it.

Even so, that afternoon, instead of going directly to his art class, Ean detoured to the Library. He almost turned back three times; at the door, before he sat down and when he activated the research interface.

It did not take long to turn up some relevant facts. Prospicient Prosthetics had been registered at Mercy Station. There were no obvious activities associated with it for the last two standards.

Loy had joined the Willow two standards ago. Ean took a deep breath and began digging further. The relief he had felt trickled away. It was Loy's company; he was listed as owner.

Ean scrabbled about for other explanations. Maybe Loy had given other people permission to use the company name. Maybe one of those people had booked the suite.

The alternative was that Loy had made the booking. He had known in advance that the Willow would be destroyed.

9

Rae tracked people. It was built into him; part of being a canine–human hybrid. Once he was sure that Ean and Loy were not on the Petunia Mae, he started getting interested in Kip's less nose-and-ear-based ways of finding them.

One of the great things about Kip was that he was not limited by his senses like other purebreds. He used any detectors available to him: telescopes; cameras; microphones; oxygen sensors; thermometers; chronometers. He even used things as detectors that weren't designed to work that way, like fluctuations in power usage, changes in background radiation and variations in electromagnetic emissions.

Then, better still, he produced displays that Rae could understand.

Yet even Kip couldn't find out what had happened to Ean and Loy. The information from the Blackjack had not helped. Their last hope of a lead was Tre 'talking to' Doctor Alexander.

Or was it? What about the minkies? Maybe one of them had heard or smelt Loy or Ean leaving the ship. Rae went back to the room where their stuff was spread out and found a pair of sleep shorts that smelt of Loy and an undershirt that smelt of Ean.

Then he headed for the minkies' levels of the ship.

He had to go towards the tail a long way, through two inversions of the gravitational field. Finally he found a passageway that reeked of minkies but as soon as he stepped off the ladder there were three males blocking his path.

One of them growled. "Not welcome," he barked.

Rae wished he had talked to Jax or maybe Mutt Tucker. He could only think of one thing to try. "I am Rae. I was introduced to the Grand-grand-grand-grandmum." He hoped he had included the correct number of grands.

They didn't let him through but one of them did walk away; Rae guessed he was going to find someone. After what felt like ages one of the Grand-grand-grand-grandmum's sons appeared, moving slowly along the corridor.

Rae explained the problem. "I hoped that someone might remember smelling one or both of them," he concluded.

The old minky's whiskers twitched. "You care about these purebreds?"

"Yes," Rae replied with conviction.

Dark, whiteless eyes, the pupils cloudy with age, studied him. Then he signalled that Rae should give the shorts and shirt to one of the other minkies. Rae complied.

"You will wait here," the old minky stated and walked away with the minky carrying the clothes.

Rae was pretty sure he was being tested. It was as if the old minky knew he hated staying still. Rae settled down; if there was any useful information available, he was determined to get it.

A long, long time afterwards he heard a purebred coming down the shaft. It was Mutt Tucker. He stepped off the ladder, nodded to Rae and vanished down the corridor.

More waiting; Rae began wondering if the minkies intended to tell him anything. Perhaps leaving people waiting was the minky version of a joke or even an insult. Rae's stomach was rumbling; he should have brought some meal bars with him.

Then, finally, Rae heard a purebred's footsteps and Mutt Tucker came towards him along the corridor, carrying the clothes Rae had brought and a thick sheet of plasticard covered with scribbles.

Rae was up, bouncing on the balls of his feet. "Do they know something?"

Mutt gave him Ean's shirt. "Nothing about this one. They never smelt him or saw him."

Rae's hope began draining away.

"This one." Mutt looked as if he was sucking something sour as he handed over Loy's shorts. "They had quite a bit to say about him."

Tre had decided to allow Doctor Alexander to stew a little. It was a better option than allowing his impatience to get the better of him and rushing into something he might later regret.

Doctor Alexander had given the impression that he had useful information but that he wanted assurances before parting with it. His gaze had gone to Tre's knife and Tre could almost hear him thinking that once a spacer gave his word he would not break it.

Jax and Kip were in the room next to Vic's workshop where Kip had set up the banks of displays and speakers. Tre stopped in the doorway; something was amiss but for a moment he was uncertain what. Then he had it; Jax did not have Rae with him.

"Where is Rae?" he asked, listening for the sound of the treadmill. He could not hear it.

Jax frowned. "I don't know. He said he had something to do but that was ages ago. Did Doctor Alexander tell you anything?"

"Not yet," Tre admitted. He continued into the room. "Kip?"

Kip's shoulders were rounded and his head down. "Nothing." He hesitated for a moment and then spoke. "Back on the Willow, Loy and Ean were arguing."

"You never mentioned that before," Jax accused.

"I only heard snatches of it," Kip admitted.

"Try and remember it piece by piece," Tre suggested.

Kip shut his eyes. The look on his face was the same as that on a cyborg's when he was accessing information on his internal data crystal array. Given the complexity of Kip's mind, maybe the process was similar. Tre listened to Kip's account. Something must have happened to make Ean reopen Kip's pod and there had obviously been a disagreement.

"Can you remember their exact words?" Tre asked.

Kip was silent for almost a minute. Tre had to put a hand on Jax's arm to stop him interrupting.

"I didn't hear Ean say anything. Loy said three things. 'This is a mistake, Ean. You are endangering Kip's life.' That was after Ean reopened the pod and they started fighting. Then, 'Think, Ean. I am doing this for your own good. It's better to be off the ship.' Then, 'Stop fighting it, Ean.' After that the lid shut again and I was pushed out."

"What do you think might have happened?" Tre asked.

Kip frowned. "Maybe Ean realised the pirates were outside picking up the pods. Loy thought we should still evacuate then and there. Ean wanted to try something else."

It fitted; Tre would have to think about it.

"The pods they were in are still on this ship," Kip insisted. "Rae confirmed that two of the Willow's pods we found smelt of them."

"The stuff they had with them when they left the Willow has gone," Jax complained. "Mutt Tucker and the minkies have looked everywhere. When Noe and I were taken off the ship, our stuff was left behind."

Tre had not picked up on that; it made even less sense than the altercation between Ean and Loy on the Willow. It was as if they had got out of the pods, taken their stuff and walked away.

He was still thinking about what Jax had said when he heard Rae running along the corridor towards them. He entered carrying a board covered with writing and sketches, which he put down on one of the tables.

"The minkies put together everything they smelt at the time and after," he told them. "Then they added in bits of gossip." He gestured at the board. "Loy walked through the ship to the docking bay. He was escorted by Doctor Alexander. He had one of the Maul's pods on a hover platform. He got onto a shuttle."

"When?" Kip demanded.

Loy? Tre gripped the edge of the table. He made himself focus on Jax. Jax was safe; that was what counted. What Loy had done and even Ean's fate were secondary; irrelevant.

Jax was talking with Rae and Kip, trying to work out how Kip had missed the shuttle docking with the Maul. From what Rae was saying it had happened during the time Kip had been cut off from the live feeds, before power was fully restored.

It didn't matter when it had happened. It had. Loy had betrayed them and Ean was part of his payment.

Ean would never accept it. Then Tre remembered placing the bottle of forgetting pills in front of Loy at the bar. A carefully controlled dose would wipe only the most recent memories. As far as Ean was concerned the Willow's destruction would be a terrible accident. He would be devastated; grief-stricken and utterly bereaved.

Loy would be there; consoling him and picking up the pieces.

"Tre?" Jax's voice sounded young and uncertain.

Tre realised that the edge of the metal table had deformed in his grasp. He loosened his grip. He would not lose his temper. Fury would not find Ean. "I am fine," he lied.

Kip already had his interfaces out, his goggles on and his earpieces in.

"Kip is going to identify the shuttle," Jax explained. He looked puzzled. "I don't understand. What was Loy doing?"

"Betraying you to the Edgers," Rae snapped.

"But…" Jax trailed off. "What about Ean?"

Tre could not talk about Ean. "It is my fault," he declared. "I decided we could trust Loy. I was wrong."

Jax opened his mouth and then shut it again. He looked at Tre with an expression that reminded Tre of Oro. "This is not the time to dwell on what went wrong. We have a job to do. We must find Ean."

Jax had taken a moment or two to catch up. Once he had, he realised that the priority wasn't Loy or even Ean. It was Tre. Someone Tre had trusted had betrayed them and, to make it worse, he had kidnapped Ean.

For a cyborg Tre was astonishingly stable. So much so that it was easy to forget his nature. Seeing the table bend had reminded Jax of the videos his uncle had shown him; the ones showing cyborgs losing control.

"I can't see it turning out well for Loy," Jax pointed out. "You aren't dead and I was never delivered to Nevin Edger. That is two enemies he could do without."

Tre inhaled more deeply than usual. "Loy knows Nevin Edger. When Nevin Edger was a boy, he used to come and stay with his sister, your father's first wife. At that time, Loy was working on a project for your father that required regular visits to Kalakmul."

Jax had not known that. However, at the moment, he was more interested in encouraging Tre to keep behaving like Tre. "Maybe Loy told Doctor Alexander something," he suggested. If Tre had to take his anger out on someone, Doctor Alexander seemed an appropriate scapegoat; it would serve him right for selling live people to organ harvesters.

Tre nodded and stood up. He glanced at Kip, who was lost in his virtual world. "Doctor Alexander first," he decided. "Then I will make a list of facts about Loy that might give Kip a lead."

Two pairs of eyes tracked Tre to the door; Rae's as well as Jax's. Then Rae's gaze went to the bend in the table. Next he looked at Jax and twitched his whiskers.

"Not my secret," Jax admitted apologetically.

Rae nodded. "Do you think Ean is out of the pod yet?" he asked.

"Probably not," Jax decided. "Loy can keep him in it as long as he wants. You weren't that surprised," Jax observed.

"I had time between the minky level and here to think," Rae admitted. "Loy liked Ean but Ean was Tre's. What about Cas?"

Jax imagined being the one to tell Cas what Loy had done and shuddered.

"You could talk to the captain," Rae suggested.

To Jax that seemed an excellent idea.

The captain listened in silence. Jax saw his eyes narrow and his lips thin.

"It is certain that Loy betrayed us?" he checked when Jax had finished.

Jax considered. "Not yet," he replied "Tre is talking to Doctor Alexander now."

The captain sighed. "Then now would be a good time to talk to Cas, to prepare him for what is likely to come."

Jax hoped the captain did not expect him to do it.

Captain Mel gave a grim smile. "Don't worry, Jax. It is my job, not yours."

Jax went back to where he had left Rae and Kip. Kip's goggles were up and he only had one earpiece in. He looked miserable.

"The trail goes to Spacestation 2. Then it vanishes," he admitted. "Spacestation 2 is a transport hub. Ships come and go from there all the time, including ones that carry passengers. Some don't have passenger manifests and the ones that do don't keep them in places where I can get to them."

Rae gave a whisker twitch that said, "Think of something to say to him because I'm out of ideas."

"Loy doesn't know we are alive," Jax began. "He thinks he is safe. He'll send a message to someone or turn up somewhere."

Kip cheered up a little. "I'll send out worms that will wend their way around the data streams looking for him."

Jax didn't have a clue what Kip meant. "You do that," he encouraged. "And you could track Nevin Edger and his men. They might be after Loy too."

Kip nodded but then paled. "The Edgers might hurt Ean," he suggested

Rae growled, which was not good. It implied that he agreed with Kip.

"Do not mention that to Tre," Jax ordered. Then he sighed; Tre was bound to think of it for himself.

Kip pulled his goggles down and put his other earpiece in. Jax watched his fingers stroking the various inputs of his interfaces. Occasionally he would tilt his head or murmur; reacting to what only he could see.

"I am going to make some tea," Jax decided. "Shall I look for something for you to eat?"

Rae produced three of Ean's meal bars as if from nowhere. "The last ones," he admitted mournfully.

Jax resolved to try to make some more. Most of the food stores from the Willow were now on the Petunia Mae.

He was boiling the water to make the tea when Noe appeared in the doorway of the small galley he was using.

"So it was Loy," Noe stated; the captain must have finished telling Cas.

"Looks like it," Jax admitted. He decided to be honest. "I didn't see that coming."

Noe frowned. "He knows Tre and yet he still decided to betray you and run off with Ean? The man must be crazy."

"He must have been absolutely sure Tre would be killed," Jax pointed out. He thought about it. "Their plan would have worked if it wasn't for Kip." He almost said more but stopped himself. He still didn't know if he trusted Noe.

Noe studied him. "Kip is something else," he suggested.

There was no arguing with that.

"Captain Mel has called a crew meeting," Noe added. "For immediately after Tre finishes interrogating Doctor Alexander."

Jax nodded. It was a good idea. They could still behave like the Willow's crew, even if they were on another ship.

Captain Mel opened the meeting by laying the Willow's log on the table.

"This Meeting is open. Present are Captain Mel, Engineer Vic, Enforcer Tre, Pilot Cas and the cats Obe, Kip and Noe. Cabin boys Rae and Jax are observing. Absent are our queen, Ean, and Medico Loy." He looked at each of them in turn. "What you may not know is that the Willow has been destroyed three times before. The Willow is not just a ship. It is a history and a tradition. It is a crew."

Jax's gaze went to Cas. He looked angry rather than sad or

abandoned.

"It is now eight days since the destruction of the Willow," the captain continued. "From what Doctor Alexander told Tre, it was up to the commander, under the guise of Interstellar Salvage, to contact the spacers' guild and record that there were two survivors and nine bodies. He never did this, presumably because he was waiting until Jax had been handed over to the client."

Jax studied Tre. He looked as he usually did. Jax wondered what state Doctor Alexander had been in when Tre had stuck him back in the pod.

"Another two days and we reach the ten day point," the captain pointed out. "As you know, a claim for compensation from our insurance provider can be registered from ten days onwards. However, if we do that Loy will have a way of knowing that we are still alive."

"It would be best not to do that," Tre stated. "Once he knows, it reduces our chances of finding him."

"That is our first vote then," the captain suggested. "I propose we delay informing the spacers' guild and our insurance provider that we are alive for now. Shall we vote?"

The vote was seven for, none against and two absent.

Following the familiar pattern was soothing. As well as that big decision they made lots of little ones about eating, accommodation and even cleaning clothes. Jax noticed that the captain looked to Cas often, silently asking him to step up and take on some of Ean's responsibilities.

Cas, to do him credit, responded; Jax was impressed.

After the meeting was closed, Cas whispered something to Obe and then walked over to where Kip was sitting. Obe followed reluctantly.

Jax stiffened. Beside him Rae bristled slightly. Kip was not in any state to deal with crew dynamics.

"We realise that you have lots to do, Kip," Cas began. "Looking for Ean."

Kip stared up at Cas, obviously lost and probably worried about where the conversation was going.

"So we won't expect you to do the usual cat duties," Cas continued. "Just look after yourself and turn up for meals."

Jax relaxed; Rae's fur settled.

Cas nudged Obe. "Yes," Obe agreed. "And thanks, for saving us. We know no one else could have done it."

Kip flushed a deep pink. "You are welcome," he stammered.

"If anyone can find Ean it is you," Cas added.

Kip did not know what to say. What if he failed? There weren't any leads. All he could do was monitor the data streams, track the Edgers and hope. Tre hadn't got anything more from Doctor Alexander, just confirmation that Loy was the traitor and that Ean had been in the pod.

Even Tre's list of stuff about Loy hadn't helped. It confirmed that Loy had lived and worked at Mercy Station, which Kip already knew. Other than that there wasn't much to work on.

Cas smiled at him and Obe looked sheepish. As they turned away and began walking towards the door, Kip felt someone grasp his arm.

It was Noe.

"I am going to look after you," Noe told him. "Until Ean gets back."

Kip knew he didn't need looking after. He needed someone like his Ma or Ean, who insisted he did the things normal people did. "Thank you," he replied, hoping that he didn't sound ungrateful.

Noe did say something else but Kip missed it because there was a double ping from his earpiece.

"Something important," he explained, fishing his goggles and interfaces out of various pockets.

He had expected it to be a query or worm yielding something useful. Instead it was a light speed video message from his parents.

It must have cost a fortune to send; Kip resolved to transfer an equivalent amount of credit into his Pa's account.

"*Kipawa, sweetie.*" It was his Ma. She only ever called him sweetie when she was really worried about him. "*Thank you for your message. I am sorry about the Willow. You can always come home. Or we can come to you. Just say. We love you so much.*"

"*Kip.*" His Pa sounded and looked serious. "*We're sending this light speed because we got a message from Ean today and you said in your message that you were looking for him. He thinks you and the others are dead.*" His Pa rubbed a hand over his face. "*Thankfully we received your message first.*"

Kip imagined what his Ma would have been like if it had been the other way around; his Pa and Grandpappy wouldn't have been much better.

"*Ean is on a liner called the Stellar Rover, travelling between Verdant and Mercy Station. He is with Medico Loy. You need to get hold of him as soon as possible, Kip, because he's in a dreadful state. We love you and are proud of you.*"

The video cut to an image of his grandfather.

"*Good work Kiplet. Keep it up. Set things straight with Ean. Safe travelling.*"

Then, all too soon, it was over. Kip resisted the urge to play it again. Instead he pulled off his goggles. The others were walking away; some of them were already out the door.

"I know where Ean is," he called.

Those close enough to hear him turned back and Rae quickly rounded up the others. The last to arrive was Tre.

"He's on a liner with Loy," Kip told them. "The Stellar Rover, en route from Verdant to Mercy Station."

"How in Known Space did you find that out?" Tre demanded.

"I didn't," Kip admitted. "Ean contacted my parents."

Tre sat down on the nearest chair. "Of course he did," he

murmured. "What's the liner's route, Kip? Are there any stops on the way?"

At first it was wonderful, everyone was smiling and hugging each other. There was even some laughter. Then Tre went quiet, followed by Jax. They had to have seen something.

Kip concentrated on the subset of the information Tre and Jax could access. There it was. All the pleasure and relief drained away.

The Orca, with Nevin Edger aboard, was heading towards the Stellar Rover's first port of call.

It was beyond frustrating. The Stellar Rover's last but one jump had taken her away from a shipping lane with light speed data relays into one that did not. Even the system it was heading for, Ellettian, did not have one; it was known for its spectacular planets and moons, not its commercial development.

Even using the Briar Rose they could not get there in time. With her head start the Orca could. She would be there before the Stellar Rover arrived.

Kip had analysed every possible gated route. He was onto working out if he could get a light speed message anywhere from which a ship could make it to the Ellettian system in time.

"What's the point of that?" Jax complained. "Who in Known Space could you hire and trust?"

It was a valid argument, even if it was one Kip did not want to hear. He resolved never to be in this situation again. He needed a network of agents in fast ships; a real version of his virtual identities.

"We will have to rely on Ean's good sense," the captain insisted.

Kip couldn't see that working. Given what Ean knew, he was more likely to try to protect Loy than run for cover.

Then he saw it. There were non-gated routes but only ships with Mulligan drives would be able to use them. Kip almost mentioned it but decided against it; Jax would probably blow a gasket. Instead Kip started looking for ships with Mulligan drives that were close enough to be useful and might be available for purchase or hire. Ideally a spacehopper ship, because that would be fast as well as not needing gates to jump through holes.

Purchasing any ship with a Mulligan drive would be difficult. They were expensive, even for him. It became the second resolution in his list; put more effort into acquiring credit.

If he could locate a suitable ship he would steal the necessary funds; he could always replace them later.

Only he could not find one to purchase, to hire or even to steal.

Kip felt the gentle pressure of a large warm hand on his shoulder; Vic. His left earpiece was tugged away.

"That's enough, Kip. You need a break."

Kip's gaze went to the chronometer in the corner of his field of view. The remainder of the afternoon had vanished; it was time for supper. He thought about objecting but he knew that Vic would not have it. If it came to it the big man would pick him up and carry him.

Noe, Cas and Obe had made a real effort to make it as like supper on the Willow as possible. The captain had invited Kurt, Owen, Medico Kem and the Tuckers.

Owen and Kurt had accepted or rather, as Jax whispered, Owen had accepted on behalf of both of them, forcing Kurt into it.

Kip sympathised; he did not want to be there either. He could not even put one of his earpieces in because Captain Mel frowned at him when he tried. Resolution three; get some earpieces that couldn't be detected.

At least Kurt, as captain of the Petunia Mae, could have a tablet on the table next to him.

They had got as far as dessert when Kurt's tablet beeped. He excused himself and stood up, picking up the tablet. Kip guessed that he would have left but Owen went after him and insisted that he at least check what was happening before leaving the room.

The two of them listened to the sound from the tablet and then started a whispered argument.

"Can we help, Captain Kurt?" Captain Mel asked.

"It's a man called Klennethon Darrent," Kurt admitted. "He wants to speak to the commander."

The name Klennethon Darrent seemed vaguely familiar to Kip. His fingers itched to construct and run some queries.

"I think he's threatening us." Owen admitted.

Tre cleared his throat. "That may be my fault. Perhaps I should record and send a message updating him as to the situation."

Kurt offered the tablet. "He's close enough on a radio link that there's no delay."

Then Kurt, Owen and Tre left to go to the control room.

The interruption sped up the end of the meal. Kip managed to slip away before anyone could suggest he should help clean up. Behind him, Jax and Rae were caught by Cas and instructed to clear the table.

Kip dived into the room next to Vic's workshop and sat well away from where he would be seen if someone opened the door.

Who was Klennethon Darrent? Why was the name familiar? How did Tre know him?

Only once Kip had the live feeds up, he was distracted by the images from the telescopes. Usually Kip didn't find ships attractive. They were merely modes of transport.

The ship that had appeared, the one that was presumably Klennethon Darrent's, was gorgeous. Kip wanted a ship like that.

Then he focused on the fact that she had, literally, appeared from nowhere. Kip was keeping tabs on all the ships coming and going from the system. Klennethon Darrent's ship had not come through any of the gates. He rechecked. The ship had not been in the Verdant system that morning. She had not entered through any of the gated holes. She was not close enough to any large ships to have been hiding in one of their docking bays.

There was only one explanation. Despite her relatively small size, Klennethon Darrent's ship had a Mulligan drive.

She was a spacehopper; exactly the type of ship Kip needed to rescue Ean.

10

As Tre accompanied Owen and Kurt to the control room, he found himself wondering about his competence. Why in Known Space hadn't he remembered to send a light speed message to Klennethon Darrent as soon as Kip was safe?

It had certainly never occurred to him that Klennethon Darrent would turn up in person.

"Would you like to use the desk in the commander's cabin?" Owen asked. "I could show you and Kurt could put the channel through."

Tre decided that he could do with any advantage available. "Thank you, Owen; that would be appreciated."

Owen set up the real time video link and stepped back. Tre caught himself smoothing his hair as Kurt's voice came from the speaker built into the desk.

"I have Citizen Klennethon Darrent for you, Enforcer Tre. Shall I put him through?"

"Please do, captain."

The display screen in front of him activated. Klennethon Darrent gazed at him. *"Enforcer Tre."*

There were very few men who could intimidate Tre but Klennethon Darrent was one of them. Tre managed to stop himself swallowing. "Citizen Darrent," he replied.

"*The situation appears to have moved on since you sent your message*," Klennethon Darrent observed.

"It evolved swiftly," Tre admitted. "I did not expect such a personal response," he added.

"*I was in the vicinity. It was fortuitous*," Klennethon Darrent replied.

Tre assumed that had to be true. Otherwise Klennethon Darrent could not have arrived so quickly, even using a space-hopper ship.

"*Do you have both Emanuel Rafael Jax Esteban and Kipawa Wheeler with you?*" Klennethon Darrent asked.

"Yes," Tre admitted.

"*Then congratulations appear to be in order*," Klennethon Darrent suggested.

Tre was less sure. The Willow was gone, along with a signifi-cant slice of his resources. Too many people knew about Jax's whereabouts. Without Ean he doubted he could care for Jax and he knew he would never cope with Kip.

Maybe Kip would be better off with Klennethon Darrent.

"Thank you," Tre acknowledged. "The people after Jax…" He paused, giving Klennethon Darrent the opportunity to contribute.

"*Nevin Edger*," Klennethon Darrent supplied.

"Quite," Tre acknowledged. "Nevin Edger had a very thorough understand of my capacity. However, he had been informed that Kip was a just a cat with an interest in technology and a talent for mathematics."

"*Ah*," Klennethon Darrent observed.

"So I should be thanking you," Tre suggested. "You suggested that we recruit him."

"*And how has that worked out?*" Klennethon Darrent asked.

Tre was not certain how to answer. He decided to be honest. "It has been educational. I think the Willow was a very suitable home for Kip. Unfortunately it has gone."

"*A ship can be replaced,*" Klennethon Darrent reminded him.

"True, but anonymity is difficult to regain once it has been compromised," Tre replied. "Also, our queen, Ean, has been separated from the rest of the crew."

"*The queen is the heart of a Traditional spacer crew,*" Klennethon Darrent quoted.

Tre could tell from his tone that this was one aspect of spacer life that Klennethon Darrent utterly failed to appreciate.

Klennethon Darrent examined his perfectly manicured fingernails. "*I wish to meet Kipawa Wheeler,*" he stated.

Tre managed not to smile.

The dishes from supper had to be washed by hand; there wasn't an automated cleaner. Jax was washing. Rae was drying. Noe was putting away. Obe had cleared the table and was now making coffee for Captain Mel, Vic and Cas.

"You know," Jax insisted. "Klennethon Darrent. There is only one."

"Who is Klenn-whatever Darrent?" Obe asked.

Jax could not believe that the others had not heard of him.

"The single most powerful individual in the Fringe," the captain informed him. "I would get his name right, Obe. He is not someone you would want to offend."

"How does it go?" Noe asked.

"Klennethon Darrent," Jax repeated carefully. "Citizen Klennethon Darrent. He is, was, a Centralite." He still hadn't got over that Klennethon Darrent was Kip's secret benefactor. He had to be, because Tre had sent a message to Kip's secret benefactor and Klennethon Darrent had arrived.

"And why is he interested in us?" Cas asked.

There was silence. Jax realised that everyone's eyes were on him. "I think Tre has had contact with him before," he admitted, which seemed a better answer than saying that Klennethon Darrent was interested in Kip but Kip did not know it.

As soon as they had finished tidying up, Jax grabbed Rae and they went to find Kip. He was hiding in the room next to Vic's workshop but, typically Kip, he was using his goggles and earpieces rather than the displays and the speakers.

He must have had one earpiece set to transmit ambient noise

because he turned around as soon as they entered.

"Look," he declared.

One of the displays activated and showed an image of one of the most beautiful ships Jax had ever seen.

"Klennethon Darrent's spacehopper," Kip told them. "We could get to Ean in time using her."

For once Jax was absolutely speechless. What was Kip suggesting? That they steal Klennethon Darrent's ship?

"You know who he is?" Rae asked.

Kip scowled. "Yes, I just looked him up. He's a typed-five genius."

Jax didn't know what a typed-five genius was.

"He's the only typed-genius operating outside Centre," Kip added. "Which means that he is the typed-five genius that the Darrenden government hired to find the anomalies, which means he's the reason I had to leave home."

Jax only understood the end of that. "He's also the most powerful individual in the Fringe," he pointed out, finally finding his voice.

Kip looked remarkably unimpressed.

"And the person who asked Tre to recruit you," Jax added.

Kip was stunned into silence. Jax was just congratulating himself on having gained the upper hand and making Kip see sense when Rae spoke.

"So this Klennethon Darrent has been messing with Kip's life."

Jax could not believe Rae had just said that. He watched as Kip's expression hardened into stubborn determination.

"He's been trying to keep you safe," Jax suggested.

"Well he should have asked first," Kip pointed out.

They would have probably argued more but Rae stopped them.

"Tre's coming," he warned.

Sure enough, Tre walked in a few moments later.

"Jax, Rae, could I have a moment with Kip alone?" he asked.

Jax nodded and Rae stood up.

"I want them to stay," Kip insisted, his chin jutting out in a way Jax had never seen before.

"Kip..." Tre began.

"What does he want?" Kip demanded. "He's already managed to get me off my home planet, away from my parents and into the crew of his choice with someone to mind me. What does he want now?"

Jax remembered Tre describing Kip as the second most dangerous person he had ever met. If Klennethon Darrent was the most dangerous, stuck between them would not be a comfortable place to be.

"What does he want?" Kip insisted.

"To meet you," Tre admitted.

"No," Kip replied. "I refuse."

Jax watched Tre tense up and remembered the bend in the table. Tre was under a lot of pressure. Jax's identity and whereabouts were known. Ean was probably in danger. Tre had asked for Klennethon Darrent's help to rescue Kip and now Kip was having none of it.

Kip didn't know that Tre was a cyborg. If he did, he might choose to be more reasonable.

Or maybe not; Kip was Kip.

Rae walked over to the display and tapped the frame to attract Kip's attention. Jax watched as Kip's gaze went to the image of the spacehopper ship.

"I'll speak to him over a video link," Kip conceded.

Tre blinked at the sudden change in position. "You will?"

"I will," Kip agreed. His chin jutted out again. "I'll give him the opportunity to persuade me to meet him."

Kip was cross. It wasn't something that happened often. Usually he avoided it. When he was cross he didn't think clearly. After he had finished being cross he would look back and realise that he had made embarrassingly poor decisions.

One part of his mind was reminding him that if he had behaved himself on Darrenden the government would have never employed Klennethon Darrent. The same small, logical inner voice was pointing out that Klennethon Darrent could have betrayed him to the government or, worse, to Centre but instead had gone out of his way to find him a crew in which he would be safe.

Unfortunately that logical part was being drowned out by the rest. This man, this Klennethon Darrent, had taken control of Kip's life. He had separated Kip from his parents. He had upset Ma. Now he wasn't willing to give Kip his ship and Kip needed that ship to rescue Ean.

At least Kip didn't think Klennethon Darrent would give him the ship. Not unless he was forced into it.

He did listen to the part of his mind reminding him that Klennethon Darrent could outthink him. Klennethon Darrent had found him on Darrenden despite all Kip's efforts to stay hidden. Kip understood why; typed-fives were better at patterns than Kip could ever hope to be.

That was as far as Kip and his Pa had got; Kip wasn't a typed-five because he couldn't detect patterns a typed-five could find. He could see them once they were pointed out, which was more than Pa could, but he could not find them.

They knew that because there were enough typed-five geniuses for studies to have been done on them and books written about them. One in one billion humans was a typed-five genius.

Neither Kip nor his Pa knew what type of genius Kip was because the only way to find out was to take the Centralite psychologists' test without fixing the answers.

Maybe he wasn't a typed-genius at all. Perhaps he had been running all his life from Centre when Centre wasn't even chasing him.

They were going towards the nose of the ship, through one of the gravitational field inversions. Once they were on the ladder, Kip had discovered that he did not want to go; at least the mission level was familiar. He had tried persuading Tre to turn back and to arrange a link from the room next to the workshop instead.

Tre had refused.

Apparently they were going to use the desk in the commander's office because that was set up for live video links.

The commander's cabin was unexpectedly nice. It reminded Kip of his Pa's study only it was much neater and the wood wasn't real.

Kip settled into the chair. In front of him detectors checked his line of vision and adjusted the camera accordingly. A large display screen activated.

"*This is Owen.*" Owen's voice came from speakers built into the desk. "*I have Citizen Darrent for you. Making the link.*"

Hearing Owen reminded Kip that the link might not be secure. Before he could do more than resolve to be careful, an image appeared on the screen.

Klennethon Darrent did not look real. On Darrenden they had storyvids that had been made for the Inner Borders and even some that had been available in Centre. The actors in them never looked real. They were just too perfect.

Kip knew the way the actors looked was due to a combination of age-retard and biosculpting. He guessed it was the same with Klennethon Darrent. The man was the wrong side of one hundred; one hundred and twenty standards to be precise. He looked a mature thirty or a wrinkle-free forty.

He was very handsome, again like an actor.

"*Kipawa Wheeler*," Klennethon Darrent acknowledged in the type of voice that connected to your gut as well as your ears.

Despite his annoyance, Kip's manners automatically cut in. "Citizen Klennethon Darrent."

There was silence. Kip did not see why he should speak first. Then, slowly, he realised that Klennethon Darrent was studying him and felt himself blush.

He was determined not to be the one to initiate the conversation. He looked away. Finally he could not resist looking back. Klennethon Darrent was smirking at him. It wasn't much of a smile but it was definitely there.

It felt like an insult; the man was laughing at him.

"*I would like to meet you face-to-face*," Klennethon Darrent stated finally.

"Why?" Kip asked. He knew he sounded sulky. He imagined what his Ma would say if she caught him being so rude.

"*You know why*," Klennethon Darrent replied. "*Do you really want to discuss it over a radio link?"*

Kip recognised a threat when he heard one. "You have to ask the queen of my crew and you can't because he isn't here."

"Ean," Klennethon Darrent stated.

"Yes," Kip confirmed. He was surprised Klennethon Darrent knew Ean's name.

"I believe that asking your captain would be equally accept-able," Klennethon Darrent suggested.

"You do that then," Kip replied. Then he was off the chair and out of the field of view of the camera.

It was only then that Kip remembered that Tre was in the room, lurking to the side. He was looking at Kip with exasperation; an expression he usually reserved for Obe. He nodded at the chair, indicating that Kip should go back to it.

Kip headed for the door. He was a cat and Tre was a senior member of crew. If Tre gave him a direct order he could not refuse to follow it. If he was out of the room he could pretend not to hear.

However, once he was in the corridor, he could not resist pausing to listen.

Tre took his place on the chair. Kip heard the sound of the camera adjusting.

"Enforcer Tre."

"Citizen Darrent. Please excuse Kip. The Willow's destruction has been traumatic for him and he misses Ean."

"I understand. Please relay a formal request for a face-to-face meeting with Kipawa Wheeler to Captain Mel."

"Captain Mel is a Traditionalist," Tre replied. "Cats do not even speak to outsiders. I could ask if he would be willing to receive you here, as a crew guest. If you were a crew guest, it would be acceptable for Kip to speak with you."

"That is not an acceptable option, Enforcer Tre, as I am sure you appreciate. Would an invitation for the whole crew to share lunch with me tomorrow on my ship be acceptable?"

"That is a plausible option," Tre agreed. "I shall put it to Captain Mel."

"I hope to see you late midmorning," Klennethon Darrent replied. "I should warn you that all my ship's systems have unusually robust shielding."

"I understand," Tre replied.

Kip didn't. What type of shielding did he mean and why did Tre say he understood?

Tre did not tell Kip off about his rude behaviour to Klennethon Darrent or for listening at the door. He merely shook his head and gestured that Kip should lead the way back to the mission level.

When they got there Tre went off towards the room the captain was using as his cabin. Kip walked slowly back towards the room next to the workshop.

Jax and Rae were still there.

"Did you get it?" Rae asked.

Kip shook his head.

"Did you ask?" Rae demanded.

"Be sensible, Rae," Jax chided. "Kip can't just come out and ask Klennethon Darrent to give us a lift to the Ellettian system."

Kip felt awful. He hadn't even tried. He had been too busy being a stroppy teenager. "We may be meeting with him tomorrow morning," he told them.

"How soon would we have to leave to get there in time?" Rae asked.

Kip admitted that he didn't know. It depended how quickly Klennethon Darrent's ship could travel between holes. She certainly looked fast.

Kip could not help but think he had disappointed Rae. Worse he had let Ean down. He had thought he was willing to do anything to get Ean back safe and yet he hadn't even been polite to the one person who could make that happen.

It was a relief when Cas put his head around the door to send Jax and Rae to bed.

"How are you doing, Kip?" he asked once they had gone.

"Fine," Kip lied. "I am sorry about Loy," he added.

Cas's expression hardened. "Loy is not worth a moment's thought. I worry about Ean. What did your parents say about him?"

"That he thinks we are all dead," Kip admitted.

"I hate Loy for putting Ean through that much more than for

anything he did to me," Cas insisted. He managed a smile. "At least we know where he is now. I only wish we could get there before the Edgers."

Kip felt even more terrible.

Once Cas had gone he set up his interfaces, put on his goggles and set out to make things right. Typed-five geniuses could see patterns no one else could, so he encrypted a message using one of those patterns and sent it to Klennethon Darrent's ship.

I apologise.

The reply did not come through until he was in his bunk. Klennethon Darrent had used the same encryption pattern rather than challenging Kip with another.

You are fifteen and hurting.

It was a surprisingly frank answer. Kip was much more impressed by it that he had been by Klennethon Darrent's looks or even his voice. He decided to go for it.

Ean's in trouble and we can't reach him in time to tell him about it or stop it. You could, in your space-hopper, but we can't.

Kip waited. At least he would be able to tell Rae that he had asked. Finally the answer came through.

I might agree to take you there. It depends on you.

Kip took his more charitable thoughts back. He hated Klennethon Darrent. **What do you want?**

The answer was immediate. **Regular contact like this. Plus some time face-to-face. I understand that the**

face-to-face time may have to wait. You are a cat in a Traditional crew.

Kip had been anticipating much less reasonable demands. **Why?**

Are you lonely, Kipawa Wheeler?

Kip didn't like thinking about that. There were times when he wasn't lonely: when he was lost in a problem he was solving; when Ean hugged him; with his Pa. He decided to be honest. **Yes.**

I have lived one hundred and twenty standards.

Kip had waited fifteen standards to meet someone else like him; Klennethon Darrent had been waiting eight times as long.

Rae was impressed. When he had gone to sleep they still had no way of getting to Ean, despite having a spacehopper ship dangling temptingly in front of them, but when he woke up Kip and Captain Mel had sorted it.

They were going to Ellettian on Klennethon Darrent's ship. While they were gone, the Petunia Mae would continue salvaging the wreck of the Willow.

As soon as they had been told, Tre had sat Rae down for a private chat. Apparently Klennethon Darrent was obsessed with security. There would be cameras and guards and probably even snipers.

"Klennethon Darrent is a very powerful man," Tre concluded. "He has many enemies. He has not lived to one hundred and twenty by taking risks. Between you and me, I am astonished he has agreed to have us on board his ship. Apparently we are even going to spend time with him. Expect massively over-the-top security. Do not move too fast or growl. If you do you will be shot through with lasers before you can apologise for twitching. Do you understand?"

Rae nodded. He understood. He would have to move like a harmless purebred or the trigger-happy guards would overreact and shoot him.

Next it was back to the cabin he shared with Jax to pack enough stuff for the trip to Ellettian and back. Jax insisted on checking what was in his backpack and Rae ended up having to repack it. He didn't get why he needed so many clothes or why they had to dress up. All that Jax would say was that Ean would want them to make a good impression.

He understood a bit better once he saw the shuttle Klennethon Darrent had sent. Every bit of it was nice in the same way as the bird carving he had bought for Jax was nice.

Not that the others seemed to notice. They were too busy staring out the viewports at Klennethon Darrent's ship, the Renaissance.

Rae could see the ship was different. It was shaped a bit like a fish, sweeping back from the nose to the tail with two side parts a bit like fins. There was a large rocket built into each fin part although Vic said the main drives, both conventional and

Mulligan, were built into the tail end of the ship, which nestled between the swept-back fins.

Down each side was a row of viewing ports and, top front, there was something Vic called a bridge.

Apparently the levels, which the captain referred to as decks, ran along the ship rather than across, each deck going nose to tail.

"Custom built gravity field generators," Kip murmured in awe. "Probably fully controllable."

The shuttle bay was in what Tre called the ventral side, which was underneath. The pilot warned that they were switching from the shuttle's gravitational field to the Renaissance's but Rae could barely feel the transition.

Once the shuttle bay had pressurised the door opened and the pilot suggested that they disembark. Waiting for them was a purebred female dressed in very neat, well-fitted grey clothes.

"Welcome to the Renaissance," she announced as they stepped off the shuttle. "My name is Elspeth. I shall be your liaison for the journey. If you require anything, please ask."

Rae soon realised that Elspeth was the purebred female human version of the Renaissance. Most of the crew smelt interested, even Kip. Kip couldn't take his eyes off her lower legs, which were covered in dark, tight-fitting, sheer stockings. The captain, Vic and Obe were focused on her breasts, although Captain Mel made a real effort to keep his eyes on her head.

Cas and Tre liked her butt, the shape of which was obvious because her skirt was tight.

Jax didn't really notice her, which confirmed what Rae already knew; Jax didn't like girls.

Noe was fixated on her shoes.

They were shown to the guest quarters, which proved to be a whole deck of the ship that came with its own servants and even had a garden.

To Rae's relief there was a gym with a treadmill.

Tre and Captain Mel had a whispered conversation and then spoke to Elspeth. Rae listened in, as always, only to discover it was pretty boring. It was decided that the crew would occupy three of the guest apartments and use certain amenities. The servants would stay out of those areas unless their presence was requested.

"But they would have cleaned and tidied," Obe objected once Captain Mel announced the decision. "They'd have probably even done the laundry."

Cas gave him a push. "Trad crews don't have servants, Obe. What would Ean say?"

Rae noticed that Cas didn't push very hard and that Obe didn't mind in the least. Both of them seem to have forgotten Elspeth.

Then Cas and Obe had a look about and consulted with Captain Mel, before deciding where everyone would sleep. Rae and Jax had a small cabin with two bunks; it was perfect. Rae glanced at Jax and then put his backpack on the upper bunk, claiming it. Jax smiled his approval, hung his pack from a convenient hook and began investigating where they could put their things.

They had to go for something called a 'reception' on the 'viewing deck' soon after they boarded. They walked up stairs rather than using ladders. Two levels up, they stepped out into a huge space. The majority of the deck, from just below the nose to the bulkhead that divided off the Mulligan drive, was open.

Obe just stood at the top of the stairs and gaped. If Rae hadn't been checking for threats like Tre had taught him, he might have done the same.

Tre had been right; there were snipers.

The room was twice as high as a usual level. The ceiling looked like the sky on Janine. The floor appeared to be made of polished wood. On the walls in front of them and behind them were display frames with pictures.

To the sides the level was split into two. Jax called the upper level a mezzanine. Below it, a little way back, were lots of doors, each made of wood. The viewing ports that Rae had seen from the outside ran the length of each mezzanine.

Rae could see that you could walk up the stairs, along the mezzanine and down the stairs at the other end. It was a bit like the promenade in the spacestation at Darrenden only much, much nicer.

Klennethon Darrent was waiting for them on the 'port' viewing deck, as Elspeth called it. There was no mistaking him. He was tall and powerfully built without looking muscle-bound.

He sure didn't look one hundred and twenty.

With him were a number of the omnipresent servants, dressed in grey like Elspeth, and another man, who Elspeth told them was Citizen Garner Parrad.

Garner Parrad was utterly focused on Klennethon Darrent. Rae wondered if he was Klennethon Darrent's bodyguard.

Klennethon Darrent, to Rae's surprise, only had eyes for Kip.

11

Tre checked each of the youngsters. Obe was still doing his imitation of a fish; Tre hoped he stopped gaping before they made it up the stairs and along the mezzanine to where Klennethon Darrent was waiting.

Noe's eyes were darting from one opulent feature to the next, as if attempting to cost the room. Jax was intrigued and yet comfortable, as if being surrounded by such wealth relaxed him. Rae was moving slowly and smoothly, confirming that he had taken in what Tre had told him about the snipers. There were four of them. Given that Klennethon Darrent had all but told Tre that he had an electromagnetic pulse generator primed, four seemed excessive. It implied that he saw Rae as a threat.

Then there was Kip. The room was an amazing mixture of craftsmanship, art and technology; Tre had expected Kip to be fascinated. He wasn't. As soon as he had spotted Klennethon Darrent, Kip had gone back to channelling sulky adolescent.

Mel had reached the mezzanine and was slowing up to allow the rest of them to catch up. Tre shepherded the youngsters up the stairs and got his first proper look at the man standing at Klennethon Darrent's side. Garner Parrad was honey-skinned, medium height and on the slight side with wrists that caught the eye and a face that was saved from looking feminine by a strong chin.

It was the man who had briefed him before his meeting with Klennethon Darrent in Tarrasade.

Although Klennethon Darrent was polite it was clear that he was only interested in Kip. Not that either could speak to the other. It was a formal occasion; the captain was bending the rules by even mentioning the cats' and the cabin boys' names.

After the introductions, Klennethon Darrent conversed with the captain and Vic about the ship while the youngsters were released to explore the viewing deck under Cas's supervision.

Tre moved to stand next to Garner Parrad, who did not walk away.

Kip sat down at one of the small, low tables and began examining the contents of a bowl. Tre had thought the pile of shapes was for decoration but it appeared not. Kip quickly converted the pieces into a cuboid. Tre saw Kip's gaze go to the next table, on which there was another bowl containing another puzzle, before he moved across and tipped out the pieces.

"He is anxious about Kip's safety," Garner Parrad stated. There was no apology for discussing one of the crew's cats, not even a preamble while he edged up to the limits of the code. Garner Parrad, despite the knife strapped to his thigh, was far more a Centralite than a spacer.

"That is understandable," Tre replied, trying to keep the discussion as neutral as possible. Kip had already solved the second puzzle. Jax was delivering a third bowl while Rae was collecting a fourth and a fifth.

"It appears that Kip is very attached to Ean," Garner Parrad continued. "And has formed a friendship with your cabin boys of the type he did not enjoy when on his home planet."

Tre assumed that meant that Klennethon Darrent thought the benefit of Kip being in the crew outweighed the risks. "Kip has settled well," he agreed.

Klennethon Darrent was continuing his conversation with Vic and Mel but Tre could tell that his attention was fixed on Kip. He even moved so that he could observe Kip solving the puzzles, using the excuse of pointing out a technical feature of the ship.

Tre belatedly realised that the puzzles were not there to provide Kip with entertainment; they were a test. "Does he only have Kip's best interests at heart?" he asked bluntly.

Garner Parrad looked shocked for a moment, but Tre decided it was only at the directness of the question. "Yes," he replied. "Adolescence is a very dangerous time. Given that Kip could not remain with his parents and grandfather, it is essential that he spends this period of his life in a substitute family unit that will stabilise him."

The diagnosis meshed with what Vic had said; he had suggested returning Kip to his parents if they did not find Ean.

Kip was struggling with the fifth puzzle, which at first glance looked like a heap of misshapen metal bits, none larger than a hazelnut. He had spread the pieces across the tabletop and was staring at them, apparently unable to discern a starting point. Klennethon Darrent excused himself from his conversation, walked across and, ignoring Mel's frown, took a seat opposite.

Garner Parrad was watching them intently. Tre wondered what happened if Kip did not solve the puzzle. Would Klennethon Darrent lose interest in him?

Kip picked out five pieces. Tre heard Garner Parrad's sudden, sharp intake of breath. Something important was happening. Kip pushed the pieces across the table to Klennethon Darrent, who quickly assembled them into a shape.

So it continued. Kip selected pieces, Klennethon Darrent assembled them. Once they had all the small pieces assembled into larger ones the process continued, building up sections of the final three-dimensional shape.

"I could order Kip to stop," Tre threatened.

Garner Parrad turned anxious eyes on him. "Please don't. He has waited his whole life for this moment."

So Kip was passing rather than failing. It was a puzzle designed to be solved by two; a typed-five genius and...?

What manner of typed-genius was Kip?

Suddenly it all fell into place. Tre's heart sped up and he felt momentarily light-headed. Kip was not worryingly unstable, he was phenomenally, amazingly, incredibly sane.

A typed-seven genius who could communicate with ordinary mortals; Centre would wipe out whole systems without blinking an eye to have one.

They would pay anything: enough to ensure Jax's future as Navaja's clan leader; enough for Tre to set up his own clan. They would probably eliminate every clan if that was the price demanded.

Not that Tre would live to appreciate it; Klennethon Darrent would kill him slowly if Ean had not gutted him first.

"Klenn said that you would work it out," Garner Parrad observed.

So Klennethon Darrent was 'Klenn' to Garner Parrad; Tre doubted there were many people who could claim such intimacy.

"Yet I am still alive," Tre observed.

"You are Kip's protector," Garner Parrad replied. "And you are a remarkably honourable man. Of all the men he has met, he believes that you are the least likely to break your word."

Tre took that as a compliment rather than an attempt to manipulate him. If Klennethon Darrent knew that much, he also understood that being a man of his word had only brought Tre pain.

Tre almost asked another question but stopped himself. Garner Parrad was collecting information for his......friend? They were three days away from Ellettian; Tre had time to think things through before he decided which questions he could risk asking.

The puzzle solvers were down to thirteen pieces. Klennethon Darrent gestured that Kip should put them together. Kip did so and placed the resulting curvy, abstract shape on the table.

"That was fun," he stated, his eyes shining.

"There is only one puzzle like that in existence," Klennethon Darrent replied. "We could design others, but we would know the solution."

Kip looked distant for a moment and then nodded.

At the end of the reception, Klennethon Darrent invited the crew to eat the evening meal with him and Captain Mel accepted on their behalf. Then he left with Garner Parrad, carrying the puzzle he had completed with Kip.

Once Klennethon Darrent had gone the snipers faded away, leaving them with Elspeth.

Vic asked Elspeth if it would be acceptable for them to stay in the room for a while. She told them that it was and ordered them refreshments, which turned out to be real coffee, a spiced milk drink Tre had never encountered and a pile of cookies big enough that even Rae could have as many as he wanted.

Once they had poured their cups of coffee, the captain pointed to the furthest table.

"Time for you to bring us up to date, Enforcer Tre," he warned. "Vic?"

Vic turned to Cas. "Make sure they don't damage anything."

Cas opened his mouth to object but chose to nod instead; he really was trying to help in Ean's absence.

The three of them settled at the table.

"Well?" Mel hinted.

"It was Klennethon Darrent who brought Kip to my attention as a potential cat," Tre admitted. "We had met once, before I joined the Willow, in Tarrasade."

"And he knows Kip how?" Vic asked.

Tre wondered how much he should say. He decided to go with a partial truth and avoid mentioning hacking; Mel would not approve of hacking. "Kip's data mining activities attracted his attention."

"Even when he was on Darrenden?" Vic queried.

Tre didn't want Vic asking questions so decided to talk about Klennethon Darrent to distract him. "Klennethon Darrent was identified at a young age as being exceptionally intelligent. The government of his home planet decided that he should go to Centre to receive what experts considered an appropriate education."

Mel frowned, obviously uncomfortable about discussing a spacer's background, even a spacer who was really a Centralite.

"It's common knowledge," Tre assured him. "Anyway," he continued, "I believe Klennethon Darrent sympathised with the Wheelers' efforts to stop the same thing happening to Kip. When Kip decided to space, Klennethon Darrent wanted to make sure he ended up with an appropriate crew."

Vic snorted. "That makes sense. Kip wouldn't have lasted two days in most crews."

"The crew you had prepared for Jax was the most likely to be the best for Kip," Mel observed. "Which means Klennethon Darrent knew about Jax."

"He knew about my connection with the Navaja clan," Tre admitted. "So he worked it out. He can work most things out."

"Kip is the same level of clever as Klennethon Darrent?" Vic checked.

"Yes," Tre lied. Centre considered typed-seven geniuses far more intelligent that typed-fives. Typed-sevens could make huge intellectual leaps; it was generally accepted that one had invented the technology required to jump a hole.

"Kip was a shock at first," Vic admitted. "But he soon grows on you. He has a good heart." He looked over to where Kip was being bothered by Noe and smiled. "You should have seen him after he had been stuck in that service duct for two solid days. He was obsessed with rescuing his crew. And he did it. He even found us a spacehopper ship so that we can reach Ean."

Tre decided not to point out that it had been Jax who had suggested that Tre should contact Klennethon Darrent.

Darting movement at the edges of Tre's field of view attracted Tre's attention. Rae was getting agitated; Tre could see him eyeing the banisters.

Mel followed his line of sight. "Time to go," he decided.

Tre agreed but he needed to speak with Kip where Rae could not overhear them. After a short negotiation it was decided that Tre and Kip would follow on behind but be back in the guest quarters for lunch.

Kip stood watching the others leave; it was obvious that he would prefer to follow Jax and Rae. Tre walked over to the remains of the refreshments; the food had gone but there was still some liquid in the insulated containers.

"Sit down," Tre told him. "Which do you want?" he added,

gesturing towards the two pots.

"Coffee please," Kip replied.

Ean would not approve. Tre poured them both a cup and carried them over to where Kip had sat down. "Time to talk," he warned.

Kip claimed one of the cups and nodded.

Tre took a deep breath and let it out slowly. "The puzzle was a test for typed-seven thinking and you solved it," he stated.

Kip gave a single, very small nod.

"Did you know?" Tre asked.

"Pa suspected," Kip answered. "I wasn't a typed-five," he added. He looked away, out of one of the viewing ports into the distance. "Does it matter?" he asked.

Tre suppressed the urge to yell. Of course it mattered. It affected every iota of Kip's life. Potentially it could affect the whole of humanity. He picked his next words carefully.

"Knowing does not change things," he replied. "You are a member of our crew."

Kip settled a little. "You aren't going to hand me over to him?"

"I think Ean and your parents would have something to say about that," Tre replied.

Kip relaxed a little more and sipped his coffee.

"Also," Tre admitted, "Klennethon Darrent thinks you are better off with us." He refrained from adding 'for now'.

"Good," Kip acknowledged. He scowled. "Most of the time I really don't like him. He's vain and acts like he thinks he's really important."

Klennethon Darrent definitely qualified as 'really important'. However Tre decided it was not the time to remind Kip of that fact.

"And he shouldn't have messed with my life without asking. Pa and I had it covered," Kip added. "If he wanted to help, he should have asked. It was rude. He's rude."

Tre wondered if Klennethon Darrent was listening; part of him hoped so.

"Then there's why he wants contact with me," Kip continued. "He told me he was lonely like me but, after I thought about it, I decided he said it to get me to talk to him. If he had wanted to, he could have stayed with the other typed-geniuses in Centre. He left."

"That doesn't mean he isn't lonely," Tre pointed out. He could not believe he was defending Klennethon Darrent. "He took that decision over a hundred standards ago, when he was eighteen. He could regret it."

Kip's chin was jutting out again. "He could have gone back. He's a citizen. He could live in Centre and go visit them. He could correspond with them like he wants to with me."

Tre made a note of that. "Maybe he does visit them and correspond with them."

Kip sighed. "Maybe the Centralite psychologists don't allow it," he admitted.

Tre wished Ean was there. He was the expert at dealing with conflicted adolescents.

"You said most of the time," Tre hinted.

Kip sighed. "He says really insightful stuff and he understands math jokes like Pa does. We played a game of speed chess over a link and he beat me. It was great. The puzzles were amazing, especially the last one." Then, as soon as it had come, Kip's elation vanished. "Only I don't think he's doing any of it because it's fun. Look at the puzzles. It wasn't about enjoying solving them; it was about testing if I was a typed-seven."

Tre remembered what Garner Parrad had said. "Maybe it's a bit of both," he suggested. "Perhaps when he was fifteen he was just like you."

Kip snorted. "No, he'd have been much more like Jax."

"You are Jax's friend," Tre pointed out.

Kip drank more coffee. "Klennethon Darrent isn't fifteen. He's ancient." He put down his cup and began gesturing above his head with his hands. "If this was a storyvid he would be the mega-baddy; the Master Puppeteer who controls everyone else's life and lives in this palace where the doorknobs are made of carved diamond."

Tre could not help but smile.

Kip's face fell. "Only it isn't a storyvid." His gaze went back to the stars beyond the viewing port. "I know I'm useless at telling good from bad or right from wrong. To me there are too many shades of grey. I ask myself what Ean would do, or Ma, and I know they would tell me to stay away from Klennethon Darrent."

"If it goes well you'll be able to check with Ean yourself," Tre suggested.

Kip's face lit up. "That would be great. We have to plan what we're going to do when we arrive. I have the specs of the Stellar Rover and of the Orca. I've mapped the Ellettian system. The spacestation is close to the gate but the hole we'll be using is over two days' travel away on the Renaissance. Klennethon Darrent has a racing yacht. Maybe he'll let you use it."

Even after twenty divs' practice, Tre still struggled to keep up when Kip shot off in a new direction. He certainly was not up to it now; he still had thinking to do about Kip being a typed-seven. Picking up their cups, he proffered them to Kip, who automatically took them and placed them on the side table with the others. "We'll talk through the plan this afternoon," Tre assured him. "Now we mustn't be late for lunch or Cas will be cross."

Cas and the youngsters were in the largest galley of the three available to them. Although it was obviously intended as a food preparation area, it did have a central table that could seat nine at a pinch.

The dining room was larger but that would separate those preparing the food from those eating it.

Obe and Cas were cooking. Jax had found a teapot of which he obviously approved and was making tea. Rae was laying the table.

Kip sat next to Noe, sliding into the narrow gap between the table and the wall where there wasn't enough room for an adult. Noe was turning one of the empty teacups in his hands.

For someone as materialistic as Noe, being on the Renaissance must be like listening to an orchestra when you had only ever heard a tune on a tin whistle.

"Is your clan rich like this?" he asked.

The question was obviously directed at Jax. If Ean or Captain Mel had been present Noe would have been told off; spacers did not ask other spacers personal questions.

Tre let it ride. He was interested in whether Jax would reply and, if so, what he would say.

"Yes and no," Jax answered. "There are a lot of people in a clan. If the clan leader's family spent this much on itself, the other members of the clan might consider it overindulgence, particularly if other members of the clan were doing without to pay for it."

It was a thoughtful answer; Tre was pleased.

"It's just stuff," Kip observed.

Noe looked at him as if insulted.

"No it isn't," Rae replied, which was unexpected because he rarely contributed to such discussions. "It matters who makes it." He picked up another of the teacups. "This was made by someone who cared how it turned out."

"An artisan," Jax supplied.

Rae stroked the top he was wearing. "And this was made by someone who cares about me."

Tre was impressed; Rae had come a long way from the feral child they had met in Carrefour.

"I get that," Kip admitted.

"And it matters how pretty it is," Noe insisted.

More might have been said but Mel arrived, followed closely by Vic, and they settled to down to eat. Tre found himself looking around the table. Despite losing their ship, even without their queen, they were definitely a crew.

"Will we beat the Stellar Rover to Ellettian?" Vic asked.

Kip nodded. "By almost a day. The problem is that the hole we will be using is a long way from the spacestation. The space-station is really close to the gate."

"So we send a message to Ean, telling him to stay on the ship," the captain pointed out. "As long as he stays on the ship he will be fine. No one is going to try and board a passenger liner. Why don't you youngsters record a vid for him this afternoon? Cas, maybe you could help them. Tre, Vic and I will add our parts later."

"There's a communications desk in the small room off the dining room," Jax pointed out. "We can use that."

Tre watched them crowd into the tiny room and begin arguing about what to do. He decided to leave them to it and head to the gym. Following up with a session in the sauna, he finished up with a shower before dressing and going to see how they were getting on. Cas had decided they needed a clip for the start with all of them in it. Tre obediently took his place standing behind the desk on Mel's right.

At least Ean was young and fit; he was unlikely to have a heart attack when he opened the message and saw them all standing there.

It was almost time for dinner with Klennethon Darrent by the time the video was complete and edited to everyone's satisfaction. Cas ordered everyone to dress neatly and congregate in the room they were using as a shared area in good time for Elspeth's arrival.

A dining table had been set up on the same viewing gallery as had been used for the reception. Tre counted eleven places, confirming that only Klennethon Darrent and Garner Parrad would be eating with them.

It turned out that Klennethon Darrent could be a gracious host when he wished. He even managed to charm Mel into giving the cats and cabin boys permission to contribute to the conversation.

Kip was quick to capitalise as soon as Klennethon Darrent enquired about their plans for when they reached Ellettian.

"Can Tre borrow your racing yacht?" he asked. "So he can reach Ean as quickly as possible?"

"Kip!" Captain Mel scolded.

Kip did not apologise or take back the request.

"Of course," Klennethon Darrent replied. "You would be welcome to use her, Enforcer Tre. Perhaps you would like to spend some time tomorrow accustoming yourself to the controls. There is enough time between two of the jumps." He smiled. "And perhaps the youngsters would appreciate a tour of the ship?"

Tre spent the next morning going over the specs of the one

man yacht, the Apus. The cockpit doubled as an acceleration tank, which meant she would be phenomenally fast even when piloted by an unmodified purebred, never mind a cyborg. The yacht would be launched from the Renaissance and then accelerate to peak velocity before beginning deceleration in time to dock.

If everything went to plan, Tre would be able to make it to the spacestation only shortly after the Stellar Rover jumped into the system.

During the afternoon, between jumps, he tried the Apus out. It was, he had to admit, exhilarating; she was delightfully responsive.

Garner Parrad was waiting for him when he exited the bay where he had re-docked the yacht.

"We will book a high security berth for you," he explained.

Tre understood; the Apus was probably worth more than most full-sized ships.

"However, the Stellar Rover does have suitable, one-craft docking bays should that prove to be the more appropriate destination," Garner Parrad continued. "Will your crew need access to the bridge or the communications deck?"

"Only your transmitter and receiver," Tre admitted.

Garner Parrad just looked at him.

"Kip has his own kit," Tre clarified. "He carries it around with him."

"A full communications system," Garner Parrad checked.

"He does need a small backpack for the data crystal array," Tre conceded. "Otherwise it fits in his pockets. Maybe Citizen Darrent should ask Kip if it would be possible to see his goggles."

Back in the improvised crewroom, the rest of the crew were talking about their tour of the ship.

"It's amazing," Jax enthused. "I mean, I know nothing could justify spending that amount of credit on a ship, even a flagship, but I can see why he wanted it."

"Up on the bridge there are viewing ports everywhere," Cas added.

"And the best captain's chair," Obe added. "Rae got to sit in it," he added with a hint of jealousy.

Rae managed not to look too smug.

"How was the yacht?" Vic asked.

"Fast," Tre admitted.

"How soon will you be able to get there?" Kip asked.

Tre wondered if he had paid any attention during the tour. "Less than a day."

"Wow, that's quick," Jax acknowledged. "It's going to take the Renaissance over two."

The next day went slowly. There were five jumps; the route Kip had found was quick but complex. Tre spent three of the jumps in the viewing gallery; for all he knew no one had seen these systems since the original Space Hoppers who had mapped them. When he arrived for the third jump he found Klennethon Darrent himself sitting on one of the couches.

That explained the snipers; presumably one of them had the controls for the electromagnetic pulse generator.

"Enforcer Tre," Klennethon Darrent acknowledged.

"Citizen Darrent," Tre replied.

"Do you know how Kip found this route?" Klennethon Darrent asked.

Tre wondered if it was a rhetorical question. He shook his head.

"Neither do I," Klennethon Darrent admitted. "It cannot be found using the standard charts." He sighed. "Unfortunately asking Kip is unlikely to yield an answer. He is still angry with me."

"He's an adolescent," Tre pointed out. "He blames you for him being separated from his parents."

Klennethon Darrent could not completely cover his exasperation.

"He knows it was not your fault," Tre added. "That does not stop him blaming you. Adolescents are like that, especially emotionally immature ones like Kip."

Klennethon Darrent expelled breath in what might have been a sigh. "You know him so well."

Tre laughed. "No I don't. Truly I don't. Anyone who claims to know Kip is either lying or mistaken. I doubt even his parents have an inkling about what goes on inside his mind."

Klennethon Darrent seemed to take some comfort in that. They sat, watching one system vanish and the next appear. If Tre had not been watching, he would have barely felt the jump, it was that smooth.

"News of this incident will spread," Klennethon Darrent pointed out once they were clear of the hole. "It will become known that Emanuel Rafael Jax Esteban is a member of the Willow's crew. People will deduce that the members of the Willow's crew may be dear to him. The strategy that has served you so well will no longer be effective."

Tre knew that. "Kip has suggestions," he admitted.

"May I ask?" Klennethon Darrent requested.

Tre had already decided that the potential benefits of trusting Klennethon Darrent far outweighed the risks. "Tarrasade," he replied.

Hints of surprise, consternation and then amusement showed in Klennethon Darrent's face. "Excellent," he acknowledged.

"And a spacehopper ship," Tre added.

This time Klennethon Darrent gave more than a ghost of a smile.

The following morning Tre took the next jump, that into the Ellettian system, in the Apus; ready to be spat out at high velocity on the perfect trajectory.

"This is Tre, checking communications."

"This is Kip. Communications are functional. The pilot is counting down to jump. Do you want connecting to the intercom?"

"This is Tre. No need."

They jumped, the docking bay opened and the Renaissance angled away while the Apus continued on its original path. As soon as he was clear of the larger ship, Tre fired the rockets.

The acceleration was harsh, even for him. He watched the gee meter, keeping the force he was experiencing well within his tolerance. Now that Loy had betrayed them there was no one to mend him if he broke.

It was a relief when he reached the planned maximum velocity and could cut the rockets.

There was the immediate hiss of a radio channel being opened.

"This is Kip with an update."

"This is Tre, proceed."

"Good and bad," Kip told him. *"The Stellar Rover hasn't arrived and her jump slot is still booked as before, so it looks like she is on schedule. The Orca is here, docked, but she is empty, sealed and shut down to conserve resources. I cannot find out where the crew is."*

"In a unit in the spacestation," Tre pointed out. Crews got fed up of the insides of their ships; it was an inescapable hazard of spacing. Unfortunately for Kip, crews often hired units anonymously. It was safer that way.

"Surely there isn't much to do in the Ellettian station," Kip commented.

The Ellettian station was full of tourists there to see the natural wonders. Many of them found spacers fascinating and lady tourists were a great deal cheaper than female whores. Not that Tre intended to explain that to Kip; Ean would not approve. "Sometimes any change in scenery is welcome," Tre replied. "I am going to get some sleep now, before deceleration. You get that message to Ean as soon as the Stellar Rover pokes her nose through the gate."

"*I've already sent it,*" Kip assured him. "*They have a mailbox.*"

Tre was not surprised; the company owning the liner would have arrangements for collecting messages for passengers.

"*I've marked it ultra-urgent,*" Kip added.

"It will be fine," Tre assured him.

If it went as planned Ean would get their message and stay on the ship. In the part Tre had recorded he had recommended that Ean go directly to the captain and ask for sanctuary.

Once Ean was safe, Tre would be free to deal with Loy.

12

Ean didn't know what to think. His mind first went one way and then another, dragging his emotions with it. What did it mean if Loy had booked a suite on the Stellar Rover three divs ago? Had Loy known that the Willow would be destroyed? Accidents weren't predictable. If Loy had known then it was at least sabotage. Even the thought of it made him want to bury his knife in Loy's guts.

Or had Loy intended to leave the Willow at Verdant, like Ben and Art had left at Mercy Station? There had been no sign of it but if what Mary had said was correct, if Loy wanted him, leaving would have been an honourable way out of the situation.

Or was it something trivial, like paying a bribe so the booking was backdated and Loy had to pay less?

Was Loy a villain trying to cover his tracks or a concerned, overprotective friend?

Thinking about it was driving Ean crazy. In the end he decided that he had to find out what Loy had to say on the matter.

He waited until they were eating in the dining room. Loy always wanted them to sit as a pair at the periphery while Ean preferred the larger, more sociable tables. That evening Ean wore the pink outfit Loy liked so much and agreed to sit with Loy in an isolated corner.

He waited until dessert to raise the matter of the booking.

"The ladies in my art class say it was amazing you got us aboard with such little notice," he began.

Loy looked a little wary, but that could be because Ean had mentioned the art class ladies. "Your welfare was paramount," he replied.

"Did you organise a swap or something?" Ean pressed, keeping his tone light. "Or use an old contact?"

"I didn't have to," Loy replied. "They had a few suites left."

Ean pretended to be eating his pie. Loy had made no mention of the suite being booked by Prospicient Prosthetics or knowing someone in the company who owned the liner or even having to go out of his way not to pay out for one of the suites available at short notice.

"But we are on the gold star package," Ean pointed out.

Loy froze for a moment before replying. "Ways and means, Ean. Ways and means."

His answer was consistent with the bribe theory but Ean's uneasiness had not been allayed. He decided to try something else.

"Psychologist Mary thinks I should talk about Tre," he stated. Saying Tre's name was harder than Ean had expected. It was all he could do to stop his voice cracking.

"Does she?" Loy queried. "I am not sure you are ready for that."

"I could listen," Ean suggested. "You knew him long before I met him. What was he like?" He glanced up from his bowl. Loy had paled. Ean waited, half expecting Loy to refuse.

Instead Loy seized the opportunity. "To Tre duty was everything." His voice was harsh; stripped of its usual honeyed richness. "When I first knew him he was sworn to Jax's father and he always followed orders. It did not matter what those orders were."

Ean discovered that he hated the edge to Loy's voice; the way he was implying Tre would do anything. Even so, he swallowed his objection. If he wanted Loy to talk, he would have to listen.

"The past thirteen standards were dominated by his oath to protect Jax," Loy continued. "The Willow, you, it was all about giving Jax somewhere to spend a couple of standards. In the original plan that would have been all; the two standards between Jax's fourteenth and sixteenth birth anniversaries. Then Jax would have gone back to his clan with Tre as his bodyguard, leaving the Willow to go on her way."

Ean remembered Loy's words in the dream. "You think he was incapable of love."

Loy's eyes hardened. "Yes. He used you, Ean. He needed a superb queen for the crew he brought Jax into. You were a perfect choice but you needed affection." He reached out and covered Ean's hand with his own. "Giving it to you made you a better queen. It made the crew better for Jax."

Ean had to stop himself yanking his hand away. Instead he slid it slowly out from under Loy's to reposition his spoon in his bowl. There was some truth in what Loy was saying but not enough. If Tre had only cared about keeping Ean happy, he would have offered Ean a love ring. Tre hadn't because his oath to protect Jax had to come first; Ean understood that. "He cared for me," Ean insisted.

"He was incapable of caring," Loy insisted. "It was pretence, Ean. A show."

"I thought you were his friend," Ean accused.

Loy's eyes went distant. "Maybe I was long ago, before…" He trailed off. "…before he changed into what he was," he finished.

Ean wondered what Loy had been going to say. In the dream Loy had told him that Tre was a cyborg. If he could get Loy to say that again, now, it would suggest that the dream wasn't a dream but a memory. "I loved him," Ean insisted. He could see Loy's mounting irritation. Maybe one more push would be enough. "I think I shall always love him."

Anger flashed across Loy's face. He leaned forward and hissed, "He killed Ben."

The bottom fell out of Ean's world. Tre had killed Ben?

Loy was still talking. "Art worked out who Jax was. He was going to sell the information. That was why he decided to leave the ship. Tre found out. He killed both of them. I tried to get him to stop at Art. After all, Ben knew nothing. Tre wouldn't listen. Killing Ben as well was safer for Jax, so he did it without a qualm. Without the slightest hesitation. That's the Tre you loved."

Ben was dead? "It isn't true," Ean whispered.

"Have you heard from him?" Loy demanded. "Ben, your best friend; has he contacted you once over the last standard? Has he answered one of the messages you have left for him at the Stellar Exchange?"

"No," Ean admitted. He had decided that Ben and Art had joined a crew and shipped out for a long haul. He made himself think about what Loy had said. "Tre told us about Jax," he objected, trying to make sense of it. Maybe that did not matter. Ben and Art had left the crew; they had become outsiders.

"No he didn't," Loy replied. "He told you that Jax was from a prominent spacer clan. He didn't tell you who he was. Art had uncovered Jax's identity. That was why he had to be stopped. Ben was just collateral damage."

It made horrible, believable sense. Ean sat absolutely still: head down; each of his hands grasping the other to stop them trembling.

"I didn't want to tell you," Loy admitted in his gentlest, kindest voice. "Only you have to see what Tre was. You have to understand that he wasn't worthy of your love."

Ean no longer cared about anything Loy could say. Ben was dead too. "I want to go back to our suite," he whispered.

Loy walked beside him, ready to steady him should he stumble, but Ean managed to make it. He sat on the couch while Loy made tea. Like most of the tea Loy made, it was slightly bitter.

"Drink it, Ean," Loy encouraged.

Ean realised Loy must have put something in it; probably some sleepdrug or another sedative. Had that been true of all the other cups of slightly bitter tea?

He decided that it didn't matter. Loy was right. At the moment Ean would welcome oblivion.

Next morning he slept late and, when he woke, he felt terrible. He lay there for a moment. He could hear Loy in the other room and Ean knew that as soon as Loy realised he was awake he would be beside him, trying to look after him.

Ean did not want that. He rolled out of the bed and managed to make it into the shower before Loy could react. He locked the door just as Loy knocked on it.

"Are you all right, Ean?" he asked.

"I am fine," Ean lied, opening the faucet fully to make as much noise as possible.

He stood under the spray, pretending not to hear Loy until Loy gave up and moved away from the door. Ean thought back to the evening before. Was Ben really dead?

Could Loy be lying? He had lied about the booking. He had lied about the double bed. What else could he be lying about? Tre? Ben?

Ean braced himself against the wall and allowed the spray to pound against his back. Was he just clutching at straws?

Why was he so keen to paint Loy as the villain? Loy was all he had left.

In the end he had to face Loy. He wrapped himself in a robe and unlocked the door. Loy immediately appeared in the doorway to the sitting room.

"I am sorry, Ean," he admitted. "I shouldn't have told you about Ben."

Ean shook his head. "Better now than later. I don't want to talk about it."

Loy nodded. "I've ordered you some breakfast. I thought you would want a quiet day."

The last thing Ean wanted was a day trapped in the suite with Loy. "I'll go to my art class and to see Mary," he decided. "Routine is good for me." He could see Loy about to object. "You could come with me to the art class," he suggested.

Loy only considered it for a few moments. "No, I am sure your old ladies will look after you."

Moulding the clay and listening to the ladies gossip was soothing. Ean was less sure about his session with Mary. Maybe he should cancel it and do something else instead.

He decided to keep the appointment. Mary never pushed. It would be fine.

To his surprise he found himself telling Mary what Loy had said about Ben. Mary was silent for a moment. Ean guessed she was shocked. In Mary's world people probably didn't go around killing each other.

"How long did you know Tre?" Mary asked finally.

Ean thought about it. "Eleven standards."

"Do you think Tre would have killed Ben?" she asked.

Ean thought about it. He could imagine Tre killing Art if Art was going to betray them but not Ben. "No," he replied. "Only Loy says that I didn't know Tre. That Tre was this cold, calculating, manipulative monster."

"Is that the Tre you knew?" Mary pressed.

"No. I'm so confused," Ean admitted. Mary did not answer. Ean studied her. "You want to say something but you are not sure you should," he observed.

She bit her lower lip. "Medico Loy may have an agenda," she reminded him.

Ean left his session with Mary more settled but with no better idea about what he did and did not believe. He did know he needed some time away from Loy, so he was glad that they were jumping into the Ellettian system the next day. Tomorrow he would leave on the Etoile for a two day tour of the moons of Ellettian. The excursion was obviously not the most exciting, even the art class ladies had recommended avoiding it, but Ean would be able to have some time alone.

Next morning he woke to a persistent, escalating buzzing. For a moment he was puzzled. Then he remembered; he had promised Bev and Geraldine from the art class that he would attend the jump breakfast that started at ship's dawn on the viewing deck. Apparently the Ellettian system was so spectacular that no one wanted to wait any longer than they had to before seeing it.

Loy was awake before Ean was out of the head.

"You are welcome to come," Ean reminded him.

Loy burrowed back under the covers. "No, I really don't have your patience, Ean. I don't know how you do it, answering the same questions about spacing again and again."

"When is your meeting in the station?" Ean checked.

"Midmorning," Loy answered. "I've booked a shuttle for ninety minutes past dawn. That will give me more than enough time. When does your excursion to the Ellettian moons leave?"

"Midmorning," Ean replied. He gestured towards his backpack, which was packed ready. "We'll be back just before midnight the day after tomorrow."

Loy shuddered. "Rather you than me. I'll see you before I go," he added.

The Stellar Rover had begun decelerating a day ago; they needed to be moving slowly enough to match velocities with the spacestation.

That meant they approached the jump gate relatively slowly, which gave ample time for many questions. Ean wished he had his teaching aids with him; giving a lesson would be a great deal easier than coming up with answers to individual questions.

They jumped at precisely thirty minutes after ship's dawn. The Ellettian system was, as advertised, spectacularly beautiful. The images in the brochure had not done it justice.

After breakfast Bev and Geraldine went out of their way to introduce him to a couple who would be going on the excursion. It was not encouraging. The lady repeatedly referred to him as a 'nice young man' and her partner, an elderly male, kept leering at him.

"You don't have to go," Bev whispered as they moved away. "You can spend the time with us instead. We're going to have painting parties here on the viewing deck."

Ean glanced back over his shoulder; the man was watching his butt. When he realised that Ean had caught him he just leered again and winked. Ean looked away quickly. Staying aboard the Stellar Rover was suddenly tempting. Was he really that desperate for some time away from Loy?

No, changing plans at the last minute was almost never a good idea.

They were all squeezed into the small room with the communications desk; no one wanted to miss the message from Ean when it arrived. Kip sat on the floor in a corner wearing his earpieces and goggles. He had the goggles set on translucent, so he could see the others through the display. They were staring at the chronometer on the wall; Kip was watching the one in the lower right corner of his field of view.

The Stellar Rover had jumped in through the gate exactly on schedule. Surely they had checked their mailbox?

Three things should happen as soon as the Stellar Rover connected to the mailbox. Their message to Ean should be recognised as urgent and relayed immediately. The secret, coded receipt Kip had built into the message should be transmitted. Thirdly, worms would burrow their way into the Stellar Rover's control and communications system. By now she should be thoroughly hacked.

Kip had mentioned the receipt to the others but not the hacking; Captain Mel would not approve of him hacking another ship except in the most desperate of circumstances.

Despite the Renaissance having covered one-third of the distance to the station, they were still eight light minutes away. Eight minutes had elapsed since the jump: nine; ten; eleven; twelve.

A ping in his earpiece; it was the receipt.

Kip opened the channel to Tre as well as speaking to the others. Tre was only forty minutes away from the station; soon he would have to make the decision of whether he was docking at the station or with the Stellar Rover.

"This is Kip. Our message has been delivered to the Stellar Rover."

"Only four minutes after jump; that's great," Jax pointed out. "No one will leave the ship in the first four minutes."

"We don't know how long it will take them to deliver the message to Ean," Vic warned.

Kip had checked the company's handbook. Messages received for passengers were logged. He changed his goggles to opaque and began searching through the information flowing in from

Stellar Rover across the covert link he had established.

Five minutes later, seventeen after jump, Kip had confirmation that the message had already been transcribed to a tape, delivered to Ean's cabin and signed for.

Relief coursed through his body; Ean had received the message before the first shuttle had left the liner.

Not that he could tell the others that, because that would mean admitting that he had been hacking.

Minutes went by: five; ten; fifteen; twenty. Shuttles had begun docking with and leaving the Stellar Rover. Kip heard the others begin shifting about. Why hadn't there been a reply from Ean?

Maybe he had fainted from the shock of seeing them alive and had hit his head.

A soft ping in his earpiece; Tre on their private channel, the one not linked to the speakers on the desk.

"This is Tre. Kip, what is happening? I need to know if I should go to the station or the ship."

Tre was eight light minutes away; they couldn't have a discussion. Kip would have to send Tre as much information as he could. He started inputting text.

Hacked in. Tape was delivered and signed for by Ean at 47 minutes past ship's dawn [0407:00]. Don't understand why he hasn't replied.

Could he get confirmation that Ean was still on the ship? Kip began searching the information for Loy's and Ean's names and relaying any relevant information to Tre.

Loy has a shuttle booked for the station for 90 minutes past ship's dawn [0450:00]. Ean is due to leave on an excursion on a ship called the Etoile midmorning [0540:00].

Kip checked the chronometer. It was 0442:00; too late to stop the shuttle, but they had time to prevent Ean leaving on the Etoile. Did he admit to the captain what he had been doing? He switched his goggles back to translucent and took a deep breath; better the captain be cross with him than they miss out on making contact with Ean.

The captain spoke to him before he had a chance to open his mouth. "We have waited long enough. Kip, open me a channel direct to the Stellar Rover. Captain to captain priority message."

Kip opened a channel and slipped a few extras into the header of the transmission so it would be promoted to the top of any queue.

"This is Captain Mel of the Willow," the captain began. "Currently travelling on the Renaissance. We sent an urgent message requesting immediate contact with our crewmate, Spacer Ean, who is travelling on the Stellar Rover as a passenger. Please confirm that Spacer Ean has received the message. It is crucial that Spacer Ean should not leave the Stellar Rover. I repeat. It is crucial that Spacer Ean should not leave the Stellar Rover. I await your immediate reply."

Kip relaxed a little. Ean was not due to leave the Stellar Rover for another forty minutes. There was ample time to intercept him.

Another soft ping in his earpiece. "*This is Tre. Based on what you know, I am heading for the station. If Ean is on the Stellar Rover or the Etoile he is safe.*"

Tre was right, their whole plan was based on getting Ean to stay on the Stellar Rover but Kip could not see that there was a problem if he was on the Etoile. What mattered was that he wasn't anywhere near Nevin Edger. That he was separated from Loy was an additional bonus.

Kip guessed that Tre was going after Loy.

❋ ❋ ❋

Ean jogged back to their suite, aware that he had agreed to say farewell to Loy before he left for the station.

Loy was ready to go but he looked flustered. "Change in plan," he admitted. "My ex-colleague has been called away. However he has left a package for me at the Stellar Exchange. Why don't you come with me to pick it up?"

The thought of walking a station appealed. "After I'm back from the excursion," Ean agreed.

"No, now," Loy proposed. "It's too late for me to cancel the shuttle without paying for it. Come with me to the station rather than being trapped with strangers on a tourist barge."

Ean hesitated, remembering the unappealing couple and Bev's invitation to the painting parties.

"Ean, think about it," Loy cajoled. "Even your art class ladies have had the sense not to go. You yourself told me that there are still empty berths on it. One more won't matter."

Ean imagined being trapped on a small ship for two days with the leering, winking man.

"Come on, Ean," Loy encouraged. "Grab the pack you've packed. Who knows, we might find some adventure and stay out a couple of days. Or maybe it'll be boring and we'll be back for dinner."

Doing something spontaneous was unexpectedly tempting. "Very well," he agreed. He began walking towards the intercom. "I'll tell them I'm not going on the excursion, otherwise they might wait for me."

"They won't," Loy assured him. "You know what it says in the brochure; all excursions leave the ship on time. They probably don't even finalise the manifest until they see who turns up."

"Even so, it's polite," Ean insisted, only to be distracted by the door announcer.

Ean opened the door to reveal one of the stewards.

"Spacer Ean," the steward greeted him. "I apologise for disturbing you."

Ean checked the name on the hat. "Steward Jerome, how can I help you?"

"Have you seen Assistant Steward Lyn?" Steward Jerome asked. "We are asking all the guests in this section."

"He's missing?" Ean queried.

Steward Jerome offered an insincere smile. "I am sure he will turn up. Thank you for your time." Then he stepped back and the door slid shut.

"What was that?" Loy asked, tossing him his pack.

Ean caught it. "Assistant Steward Lyn is missing."

Loy shrugged. "Maybe he's decided that stewarding is not for him and he's stowed away on a shuttle."

That did not seem very likely; Assistant Steward Lyn had always appeared very attentive to his duties.

"Ean, he's probably been reassigned and there's been a communication failure," Loy pointed out. "Come on. Every minute the shuttle waits costs."

"But I haven't told them I won't be on the Etoile," Ean objected.

"I did it while you answered the door." Loy had his pack on and was out the door. "Come on, Ean."

They ran and made it on time, which was good because there were so many shuttles coming and going that any delay would have caused a problem.

"Two?" the shuttle pilot queried.

"I paid for a shuttle," Loy pointed out. "It seats up to six."

Ean looked over his shoulder at the queue of people waiting.

"No, Ean," Loy insisted. "If they wanted to avoid the queue they should have planned ahead."

Ean decided Loy had a point and, anyway, he was paying.

He followed Loy aboard and heard the airlock door close behind him.

Ean secured his pack, picked a seat in the second row of three and strapped in. Loy was doing the same. Ean watched him lift his pack into one of the overhead lockers. It looked heavy; Ean guessed Loy had packed it at the last minute rather than thinking through its contents.

To his surprise Loy took a seat in the front row rather than beside him. Studying Loy's profile, Ean thought he looked sweaty and pale.

They had not run that far or fast; Ean wondered what was bothering him.

"This is your pilot. Please be aware that we will be exiting the Stellar Rover's gravitational field and then entering that of the spacestation. Fluctuations in gravitational field intensity are normal under these circumstances. Please stay strapped into your seat."

They began moving away from the ship.

There was a display screen built into the back of the seat in from of him. Ean began investigating what the station had to offer. Not much, it appeared. He wondered what the 'genuine spacer club' would be like. Not that genuine, he suspected. It was probably packed with spacers hoping to persuade a female tourist to give them a freebie.

"What's the schedule?" he asked.

Loy jumped and looked over his shoulder as if not expecting to see Ean sitting there.

"You all right?" Ean asked.

"I'm fine," Loy assured him.

"Plans for when we reach the station?" Ean hinted.

"I thought we would get my business out of the way first, so that's a quick trip to the Stellar Exchange to pick up the tape my ex-colleague left and then a detour to the medical centre."

"Medical centre?" Ean queried.

"It won't take long. Just a few minutes. I want to check something and it's the quickest way." Loy forced a smile. "After that business will be over and we can have fun."

Ean resisted the urge to ask more; spacers should not pry and Loy was much more likely to share if he was not nagged. "Fine," he agreed.

The trip was short. They disembarked at the shuttle bay. It was weird to arrive at a spacestation and not be in the spacer quarter. The corridors were full of tourists and residents.

Ean scanned the walls. Sure enough there were signs for the Stellar Exchange.

"This way," he announced and set off.

Loy quickly caught up. "Maybe we should go to the medical centre first," he suggested.

Ean scowled at him. "There might be something relevant on the tape. Then we'll end up going to the medical centre twice."

Loy relaxed a little. "True. Stellar Exchange first, medical centre second."

Seeing the signs for the Stellar Exchange had reminded Ean of his promise to Kip's parents. Once they were back on the ship he would go through his memory dodecahedrons and transfer the images of Kip to a tape. Then he would either take the tape to the Stellar Exchange himself or send it by courier.

Thinking about it, it would be more sensible to wait until they reached Mercy Station. A tape dispatched from there would reach Darrenden much more quickly.

They were entering an intersection that had been enlarged to make a plaza. It was nicely set out with benches and plants as well as small carts selling snacks or knickknacks.

Ean paused at an information screen. Apparently there were concerts there in the evening. Loy was more interested in checking a map on the wall.

"There," Loy stated, pointing across the corner of the plaza towards another corridor bearing another sign for the Stellar Exchange.

They crossed the plaza and entered the corridor. The Stellar Exchange was a little way along to their right. Opposite there was a nice looking bar. Ean wondered if he could persuade Loy that they could stop at it once he had picked up his tape.

As they approached the doors to the Stellar Exchange a spacer crew came out of the bar. Ean was surprised; crews were rarely out his early, especially not a clan crew like this one. He tried to make out their insignia without appearing to stare. Chielo? Edger?

The touch of a hand on his arm; Loy had stopped. Ean turned towards him to ask what was wrong. Loy was staring at the clan crew. His face had drained of all colour. Ean had never seen a grown man so frightened. He turned desperate eyes to Ean.

"Run, Ean. Now. For your life. Get back to the Stellar Rover."

Ean looked back at the crew. He had never run from anyone in his life and he didn't intend to start now. There were eight, maybe nine, of them and, except for two, they all looked like enforcers.

The one in the middle, a dark, grim-looking man, was looking directly at them.

A movement to Ean's right. Loy had gone; hightailing it back along the corridor towards the plaza.

The grim-looking one was giving orders.

In all the training Tre had given him, they had never covered what to do when your crewmate ran out on you. Ean made himself think. Either he stood his ground, hoping to talk his way out of the situation, or he followed Loy's example. Fighting was not a realistic option. It didn't look like there would be any formalities and, as good a knife fighter as he was, there were nine of them and one of him.

He turned and sprinted after Loy.

There were shouts behind him; they were chasing him. What should he do? Not follow Loy; he had a better chance of escaping with only half the pursuers and there was always the chance they were only interested in Loy.

Loy had chosen the familiar path, heading for the corridor they had walked through. Ean ran across the plaza instead: weaving his way between the benches, plants and carts; relying on the people to move out of his way. He was fast, he knew that. He could outrun them. Once he was two corners ahead of them he would duck into a shop. A clothes shop might be best. A clothes shop would have changing rooms; maybe a store room.

He wished he had decided that before heading diagonally across the plaza.

The people in front of him were moving out of his path but their eyes weren't on him, they were on the people chasing him.

He was two-thirds across the plaza, focused on the mouth of a corridor and the shops beyond, when he spotted a movement front and left; someone heading towards him rather than away. How had they got someone into position to outflank him?

They must have had people already in the plaza. Veering right, he headed for the next corridor around. He couldn't see what was along it. He would just have to hope there were some shops or maybe an eatery.

He had no idea why a Chielo or Edger crew were after him but they were. Loy had told him to run for his life. Had he meant it literally? Were they going to kill him?

It wasn't fair. He hadn't done anything to deserve this, just like he hadn't done anything to deserve losing everyone he cared about.

Those behind him and to his right weren't closing on him; he was sure he could make it to the corridor. Then he caught another movement towards him from his left, out on the edge of his field of view.

This one was moving really, really quickly. There was no way Ean could outrun him. Ean managed one last, desperate burst of speed.

It was hopeless. The man was closing ridiculously fast. Ean expected to be tackled at any moment.

Instead an arm went around his waist: controlling the impact; gently plucking him off the ground; a familiar arm pulling him towards an impossibly familiar chest. Ean looked up.

It was Tre. It was Tre. It was Tre.

Ean had his legs around Tre's waist and his arms about his neck even before Tre had managed to slow to a stop. Ean breathed in the familiar scent and clung.

A hand rubbed his back. It felt so, so good. "I have you," Tre assured him. "You are safe now."

"You're alive," Ean accused. "You're alive," he repeated, struggling to believe it was true.

Tre pulled him close and kissed him on the lips: ardently; passionately. Ean kissed back, hugging even tighter.

A harsh voice interrupted them. "Put him down, spacer, he's ours."

Ean reluctantly broke the kiss and looked over his shoulder. Four of the Chielo, no, Edger crew were fanned out in front of them. Ean unwound his legs from Tre's waist and released his grip around Tre's neck, sliding down and around his body to stand beside him; if Tre had to take them out, Ean didn't want to get in the way.

"No," Tre replied in his most menacing voice. "He is mine and you shall not have him."

They all looked suitably wary, which showed they weren't stupid. Then the oldest paled. "Colonel Reyes?" he stammered.

Who was Colonel Reyes? The man had been looking directly at Tre when he said it. Ean searched Tre's face, trying to judge his response.

Tre was looking at the man coldly. "No one has called me that in a very long time. Is Nevin Edger with you?"

So Tre had been this Colonel Reyes but who was Nevin Edger, other than an Edger?

Ean knew he could not afford to be distracted by such questions. These were just people who had known Tre from long ago, like Loy. What mattered now was the two of them surviving the encounter, preferably without covering the pretty, touristy plaza with blood.

Ean looked back at the man who had recognised Tre. He was deciding whether to answer Tre's question about Nevin Edger.

"Yes," he replied.

"Then you had better take me to him," Tre suggested. "Otherwise I might have to rip the entrails out of each of you for what you did to the Willow."

"Shall I shoot him?" one of the younger ones asked, drawing a laser pistol from a holster inside his jacket.

Ean scowled at him. For a spacer he certainly lacked manners or even the most basic appreciation of the code.

Before the older man could answer, the rest of the Edger crew approached from the far side of the plaza. One of them was the man who had been giving the orders outside the Stellar Exchange; Ean assumed he was Nevin Edger. Two others were dragging Loy, who looked like someone who had fallen heavily more than once.

"Put it away, Flint," Nevin Edger ordered.

The young man, Flint, slid the laser pistol back into its holster.

"It probably would not kill him anyway," Nevin Edger added. "Alejandro Reyes," he acknowledged. "I am certain I recall receiving notification of your memorial service fifteen standards ago." He glanced at Loy. "It would have been useful to know that you were the boy's protector."

"Nevin Edger," Tre acknowledged with the slightest bow. "You were not misinformed. Alejandro Reyes died fifteen standards ago. I am Enforcer Tre, of the Willow. However, this once, I shall speak as Alejandro Reyes. The man responsible for your nephew's death and your sister's grief is dead. The boy is not responsible. You made a play for him and it failed. Leave it at that and hope that your indiscretion is not brought to your brother's notice."

"Jose Eduardo Gil Hierra is looking for the boy," Nevin Edger pointed out.

Alejandro, Jose Eduardo, Reyes, Hierra; those were Navaja names. Ean suddenly realised who Jax had been or rather, from the way Nevin Edger was talking, who he was.

Jax was alive? Was he safe? Had any of the others made it?

Ean stared in disgust at Loy. He had told Ean again and again that they were all dead; that he had seen their bodies.

Tre was answering. "That is a clan matter, between a boy and his uncle."

Nevin Edger hesitated for a moment and then nodded. "What about him?" he asked, gesturing towards Loy.

"You can keep him," Tre answered. "Feel free to use him to vent your frustration."

Ean had spoken before he could stop himself. "I want to know why he did it."

Nevin Edger almost sneered but stopped himself when Tre gave the smallest of warning growls. "This is Ean," Tre stated. "He is queen of the Willow and someone who is dear to me."

Warmth pooled in Ean's gut at the acknowledgement.

Nevin Edger gave Ean a slight nod and then signalled the men holding Loy. One of them buried a fist in Loy's gut, doubling him up and knocking the breath out of him.

"Your face will be next," Nevin Edger warned. "Answer Spacer Ean's question."

They waited until Loy had finished gasping and could speak.

First Loy looked at Ean with those gorgeous, bedroom eyes. "I did it for you, Ean. To get you away from him." He glared at Tre. "I hate him. He pretends to be human and he isn't. He can't be. None of them are. They are just shells with machines inside; automated killers disguised as humans."

Ean shivered at the thought of it. Then he pulled himself together. Tre, his Tre, was nothing like that.

Nevin Edger snorted. "If they are, it was you who did it to them, Me-di-co Loy."

Loy flinched at the disgusted disbelief Nevin Edger had put into his title.

"What do medicos promise?" Nevin Edger sneered. "To do no harm? How many men died on your operating table? How many survived only to be reduced to those crazed killers you describe? Is that why you can't live with him?" He pointed towards Tre. "Because if Alejandro Reyes is still Alejandro Reyes after being under your knife then maybe the others were still there, trapped inside those pathetic relics of humanity."

Loy stared at Nevin Edger: silenced; eyes wide in a chalk white face.

"That's enough, Nevin," Tre ordered. "Whatever he did before or has done since, I owe my life many times over to his skill."

Nevin Edger turned to Ean. "Spacer Ean, he did it for credit. Like he turned good men into insane killing machines for credit. Because he is a vain, shallow man who cannot bear the thought of getting old and wants to be surrounded by the trappings of the rich and powerful." He looked at Tre. "It was easy. There was a rumour that at least one of the men protecting the boy was a cyborg. So I sought out Loy. He has been in contact with me whenever he could since you recruited him. I confess I did not know it was you. I thought you were dead."

Tre nodded but his eyes were not on Nevin Edger, they were on the far side of the plaza where some security guards were deciding whether they really wanted to interfere with a spacer crew and its business. His hand moved to Ean's back.

"Time we were going," he announced.

Nevin Edger nodded. He gestured that the two men guarding Loy should bring him. They reached for him but Loy lunged forward, towards Ean.

Tre moved so fast that all Ean saw was a blur. Loy was hanging by his neck from Tre's hand. His face was turning purple. His legs began to kick.

Ean touched Tre's arm; Tre had said he did not want to kill him.

Loy was dropped to sprawl gasping on the floor. Tre was already turning away and Ean followed.

"Ean!" Loy called, forcing the word from his damaged throat.

Before he could stop himself, Ean had looked back.

"He will abandon you," Loy croaked. "You deserve more. Better."

Ean stared directly into Loy's eyes. "By no measure are you more or better."

Loy could not hold his gaze; he looked away.

"Well said, Spacer Ean," Nevin Edger acknowledged. "Colonel Reyes," he added.

Tre turned back. "Enforcer Tre," he corrected. "Alejandro Reyes is long gone. Please give my regards to your sister and your brother."

They left, dragging Loy with them.

Ean did not bother to watch them go. He had more important things to think about, like the rest of his crew; his family. He caught up with Tre, who had already started walking.

"Are any of them alive?" he asked, unable to keep the tremor from his voice.

Tre looked towards him. Every trace of Alejandro Reyes, every hint of a killing machine, had gone. All Ean saw was the Tre he had known for the last eleven standards. "Everyone's fine," he replied. "We sent you a vid. Didn't you get it?"

13

Inside, carefully hidden, Tre was still reeling from the shock of seeing Ean running from those men; the urge to rip their heads from their shoulders had been overwhelming.

Holding Ean, kissing him, had helped. Ean's Tre was incompatible with the killing machine. He had regained enough control to play the part of Alejandro Reyes; to remind Nevin Edger of his honour and his duty.

He knew he would regret letting them take Loy but it was the easiest of the options available. Nevin Edger would walk away. Tre could concentrate on Ean and Jax. He would not have to fight his desire to destroy Loy piece by piece.

Despite what he had done, Tre still owed Loy the life to which he had clung twenty standards ago.

"Are any of them alive?" Ean asked, his voice shaking.

Tre realised that Ean did not know that the others were safe. His eyes went in the direction of Loy's departure. His fingers itched to rip and shred at the thought of what he had put Ean through.

Instead he smiled. "Everyone's fine. We sent you a vid. Didn't you get it?"

Ean hit him on the chest: as Tre had hoped he would; as he always did whenever Tre made light of things.

"No, I did not. No one is hurt?" Ean checked again.

"I imagine they are more than a bit tense at the moment," Tre admitted. He gestured towards his earpiece. "Kip was hoping that this short range radio would link with the ship I used to get here but the secure berth it is in is too well shielded."

"You are out of contact?" Ean queried.

Tre nodded.

"Are they close?"

"No, over a day away."

Next thing Tre knew he was being dragged across the plaza.

"Where are we going?" he asked.

"The Stellar Exchange," Ean told him. "We can hire a booth to record and send a message. Then we can wait for a reply."

Tre followed obediently, revelling in being with his Ean, the one he would never have entirely to himself because Ean was always thinking about his crew; his family.

It was what made him Ean.

"Nice pants," he observed; being led gave him an excellent view of Ean's butt.

"Don't you start," Ean complained. "Loy had clothes made for me and they all fit like this." He glanced back. "That jacket is new and those boots must have cost."

"The leader of the pirates was exactly my size," Tre told him. "He has no more need of them."

"Pirates?" Ean queried.

"I'll fill you in later," Tre promised. "The Willow is gone, Ean. We're salvaging what we can but she's gone."

Ean sped up. "Each person is worth far more than the ship," he replied.

They recorded a vid, or rather Ean spoke while Tre sat there and pressed the buttons. Once it was sent Tre pulled Ean onto his lap.

Ean normally would have slapped his hands away and scolded him for trying to make out in a public place. This time the relative privacy of the booth and the latched door was enough.

Tre realised that Ean's enthusiasm was probably a reaction to being chased but he had every intention of taking full advantage. He managed make it as far as unbuttoning Ean's fly before Ean began objecting.

"We'll make a mess," Ean complained.

"No we won't." Tre assured him, lifting Ean from his lap to the counter. He smiled. "I'll be careful."

Ean had just finished returning the favour when the incoming message light started flashing. Tre accepted the message and the display screen activated.

They were all crowded on and around the desk in the small room off the dining room of the main apartment. Tre barely noticed the vid. He was too busy watching Ean, whose eyes were darting from face to face, drinking in the images as if they were water and he was dying of thirst.

"Kip is far too thin and pale," he complained. "And the captain looks stressed. Cas looks better than I expected," he added.

"I think he's turned to Obe," Tre admitted.

"Then we better get Obe promoted before that becomes a problem," Ean replied. "What about Obe's knife fighting skills?"

"Adequate," Tre acknowledged. "They aren't going to improve significantly in the short term. What next?" he asked.

Ean considered. "I think I should go back to the Stellar Rover and sort things out with them."

Tre's lips managed to find their way to Ean's neck. "Is that urgent? We could check into a unit or hotel room here."

"I want to sort it," Ean insisted.

Being Ean they had to do everything properly. They contacted the Stellar Rover to discuss a day pass for Tre. Tre listened to Ean reminding the petty, stuck-up, self-important nonentity on the other end of the link that the 'gold star package', whatever that was, included two day passes for family members.

What followed was a lengthy discussion about what constituted family. Ean wore the man down, as Tre had known he would, but it took so long that Tre was ready to pay the extortionate price they wanted to charge.

Then they had to sit in a queue for a shuttle with a load of tourists, each of whom knew Ean's name and wanted to be introduced.

Matters did not improve when they reached the ship. Someone had assaulted one of the staff, shooting him full of sedative and forgetting juice before hiding him in a storeroom.

It did not take much insight to work out that it had been Loy intercepting their message to Ean. Unfortunately Ean had to share that deduction with the officer in charge of the investigation. That led to more lengthy explanations, a visit to the ship's medical centre and offering the young man compensation.

Luckily it was only a gentle sedative and a light dose of forgetting juice. Also Assistant Steward Lyn clearly adored Ean and said he was willing to forgo the compensation.

Ean, being Ean, insisted on paying.

Then, finally, they started on what they had been intending to do when they arrived. Packing up Ean and Loy's stuff only took a few minutes; Loy must have had most of his things with him.

There were another five versions of the outfit Ean was wearing in a variety of colours that suited Ean but he usually refused to wear. Tre insisted they took all of them, using the 'waste not, want not' argument of which Ean himself was so fond.

By the time they finished the ship was serving dinner and, somehow, Ean managed to persuade him they should attend.

As Ean had told him, the food was excellent. However a tasty supper did not compensate for having to be polite to an endless stream of people, each of whom was determined to speak to Ean before he left.

At least they were almost all women. Tre tried to pay attention. He managed to get Bev, Geraldine and Su's names the right way around because Ean obviously cared for them and they for him. The well-dressed and kindly looking woman seated on Ean's left was introduced as Psychologist Mary Bernard.

"Mary had been my bereavement counsellor," Ean explained. "She had been exceptionally professional and caring."

Tre did not miss the warmth in Ean voice; this woman had helped him. "Psychologist Bernard," he acknowledged with a small bow.

"Enforcer Tre," she replied. "It is as wonderful to see you as it is unexpected. We all wish Ean a happy reunion with the rest of his family as well as a safe and prosperous future."

Tre did not say anything as they walked back to the suite to pick up the bags and, finally, leave. Hopefully Ean would talk about what had happened between him and the psychologist.

"I had no memories of what happened to the Willow," Ean began. He sighed. "Given what he did to Assistant Steward Lyn I guess Loy gave me forgetting juice." He glanced across at Tre. "Loy told me a lot of lies, both about what had happened and about you."

Tre wondered what Loy had said.

"I had daily sessions with Mary," Ean admitted, his voice shaking slightly. "She made me see that I should value my opinion of you over Loy's."

Tre managed not to flinch. There was still much about him that Ean did not know including many things he hoped Ean would never find out.

"She was right," Ean continued. "It doesn't matter what happened before. It doesn't matter if you were once Colonel Alejandro Reyes. It doesn't matter if you had stuff done to you to make you a better fighter. You are Tre. I know Tre."

Tre wondered if Ean had the slightest idea what being transformed into a cyborg entailed or meant. He assumed not. Ean was looking at him again, expecting some manner of response.

Tre concentrated on how lucky he was, caught hold of Ean's hand and pulled him close for a kiss.

They managed to catch the last scheduled shuttle between the liner and the station, which was close to empty. They sat side-by-side at the back.

Ean stroked his arm. "I know you suggested we get a unit, but couldn't we just go to the ship you have berthed and head out? That way I could see the others sooner."

"Sorry, Ean, but it's a one man racing yacht," Tre explained.

Ean frowned, "Where in Known Space did you get hold of one of those?"

Tre realised that Ean had done almost all the talking since they had met, which was not unusual but did mean Ean had no idea about what they had done to reach the Ellettian system. Checking that no one was listening, he filled Ean in on the basics.

"Klennethon Darrent dropped everything and came running because Kip was in danger and then gave you all a lift on his spacehopper ship just because Kip asked," Ean summarised.

"That's about it," Tre admitted.

Ean just looked at him.

Tre thought about explaining about typed-sevens and typed-fives but decided against it. Instead he shrugged.

Ean's eyes narrowed and he scowled. "Is he going to try to take Kip away from us?"

"No," Tre replied but he could see that Ean was not convinced. "I have spoken to him about it. He thinks Kip is best off with us, specifically you."

Ean flushed. "Good," he acknowledged. The scowl faded into anxiety. "How are we going to look after them, Tre? We haven't got a ship. And those men knew about Jax. Isn't that going to change everything?"

It was but Tre was not ready to discuss it yet. "We will need to talk about that as a crew." He decided to change the subject. "What was happening this morning? Why were you in the station rather than on your excursion to the Ellettian moons?"

"Loy persuaded me to come with him instead," Ean admitted. "First he said we were just picking up a tape from the Stellar Exchange but then he started talking about dropping in at the medical centre."

Given Loy's track record and the fact he had almost all his stuff with him, Tre could fill in the rest. Loy would have given Ean another dose of forgetting juice, probably a larger one this time, and stuffed him into a pod.

"Why me?" Ean asked.

Tre had been thinking about Loy's chances of escape with him, Nevin Edger and Klennethon Darrent after him; they were nigh on zero. "What do you mean?" he queried.

"Me. I understand about Loy wanting credit but why bother with me?" Ean hesitated before continuing. "Mary said he was besotted with me but why?"

One of the best things about Ean was that he had no idea how amazing he was. On the other hand, knowing Loy, there had probably been more than a bit of wanting Ean because he was someone else's. Not that Tre intended to mention that. "You underestimate yourself."

Ean looked unconvinced. "And did he really need credit so badly? Loy always acted as if he was rich."

In Tre's experience people who spent credit as if it was inexhaustible did not stay rich very long. The only exception he knew of was Klennethon Darrent.

Loy had earned a massive fee for each human he had converted into a cyborg but the last one, Tre himself, had been twenty standards ago. A man with expensive tastes, especially one who wanted to stay young, could get through a lot of credit in two decades.

"Tre?" Ean queried.

"The age retard treatments must have cost a lot, even for a medico," Tre pointed out.

"Age retard? How old is he?" Ean asked before realising he was breaking the code and flushing. "Forget I said that," he added.

Tre considered. Loy was at least fifteen standards older than him, probably more. "Pushing sixty," he replied.

Ean's eyes and mouth were momentarily circular before he recovered. "Don't tell Cas that. Never tell Cas that," he insisted.

"I won't," Tre promised.

It was late so they decided to try a hotel rather than trying to locate a unit. It turned out that tourists were inclined to change their minds and even the best hotels had the occasional empty room that they would much prefer occupied.

They had checked in, picked up their key and were walking along the corridor towards their room. Tre was imagining sharing a bath and then a bed with Ean. Maybe he could even persuade Ean to stay in bed the next morning; the Renaissance would not dock until the afternoon.

He opened the door to the room and stepped aside so Ean could enter first. It was perfect; decorated exactly to Ean's taste.

Only Ean said nothing and Tre belatedly realised that he had been too quiet for some time; probably since they had left the shuttle. He scolded himself for not noticing; for being too distracted by thoughts of what they could do in a big bath and a comfy bed.

"Ean?" he queried.

Ean took off his backpack and put it on the side but said nothing.

"You've been through a lot," Tre pointed out. "Sit down. I'll make you some tea or get room service to bring some."

"I don't want tea," Ean replied. "Tre, I know Loy told me many lies but there is one I have to check with you."

Tre steeled himself. What had Loy told him?

"Did you kill Ben?"

❋ ❋ ❋

Ean had not thought about Ben until he saw Mary. Even then it had only been a fleeting thought. Only it kept coming back, throughout the evening, and each time it was louder and more insistent.

Then, once they had selected the hotel and were heading there, Ean realised that the sooner he and Tre talked about it the better. If he left it, the doubt would fester and grow.

So, as soon as they were over the threshold of their room, before Tre could start pampering him, he asked.

"Did you kill Ben?"

To his horror Tre didn't answer immediately. He didn't look insulted and tell Ean he was an idiot for believing such a thing. Instead his expression closed down, as Ean had seen it do a thousand times before.

By the Lady, what was he going to do? Could he stay with someone who had killed his best friend?

"Tre, answer me!" he demanded.

"Ben is alive," Tre insisted. "So is Art."

It was a massive relief. Whatever Tre had done, he had not killed them.

"They are podded and stored at Mercy Station," Tre admitted.

Ean sat down on the bed. Ben wasn't dead. On the other hand, was what Tre had done to Ben and Art any different from what Loy had done to him?

"At the time, it was better than the other options," Tre told him. "Art was going to sell Jax's true identity. I decided to leave them podded until no one wants to buy what Art is selling. Then I don't need to kill him and Ben gets to choose between going with Art or staying with us."

Ean was struggling to keep up. "Ben already made that choice," he snapped.

Tre frowned at him. "Podding Art was the only realistic alternative to killing him," he insisted.

"Are you sure?" Ean asked.

"Completely," Tre replied. "Ean, I am sorry that I had to include Ben but all the other options involved separating them and then lying to Ben about what had happened to Art."

At least it was obvious that Tre had never considered killing Ben.

"I did think about killing Art in some way that looked like an accident; maybe when he went off to try to sell his information to the highest bidder."

Ean imagined Ben's grief and his reaction if he had ever learned that Tre was responsible. Yes, Ben would have come back to him but, from that point forward, their relationship would be based on a lie. "So we go to Mercy Station, unpod them and talk to them," he insisted. "We'll have to come up with enough credit to pay them compensation for taking away fourteen divs of their lives."

Tre scowled at him. "They've been in stasis, Ean. It isn't lost time; just delayed. And I am not paying Art. He is not going to benefit from deciding to sell out a member of his crew. The only reason he isn't dead is that Ben loves him."

"But we go to Mercy Station, unpod them and talk it through," Ean insisted.

Tre shook his head. "Ean, we haven't got a ship and, when we do get one, every journey, every jump, is going to be risky. It is out that Emanuel Rafael Jax Esteban, the missing heir to the Navaja clan, is a cat on the Willow's crew. That news is going to spread. Going to Mercy Station may have to wait."

It was not a matter of what was convenient but what was right. "But…"

"Ean, please," Tre asked. "Leave it for now. We will sort it out, like everything else, but maybe it'll have to be lower on the list than keeping everyone alive."

Tre looked weary and haggard. A large part of Ean wanted to try to kiss his troubles away. Another part shared his anxiety. Then there was the third, the part that resented all the secrets Tre had kept. Not about his life before, Tre had a perfect right to those, but the ones about the life they now shared.

He had knocked Ben out and stuffed him in a pod; whatever

Tre's reasons, it would take Ean some time to get over that.

"I am going to have a shower," he announced. Then, before Tre could suggest anything else, Ean walked into the bathroom and locked the door behind him.

He did have a quick shower but then he filled the bath and climbed in. The warmth of the water and the scent of the bath oils were soothing. The bath was huge, easily big enough for three or four. He straightened out, allowed himself to float, and tried to relax enough to think.

Jax wasn't just a 'boy from a prominent spacer clan', he was heir to the Navaja clan. What made it worse was that he was the missing heir to the Navaja clan. Ean tried to recall the details; what Tre had said to Nevin Edger helped. The clan leader, Jax's father, had been murdered by his wife's brother, who had taken control.

So Jax's uncle had to be after them; along with every other clan, each one of which would see Jax as potential source of power. Then there would be the reporters. And the kidnappers.

Anyone Jax was close to would be a target; a commodity that could be bought and sold. If any of them decided to walk away, he would need a new identity; preferably in a different sector of the Fringe.

Ean groaned. He had not signed up for this; none of them had.

A tap on the door; Tre.

"Are you all right?"

"Of course I'm not all right," Ean retorted. "I've just worked out that I've completely lost control of my life."

There was silence before Tre spoke again. "Can I come in? Please?"

"The door is locked and I'm not getting out," Ean replied.

Tre took that as a yes, as Ean had known he would. At least he bothered to find something to turn the latch from the other side rather than breaking the door. Ean did not move; he stayed floating and watched Tre from under half-closed eyelids.

He had taken his jacket off but, other than that, he was still fully clothed. Ean knew that meant he was uncertain of his reception, which was good because Ean did not feel like forgiving him anytime soon. Tre chose to sit on the stool, close to the door, and waited.

Ean knew he was being unreasonable. This morning he had thought he had no one other than Loy, whom he couldn't trust. Now he had his family back and confirmation that Ben was alive.

He should be grateful. Instead he felt like screaming.

"Ean, what did you dream of being when you were a boy?" Tre asked.

Ean gazed at him through his eyelashes. What was Tre up to? "You know what. A teacher. Not that someone like me could ever become a teacher on Nova Tremaine."

"But being queen of the Willow has not been a disappointment," Tre pointed out.

Ean sat up, sending a small wave of water over the edge of the tub. "Of course not. It has been an honour and a privilege. I could not wish for more."

"So sometimes the future can be good, even if it is not the future we dreamt of or anticipated."

Ean could not help but smile. He had been caught. He leaned back again. "You should have come up with a better solution for the Art problem," he scolded.

"Yes, Ean," Tre answered with exaggerated contrition. "I'll try to do better next time."

Ean sighed because Tre's promise fitted their situation exactly. On this crazy journey there would be many 'next times' when they could only choose to do the best possible rather than what was right.

Hopefully they could stay within the limits of the code.

"Shower first," he ordered.

Ean would have sworn Tre was out of his clothes, through the shower and into the bath in less than a minute.

Jax was delighted that Ean was safe. He was a lot less happy that Loy had been given over to the Edger crew. He would have words about that with Tre.

It had been a rough morning. They had been high on excitement when Kip had confirmed that the Stellar Rover had received their message for Ean, uncertain when he had not replied and despairing when the captain of the passenger liner had confirmed that Ean was not on the Stellar Rover or the

Etoile.

Then they had lost contact with Tre once he had left the Apus. It had not helped.

Kip had looked progressively worse with every minute that had passed. Jax had begun to think what would happen if Ean was killed by the Edger crew. What would they do if Kip fell apart?

All he had been able to think of was sticking Kip in a pod and shipping him back to Darrenden. Or maybe, since Kip had left Darrenden for a reason, sending for his parents.

Then, thankfully, Ean's message had come through and they had sent their reply.

After that Cas had insisted they all had lunch together. Jax watched Noe trying to coax Kip to eat with only limited success.

Jax looked at Rae. Rae looked back and gave a whisker twitch that meant, "He's our friend. It is up to us to do something."

"Cas, do we have any duties this afternoon?" Jax asked.

Cas looked surprised to be asked; he still had not got used to the idea of filling in for Ean. "No. Once the lunch dishes are done I think we could all do with some rest time." He looked to the captain.

"That sounds good to me," Captain Mel agreed.

"Kip, do you want to hang out with Rae and me in our den?" Jax asked.

There was silence. Obe almost broke it with an exclamation of disbelief but Cas managed to stop him with an elbow in the ribs.

Kip blinked at Jax in surprise. Then he smiled, which was great, before looking towards Noe, which was not. Jax really didn't want Noe there.

"I'm going to soak in that bath with all the jets," Noe announced, which was a relief.

"Thanks, Jax, Rae, that would be great," Kip replied.

Jax sent Rae to collect cushions and a blanket while he raided the galley for supplies. Then they piled onto Jax's bunk. Kip still had an earpiece in but Jax decided not to suggest he took it out.

"What are we going to do?" Kip asked. "We could watch a storyvid but there isn't a screen."

Jax hadn't got as far of thinking about what they would do. Did Kip like storyvids? Jax had never been allowed to watch them; his parents had not approved of fiction. "We might go do that later," he suggested.

"Yes," Kip agreed. "We could ask Noe. He'll be out of the bath by then." Then his eyes went distant, like they did, before coming back into focus. "Maybe we should tell each other another secret."

It wasn't the direction in which Jax had intended to go but he could live with it. Giving Rae more information about his background wouldn't be such a bad idea. He checked with

Rae. Last time Rae had been hesitant. This time he appeared fine with it.

"I'll go first," Jax volunteered. "I am Emanuel Rafael Jax Esteban, son of Joaquin Oro Sebastiano Socorro and recognised heir to the Navaja clan leadership."

He looked at Rae, who gave a 'what in Known Space does that mean' whisker twitch in reply.

"The plan was that I would spend my first thirty standards seeing if I came up to my father's expectations. Then, if I made the grade and survived, I would take over the clan when he died." Jax sighed. "Only it isn't working out like that. My Uncle Gil, my mother's brother, killed my parents and took control of the clan. I've been running ever since."

"Does your uncle want to kill you?" Rae asked.

It was a question that Jax had never thought of asking. "I guess so," he replied. "Your go, Rae."

"Mutt Tucker thinks my maker's mark may be real," Rae told them. "He thinks there could be a breeding colony of hybrids like me somewhere."

Unlike what Jax had said, Rae's secret really caught Kip's attention.

"Like the minkies?" he queried.

Rae nodded.

"Wow," Kip exclaimed. "A colony of Bara hybrids? That would be amazing."

"Probably not true," Rae pointed out. His whiskers drooped

slightly. "Medico Loy said my sex-bits will work for fucking but not for breeding."

"Well Loy was a lying traitor so we're not going to trust what he said," Jax reminded them.

"He might have just have been saying what he knew was true of modern hybrids," Kip added. "If you want, I could have a look at the scans."

"No!" Rae squeaked. Then he flushed. "Medical stuff like that is private."

Jax had a shrewd idea that 'private' didn't mean much to Kip but if Rae had told him to stay away from it, he would. He turned to Kip. Kip would have never suggested telling secrets unless he had one he wanted to share.

"I think in different ways to most people," he began.

Jax stopped himself commenting about how not-a-secret that was.

"Only one in ten trillion people think like me," Kip added.

That was different. It was almost impossible for Jax to get his head around and Rae obviously didn't have a clue.

Kip tried again. "At the moment there is only one other person alive who thinks like me. And she's completely crazy. Like every other person who thinks like me has been crazy, back across at least the last fifteen thousand standards."

Jax got it. Kip was scared he would go crazy, like all those other people had. "You sure?" he asked.

The puzzle Klennethon Darrent and I did together, it was to

test whether I thought in the one-in-ten-trillion way; the way that sends a person crazy."

Rae twitched his whiskers. "You aren't crazy," he stated. "I've met crazy people and you aren't one of them."

Kip smiled. "Thanks Rae."

Jax thought about it. "Did they go crazy or did they start crazy?" he asked.

"They started crazy," Kip admitted.

"Then you are different," Jax pointed out.

Kip considered. Then he reached for one of the nut clusters that Jax had taken from the galley. "Yes, I am different from them," he agreed.

They ate more treats, had a pillow fight and then Kip fell asleep. Jax decided to go and investigate if it was possible for them to watch a storyvid together. Noe was on one of the couches in the shared area painting his toenails, which would have earned him a scolding from Ean.

Jax didn't mention it. Instead he told Noe about Kip wanting to watch a storyvid.

Forty minutes later they had a three dimensional projector set up in one of the rooms they weren't using. Noe had asked Vic and Vic had asked Elspeth.

Not that Kip was in any state to watch it; he was curled around a pillow on Jax's bunk, snoring gently. Rae had even managed to remove his earpiece without waking him.

They watched the storyvid in the evening instead, after supper.

Jax understood the part where they piled onto the couch or sat on the floor nearby, passed around treats and made comments.

He didn't get why Kip, Rae and Noe liked the story. It had infeasible creatures and magic and a ridiculous number of coincidences. It was like the stories his niñera had told him when he was little; the ones his father had told him were for babies.

Only the others did like it, so he enjoyed watching them instead.

14

This morning breakfast was different. Rae could tell that Ean was trying to behave as if it was a normal day when it wasn't. Today was the day when the captain was going to wake Ben and tell him what Art had done.

Ean wanted Ben to come back so much. Rae could see it in Ean's stiffness, hear it in the way Ean was breathing and smell it in Ean's sweat.

They were still on the Renaissance. Klennethon Darrent wasn't. He and Garner Parrad had left in a tiny spacehopper ship called the Dart. It was great being ferried around by the Renaissance and its crew but the mere thought of it made Tre jumpy. Jax had explained. It was about being beholden to people who might want something in return.

Rae could see that. In the future Klennethon Darrent might want Jax to do something that Jax didn't want to do; maybe even something he shouldn't do.

Ean had called a Meeting for the day after he and Tre had joined them on the Renaissance. The crew had decided to accept Klennethon Darrent's offer to stay on the Renaissance for up to but not exceeding thirty days. Within those thirty days they would return to Verdant to resolve what to do about salvaging the Willow, complete their business at Mercy Station and travel to Tarrasade.

Yesterday they had reached Mercy Station.

Rae watched Ean say goodbye to Tre, who was going with the captain to the spacestation. The words sounded right but Ean turned away when Tre began to take a step towards him.

Things hadn't been the same between Ean and Tre since Ean had returned to the crew. Rae wasn't sure why. Maybe sex-stuff had happened between Loy and Ean before Ean found out Loy was lying to him. Maybe it was because Ean had found out that Tre had stuffed his best friend in a pod. Maybe it was because Ean now knew who Jax was. Maybe it was all three.

Maybe it was just losing the Willow.

Whatever it was, Ean and Tre fucked even more but many of the little, everyday things were missing. Ean did little things for everyone all the time. Favourite shirts were accelerated through the laundry. Extra seasoning was added to someone's plate. Collars were turned down properly. The list was endless.

Ean was doing fewer of those little things for Tre.

Maybe after today, when it was resolved whether Ben was coming back or not, things between Tre and Ean would go back to normal.

Rae hoped so.

Rae knew that Ean had wanted to go with the captain and Tre but it had been decided at the Meeting that Ean should stay on the ship. Tre was only going to open up the unit. The captain was going to wake Ben and speak with him. Then Ben would decide what he was going to do and what should happen to Art.

After the captain and Tre had gone, Ean told Rae and Jax to clean up the galley and go about their usual morning duties. Like most mornings, Rae had the first session in the gym and Jax had the second.

Jax went to find Noe to help with the laundry or the mending or both.

Rae didn't go to the gym. Instead he followed Ean.

Following Ean's trail was easy; his scent was fresh and stank of tension. Rae soon realised that Ean was heading for the big dining room with the viewing galleries. Sure enough, Ean was there, up on the mezzanine level where the viewing ports faced the station.

Rae sat on the stairs, out of sight but there in case Ean had need of him.

Ean and Ben were best friends, like him and Jax. Rae tried to imagine what he would feel in Ean's place but failed. He would want to kill anyone who had pretended that Jax had left but had really stuffed him in a pod. Only Ean loved Tre. Could Rae love someone who had stuffed Jax in a pod?

Would Jax ever choose someone else over Rae, like Ben had chosen Art over Ean?

Maybe not someone but something. Being Navaja clan leader was a lot more important than being Rae's best friend.

Rae didn't want to think about that. Instead he went over what had happened recently, checking that he hadn't missed something. Loy had been taken by the Edger crew, which was bad; Rae thought Tre should have killed him.

Too many people knew that Jax had been on the Willow: Nevin Edger and his crew; the crew of the Talon; the minkies; the Tuckers; the crew of the Petunia Mae.

Rae wasn't too worried about the minkies or the Tuckers; they lived in their own world, not Jax's. He was confident that Medico Kem, Owen and Kurt could be trusted.

Kip had this model. It showed how quickly the news about Jax was likely to spread. There were lots of variations but they all had one thing in common; the information spread too quickly.

They needed a safe den and they needed it now.

They had a two-part plan. A new Willow was going to be built at a shipyard in a system called Potash. She would be mostly new, paid for by their compensation, but she would incorporate the components the minkies had salvaged and the Petunia Mae would deliver to Potash.

She would also be built with space for an extra drive; a Mulligan drive. Kip would own the Mulligan drive. The Willow's crew would hire the drive from Kip for what Jax called a nominal fee.

So the new Willow would be a spacehopper ship, which solved the problem of avoiding the people who would be lurking at every gate, hoping to grab Jax.

The captain had checked that Kip was actually buying the Mulligan drive in his own right and not getting it from Klennethon Darrent. It turned out that Kip had decided that huge quantities of credit were useful and would be mega-rich by the time the Mulligan drive had to be paid for.

Ean had gone into a panic, thinking he might be stealing, but Kip was earning it by buying and selling things, like all spacers, just very quickly and across many different systems.

The new Willow, with its Mulligan drive, wouldn't be ready for five divs. Vic had been astonished that it was only five divs but it was pretty clear that Klennethon Darrent had talked to the owners of a shipyard on Potash.

Meanwhile, they were going to Tarrasade because Kip thought that Tarrasade was the place Jax should be when he was being the heir to the Navaja clan rather than a cabin boy in the Willow.

Rae thought of Tarrasade as a potential den and he was yet to be convinced it was suitable.

A hitch in Ean's breathing; Rae hoped that he wasn't going to start crying. Rae didn't know what to do when people cried. Instead he heard Ean get up from where he had been sitting and walk towards the balustrade.

Rae wondered if he should run. Instead he stayed where he was and looked up as Ean looked down.

"I thought you were going to the gym," Ean observed.

Rae settled for a whisker twitch.

"Up you come then," Ean decided.

As Rae climbed the stairs Ean went back to his seat. Rae realised that he had been staring out the viewport towards the spacestation, willing Ben to decide to return rather than going with Art.

Rae went over and stood close, knowing that would distract Ean from worrying about Ben.

Ean reached out and pulled down Rae's jacket, which just made the sleeves look even shorter. "You need new clothes again," he observed. "I'll have to make the next ones with deeper hems. You are going to be so tall." Ean's fingers smoothed his head fur and frowned at the texture. "Have you been brushing your fur properly?"

Rae hated brushing out his fur. Either it took ages or it hurt. "I'll go get a brush," he announced and set off at a run.

He was back quickly, even for him. He sat down next to Ean on the couch and handed him the brush. Ean set to work, patiently working out each tangle.

It never hurt when Ean did it. It did take ages but this time that was good because it distracted Ean from staring at the station. Also, if Rae was honest, having someone else do it was nice; he had to stop himself purring.

Ean was working on the last of the tangles when they saw the shuttle and had been just brushing for five minutes when the door downstairs opened and closed. Rae could hear one person crossing the floor and starting up the stairs but it was the captain, not Ben. Rae watched Ean's expression as hope give way to disappointment.

The captain walked along the mezzanine towards them. "I need a word with Ean, Rae."

Rae reclaimed the brush and set off for the stairs. As their paths crossed, the captain reached out and patted his shoulder.

"Good work, Rae," he acknowledged.

Rae twitched his whiskers in reply and started down the stairs, moving silently with his ears pricked. Sure enough, the captain started talking to Ean before Rae was out of range.

"Ben sent you a message, Ean. He said that a person gives the benefit of the doubt to someone he loves. He believes that you will understand."

Ean's breath caught. "You told him what Art was planning to do?" he checked.

"I did but you know how it is, Ean. Art never did it because Tre did not give him the chance. I gave Ben the tape with the evidence Kip put together but I doubt Ben will look at it. I waited outside while Ben woke Art, told him the situation and listened to what Art had to say. Ben chooses to believe Art's assertion that it is all a misunderstanding."

Ean snorted. "If Art was innocent he would be demanding compensation. The fact he isn't means he is relieved to have got away with it."

The captain sighed. "You know that, I know that and probably, deep inside, Ben knows that. Love can make a person foolish, Ean."

"You gave him my present for him?"

"I gave it to him and I made sure he knew the details of how to contact us through the Stellar Exchange by heart."

"And he knows I knew nothing about it?"

"I told him and he believes that you knew nothing about it. I told him that you wanted to come in person but the crew would not let you."

Maybe Rae would have heard more but at that point he realised that Tre was around the next corner. Tre wouldn't have to ask why Rae was walking so slowly because he would know Rae was eavesdropping. Rae sped up to his normal walking pace and passed Tre leaning on a wall waiting for the captain to finish speaking to Ean.

Tre looked from the brush in Rae's hand to his head and then nodded, as if thanking him. Rae didn't see that letting Ean brush his hair was a big enough thing to thank him for.

Then he caught sight of himself in one of the many mirrors and stopped in his tracks. His head fur was sticking straight up and out. Rae had known that it was longer now but he had not appreciated how long.

He tried smoothing it down but it just stuck to his hands and then sprung up again. Rae tried again but it was hopeless. Perhaps putting his head under a faucet would help. He decided to hurry back to their den and try that.

Unfortunately he did not make it without passing Vic, whose eyes went straight to his head, followed by Obe.

"Nice hair, Rae," Obe commented with a grin.

Rae didn't even point out it was fur not hair; he was too intent on finding that faucet. He wove his way to their den, managing to avoid meeting anyone else, only to find Jax sitting on his bunk reading.

"Wow," Jax exclaimed, his eyes riveted to Rae's head.

"Going to wash it," Rae explained.

"Come here first," Jax ordered.

Rae reluctantly obeyed and sat on the edge of Jax's bunk. Jax put out a hand and ran it across the sticking-out ends of Rae's fur.

"It's so soft," he observed. "And being spread out means you can see all the colours in it; all the different browns and golds. How in Known Space did you get so much static into it? Did Kip link you up to some kind of voltage generator?"

"Ean brushed it," Rae admitted. "He kept brushing," he added.

"You were with Ean?" Jax queried.

"Went to check on him," Rae admitted.

Jax frowned a little, as if trying to decide what he thought about that. "Good," he decided. He leaned across to his locker, opened it and brought out two objects.

Rae whimpered at the sight of another brush and a comb.

"This is a natural bristle brush," Jax told him, "and a metal comb. Both are meant to be good at preventing static but I don't know if they will disperse it once it is there."

Rae edged away. "I'll wash it."

"Let me comb it through first," Jax insisted. "It'll be like an experiment."

He was dreading Jax dragging the metal comb through his fur but the absence of tangles meant it was fine.

"There," Jax announced after a minute or two.

Rae went across and peered into the mirror on the wall. Instead of standing straight up, his head fur was swept back from his face. Even so, it still looked like there was twice as much of it than was usual.

"It looks like a lion's mane," Jax told him.

Rae studied his image and wondered if that was good or a bad thing.

"It looks good," Jax added. "Try leaving it like that."

Weirdly, when the others saw it at lunch they agreed; even those who had seen the sticking-up version. Noe was particularly taken by it and began talking about hair combs and plaiting and other stuff that Rae suspected was girly.

Cas sighed. "Do you think we'll be able to go clubbing when we get to Tarrasade?" he asked.

Rae was a bit surprised by the change in subject but he was interested in the answer. Would they be safe enough in Tarrasade to do the things normal crews did?

"Tre will have to assess the situation when we get there," the captain answered. "The spacer quarter of Tarrasade is run strictly to the code and most of the residential areas are very ordered."

"We could spend this afternoon learning about Tarrasade," Ean suggested.

Rae, like the others, knew that wasn't a suggestion at all; Ean's lessons weren't optional. Not that he minded and it would help keep Ean's mind off Ben.

"Cas and Obe, perhaps you would like to help me lead the session," Ean added, which was Ean's way of telling Cas and Obe that they needed to learn about Tarrasade too.

Obe wasn't a cat any more, so he, like Cas, didn't have to attend Ean's lessons. By the time Ean had rejoined them, it had been clear that Obe and Cas were lovers. Ean hadn't been willing to turn a blind eye like everyone else. Instead Obe had been promoted and they had settled for a crew celebration rather than going clubbing.

Ean hadn't been willing to put up with the accommodation either. Rae and Jax had their den and the captain still had the small apartment. Everyone else was in the largest bedroom, which had been converted into a crewroom, and Ean had closed off most of the other rooms.

As he had said, a Traditional crew lived in the Traditional way.

Once the debris from lunch had been tidied away, Rae expected everyone to settle back down around the table like they would have done for a lesson on the Willow. Instead they went to the room where Vic had set up the three dimensional projector for showing Kip the storyvid.

It had been one of the rooms that Ean had locked.

Three extra chairs had appeared. Cas and Obe took the two that were side by side while Ean sat on the other. The rest of them were on the couch, with Noe on one end and Rae on the other with Kip and Jax between them.

Rae soon appreciated why Ean had wanted to use the projector; Tarrasade was complicated. Instead of being one disc, like Carrefour and any other spacestation Rae knew about, it was made up of four. Then there was the sticky bit in the middle, which passed through the centres of all the discs and had a ball at one end.

"Let's make a start by finding out some of what everyone knows," Ean began.

The 'some of' had appeared in Ean's introduction after Kip joined the crew. Kip's job was to only share useful information that the others would understand.

"Jax?" Ean encouraged.

Jax was happy to oblige. "There has been a spacestation in the Tarrasade system longer than in any other Fringe system. Tarrasade is Inner Fringe and, as such, is neutral territory for all the spacer clans." He frowned, as if trying to recall something. "Tarrasade is one of the Five. The Five play an important part in the production of gravity field generators but I'm not sure what."

Kip leaned forward as if keen to discuss gravity field generators but Ean did not give him the chance. "We'll come back to the Five and gravitational field generators later," he said quickly. "Anyone else other than Kip? Cas and Obe, feel free to contribute."

"There are lots of holes," Obe volunteered. "That explains how it became such an important system when it hasn't got even a single planet and its sun's radiation is too high energy for comfort. Four of them are gated."

"Six," Kip corrected. "Six are gated but two of the gates aren't used."

There was silence. Rae understood. Gates cost a fortune. To have a gate and not use it was just plain wrong.

"Why haven't they sold them on if they aren't going to use them?" Noe asked.

Ean sighed. "Kip, you will have to answer that one. I only knew about the four functional gates."

Kip frowned. "No one is exactly sure who owns them, so no one can sell them," he told them. "Rumours are that one leads to a route that gets to Centre too quickly; if it were opened up Tarrasade would be Borders and spacers don't want that. The other is meant to be Tarrasade's bolt-hole; if all else fails the population will be evacuated through it. Where it leads is a closely guarded secret. It was put in place after the population of Tarrasade was almost wiped out by the Black Marauder fleet."

A good den should always have a bolt-hole; Rae approved. He wondered if Kip could open a closed gate. If anyone could, it would be Kip. "How many of the holes will we be able to use in our spacehopper ship?" he asked.

Ean nodded his approval of the question and indicated that Kip should answer.

"A spacehopper ship can't use a gated hole. I mean, it can go through the gate but it can't switch on its Mulligan drive when it does or the two fields interfere." Kip's eyes went distant for a moment. "There are another eight holes that could be used but only four are mapped, including the one we will be using."

An unmapped hole was one where no one knew where it went. Jumping through an unmapped hole was risky; the other side could be too close to a star or some other hazard.

"Good," Ean acknowledged. "Now, back to the station. We have mentioned connectivity. What else?"

There was silence. Kip wasn't allowed to answer unless called upon and Jax had already made a contribution. Rae was just about to say something when Noe decided it was his turn.

"Population," he answered. "How many people live there and how they are supported."

"And does anyone other than Kip know anything about that?" Ean asked.

Jax's brow puckered. "Isn't Tarrasade unusual in that they only live on one side of the disc?"

"Yes," Ean agreed. "Kip?"

"The local sun is heavy on high energy radiation and has cycles of high activity sunspots," Kip began. "Rather than spend a fortune trying to shield the residential parts of the station, they decided to orientate the station so that one side of the main disc got the full impact of the radiation but the other side would be safe."

Kip fiddled with an interface to make the projected diagram show what he meant. The ball end of the stick was towards the sun and the flow of sparkles representing the solar radiation hit one side of the first of the discs, the biggest. "People can live on either side of these other discs," he continued, pointing at the three progressively smaller discs. "They are sheltered by the big disc."

"So, in this situation, what types of things would you site on the sun-side of the large disc?" Ean asked. "Rae?"

Rae wished he had volunteered earlier. At least Ean had asked him first, before all the easy answers had been used up. "Energy harvesting and food production." He decided to add something else. "Possibly the docks because ships are really well shielded."

Ean's smile confirmed that he was impressed. "If you had to add something else, what would you choose? Noe?"

Noe's expression suggested he didn't care about coming up with a correct answer but Rae knew different from his scent. "Manufacturing?" he suggested. "But you would have to shield the workers and maybe the equipment."

"Excellent, Noe," Ean confirmed. "Jax?"

Rae saw Jax trying to work out why Noe's answer had led Ean to him. "They manufacture gravitational field generators?" he suggested.

"Exactly," Ean replied. He shifted in his seat slightly and Rae braced himself; Ean was entering lecture mode. "By spreading the manufacture of gravitational field generators over at least five different locations, spacers ensure the supply of this essential component of ships and spacestations. The five factories are owned by all spacers and overseen by the same organisation that provides our insurance. Other companies are welcome to produce gravitational field generators but it can be difficult for them to compete with the Five as far as the basic models are concerned. Cas, do you have anything else to add?"

Cas smiled, suggesting that he was honoured to be offered the opportunity to finish the lecture.

"The same system works for the basic models of other essential components of ships or spacestations: conventional drives, air scrubbers, guns, shielding materials, rockets, transmitters, receivers, telescopes and scanners."

A list; Rae wasn't keen on those. He could only remember the thing at the start and the thing at the end. Ean usually avoided lists.

"It's only the gravitational field generators and the conventional drives where the spacer-owned rather than privately owned factories dominate the market," Cas continued. "Even so, the spacer-owned factories keep producing so that no one can take over the supply and drive up the prices."

Rae thought he understood. It was different if you lived on a habitable planet. On a planet with liquid water and a breathable atmosphere you could survive with very little technology. In space if someone drove up the price of some piece of technology you needed, you had to pay it.

"Thank you, Cas," Ean acknowledged. "Right, Kip, take it away but keep it simple."

Ean was letting Kip off the leash and that always meant a cascade of facts in an order that made more sense to Kip than anyone else. Kip produced a pair of control wire gloves from a pocket and put them on. A few hand gestures confirmed that he had the projection under control.

"The Sphere is the original Tarrasade spacestation," he told them. "It's got a single gravitational field generator at its core, generating a one thousand gee field at one metre." His eyes were shining. "Isn't it amazing? It's been functional for thousands of standards. Anyway, as we all know, disc stations with arrays of gravitational field generators give a lot more usable area, so next they build these two discs." Kip rotated the image to show the big disc and the smaller one above it. "Weirdly they call the different areas levels, even though they aren't. I guess that's because the original sphere station had levels. The residential side of the big disc is divided into four concentric areas. Working from inside out they are Level 6, Level 5, Level 4 and Level 3. Level 3 is essentially the spacer quarter. Level 6 is high density residential accommodation. Levels 5 and 4 have everything you would expect in the transition between those two."

Rae tried to commit the most useful bits to memory. Spacer quarter was at the edge of the disc; only ressies lived in the middle. Kip was continuing.

"The sunside of the smaller disc is known as Level 2 and the starside as Level 1. For over a millennium Level 1 was the most upmarket part of the station and it is still the most prestigious place to live. However, five hundred standards ago they built this disc. The sunside is called the Outer Residential Ring and the starside is called the Inner Residential Ring. Both are residential areas for rich people. Then, fifty standards ago this smallest disc was built, which is called Prime.

"The cylinder in the middle is called the Hub. It contains ladders so people can get from disc to disc and a really neat set of chutes for the transfer of goods. There are also two elevators between the two main discs and separate elevators going to the new discs."

That was the point Rae stopped listening; it was like his brain had been saturated with information. He studied the projection while Kip went on about the chutes. He wondered where they would live. It depended on whether Kip was right and Jax had a claim on part of the station. Maybe part of Level 1; Jax's family was probably old enough to own a bit of that.

Ean called it a day when Jax's eyes started to glaze over.

Kip was still enthusing about Tarrasade as the four of them helped Ean make supper. Kip and Noe were at the table preparing ingredients. Jax was cleaning up anything Ean had finished with. Rae was relaying stuff between the table, the stove and the sink.

Rae wasn't listening to Kip. He wasn't sure anyone was; not even Jax. Finally Noe decided to change the subject.

"Will we ever be able to leave where we're living?" he asked. "I mean, if reporters and challengers and would-be kidnappers are going to be waiting for Jax around every corner?"

There was a short silence that Ean broke. "As the captain said, Tarrasade is one of the most civilised spacestations."

Noe finished popping the peas out of one pod, discarded it and picked up another. "Jax does not look like you would expect him to look," he observed.

How was Jax meant to look? Jax looked like Jax.

"Jax the Willow's cat could continue to look as he does," Noe suggested, "but the missing heir to the clan could look as people expect him to look."

Kip froze for a moment and then exploded. "That's a fabulous idea. We can make two people. We could probably back engineer all manner of records to suggest that they joined the crew at different times. How is your disguise maintained?" he asked Jax. "Is it nanobots?"

Jax smelt a bit reluctant to answer but he nodded.

"There won't be any problem with vids," Kip assured them. "I can manage those. Face to face it'll be more difficult unless we can switch the nanobots on and off. I'll investigate. See, Ean, bringing Loy's kit with us rather than sending it to Potash was a good idea."

Rae wasn't really listening. How was Jax meant to look? They finished helping Ean with the supper and laid the table.

"Supper won't be for another twenty minutes," Ean pointed out. "Rae, why don't you and Jax spend that time tidying your den? Kip and Noe can help me finish cooking and serving."

Rae was about to say that their den was always tidy because Jax liked it that way when Jax's hand on his arm stopped him. Instead Rae nodded. "Thanks, Ean," he acknowledged.

As soon as they were in their den Jax shut the door and turned to him. "What's wrong, Rae?"

Rae thought about refusing to reply but he knew Jax would just keep on at him. "How are you meant to look?" he asked.

Jax sighed, sat down on his bunk and then leaned over to get a tablet from his locker. "I have lighter hair and different colour eyes." He activated the tablet and brought up an image. "Here.

That was taken two and a half standards ago."

The image showed a boy with short blond hair, pale skin and bright green eyes. At first glance Rae could not see any similarities to Jax but as he studied it he started to see that some of the shapes were the same.

"Of course I was younger then," Jax pointed out.

Rae pulled himself together. If they bleached Jax's hair and gave him green contact lenses he would still be Jax. He would sound the same and move the same.

Most importantly, he would smell the same.

"You are Jax," Rae stated firmly. "It does not matter what colours your hair and eyes are."

Jax smiled. "Best friends?" he checked.

"Best friends," Rae confirmed. "Always."

15

Jax looked in the mirror to see a stranger looking back at him. His hair was silvery blond and straight. Jax brushed it back and secured it with a clip at the nape of his neck; by having it close to his scalp it made him look more like the boy he had been when his hair had been cut short. His eyes were bright green and his skin was paler.

He was reminded of the images of his half-brother he had found in the Navaja archive or images of his father as an adolescent.

Of course that was to be expected; genetic engineering ensured it.

Kip had worked on Jax's cosmetic nanobots while they travelled from Mercy to Tarrasade. He had relished the challenge of reprogramming them. It had quickly mastered Loy's equipment, analysed Jax's nanobots and produced versions that could be switched on or off; ten days to go from novice to ground-breaking expert.

The difficult part had been clearing Jax's skin, eyes and hair of the brown pigment the old nanobots had produced. The new nanobots could release brown pigment and then sequester it again. It took less than twenty minutes to change from Jax to Emanuel Rafael Jax Esteban. The change back was even quicker.

Now, four days after the Renaissance had dropped them off at Tarrasade, Emanuel Rafael Jax Esteban could be produced on demand.

Jax dressed in the clothes Tre had chosen for him; a dark green tailored jacket with black pants and knee high boots. It was very stylish and ultra conservative.

He then picked up the small tablet he had prepared. It had relevant information Kip had collected about his claim to part of Tarrasade and a detailed profile of Leveret Poe, the Navaja clan's agent in Tarrasade. Jax checked the images that accompanied the profile: greying brown hair; pale tan skin; brown eyes; average height, weight and build; no remarkable features; not a spacer or even an ex-spacer. Kip had discovered that Leveret Poe was a professional agent, working on behalf of a wide variety of clients.

Jax had queried that. What if the clients' interests clashed? Also, from what Kip had dug out of the Navaja archive, the clan paid the man a hefty salary.

Finally Jax threaded his father's ring onto a chain, hung it around his neck and tucked it away under his jacket.

It had been decided that they could not risk hiring a unit anywhere in the main disc; it was too vulnerable. The cheapest unit available elsewhere had been in the Outer Residential Ring. It was both tiny and ridiculously expensive. Ean had looked as if he would have a meltdown when he had been told the cost.

The captain had the smaller of the two bedrooms while everyone else shared the larger; Rae and Jax's den was a closet.

There was a sitting room that they could all sit in at a pinch and a kitchen where two people could work side by side provided they coordinated their movements.

The captain had his own head and shower but the rest of them had to share the ones off the main bedroom.

Four days had been too long; the sooner Jax found out if he had a claim to any part of Tarrasade the better.

Rae put his head around the door and twitched his whiskers. Jax interpreted the twitch as a reminder that everyone was waiting. He took a deep breath, picked up his cloak and followed Rae out.

Everyone else was waiting in the sitting room. Tre looked magnificent. His hair was pulled back and his face was painted with strategically placed black lines to emphasise the threat he represented.

He was wearing the most severely formal of the outfits he had acquired from the pirate commander. Jax noticed that Ean had embroidered the Navaja insignia on the collar of Tre's jacket; it was a nice touch.

"Time to go," Tre told him

Jax nodded. He put on his cloak and pulled up the hood.

Rae gave the tiniest of whimpers. Jax understood; Rae wanted to be strong enough to take Tre's place.

"I'll be back soon," he whispered and Rae nodded.

They walked along the corridor towards the Hub. Jax had

been concerned that the security guards would be curious but one glimpse of Tre was enough for them to melt away.

As they approached the Hub the corridor floor curved but the gravitational field remained constant, so it felt flat. Tarrasade had carefully tailored gravitational field generators built into the Hub so that there was a constant force of one half gee pulling towards the Sphere. In the more upmarket discs, like the one they were living in, other specially built field generators controlled the transition between disc and Hub.

They paid for a whole elevator car to take them to Level 2; it was more secure than sharing a car or using the ladder. Then it was through one of the flat-feeling curves into the sunside of the second disc.

Here the security guards held their posts rather than retreating. Tre kept up a measured pace and Jax walked as he had been trained to do, on Tre's left within arm's reach.

Tre had insisted that they rent a secure meeting room close to the Records Office for their first interaction with Leveret Poe. He had tried suggesting that the agent pay for it only for Leveret Poe to refuse on the grounds that Jax had yet to establish his identity.

In response, Jax had copied the man's contract onto his tablet and studied it closely.

At least the man was already there, along with two bodyguards. Jax looked them over and had decided that they were muscle-for-hire even before Tre's hand signal.

Jax lowered his hood and spoke as soon as the door slid closed behind him. "Agent Poe."

Looking almost identical to your father, grandfather, great-grandfather and great-great grandfather meant that no one failed to recognise you. The bodyguards tried to keep their attention on Tre but failed miserably. Leveret Poe did not even try not to stare.

However, he did have the presence of mind not to say anything, just bow and indicate a small device on the table that bore the Navaja clan symbol.

If the device was genuine, it should respond to the ring. If it was not…

Jax decided not to think about that. Instead he brought the ring out. Provided he was holding the ring it should work; there was no requirement for him to have it on his finger. The chain was long enough for him to touch the ring to the top of the truncated cone, which obligingly glowed and made a pleasant bell-like sound.

"Emanuel Rafael Jax Esteban," Leveret Poe acknowledged immediately.

Jax tucked the ring back inside his jacket. "We will meet regularly," he announced. "However today you will accompany me to the Records Office."

The plan for today was to keep it simple; establish his identity and visit the Records Office to look at the hardcopy of the ownership document. Leveret Poe walked ahead with his bodyguards so that Tre could watch them.

When they arrived Leveret Poe, as a professional agent, vouched for them. As planned it was enough to get them through the outer layers, past the well dressed young people on the reception desks and a quiet, intense researcher, without revealing Jax's identity. Ensuring the attention of an archivist obviously required more; the implacable middle-aged woman in front of them was insistent that they would have to make an appointment at a future date.

Jax made the decision to lower his hood at the same moment that Tre signalled he should do so.

The woman's eyes widened.

"This is Emanuel Rafael Jax Esteban," Leveret Poe stated. "He wishes to consult an archivist on a matter relating to Navaja clan business."

"I shall ask Archivist Dorn if she is available," the woman replied immediately.

Archivist Dorn was a tiny and ancient woman. She was no taller than Jax and showed no sign of being impressed by his identity or heritage. She did, however, admit him and Tre to a private consulting room.

Jax did not waste time. He used his tablet to access the electronic record that Kip had dug out, the one that referred to an ownership document, and showed it to the woman.

Archivist Dorn smiled. "This is going to be interesting," she stated and vanished through one of the doors.

They waited in silence; too wary of microphones and recording equipment to speak. Jax looked about the room. There was nothing other than a large table with a shelf beneath it and a bench on either side. On the table were eight small cubes with rounded corners and a loop on the top face.

Jax wondered what they were for.

Ten minutes later Archivist Dorn reappeared bearing a cylindrical tube a hand's length in diameter and half as long as she was tall. She did not say anything. Instead she popped the lid off the end of the tube, which revealed two concentric compartments. From the outer she slid a large sheet.

Placing the cylinder on the shelf under the table, Archivist Dorn spread the sheet on the tabletop, weighing down each of the corners and the midpoint of each curving side with one of the cubes.

"This is the property deed to which the electronic record refers," she told him. "Of course clans cannot own property in Tarrasade. That is part of our charter. Only named individuals can own and inherit property. The property in question is now owned by you. You inherited it from your father, who inherited it from his father and so on back through the generations. Any dispute about who leads the Navaja clan will not affect this ownership issue."

What Archivist Dorn was saying was consistent with what Kip had told him. Jax began scanning the document, eager to find out what bit of Tarrasade he owned. However, he was prevented from doing so by a sheet of fabric that Archivist Dorn whipped from the shelf and draped over it.

He was about to object when she grasped the cylinder, lifted it up and tipped the contents out onto the fabric. There was a cascade of small boxes. Most were the standard size to contain old fashioned message tapes but there were several smaller ones, probably containing data crystal wafers.

"This is all the associated documentation," she told him. "For convenience the boxes have been colour-coded. Purple is for warnings issued by the Committee. Red is for official notification of fines. Orange is for charges for essential works carried out. Black is everything else."

There were a lot of purple, red and orange boxes.

"Now that you, the owner, are in Tarrasade you have ten days to present your plan for resolving all outstanding issues to the Committee. After that they will begin proceedings to recoup their costs. I have already informed the Committee that you are in Tarrasade and are aware of the deed, as I am required to do."

Jax was pretty sure Archivist Darn was enjoying herself. He took a deep breath, leaned forward and gathered together the corners of the fabric, followed by the sides, so that it contained the boxes.

Archivist Dorn proffered something. It was a clip. Jax accepted it and used it to secure the neck of his makeshift bag. Then he transferred the bagged boxes to the shelf and went back to studying the deed.

It was the Sphere; he owned the ball at the end of the Hub.

Other than an ancient one thousand gee gravity field generator, Jax had no idea what was in the Sphere. None of Ean's sessions on Tarrasade had mentioned it. As far as he knew, it had been abandoned when the discs had been built.

On the other hand, it had been a spacestation in its own right. It must still have the potential for occupation.

"A piece of advice," Archivist Dorn began.

From the tone of her voice, Jax knew he was not going to like what the old woman was about to tell him.

"The Scavengers aren't like the squatters," she continued. "They have rights."

It was almost lunchtime before they had finished copying each of the tapes and the wafers onto the tablet. Archivist Dorm had provided them with a tape reader and there was a data crystal wafer reader built into the tablet.

Jax stared at the totals. The Committee had spent over five teracredits in essential maintenance costs. Then there were the fines and the interest. Compound interest was vicious in the short term, never mind over centuries.

He owed two point three petacredits. You could buy a Mulligan drive for a petacredit; a gate only cost five.

And, as far as he could tell, selling the Sphere was not an option. No one would want it. It was falling apart, filled with squatters, and the Scavengers, a group of people Jax had thought fictional like ghosts and ghouls, had the right to live there permanently.

Kip's idea of coming to Tarrasade no longer looked so good.

Jax handed the tablet to Kip as he came through the door of the unit. Then he went directly to his and Rae's den, grabbed one of the hyposprays Kip had prepared, pushed it against the skin of his neck and activated it.

Rae had followed him and was watching him from the upper of the two undersized bunks Vic had managed to cram into the closet. Jax's folded up against the wall, liberating enough standing room for them to dress and undress.

Within another minute Emanuel Rafael Jax Esteban's clothes were on a hanger and covered by a bag. Then the hair clip and the ring were returned to his lockbox.

Jax glanced in the mirror between pulling on the various garments he usually wore. His skin was darkening and the green of his eyes was already murky. Then his hair started to curl before turning from silvery blond to glossy chestnut.

He looked up to Rae, who twitched his whiskers.

"Don't ask," Jax warned.

Lunch was ready by the time the transition was complete. One by one they told Ean what they wanted from the selection laid out along the counter in the kitchen. Ean made up a plate that Noe placed on a tray before adding cutlery, a drink and a napkin. The tray was then passed hand to hand until it reached its destination.

It had been novel the first time, like a picnic. Now Jax hated it, like he hated everything else about living with nine other people in such a tiny space.

After lunch Tre took Rae to one of the public gyms; there had been one day when Rae had got no exercise and it was not an experience any of them wished to repeat. Ean turfed Vic, Cas and Obe out of the unit with strict instructions not to spend too much. Then, at the last minute, the captain decided to accompany them.

Once occupancy was down to four, Jax felt like he could breathe.

"Noe and I will tidy up," Ean decided. "Jax, you and Kip talk about what happened this morning."

Jax wondered how Ean knew it had not turned out as expected; possibly Tre had said something. Ean and Noe went into the main bedroom. Kip sat on the couch and produced the small tablet Jax had handed him.

Kip looked like a puppy that had been kicked. Jax resolved not to talk about blame and sat down beside him.

"I'll find the credit," Kip began. "It'll be a bit tricky. I may have to take a few more risks, but I can do it."

Jax sighed. "This isn't like the drive, Kip. This is my debt. I have to find a way of paying it. Also, you set the level of risk to what was safe for you. Increasing it is a bad idea and we both know it."

Kip was silent and Jax waited. After what was probably less than a minute but felt much longer, he spoke. "If it wasn't for the debt, owning the Sphere might be a good thing."

Jax lost control before he even realised his grip was slipping. "How in Known Space can it be a good thing?" he demanded. "It's full of squatters, there are whole sections shut down because there is no life support and Scavengers have an inalienable right to live there. Scavengers!"

"They're just people," Kip whispered, shrinking away from him.

"No they aren't. They eat people. Everyone knows that," Jax retorted.

"It's just a myth," Kip murmured.

Jax wanted to get hold of Kip and shake some realism into him. Instead he jumped to his feet. "The Scavengers aren't a myth. They are there. In my Sphere. Forever. And if we hadn't come here I wouldn't know and I wouldn't have to pay a debt that is so ludicrously massive that even Papá would have struggled to pay it!"

Kip looked awful. He was horribly pale and totally motionless. Jax knew he should stop but he was so angry: about losing the Willow; about Loy; about being stuck in a tiny unit; about what had happened his morning; about having to be Emanuel Rafael Jax Esteban when all he wanted to be was Jax. "I wish you'd…" he began.

"Jax!"

Ean's authoritarian tone stopped Jax in his tracks. The anger drained away as quickly as it had come to be replaced by shame. A leader should never lose his temper. He should never blame people for circumstances beyond their control. He should never forget that people with special talents, people like Kip, were always far more fragile than they appeared.

Jax stood straight and bowed to Kip. "I apologise. My words were inspired by anger rather than truth. Please inform me how I can repair any damage I have caused." Kip did not respond immediately so Jax turned to Ean. "Thank you, Ean, for terminating the situation and reminding me that my behaviour was unacceptable."

Ean's stern expression had already softened. "Maybe Kip

would appreciate a less formal apology," he hinted.

Jax forced himself to relax. "Sorry, Kip. I lost it. None of this is your fault. I know how lucky I am to have you as my crewmate and my friend. Please forgive me."

A hint of colour had returned to Kip's face. "It was my idea to come to Tarrasade," he whispered.

Jax knew he had to do more to make good. He crouched down in front of Kip and smiled. "We're only alive and together because of your ideas, Kip."

Kip smiled uncertainly in return.

Jax watched Ean guide Kip into the bedroom. Ean was pretending that he needed help cleaning the bathroom but Jax knew it was because Ean did not trust him to treat Kip properly. To make it worse Noe was standing on the other side of the room, studying him. Jax steeled himself for some cutting comment, knowing that he deserved it.

Instead Noe came over and picked up the tablet. "Tell me what's wrong," he ordered.

Jax explained and Noe listened. Once he had finished, Noe stared at the displayed calculation. "The numbers are too big for me," he admitted. "How does what you owe now compare to credit they spent on repairs?"

"It's over two thousand times as much," Jax admitted.

Noe's eyes widened briefly. "That's..." He trailed off and tried again. "Even the worst loan sharks don't charge that much interest."

"It's been hundreds of standards," Jax pointed out.

"Did they ever send an invoice?" Noe asked.

It was an excellent point. The Committee must know that Kalakmul was the home planet of the leader of the Navaja clan. Kip had a copy of the clan archive; they could check.

"If I were you, I would try to get the debt reduced to the cost of the repairs," Noe suggested. "The rest isn't real; it's just numbers they decided to add on. Could you pay that much?"

Jax sighed. "No. It's five trillion credits." He thought about it. Kip was raising one petacredit within five divs; this was one two-hundredth of that. "It isn't impossible like two point three petacredits."

Noe frowned. "It sounds a lot for repairs when it's been left in such an appalling state. I would ask to see the itemised break-down for each job. Also, why didn't they force a sale once the debt was equal to the worth of the Sphere? I mean they are spacers. That's what happens when a crew's debts outweigh the value of their ship."

"Who would want it?" Jax queried. "It's full of Scavengers and squatters."

Noe shrugged. "Did they try? If not why not?"

Talking to Noe helped. Noe wasn't blinded by the enormity of the amounts or horrified at the potential dishonour of being declared a debtor or even distracted by the idea of Scavengers. He focused on the practicalities and made sensible suggestions.

Then Ean came back with Kip and Jax made the four of them tea. When he returned with the tray Noe had finished reciting his version of the situation.

Ean claimed the pot and poured. "Tarrasade is a spacer station," he reminded them. "The Committee will expect to negotiate a settlement. How many days do you have, Jax?"

"Ten including today," Jax replied.

"I imagine it would be a good idea to have some preliminary meetings before then," Ean suggested. "Kip can help with digging out all the relevant information. Maybe I can help by going to the Sphere and getting some idea of how bad conditions are there."

Jax didn't like the idea of Ean going somewhere infested with Scavengers.

"Perhaps Agent Poe can help," Ean proposed. "Did you speak to him about it?"

Jax sighed. "Yes, he was waiting when we finished consulting with Archivist Dorn. Clans can't own property in Tarrasade, so I own the Sphere as an individual. Agent Poe said that he could not act on my behalf as an individual because that represented a conflict of interest, so he is unable to discuss anything relating to my ownership of the Sphere."

Ean's eyes narrowed. "That sounds to me like someone hiding behind semantics to evade responsibility. I think you, as heir to the clan leadership, should ask to see those of his records that pertain to Navaja business."

Kip blew on his tea. "We can compare the records he tries to fob us off with to the ones he had sent into the Navaja archive and those he's filed with the Committee. What do you think are the odds of all three tallying?"

They were two more excellent ideas. By the time Rae came

back with Tre Jax was feeling a great deal better. They had the beginnings of a plan for dealing with the Committee.

Better still, he had made up with Kip.

16

Ean had insisted on meeting with Agent Leveret Poe alone. He made the appointment for the first part of the morning and suggested that Tre use the time to take all the youngsters to the gym. Jax, Kip and Noe might not show the symptoms of becoming stir-crazy, like Rae did, but they still needed exercise.

It was Ean's first time in Level 2. The transition from the Hub to the Level 2 corridor was fascinating; his eyes and even the flex of his feet told him he was walking around a steep curve but the rest of his brain was convinced it was flat.

Level 2 was nice. It was clean, safe and spacious without trying too hard to be upmarket like the Outer Residential Ring.

He quickly found Agent Poe's office, which was located in the complex of rooms that Kip had discovered were paid for by the Navaja clan. They even held the lease.

Ean went from room to room with Leveret Poe trailing behind him. There was a substantial apartment, currently occupied by Leveret Poe, alongside spacious entertainment rooms and Agent Poe's offices. Compared with their tiny unit, it was palatial.

"This will do very nicely," he acknowledged. There would be no problem fitting in the living accommodation for the crew alongside an office and meeting room for Navaja business. There might even be enough space for Agent Poe.

Agent Poe's attitude oscillated between resigned, when he was thinking about losing his home, and grateful, when he remembered that Jax had said he would not publish Kip's forensic analysis of his accounts. There had been, as Kip had suggested, three versions; the ones he had chosen to give Jax, the ones he had sent to Kalakmul and the ones he filed with the Committee in Tarrasade.

There were interesting differences between the versions. For example Agent Poe and his predecessors had made a charge each time they had refused to deal with a communication about the Sphere. This was hidden under 'general expenses' in the version sent to Kalakmul but was specified in the one submitted to the Committee.

Anyone would think not mentioning the Sphere in the information sent to Kalakmul was deliberate.

In Agent Poe's defence, he had only continued the patterns established by his predecessors centuries ago. Also he had not quibbled when Jax pointed out that the Navaja clan paid for the apartment in Level 2 precisely so that Navaja clan members or their guests could be accommodated. Also, Agent Poe understood Tarrasade, which they did not; Ean did not wish to alienate him.

"We won't need all of it," Ean told him.

Agent Poe perked up. "You won't?"

"Are there any restrictions on remodelling or refitting?" Ean asked.

"No, none at all. It is a long term lease," Agent Poe assured him. "Centuries long," he added.

"Let's look over the floor plan," Ean suggested.

They quickly worked out how comfortable quarters for the Willow's crew, an office for Navaja business, a secure meeting room and a modest apartment for Agent Poe could fit into the space.

"There is no entertaining area," Agent Poe pointed out. "Surely that will be needed."

According to Agent Poe's accounts, the formal entertainment rooms were empty except for a handful of days per standard; Kip suspected that Agent Poe offered them as a venue to his other clients in return for a substantial fee.

"Emanuel Rafael Jax Esteban will be expected to receive guests of influence," Agent Poe emphasised.

Ean thought of where they were living at the moment. "Then you will have to hire a suitable venue should the need occur, Agent Poe," he decided. He peered at the arrangement they had agreed upon. "Unless you wish to move out to liberate the required space."

Agent Poe was silent for a moment before replying. "I can think of a number of pleasant and secure venues that would be suitable should the need arise."

Ean smiled at him. "Excellent. Let's talk about fitters. This firm you have suggested seem rather expensive. Do you think we can negotiate a better rate or should we look for an alternative?"

Ean carried the plans back to the unit like a prize. He put them up on the display frame in the sitting room and watched everyone gathering around. Sure enough, they were received with delight.

"When will it be ready?" Jax asked.

"The structural changes will be completed in five days' time," Ean replied. "Agent Poe will be paying out of the Navaja funds Kip located."

Kip had found ten megacredits tucked away in an account; the interest had been paying Agent Poe's salary and other expenses.

It had not escaped Ean's notice that the sum of Agent's Poe salary plus his expenses always totalled a sum that was a few hundred credits short of the interest. In Ean's eyes it was tantamount to robbery; Leveret Poe and his predecessors had been paid more than a hundred thousand credits a standard, sometimes close to two hundred thousand, for doing next to nothing.

"We won't be able to move in immediately," Tre warned. "Making sure everything is secure will take at least another two days."

There was a momentary lull as everyone contemplated another seven days in the tiny unit. Then Rae asked a question about the new gym and Ean could see them deciding to focus on the more promising future rather than the difficult present.

He left the others poring over the plans and went into the kitchen to put the kettle on. Tre followed him, taking advantage of the limited space to press him up against the counter from behind.

Ean decided not to object. Instead he pushed back, evoking a groan of desire from Tre who wrapped his arms around Ean and nuzzled his neck.

"No poking in the kitchen," Ean reminded him. "And distracting me is not going to stop me going to the Sphere this afternoon." He was determined to see the Sphere before they finalised the plan Emanuel Rafael Jax Esteban would present to the Committee. Given that they intended to do that in three days' time, the sooner he did so the better.

"What if I refuse to go with you?" Tre threatened.

Ean twisted away to fill the kettle. "Then I shall go alone."

Tre suppressed a groan, caught between aggression at the thought of Ean in danger and pure, unadulterated desire.

Ean had been amazing since he rejoined the crew. Tre had worried that he would struggle when faced with powerful individuals like Klennethon Darrent or a sophisticated station like Tarrasade. Instead he had faced every setback head on, armed with the information Kip had given him, and one by one they had crumbled in the face of his integrity and patience.

Now, having mastered Agent Poe, Ean's attention had turned to the Sphere.

"You are not going to the Sphere alone," Tre growled.

Ean smiled. "Then come with me."

Tre gave in to the inevitable. "Very well," he conceded. "Do you have a plan?" He reviewed what he knew about the Sphere, which was not much: stay out of Sublevel A and B where the Scavengers lived; avoid Sublevel C because it was full of squatters; the only other people who went there were the Recyclers and the Technicians, who were part of Station Services.

Of course Ean had a plan.

"I thought we would start with the Recyclers," he explained. "They have a permanent facility in the layer above Sublevel A, close to the Hub where the rest of the Sphere shields them from the radiation. I sent them a tape."

Tre agreed; it was the only place to start. "Did they reply?"

"No," Ean admitted. "But if they read it they will know we are coming this afternoon. I am hoping that one of the Recyclers will agree to show us around the Sphere."

Tre was stuck between hoping that they would refuse and fearing that Ean would insist on looking around anyway.

They set off immediately after lunch. Ean chose the ladder rather than the elevator, which was fine. Tre put on his gloves and followed. They climbed down to the Level 2 landing with Ean going first. By the time Tre stepped off the ladder, Ean was heading for the 'Down Fast' ladder that led to the main disc and then on into the Sphere.

"Not that one," Tre warned.

Ean stopped and turned. "Why not? Surely we aren't considered slow."

"Next to the hybrids who specialise in carrying loads up and down the Hub we are," Tre explained. "They are paid per load and they do not like slowing down. You might be able to hang on to the ladder as they go past you but it isn't worth the risk."

Ean nodded and headed for the other door, marked 'Down Slow'.

Things deteriorated as soon as they passed the main disc. The ladder was still structurally sound but the finish on the rungs had worn away; Tre was glad of his gloves. The lighting level was too low; more like station night than station day. Worst, an unpleasant aroma was drifting up from the Sphere, becoming more intense with every downwards step.

As they approached the next landing, the first in the Sphere, Tre spotted a notice on the wall of the shaft.

WARNING

NO ACCESS BEYOND THIS POINT

DO NOT ENTER THE SUBLEVELS

GET OFF THE LADDER AT THE NEXT LANDING

AND TAKE AN UP LADDER BACK TO THE DISC

Ean had stepped off the ladder onto the landing. For a moment Tre thought it might be because of the warning but then he realised that this was where the Recyclers were to be found. Below the large notice was a small sign that read 'Recycling' and an arrow. Ean entered the indicated corridor and Tre followed. It led to a closed door with a shuttered window. Ean had pressed the announcer before Tre could close in behind him.

The shutter slid open immediately revealing closely-spaced bars and a woman's face.

"Yes?"

"My name is Spacer Ean and this is my crewmate Enforcer Tre. We wish to speak with someone. I sent a tape."

The woman looked them up and down. Then she gazed at Tre for a moment with undisguised disapproval before turning to Ean with a relatively neutral expression.

"State your business."

"I do not know if you have heard, but the owner of the Sphere is in Tarrasade," Ean began.

There was definitely a small spark of curiosity in the woman's eyes.

"I am here to investigate the situation within the Sphere on his behalf," Ean continued. "Is there anyone I could speak with who would be able to tell me about the Recyclers and their important work?"

"Wait there," the woman ordered and slammed the shutter closed.

Tre did not say anything; he knew how much Ean detested rudeness. He wondered how long it would be before Ean pressed the announcer again and decided it would be four minutes, possibly five.

The door opened in three and a middle-aged man invited them to enter.

"My name is Chief Recycler Nash. Please follow."

Nash was small, slightly plump and distinctly unhealthy looking. He limped along the corridor towards an open doorway and gestured that they should enter.

Inside was a table with chairs around it. Ean entered, took off his backpack and sat down. Out of habit, Tre waited until Chief Recycler Nash entered to follow.

Ean opened his backpack and reached inside for a lidded plasticard box. Tre recognised the first step in one of Ean's charm offences. Offer them something you think they will appreciate. If you do not know them, fall back on cookies. He slid the box across the table in Nash's direction.

"My name is Spacer Ean. I am queen of the Willow's crew. This is my crewmate Enforcer Tre. Thank you for agreeing to see us. Please accept this small token of appreciation. Perhaps you would like to share them with your fellow Recyclers."

Recycler Nash reached out and lifted the lid of the box, revealing the cookies within. Tre saw his surprise, even though he tried to cover it.

"Thank you, Spacer Ean. I can honestly say that in all my standards of working as a Recycler, no one has ever brought me cookies."

Tre tensed. Was Nash's tone slightly sarcastic? Had be expected a boxful of credits rather than cookies?

Nash smiled, revealing less than perfect teeth. "They smell delicious."

Twenty minutes later half the cookies had gone, they had been offered a mug of something Chief Nash referred to as tea and they had a much better idea of how the system worked.

The Scavengers collected everything the people of Tarrasade discarded. Anything that was put into one of the chutes was theirs. Having sorted the rubbish, they traded it with the Recyclers, who refined it further before selling it on.

"Will it be possible to meet a representative of the Scavengers?" Ean asked.

"No," Nash replied bluntly. "They will not speak or interact with Outsiders." He paused before continuing. "Are you really here from the person who owns the Sphere?"

"Yes," Ean confirmed. "He is too young to visit the Sphere himself. We are representing him. Please understand that he only realised he owned the Sphere a handful of days ago."

Chief Recycler Nash nodded. "The only way to communicate with the Scavengers is through a Discard."

Tre saw Ean tense; he hated even the thought of someone being referred to by such a disparaging term.

"A Discard?" Ean queried.

Recycler Nash put the lid on the box of cookies with obvious reluctance. "I'll show you around the recycling facility. After that you'll be in a better position to understand."

Despite the air scrubbers, which from the sound they were making were working at full capacity, the whole facility stank. Tre wished he was wearing a gasmask and decided to invest in some nose filters before his next visit.

The containers of sorted materials were exactly what he expected.

The bodies were not. However, thinking about it, Tre was not surprised. In a station as large and diverse as Tarrasade there would always be bodies needing disposal.

"We pay well over the odds for complete bodies," Chief Nash explained. "It isn't because they are intrinsically valuable because by the time we get them they've been dead too long for that. It's so that we can monitor and record who has been fed down a chute."

Ean looked as horrified as he doubtlessly was. "Fed down a chute?" he whispered. "Are they alive or dead when that happens?"

"It varies," Chief Nash admitted. "The living ones don't last long. The official line is that they die during their trip down the chute."

"And the unofficial line?" Tre asked.

"We pay for dead bodies, not living ones," Recycler Nash replied.

So the Scavengers killed them.

"And a Discard?" Ean asked.

"A baby who survives the chute. Usually in its mother's womb."

Tre watched Ean's face; disbelief was replaced by horror that then gave way to disgust before his expression settled on determined. Tre had seen that look on Ean's face before and it was not a good sign. The last time had been when he had refused to let Tre fob Noe off on another crew.

Sorting out the Sphere was now about more than getting Jax out of the two point three petacredit debt.

❊ ❊ ❊

Ean felt sick. Then he wanted to scream. What monsters fed heavily pregnant women and babies down disposal chutes?

"The Scavengers raise them but not as one of their own," Chief Recycler Nash told them. "They are raised as Discards. The whole purpose of a Discard is to act as a communication channel with Outsiders. He will never be accepted into Scavenger society. He will never be allowed to marry a Scavenger girl or be a trolley pusher."

Ean wondered what a trolley pusher was but decided it was not the time to ask.

"On the other hand," Chief Recycler Nash continued, "Discards are expected to read and write, which Scavengers are not allowed to do, and they are permitted to use technology. They become Technicians or Recyclers. Occasionally they leave the Sphere completely." He smiled, displaying his yellowed, crooked teeth. "Some of us do rather well."

Chief Recycler Nash had been a Discard? Ean was impressed.

Also, Chief Recycler Nash was open about his origins and proud of what he had achieved, which Ean approved of greatly.

Ean smiled in return. "You must come to Level 2 and meet with the Sphere's owner," he suggested.

Chief Recycler Nash went white, then red, then white again before regaining his previous pallor. Ean checked with Tre. Had he crossed a line he had not known was there?

It did not look like it; there was a trace of a smile around Tre's lips and a twinkle in his eyes.

"He won't want to meet with a Discard like me," Recycler Nash objected.

"Nonsense," Ean declared. "He will be grateful for your expertise."

After that Chief Recycler Nash could not be more helpful, even agreeing to show them Sublevel C. Tre tried to object, suggesting that they leave the tour for their next visit, but Ean was having none of it. They needed to see how bad the situation was before finalising their presentation to the Committee.

As they climbed down the ladder, past Sublevel A and then Sublevel B, the stench became almost unbearable.

"Sublevels A and B are where the Scavengers live and work," Chief Recycler Nash told them when they reached the landing marked 'Sublevel C'. "They used to work in Sublevel A, which is where the chutes end, and live in Sublevel B but with so many areas sealed off because of lack of life support they had to start living in the good parts of Sublevel A. They don't like that. There is vicious competition between the families to live in Sublevel B."

Ean made a note of that; renovating Sublevel B would probably go down well.

"Sublevel C is overcrowded and the gravity's a bit high but the people living here really don't have anywhere else to go. Some try living in the Upper Services, above Sublevel A, despite the radiation. We can't have that because they start disassembling the equipment and trying to sell the parts. Station Security comes down and forces them back into Sublevel C."

Ean didn't have to ask what happened to the people who ended up in Sublevel C. You could tell from the smell. They died; some quickly and some slowly.

It was appalling; by far the worse experience of Ean's life. Sublevel C was filled with the old, the sick and the injured. Almost half the people were hybrids. He saw one dead body and then another. It was hard not to think that they were the lucky ones.

"A group of Scavengers make the rounds at station dawn," Chief Recycler Nash told them. "They take away the bodies."

"We've seen enough," Tre stated firmly. He put his arm around Ean's waist and began guiding him back the way they had come.

Ean did not resist. He felt drained; empty.

Then he heard it; a boy's high, clear voice raised in anger. He twisted out of Tre's grasp and turned to Chief Recycler Nash.

"There are children here?" he demanded.

"Ean," Tre pleaded but Ean warned him with a raised finger

to be silent.

"Not often," Chief Recycler Nash replied. "Most parents have the common sense to give them to someone else or put them in the orphanage before coming here."

"What happens to them?" Ean asked. "After the parents are too weak to look after them?"

Chief Recycler Nash shook his head. "Just because people are dying doesn't make them any nicer than when they were healthy."

Ean followed the sound of the boy's voice. He was attacking an old, tall, one-legged hybrid who was leaning on a crutch and biting into a lump of something that Ean guessed passed as food.

"That was mine!" the boy shouted. "I worked for it."

The hybrid took another bite, ignoring the boy's futile attacks.

"Give it back or else!"

The hybrid stopped chewing long enough to laugh before biting into the lump again.

Then the boy screamed and kicked the hybrid's crutch away.

The hybrid flailed about for a moment before erupting into a maelstrom of fury and lunging at the boy. Clawed hands swiped at where the boy's head would have been if Ean had not dived in and pulled him away. Teeth snapped close enough to Ean's face for him to smell the hybrid's breath.

Ean wrapped his arms around the boy and sheltered him with his body but the second attack did not come. Instead there was the thud of something heavy hitting a wall and a whoosh of expelled breath. Ean risked turning his head and saw the big hybrid pinned to the wall with Tre's forearm across his throat.

The hybrid was bucking and writhing, as if he could not accept that a flimsy-looking purebred was so strong. Tre waited and, after a few more attempts, the hybrid stopped.

"Better," Tre acknowledged. "You are going to accept that what you got was fair payment for what you did. Do you understand me?"

The hybrid managed a small nod.

"If you attack when I release you I will kill you," Tre warned.

Ean turned his attention to the boy; if the hybrid misbehaved he would be dead in seconds, like when the Saber's crew had challenged them.

"What's your name?" he asked.

The boy was staring at Tre, his mouth hanging open.

Ean tried again. "My name is Ean. What is yours?"

"Wes," the boy whispered, still staring at Tre.

Ean turned to the boy and crouched down so that they were face to face. "Wes, I want you to go and pick up the crutch."

The boy looked at him in disbelief.

Ean had no intention of giving in. There were some things you did not do and kicking away a cripple's crutch was one of them.

"Go pick up the crutch," Ean repeated. "What you did was wrong."

"But…" Wes objected.

"The crutch," Ean insisted.

He looked over to Tre and the hybrid. Tre had released his grip and the hybrid was leaning against the wall. He did not look like he would attack.

Wes had retrieved the crutch and brought it back to Ean. Ean thought about forcing Wes to return the crutch and to apologise but the situation was too volatile. Instead he took the crutch from Wes and handed it to Tre, who gave it to the hybrid.

The hybrid stomped away.

"Where are the people who look after you, Wes?" Ean asked.

The boy looked away. "Mama died the day before yesterday."

Sympathy and fury warred for dominance of Ean's emotions. Fury won; it was probably a good thing the woman was dead because if she had been alive, Ean thought he might have strangled her. How dare she bring Wes here rather than leaving him at an orphanage? What kind of mother did that?

Wes could not stay here. If they had not intervened he would he dead already; one blow from the hybrid would have been enough. "Gather up your things," he told the boy.

"Ean!" hissed Tre.

Ean turned on him. "Don't say it," he warned. "I do not want the memory of those words coming out of your mouth."

Tre paused for a moment, obviously rethinking what he had intended to say. "We can't just walk off with a child," he argued.

Ean heard the slight whine in Tre's voice; he had already given in even if he did not want to admit it.

"Yes you can," Chief Recycler Nash encouraged from where he was standing in an alcove. Ean noticed that he had only caught up with them once the altercation had been resolved. "It's the best idea I've heard in a long time."

Wes looked from Chief Recycler Nash to Ean and then to Tre, who pointedly ignored him. For a moment Ean thought Wes might refuse to go with them but then he nodded. "I'll get my stuff," he agreed and dashed off.

Tre's expression was blank. Ean imagined what was going through his mind; despite his certainty that they were doing the right thing, it was all Ean could do not to cringe. He wondered how long it would take before Wes returned.

"We cannot take him back to the unit," Tre stated.

Ean opened his mouth to object.

"No, Ean. He's far too young and, even if he wasn't, it would not be fair on the others. They are barely coping as it is."

Ean knew Tre was right. The unit was tiny. The only reason they were doing as well as they were was because they knew each other well enough to avoid potential flash points.

"We go to the main disc," Tre told him. "We clean him up, get him a decent meal and maybe buy him some stuff. Then we take him to an orphanage, like his mother should have done."

Ean opened his mouth to object but then closed it again. He

imagined turning up at the tiny unit with Wes. Tre was right, it would be a disaster. "Can we at least try to find a decent orphanage?"

Chief Recycler Nash cleared his throat, attracting their attention. Once they looked in his direction he spoke. "The Foundlings' Home does a good job. I get apprentices from them."

Ean shut his eyes for a moment. There were much worse places to be than a good orphanage; he knew that. "That's the plan then," he agreed.

The words were barely out of his mouth when Wes reappeared with a tatty bag. At least it had a strap so that he could sling it across his back.

It smelt even worse than Wes himself, which was an achievement.

Ean crouched down so that their eyes were level. "Wes, for now, we can only take you out of here. The place where Tre and I are staying is only temporary and it is not suitable for a child. We are going to take you to The Foundlings' Home, which Chief Nash here says is a good place. He has known boys who have lived there."

Wes's face fell. "An orphanage? Mama said that orphanages were awful places where they beat the children."

Ean wanted to hug him, but it would only make things worse. "Chief Nash says that The Foundling's Home is a good place," he repeated.

Tre stepped forward. "Let's go, Wes, I'm going to give you a piggyback up the ladder."

Wes's grubby face lit up. "You are? Thank you, Enforcer Tre. That would be awesome."

Ean watched the boy scrambling up onto Tre's back and blinked back tears.

17

Tre barely noticed the boy's weight as he climbed, although he could not ignore the way Wes clung to him. Then there was the stink; Tre was glad that his sense of smell was unenhanced.

Removing Wes from the Sphere had been the inevitable outcome; that had been why Tre had tried to steer Ean away from the sound of the boy's voice. Ean was Ean. The qualities that made him so apt at dealing with Agent Poe and Chief Recycler Nash, the reasons Tre had picked him as queen for the Willow's crew, meant that Ean would never leave a child in a place like that.

Like Nash, Tre could have walked past.

If they had not interfered, Wes would be dead; killed by the hybrid. It would not have been their fault. It would have been the hybrid's fault for not controlling his temper. It would have being Wes's fault for being stupid and kicking the hybrid's crutch away. Mostly it would have been Wes's mother's fault for taking her son to Sublevel C when there had been an alternative.

Even so, now that Wes was a real boy rather than merely a voice Tre felt guilty about wanting to leave him in such an awful place. The least he could do was make Wes feel as positive about the orphanage as possible.

He decided to start by finding out a bit about the boy; a first step to being able to influence him.

"So, Wes, how in Known Space did you and your mother end up in the Sphere?"

"Papa stopped sending credit," Wes admitted.

So there had been a father who had acknowledged Wes and paid to support him. It was a start. "Do you know why he stopped?"

"Mama didn't know." Wes's grip tightened. "She didn't even tell me. One day Principal Cole called me to his office. He told me that he was sorry but I would have to leave. My fees hadn't been paid. He said that he would have preferred Mama to tell me but she refused to communicate with him."

Tre decided not to dwell on Wes's mother's shortcomings as a parent; he was more interested in this Principal Cole. If Wes had been attending a school, it might be an alternative to the orphanage. Sure, there would be fees to pay but they were unlikely to be high. Wes did not strike Tre as a boy who had attended a school for children of wealthy parents. "So you were attending a school?" he queried.

He felt Wes nod. "Yes. Cole's School for Boys. It's in Level 4."

There was regret in Wes's voice; he had liked school, even only if in retrospect. Now what Tre needed was a big slice of luck. "Do any of the children live at the school?" he asked.

"About a third," Wes replied.

Tre thanked the Lady. He almost asked more but decided against it. He did not want to raise Wes's hopes or, more importantly, Ean's. "You were telling me about how you ended up in the Sphere," he encouraged.

The story was one Tre had heard before. Wes's mother had lived her life as if the credit arriving each div from Wes's father was a sure thing. Worse, she had continued to live that life once the supply had dried up.

The debt collectors had taken everything.

Wes did not give many details. Tre filled in the gaps. Instead of working her butt off to support herself and her son, Wes's mother had hidden behind uppers that made the days bearable and downers that let her sleep at night. No longer able to afford an apothecary, she had bought from anyone and, inevitably, poisoned herself taking bad stuff.

On the day they climbed down the ladder to Sublevel C Wes's mother had told him that he was all she had left and she could not bear the thought of life without him.

Tre felt moisture on the back of his neck; a few of Wes's silent tears had found their way under his collar.

Some people did not deserve to have children.

Unbidden, memories of his own mother crept into Tre's mind: the way she had cared for him and his sisters; how hard she had worked to support them after his father had hanged himself; her fight against the inevitability of the obvious solution; her red-rimmed eyes the day he had said goodbye to her.

It was the first time he had thought about her in a long time.

When they reached the main disc, Tre stepped off onto the landing and swung Wes down from his back. Against the cleaner air, the stench coming off Wes was even worse; as they emerged from the Hub every head turned in their direction.

"Operation Clean Up," Ean stated, referring to the procedure they used when one of the crew threw up or, on the odd occasion, ended up bleeding.

"Operation Clean Up," Tre confirmed. "Don't forget the airtight bags." He needed to try to make contact with this Principal Cole. "Then we'll find a Stellar Exchange and I'll contact the unit to tell them we're going to be longer than planned and they should eat without us."

Ean nodded.

Tre held Wes's hand every time Ean went into a shop to buy something. It was partly because he was worried that Wes would make a run for it but mostly so that people associated Wes with him; hopefully they would be too intimidated to make nasty comments.

It was weird to have a child's hand in his.

Once Ean had everything he needed, they ducked into a public convenience to clean Wes up enough to stop the unwanted attention. Tre leaned on the doorjamb at the entrance and suggested that people go elsewhere while Ean stripped Wes, washed him down and rubbed him over with medicated cream. With a few minutes Ean had him dressed in new clothes and was washing his hair.

Tre listened to their interactions and suppressed a smile; Wes was repeatedly objecting about being treated like a baby and Ean was acknowledging his objections whilst continuing to manhandle him.

It was a public convenience; the less time they spent there the better.

The towels and any clothes Wes said he did not want went down the disposal chute. Ean asked him if there was anything he could not do without for a few days and Wes picked out some small items; Tre did not see what. The rest went into airtight bags in Ean's backpack.

Wes was scowling when they emerged.

"That's better," Tre observed.

"I can look after myself," Wes complained.

"Public conveniences are just that; public," Tre reminded him. "We had to be quick. Ean knows how to be quick, you don't. Now we can take you into a shop or into an eatery for a meal."

Wes's eyes widened at the mention of food. Tre remembered that Wes had attacked the hybrid for food and felt guilty about being more concerned about the way the boy smelt than how hungry he was.

He bought a small bag of nut clusters from the next stall they passed and handed it to Wes. He did not check with Ean. Ean would point out that they should wait and make sure Wes had a proper meal.

Sure enough, Ean scowled at him.

They had no problem finding a branch of the Stellar Exchange. Ean and Wes sat in the waiting area while Tre searched for an empty booth within line of sight.

He left the door open so that he could keep an eye on them.

First on his list was speaking with Kip. Sure enough, Kip hijacked the link as soon as Tre contacted the unit and asked for him.

"*You want to know about Cole's School for Boys and The Foundlings' Home?*" he checked.

"Yes," Tre confirmed. "Can you put Cas on while you are doing that?"

By the time he had told Cas that they would not be back for supper, information about the two organisations had started to appear on the display screen. The school was affordable and looked fine. As Tre read, less easily available information appeared. The general opinion was that Principal Cole was a decent man who managed to combine making a living with giving boys a good education.

Opinions of The Foundlings' Home were more mixed. It was strict, which was understandable given the types of children it had to deal with. Some of them were probably feral, like Rae had been.

Tre was not convinced that Wes would respond well to that approach. Wes was more like Obe, who had been traumatised by his three standards in an orphanage before Ean had picked him out to be their cabin boy.

Tre decided to take the plunge and contact Principal Cole.

Contacting the school proved to be easy and, after a brief conversation with an assistant, the principal took the call himself.

Principal Cole was exactly what Tre had expected; elderly but hale with experience and confidence. What he said about Wes fitted with what Tre had seen. Principal Cole confirmed that the only obstacle to Wes rejoining the school was someone paying the fees and that they would make a boarding place available. Faced with the need to make a decision, Tre went for it and undertook to pay a standard's worth of fees in advance; he could always contact Principal Cole again and explain that it had not worked out as expected.

Before breaking the link he even remembered to ask if there was a list of items boarders needed.

Tre headed towards where Ean and Wes were sitting; time to find out if he had read the situation correctly.

Wes jumped up as he approached but sat down again when Tre took a seat. Tre looked the boy in the eyes.

"How would you feel about going back to your old school rather than to the orphanage?" he asked.

Suddenly his arms were full of boy. Wes's arms were around his neck and he was being hugged.

"Yes, please. I would like that so much," Wes declared. Then the hug loosened and Wes stepped back. "I can't. They don't take charity cases."

"I have spoken to Principal Cole and sorted that out," Tre assured him.

This time Tre was ready for the assault. He gave in and hugged back.

❊ ❊ ❊

Ean was stunned but it was a good stunned. Once he was over the shock he was delighted. Not only had Tre managed to find out that Wes had been to a school, he had found out which one and sneaked in a conversation with the principal.

It made up in all ways for him trying to steer Ean away from the sound of Wes's voice.

"I love you," Ean mouthed.

Tre didn't reply but he did smile. He held out the small tablet he carried in the inside breast pocket of his jacket. "This is the list of the things he needs."

Ean wanted to kiss him.

It was a rush but they managed to get the essentials from the list before the shops closed; Ean promised to purchase the rest and have them delivered. Then the three of them had a simple but tasty meal of soup and bread before taking Wes to the school.

According to Tre, Principal Cole had promised to make himself available, even though he would normally be off duty in the evening. Ean saw that as a good sign; he cared enough to put himself out.

The school made a good first impression, from the secure entrance and the nicely decorated lobby to the high, happy-sounding voices that Ean could hear coming from the rooms beyond. As they waited, a door cracked open and a boy peered out at them.

"It's Wes," he whispered excitedly to whoever was behind him. "With two spacers."

"That's Tim," Wes told them. "He's a friend of mine."

The door to the principal's office opened before Ean or Tre could reply. Ean saw the other door shut and the scampering of boys running away.

"Enforcer Tre," the elderly man acknowledged.

"Principal Cole," Tre replied. "This is Spacer Ean. He is queen of my crew."

"Spacer Ean." Principal Cole was relaxed in their presence; Ean wondered how many of the boys had spacer connections. "Please come in. Wes, I want you to wait out here."

"Yes, Principal Cole," Wes replied respectfully.

Tre went straight to the point as soon as they were settled into chairs with the door closed.

"If you have a token reader, I am ready to pay upfront."

Principal Cole frowned slightly. "No rush." He studied Tre for a moment. "I would like to assure you, Enforcer Tre, that if I had known your identity I would have attempted to contact you as soon as Wes's mother stopped paying his fees."

Ean realised that Principal Cole thought that Tre was Wes's father. Perhaps that was common amongst the boys at the school; an absent spacer father and a local mother.

Tre took a little longer to catch on. "No, I am not Wes's father," he insisted. Then he paused as if trying to decide how much to say. "I am merely someone who has taken on his father's financial commitment."

Again, maybe that was not unusual. Principal Cole might think that Wes was Tre's crewmate's child, or even the son of someone Tre had killed.

"I understand," Principal Cole replied in a tone that suggested he was reading far more into Tre's words than was actually there.

After a quick tour of the school they were ready to leave; Wes was already soaking in a bath after being looked over by the school medico.

The school had a medico, which was another promising sign.

"That went well," Ean acknowledged as they walked away. "Wes was pleased to see those other boys and they were pleased to see him."

Tre nodded. "Better than an orphanage where the staff do not know him."

"Much better than that," Ean agreed. He thought of Wes riding Tre's back and holding his hand. Then there was the way he had hugged Tre when Tre told him he could go back to school. "You are Wes's hero," he pointed out.

Tre grimaced. "You saved him, Ean," he objected. "You pulled him out of the hybrid's reach." He paused and then said it. "I would have left him there, Ean. You know that."

Ean appreciated him admitting it. "It's the way Wes sees it that counts. You subdued the hybrid and arranged for him to go back to school. You even bought him nut clusters."

Tre shook his head before pulling Ean close and nuzzled his neck. "Let's go clubbing."

Ean pushed him away but hung onto his arm. The last thing he wanted was to go clubbing. He wanted to go home to his family. "I'm too tired, Tre. It's been a big day." He could see that Tre was disappointed. "Let's have a few drinks in a bar and then go home."

It would have been more than a few drinks but Ean managed to persuade Tre to stop by agreeing to buy a bottle of his favourite whisky. The alcohol, as always, made Tre introspective and morose; Ean could never work out why he liked drinking.

They took the elevator up to the Outer Residential Ring and were soon at the unit. Tre grabbed the bottle of whisky out of Ean's backpack before Ean could take it off and took it into the kitchen.

Ean exchanged looks with Vic, who got Captain Mel out of his room and then followed. Ean saw the three of them lining glasses up along the counter with stools in front, like at a bar.

He sighed as Vic slid the door shut; better Tre drink a third of a bottle rather than the whole of one.

Ean took his backpack to the cupboard that housed the clothes cleaner; maybe if he opened the airtight bags within the machine he could minimise the smell.

"What's that stink?" Cas asked as soon as he opened the first one.

"I'll explain in a minute," Ean replied, keen to get everything washable into the machine as quickly as possible. "Where did we put those odour-absorbing granules? The ones we put in stinky boots?"

Luckily they had a whole tub. Ean started the machine and then added a generous helping of the granules to each of the bags that held items he could not wash.

At least Wes had agreed to him putting most of his clothes down the disposal chute. Except for a few toys, most of the things they were keeping had belonged to Wes's mother.

He could feel Cas's eyes on him, asking why he was washing a woman's belongings.

"Where is everyone?" he asked.

"Jax and Rae are in their den. Kip's trying to pretend his bunk is a simulator. Obe is having his turn in the shower and Noe is sewing."

Ean decided to give Cas the short version of what had happened. After that, hopefully, Obe would be out of the shower and he could wash away the stink of Sublevel C before turning in.

✳ ✳ ✳

Tre woke the next morning with a hangover. Loy had always told him that it was only in his imagination; his nanobots dealt with any side effects of imbibing alcohol.

Thinking about Loy did nothing to improve his headache. Tre rolled out of his bunk and headed for the shower; if there was anyone in there he would have to share. His luck held and it was unoccupied. Tre stood under the less than impressive spray and hoped Ean was too busy to complain about the amount of water he was using.

It was his own fault he felt this way. Ean had allowed him to buy the bottle of whisky on the promise it would last longer than a single evening.

It had been empty before he and Vic had retired to bed.

Jax and Kip were already in the sitting room working on Jax's presentation to the Committee. Ean was in the kitchen so Tre joined him. Ean put a cup of coffee on the counter. Tre lifted a stool off its hook on the wall, unfolded it and sat down.

"Where's everyone else?" he asked.

"The captain took them out," Ean told him. "They are going to the gym, mainly for Rae, and then shopping."

Tre did not like cats or cabin boys going out without him; there was always the possibility of a challenge. At least Jax and Kip, the two high value targets, were still in the unit.

"They will be fine, Tre," Ean assured him. "I made them promise not to leave this disc. Cas and Noe are going to make sure we get everything else on Wes's list." He rubbed Tre's back. "We need time this morning to work up the proposal. The plan is to present it to the rest of the crew this afternoon. Then tomorrow we should arrange a meeting at Agent Poe's offices for a final run through. We could invite Chief Recycler Nash. He or Agent Poe may have some useful comments."

Tre watched Ean making toast. Ean had not mentioned the whisky. Was it better to bring it up or let it pass? In the end he decided better out than in.

"I did mean the whisky to last more than one evening," Tre began.

Ean kissed his cheek. "Vic and the captain both explained that they helped you finish it."

Tre took another sip of coffee; he would have to thank Vic and Mel later.

After he had finished his toast and had another cup of coffee, they joined Kip and Jax in the sitting room. Ean began by giving an edited version of their experience of the Sphere.

Tre watched Kip's face; he obviously knew that Ean was pulling his punches.

"What will happen if we stop the squatters getting to Sublevel C?" Jax asked. If he was affected by what Ean had said he did not show it.

Tre doubted he was. Oro and Mya had raised Jax to be hard; it was a miracle that he cared for anyone.

"They will have to find somewhere else to die," Ean replied.

"Which might be a good thing," Tre admitted. "The current situation suits Station Services because it displaces the problem. If people were begging in the corridors or dying in the plazas they would have to do something about it."

Kip was too quiet.

"Kip?" Tre queried.

"The Committee isn't going to like our plan if it displaces the squatters," he pointed out. "It might be better to manage the problem where it is."

Jax snorted. "Why in Known Space should I let the squatters stay? It's bad enough that the Sphere is full of Scavengers. At least I can get rid of the squatters."

Kip scowled at him. "Because if you don't come up with something that satisfies the Committee they might decide that you have a two point three petacredit debt to work off."

Jax scowled back.

Tre and Ean exchanged looks.

"Let's hear the plan so far," Ean suggested. "Kip's latest proposal," he clarified.

Kip activated a box on the table. It projected a three-dimensional diagram of the Sphere above it. Tre was impressed. He wondered if Kip had bought the projector or made it.

"My proposal is based on a complete renovation of the Sphere," he began. "I believe that the Committee will forgo the fines and the interest, perhaps even delay repayment of the five tera-credits, if they believe Jax is serious about doing this. In its current state, there is a very real possibility that the Sphere will fail and that would mean, at the minimum, completely redesigning the station's waste management systems and then running them without the Scavengers, who are a remarkably cheap solution to the problem."

"How will Jax fund the renovation?" Ean asked.

"Let's leave that for now," Tre suggested; Jax could no more fund the renovation than he could pay the outstanding debt. "Let's hear the rest of Kip's proposal."

It was nice: a segment of the Sphere converted into secure accommodation in return for overhauling the systems and returning the other parts to their original condition.

"I am not sure that taking any of Sublevel B away from the Scavengers is a good idea," Ean warned. "Chief Recycler Nash says that they are very attached to it."

"Only forty-two per cent of Sublevel B is functional at the moment," he replied. "Under this scheme they would have three-quarters."

"Sublevel B is by far the best territory," Jax pointed out. "The gravitational field there is one gee."

Tre liked the idea of having a whole segment; a multi-level block was easier to make secure.

Kip frowned slightly. "Given what Ean told us, I think we should consider offering to lease out Sublevel C to a charity specialising in caring for the destitute."

Tre watched Jax's expression, which was becoming progressively stormier.

"Does such a charity exist?" Ean asked.

"Probably not," Kip admitted. "Creating one would be interesting," he added.

Tre decided to intervene before Jax could say something he would regret.

"Let me summarise," he offered. "The plan is to try to persuade the Committee to forget about the fines and the interest by offering to completely renovate the Sphere. We will try to persuade them to delay payment of the five teracredits of maintenance charges by pointing out that the renovation will proceed much more quickly if those five teracredits are available. If they ask to see the specific plans we point out that they have not been finalised because they need to be negotiated with each interest group, starting with the Scavengers, the Recyclers, Station Services and Station Security. If they ask about the squatters, we will float Kip's idea about the charity, which I believe will be sufficiently novel to impress."

Ean nodded. "That seems clear. Not giving detail unless they demand it is a good idea. I suggest we break into two pairs. Kip and I will work on the presentation while Tre and Jax think things through from a Navaja point of view." He smiled at Kip. "Kip and I will need to be in here with the projector."

Tre could have hugged him; trust Ean to realise that he needed a private word with Jax.

He guided Jax into the crewroom, shutting the door behind them. Then he pointed to a chair. Jax sat on it while Tre found another and placed it so that they were sitting face to face.

"In all but name, the Sphere is Kip's," Tre began.

Jax opened his mouth to object and then shut it again.

"That is the reality of the situation," Tre continued. "He can pay the outstanding maintenance costs and for the renovation. You cannot. However, I don't want you to sell the Sphere to Kip because owning part of Tarrasade gives you influence. Once the outstanding matter of the debt is resolved you will get a representative on the Committee. That will open many doors. Do you understand?"

Jax nodded reluctantly.

"Good. Renovating the Sphere would be popular," Tre informed him. "It would help build you a reputation for being constructive. How is the Navaja clan seen by other spacers?"

Jax looked puzzled by the change in subject. "A Navaja keeps his word," he replied.

Tre just looked at him.

Jax flushed. "Ruthless," he admitted.

"Better," Tre acknowledged. "Now imagine you are known to have renovated the Sphere for no other reason than it was the honourable thing to do. You have done it in a way that is sympathetic to the Scavengers and encourages charities to care for the destitute."

"They would think I was soft," Jax growled.

Despite his colouring, it could be a younger version of Oro sitting there. Tre tried again. "Members of the Navaja clan might think you were soft. Other spacers, spacers like Ean and Captain Mel and Vic, would think more of you than they did of your father or your grandfather."

Jax was silent for a moment. Tre could see him weighing what he wanted to do against what Tre, Kip and Ean were recommending.

"I thought we were renovating the Sphere to get a base for operations," he challenged.

"The need is less acute because we now have access to the accommodation in Level 2," Tre reminded him. "Owning the Sphere gives you influence, Jax. Assuming the outstanding matter is resolved, you will have a representative on the Committee. That will give you a say in how the station is run. Better still those things are yours as an individual rather than as the Navaja clan leader. You may need that. What if you don't regain control of the clan for ten standards? Or twenty? Or fifty?"

Jax's expression was priceless; he had obviously never considered that possibility.

"List the potential benefits of Kip's scheme," Tre ordered. "Start with the one you judge to be most important."

Jax thought for a few minutes before speaking, which was promising. "Not having to pay a two point three petacredit debt," he began. He sighed. "I had decided that it was just a threat, that the Committee would know it was pointless trying to collect, but Kip came up with a scheme for me to earn it within a blink of an eye."

Tre was intrigued. He did not think any of the clan leaders would pay that much for Jax. "Should I ask?"

Jax shuddered. "Porn vids. A series. He constructed a financial model. It looked sound."

Tre shut his eyes to ride out the surge of adrenalin-fuelled fury; only over his dead body, and Rae's, and probably Ean's.

"It helped," Jax admitted. "I must not get complacent or over-confident. Don't be angry," he added. "It's the way Kip's brain works; you ask a question and he comes up with answers."

Tre focused, calming himself so that the anger drained away. His fury had not been directed at Kip or at any individual. It had been triggered by the thought of Jax being harmed.

"Kip is Kip," he agreed. "What about those other benefits?"

"The influence owning part of Tarrasade will bring me," Jax continued. "I wouldn't have put that as high as second but after your explanation I understand better. Third would be having accommodation and facilities in Tarrasade that we own rather than lease. The secure facility Kip has in mind would be great. We would have our own docking bay and enough accommodation to expand."

Tre realised that Jax had particularly liked that part of Kip's plan, which was why he had reacted so badly to the thought of giving Sublevel B entirely over to the Scavengers. "Anything else?" he asked.

Jax considered. "Kip will enjoy doing it," he decided.

Tre thought about it and realised that Kip was not the only one. He could not help but smile. "So will Ean."

18

Kip kept looking towards the closed door to the crewroom. He was pretty sure Tre was telling Jax off. Jax had been in a foul mood all morning. Once he heard that Sublevel B might have to be given over to the Scavengers and that the squatters would probably have to stay in Sublevel C he had started to lose it.

It had been a relief when Ean had suggested Jax and Tre go into the crewroom.

Jax was short tempered most days. Kip sympathised; the unit was far too small and owning a part of Tarrasade was looking like it was more trouble than it was worth. Even so, he wished that Jax could be more grateful for what they had. They were all alive and together. They were in Tarrasade, their space-hopper ship was being built and Jax owned the oldest function-al sphere spacestation in Known Space, even if it didn't work very well.

Kip wanted to revel in the anticipation of what was to come, not spend his time trying not to annoy Jax and failing.

He felt Ean's hand on his arm. "It will be fine, Kip."

As always, that made Kip think about all the ways it might not be fine. "If he has to pay the two point three petacredits, I'll work out a way," he promised. There were other options than the porn vids he had suggested to shock Jax. Jax was the missing heir to one of the five ancient spacer clans. Better still, the Navaja clan had brand recognition utterly sorted; a mere glimpse of the silver-haired version of Jax was enough to know who he was. The merchandising opportunities were too numerous for Kip to have finished listing them.

Ean smiled at him. "I am sure you won't have to, Kip. At worst we'll have to come up with the five teracredits for the maintenance work that has been carried out." He laughed; a soft, gentle sound that Kip had missed when Ean had been absent. "I can't believe I am talking about five teracredits as if it is affordable." He looked at the projection. "Let's carry on deciding what should go into the initial presentation and what would be better held in reserve."

They had cut it down to the barest essentials when the door to the crewroom slid open. Ean went to make tea and Tre followed him into the kitchen. Jax sat down next to Kip.

"Kip?" he queried.

Kip focused. Jax could do that; make him focus just using a single word and his presence. Kip guessed it was a useful quality in a leader.

"I wish I could give you the Sphere," Jax told him. "I shall change my will so that you will get it if I die, I promise."

"You have a will?" Kip queried. He thought about his numerous projects spread across Known Space; maybe he should think about what would happen to them if he was suddenly gone.

"Kip!" Jax called. Once Kip had refocused Jax continued.

"And we should have an agreement that I won't sell to anyone else."

Kip didn't want to own the Sphere, at least not now. A youngster from Darrenden who was unusually good at math but had decided to follow his grandfather into space would not own a chunk of Tarrasade by the time he was sixteen. Jax owning it was fine; he was heir to the Navaja clan leadership.

Even so, he would be cross if Jax sold the Sphere. "Yes, I would like an agreement that you will not sell to anyone else," he confirmed.

"Good, we will do that," Jax confirmed. "And I am fine with any outcome that means I don't have to pay off the two point three petacredits making porn vids. I realise that getting the base in the Sphere is a bonus rather than a prime objective."

What had Tre said? Kip wished he had similar skills for adjusting Jax's point of view.

Jax smiled at him. "Good. Now show me how far we have got with the presentation."

That afternoon they ran through the presentation with the rest of the crew as the audience and it went well. Kip realised that Ean had judged the level of detail perfectly; they were intrigued and had enough information without being overwhelmed. As requested, everyone asked questions from different points of view. Nothing came up that Jax or Ean could not answer.

"Is Kip going to the actual Committee meeting?" the captain asked as soon as they stopped pretending it was a real presentation and started talking about how it could be improved. "Given how well briefed Jax and Ean are, it may not be necessary."

Did the captain think he would make that bad an impression?

Ean smiled reassuringly at him. "The captain does not like the idea of even Jax going. Cats and cabin boys do not speak to outsiders."

Kip had forgotten that. "Jax isn't going," he pointed out. "Emanuel Rafael Jax Esteban is."

"Also Kip's like our secret weapon," Obe declared. "The fewer people who catch on to what he can do the better."

Kip felt himself flush, pleased that Obe had started to think of him as useful rather than just weird.

"Kip?" Jax asked. "Would you mind not going?"

"No, I don't mind," he admitted. He would probably only alienate the members of the Committee. He considered. "I would like to talk with Chief Recycler Nash, if that were possible."

"The Scavenger?" Jax queried.

Ean frowned at him. "Chief Recycler Nash was careful to explain that he is not a Scavenger. However he can communicate with the Scavengers, which is something we will be unable to do."

"The whole scheme will fail if we don't get the Scavengers' cooperation," Kip pointed out. "They've been on strike twice since the main hubs were built. Both times the Committee gave them what they wanted within days but it took divs to sort out the problems the strikes caused."

Ean looked concerned. "You didn't mention that before, Kip," he reproached.

There was so much information in Kip's head; sometimes it

took the right stimulus to bring it out. "Sorry, Ean."

"Well we know now," Ean replied. "I think Kip should come with us tomorrow when we do the run through for Agent Poe and Chief Recycler Nash. Then, if that goes well, we will ask Agent Poe to leave and Kip can ask Chief Recycler Nash questions."

Kip was fine with that.

Before Kip knew it the next morning had arrived and Noe was fussing about how he looked. Kip didn't get it. He was clean and he had put on the clothes Noe had chosen for him. What more was there?

Apparently quite a lot and most of it was to do with his hair, his face and his nails.

"You need to start thinking about getting your knife," Noe announced as he finished brushing Kip's hair and separated a section out for plaiting.

Kip had not been prepared for the sudden change in subject but he went with it.

"Because if you don't you will need a bodyguard and that's like having a flashing sign above your head telling everyone you're important," Noe pointed out.

That was something Kip had never considered.

"Or we could pass you off as the crew's floosie but that would take a lot of work," Noe added. "You aren't very promising floosie material."

No crew run by Ean would ever have a floosie. Anyway, Kip didn't think he could bring himself to tell his Grandpappy that he couldn't make the grade as a spacer.

"How is the training with Tre going?" Noe asked.

There hadn't been much of it lately. "It never goes well," Kip admitted.

"Have you ever watched Ean working out?" Noe asked.

Kip hadn't.

"He's skilled with a knife. Better than anyone else on the crew other than Tre and maybe Rae. You should suggest to Tre that Ean trains you. You would find it a lot easier to learn from Ean and you could practise with me."

It was a really good idea; Kip resolved to do it. "Thanks, Noe."

"Anytime," Noe replied. He tied off the end of the narrow plait, pulled back the rest of Kip's hair and fastened it with a clip. "There. Stand up so I can look at you properly."

Noe made him stand in front of the full length mirror; Kip usually avoided mirrors. The image showed someone who looked like him but rangier and less peculiar looking than he remembered. The jacket Noe had picked out for him, maybe even altered to fit him, made his shoulders look broader and his neck less scrawny. The silver wire woven through the narrow plait drew attention to his hair, which had been brushed until it shone.

"A touch more muscle and you would look just fine," Noe told him. "Obe said your father was handsome. Looking at that…" He pointed at the image in the mirror. "…I can believe it."

It was a bit embarrassing because people kept paying him compliments, which Kip decided meant he usually looked a mess. Ean even insisted on taking some pictures to send to his Ma.

When Jax appeared it was as Emanuel Rafael Jax Esteban. Maybe it was the silver hair and piercing green eyes that made him look so stern but Kip wondered how much of it was subjective; you saw him and you thought Navaja.

At least Jax relaxed enough to hug Rae, whose whiskers were dropping at the thought of being left behind.

Kip carried the satchel, because he was playing the role of Ean's assistant. He walked on Ean's left, like Jax walked beside Tre. They took the elevator, because Tre thought that was more secure, and were soon at the entrance to Level 2.

They were meeting Chief Recycler Nash there, so that they could make sure that the security guards did not give him any hassle.

He was waiting for them; a middle-aged, dumpy man wearing a grey uniform with a shiny metal badge that identified him as a member of Station Services and stars on the collar that indicated managerial or leadership responsibility. Chief Nash had three stars; Kip didn't think that Recycling was a big enough department to have a position that merited four or five.

Ean stepped forward. "Chief Recycler Nash; how nice to see you again. Please accompany us to the room in which we will be meeting and where proper introductions can be made."

Chief Nash nodded and Kip could see that he understood;

having Jax's identity announced in a corridor was not an option.

Even Kip could tell that Agent Poe's receptionist and his secretary as well as Agent Poe himself were stuck between amazed and disgusted to be meeting Chief Recycler Nash in person.

Kip had looked him up. Chief Nash was the highest ranked Discard in Station Services. A Discard might not be a Scavenger but it was too close to one for most people's comfort; he had been raised in a Scavenger household. If they had eaten human flesh it was likely that he had too.

He wouldn't have of course; Scavengers only ate bits of dead people when there was no other option and Kip knew that was true of humans everywhere.

He looked sideways at Jax, who was taking off his cloak. Jax had better not be rude to Chief Nash or Ean would be furious; Jax would be scrubbing heads for eternity.

Ean stepped forward. "Chief Recycler Nash. This is Agent Leveret Poe, who represents Navaja interests in Tarrasade, Kipawa Wheeler, a youngster in our care, and Emanuel Rafael Jax Esteban, the owner of the Sphere."

Agent Poe managed a nod of acknowledgment.

Kip bowed politely. "It is an honour to meet you, Chief Nash."

Jax's bow was midway between Agent Poe's and Kip's. "It is an honour to meet you, Chief Recycler Nash. I thank you for your lifetime service to the Sphere and those living there."

Based on Chief Nash's reaction, Jax wasn't going to be scrubbing heads or at least no more heads than usual. Chief Nash went a bit pink but it was a pleased pink.

One of Agent Poe's staff brought tea and Ean gave her a box of small, melt-in-the-mouth cookies to put on a plate before explaining that they were going to show them the presentation Jax intended to make to the Committee the next day.

That wasn't entirely true; the presentation to the Committee would include more references to the debt while this one concentrated on the Sphere.

Kip placed the projector in the middle of the table, activated it and gave the small, handheld interface he had built to Ean.

Agent Poe was distracted by the projector. Kip could almost hear him wondering from where Jax had obtained it and whether he could afford one. Of course he couldn't, because it was a one-off built by Kip.

It did suggest that it had potential as a product.

Chief Nash wasn't interested in the projector. He was only interested in one thing; the renovation of the Sphere.

"You intend to restore the Sphere to its original condition?" he asked.

Jax almost said yes but he did check with Kip first. Kip moved the middle finger of his left hand; their signal for tread carefully. "Fully functional condition," Jax replied, which was what he had said in the presentation. "The details will need to be negotiated."

At that point Ean decided to intervene by asking Agent Poe if he would mind if they moved to the second stage of the meeting, during which they would discuss the technicalities of the plan with Chief Nash.

Agent Poe was happy to escape.

Once he had gone, Kip switched the projection to show the fine detail of the Sphere in its current state.

"We will be using modern technology to renovate the Sphere," Jax stated. "However, we believe that the Scavengers will want their areas to look and function in the same way as they did in the past."

"You care about the Scavengers?" Chief Nash checked, looking at Jax.

Jax was careful not to lie. "I understand how important the Scavengers are to Tarrasade. I have listened to those who have told me that they want to lead their own lives rather than the lives other people think they should lead."

Chief Nash studied him for a moment before nodding. "That will be a sound basis for negotiation," he confirmed. "Now this new installation you mentioned in passing. Exactly where do you intend putting it?"

Kip raised the little finger of his left hand; the signal they had arranged for when he wanted to get involved. Ean checked with Tre and then nodded. Kip then switched the projected image to show a disembodied segment.

"This is the aim for the new installation," he admitted.

Ean followed up. "I suppose the first question is whether such an installation is even plausible. How will the Scavengers react to other people living in the Sphere?"

Chief Nash considered. "They put up with the Recyclers and the Technicians. They even tolerate the squatters as long as they stay in Sublevel C. They do not see the Sphere as theirs. They see parts of the Sphere as theirs."

It was a hopeful start. "This installation includes part of Sublevel B," Kip pointed out. "Is there anywhere in the Sphere we could locate it that would make that acceptable?" He showed a succession of images that had different shaped segments located in different places in the Sphere. "I have already worked out that these only cut across areas of Sublevel B that are currently sealed off."

"Clever," Chief Nash admitted. "Show me again."

Kip put up each of the options in turn.

"The fourth," Chief Nash decided. Kip selected it. "Now you need to change the shape a bit," Chief Nash explained. "Can you show me Sublevel B in more detail?"

Chief Nash gave very precise instructions as to what part of Sublevel B should be included. When projected out to the shell and in towards the core it produced an irregular but contiguous shape. Kip expanded and neatened up the boundaries on all the other levels while keeping the irregular shape of the Sublevel B layer.

"That's your best chance," Chief Nash informed them.

Kip studied it. It wouldn't have been his first choice. It did not have easy access to the Hub but they could deal with that by building a secure corridor in the Outer Services level or even the Inner Shell. It was also on the sunside, which would mean boosting the shielding if they wanted to use the outer layers of the Sphere.

"Can we ask why?" Ean asked.

"The Scavenger families who occupied those areas are gone," Chief Nash explained. "They died out. If those parts of Sublevel B were available again it wouldn't be clear who should occupy them. The other families would fight over them. It would go on for generations. If you take them, it would avoid all that conflict."

Ean was asking questions about negotiating with the Scavengers but Kip's attention was on the Scavenger families that had not made it.

When Ean had finished Kip asked, "Were all the families that died out located in the area you have specified?"

Chief Nash studied him for a moment and then nodded. "Sunside, furthest from the Hub and none of the chutes deliver to that part of the Sphere. During the bad times, they had it worst and maybe some of the radiation made it down to at least Sublevel A."

Kip resolved to improve the specification for the new shielding.

"So will the person who takes that area be seen by the Scavengers?" Tre asked. "Will they resent him? Or will they appreciate that he only took the part of Sublevel B with no living family to occupy it?"

Chief Nash smiled. "He'll been seen in different ways by different families. Not that the Scavengers would think about him much, because he'll still be an Outsider."

When they got back to the unit Kip sat on his bunk thinking about the changes he would need to make to the plans while Jax described to Rae and the others the start they had made towards finding a solution that the Scavengers could live with.

Noe came over and sat on the edge of his bunk. He didn't ask permission; he never did. Kip changed his goggles to translucent but didn't take them off.

"Did you hang up your jacket?" he asked.

Kip had. He nodded.

"And did you talk to Tre about Ean training you?"

"No chance yet," Kip replied.

"What was Chief Recycler Nash like?" Noe didn't call him 'the Scavenger' or 'the Discard'; Kip liked that.

Kip thought about it. "Clever. Dedicated. I liked him."

"What did he look like?"

"Nothing special," Kip admitted, remembering the dumpy man with his iffy leg and crooked teeth. "I think he is though," he continued. "I think Chief Recycler Nash is exceptional."

Kip decided to talk to Tre because otherwise Noe would keep asking him, probably three times a day, if he had done it. As always, Tre was amused that Kip was seeking him out rather than avoiding him.

The words all tumbled out badly; again something that happened when Kip was talking to Tre about himself rather than a problem that needed solving. Halfway through Tre cottoned on.

"You want Ean to train you instead of me," he checked.

Kip felt himself flush. "Just the knife fighting part," he clarified. He would much prefer Ean to oversee all his training but Ean was too busy and, anyway, it was Tre's job.

"It might work," Tre admitted. He studied Kip. "It's good that you are keen to get your knife."

"I want to be able to tell Grandpappy I did it," Kip admitted.

Tre must have talked to Ean because Ean brought the subject up when Kip was helping him prepare supper that evening.

"I am honoured that you should want me to be your trainer for knife fighting," he began. "I am looking forward to our sessions together."

Kip was relieved; he had been worried that Ean would be too busy.

"I suggest we begin once we move to the new apartment." Ean smiled. "Not too long a wait now, only another five days."

Five more days with everyone falling over each other; Kip told himself they were lucky it wasn't ten or even longer.

"Kip, why are your training sessions with Tre so unsuccessful?" Ean asked.

Like always, Kip's mind was immediately filled with answers. He shifted through them. "Tre frightens me," he admitted. "He's lethal. I can forget that most of the time but not when every word and movement is about combat."

Ean's eyes softened. "Anything else?"

Kip considered. "He forces me to my limits every time. There's all this adrenalin coursing around my body and my brain doesn't work right." He knew he was making it sound as if Tre had been mistreating him when that wasn't the case. "He has helped me deal with crisis situations."

"Yes," Ean acknowledged. "You have come a long way." He rubbed Kip's upper arm. "Look how well you coped when we were attacked. I am so proud of you for that."

Kip felt himself flush.

"I think we'll start by increasing your fitness by another notch and improving your strength," Ean told him. "Then we'll move on to using a knife."

It sounded like Ean was going to be overseeing all his physical training. "Will I be having any sessions with Tre?" he asked cautiously.

"Occasionally," Ean told him. "I shall ask him to concentrate more on fitness rather than combat. Now, what types of exercise do you like best?"

Kip's mind was full of experiences he had hated. He concentrated on the few he had enjoyed. "I like swimming," he admitted. "But not competitively," he added hastily. He could not think of anything else. "Sorry, Ean."

Ean looked defeated for a moment but then his eyes lit up. "You like music, so what about dancing?"

Kip did remember dancing around the house with his Ma when he was little. "Maybe," he admitted cautiously.

"We'll try that then," Ean decided.

The meeting with the Committee was the next morning. Ean, Tre and Jax set off in good time. Kip watched them go, hoping that it would go well.

Rae was sitting in a corner looking small; his ears slightly back and his whiskers drooping. He really hated it when Jax went out without him.

"Come on Rae," the captain called. "I'll take you to the gym. Then you will be back well before Jax returns to tell us what has happened."

Rae jumped to his feet and dashed off, presumably to his den to get his kit.

Kip checked with Cas that there wasn't anything he should be doing and then went to sit on his bunk. First of all he looked to see whether he had a message from Klennethon Darrent. After all, that had been their deal; the crew of the Willow would be ferried around on the Renaissance in return for Kip being in regular contact.

Every three days Kip had composed a message and sent it to the Stellar Exchange as they had agreed; thirteen so far. It was usually a puzzle, a joke or pointing out something interesting he had come across. He had yet to receive a reply and he had assumed that the Dart was travelling a route without gates, never mind light speed data relays.

Today was no different; that mailbox at the Stellar Exchange was empty.

Next he went through the various stock markets and futures exchanges he was using to generate credit. It was much more boring than his other projects but was working; the credit was building up.

He swept five teracredits into a Belmenth account ready for Jax to pay the Committee. Then he checked how his Mulligan drive fund was going. A few of the stocks had done a little worse than he had anticipated but that was easily outweighed by others that were doing better; he had been conservative in his predictions.

Then he scanned the results of his latest batch of searches to see if there were any stocks available that fitted his criteria for short term profit. He picked out five and spread the buying as wide as he could, always buying under different identities and, if possible, spreading the purchases across different markets.

Satisfied that he had dealt with everything that was urgent, Kip went on to the much more intriguing task of working out how Jax could earn two point three petacredits. Even if the Committee decided they would forgo the fines and interest, a couple of petacredits would be a good start for Jax to fund his campaign to regain leadership of the Navaja clan.

Jax could sell the rights to an exclusive interview but Ean would never allow that before Jax was sixteen. Maybe they could take advantage of Jax's low profile by selling the publishing rights to some official images.

Kip imagined Emanuel Rafael Jax Esteban staring out from hordes of pre-adolescent girls' bedroom walls. Yes, that would work and they could follow up with some short vids. That should whet the public's appetite nicely for the interview for when Jax hit sixteen.

He was working through some models, trying to decide whether it was better to create a new public relations company or use an existing one, when Rae returned. He obviously didn't want to be alone because instead of going into his den he came and stood a few paces from Kip's bunk.

Kip removed his goggles and took out his earpieces; Rae didn't come to him for company very often. He gestured that Rae should join him. Rae was there, sitting cross-legged at the foot of Kip's bunk, in the blink of an eye. Kip didn't know what to talk about so he brought out the small prototype of the larger projector that Ean had taken to the meeting.

As he had thought, Rae was content to look through three dimensional diagrams of the proposed renovations to the Sphere and ask the occasional question.

At least he looked less tense than before he had gone to the gym but his ears kept twitching; Kip guessed he was listening for Jax.

So it was no surprise when Rae leapt off the bunk and dashed out of the crewroom. Kip put away the projector and followed.

"How did it go?" Cas asked almost before the outer door of the unit was shut; certainly before Jax had his cloak off.

"Well," Ean replied. "At least it seemed that way from our point of view. They will send us the outcome of their deliberations this afternoon. It will either be their final decision or a request for more information."

Jax headed for his and Rae's den, with Rae ahead of him. "I'll be a few minutes," he called back over his shoulder.

Kip had noticed that Jax always wanted to get rid of Emanuel

Rafael Jax Esteban as quickly as possible.

"We had some unexpected support," Tre told them.

"It turns out that Klennethon Darrent owns Prime," Ean explained.

Prime had been built sixty standards ago; Kip wondered if Klennethon Darrent had been responsible or whether he had bought it more recently.

"Apparently he does not usually attend Committee meetings himself, he sends a representative but he made an exception this time," Tre added. "He asked about you, Kip."

Kip nodded but he was wondering why Klennethon Darrent had not replied to his messages. He flushed. Maybe Klennethon Darrent had read them and laughed at how childish they were.

Jax reappeared as Jax rather than Emanuel Rafael Jax Esteban and the whole crew sat together in the sitting room discussing what had happened at the meeting. Apparently the Committee members had been sceptical at the start. They had thought that Jax's offer to renovate the Sphere was merely a ruse to distract them from the debt.

It was Ean who had convinced them the proposal was genuine; apparently the turning point had been when Ean mentioned that they had visited Sublevel C and that they had already spoken with Chief Recycler Nash about the plan.

Even Tre was hopeful that the Committee's response would be positive.

After lunch it was just a matter of waiting for the Committee's response. Kip went back to sit on his bunk; there was always a new identity to create or a project that needed tweaking.

As soon as he linked to the data streams he saw it; a message from Klennethon Darrent. He opened it tentatively.

We jumped into the Tarrasade system last night. I saw your messages but also the agenda for the Committee meeting. It was more urgent to get to Tarrasade in time to take my representative's place at the meeting than to reply to you. I apologise.

It never occurred to me that you were coming to Tarrasade because Jax owned part of it. It must have been a shock to discover it was the Sphere with all the problems that came with it. Impressive plan for the renovation; I assume it is yours.

I shall now have some lunch and look through your messages before the Committee reconvenes to discuss the proposal. If they decide to insist on payment I am willing to lend you the credit. Not Jax. You may then wish to lend it to him.

I look forward to your next communication.

KD

It was a nice note and after it in the queue of communications awaiting Kip's attention were replies to each of Kip's thirteen messages. Kip was surprised at how much better he felt.

As for Klennethon Darrent's offer, Kip was determined not to borrow credit from the man; he was beholden enough to him already.

Halfway through the afternoon, Kip found his attention wandering. He guessed he was beginning to worry about what the Committee would decide. Maybe Ean had not been as persuasive as Tre and Jax had thought. Perhaps having Klennethon Darrent in favour of the plan would turn the other Committee members against it.

He decided to go and find out what was going on. He found everyone else in the sitting room. Jax had his tablet out on the table, presumably already connected to Emanuel Rafael Jax Esteban's account at the Stellar Exchange.

The Committee had specified this afternoon. Kip's gaze went to the chronometer in the corner of the room; there were only another one hundred and eighteen minutes until station's dusk.

Noe had just finished making another pot of tea and Obe had brought out a pack of cards when the tablet gave a soft ping. Jax snatched it up.

"It's the final decision," he told them. "It is an image of a written document."

"Send it to the display frame," Ean ordered.

All eyes were on the image as it appeared on the wall.

Decision of the Committee for the Efficient Operation of the spacestation Tarrasade

Issue: Inadequate maintenance and outstanding debts

Owner: Emanuel Rafael Jax Esteban

Property: The Sphere

This decision was published on 23,740:06:22

Records in the archives of the Tarrasade Record Office confirm that neither Emanuel Rafael Jax Esteban nor any of the previous thirteen owners received notification of outstanding or occurring debts associated with the ownership of the Sphere. Therefore the fines associated with the currently outstanding debts, as well as the interest associated with those fines, have been nullified.

The charges for maintenance work carried out by Station Services on behalf of Emanuel Rafael Jax Esteban and previous owners for the last 525 standards have been reviewed. It has been decided that Emanuel Rafael Jax Esteban will pay 26.3 million credits towards these costs. This must be paid to Station Services within 5 days. The Committee for the Efficient Operation of the spacestation Tarrasade will bear the balance of the maintenance costs.

The interest owed on these 26.3 million credits, based on a 4.0% annual interest rate, is 1.14 petacredits. Payment of 99.58% of this debt will be delayed for five standards. If the Sphere is fully renovated by Emanuel Rafael Jax Esteban or future owners within these five standards, this delayed debt will be written off.

A sum of 4.9 teracredits, 0.43% of the interest owed, must be paid within 60 days. This will be deposited by the Committee for the Efficient Operation of the spacestation Tarrasade in a specified account and

used as it sees fit to support the renovation of the Sphere.

The decision of the Committee for the Efficient Operation of the spacestation Tarrasade is final. If 26.3 million credits is not paid to Station Services within 5 days and 4.9 teracredits is not paid to the Committee for the Efficient Operation of the spacestation Tarrasade within 60 days, Emanuel Rafael Jax Esteban will be held liable for the previously outstanding debt of 2.3 petacredits.

The numbers had been plucked out of empty space but Jax would have to pay close to five teracredits, which was what they had anticipated. The fact that the Committee were going to use most of this to support the renovation was unexpected and encouraging. Kip was pleased.

He looked towards Jax, who was explaining the Committee's decision to Rae with Noe and Obe listening in to check they had understood what they had read. He was slightly flushed but looked happy. Kip guessed he was relieved.

Ean stood up. "Special supper to celebrate," he announced. "Cas, would you be willing to partner me in the kitchen?"

Cas smiled. "I would be honoured."

Soon the aromas of spicy stew and apple pie filled the unit. Kip's mouth watered in anticipation. For once he didn't want to escape into his virtual world. He was happy here, with his crew, anticipating a tasty meal and an exciting future.

19

Jax looked into the mirror and took a few deep breaths. At least it was him looking back. He was fed up with seeing Emanuel Rafael Jax Esteban's reflection. To make it worse, Obe delighted in showing him objects with Emanuel Rafael Jax Esteban's image emblazoned across them.

Kip had been correct, there was a huge demand. Unfortunately they had not been the only ones to spot the opportunity. Before they could release the official portrait there had been an abundance of others; some of them only bearing a passing resemblance to the reality.

Yesterday Obe had come back from the market with a pair of girl's panties with Emanuel Rafael Jax Esteban's face on each butt cheek; Jax shuddered at the thought of it.

At least the authorised merchandise was also selling well.

He heard one of Rae's interrogative growls from behind him; Jax looked around and up to where Rae was sitting on his bunk. Rae twitched his whiskers, a 'What is wrong?' twitch, and jumped down to stand behind him.

Jax was still unaccustomed to Rae being taller than him; they had both shot up over the last five divs, since they reached Tarrasade, but Rae's had been a hybrid's growth spurt while

Jax's had been a purebred's. Rae was at least a hand's breadth taller than him, possible a hand's length if Jax could bring himself to admit it, and was leggy in a way that would be strange in a purebred but fitted him perfectly.

"No more den after today," Jax admitted. Cats lived in the crewroom.

Rae began massaging his shoulders. Jax relaxed into it. It was one of the things that cats were expected to do, give a good massage. After Cas's lessons Jax was competent, better with feet, but Rae was amazing.

Which was probably a good thing because blow jobs were never going to be Rae's forte; not with those teeth.

Jax's birth anniversary had been five days ago. He had expected it to pass unremarked, as had the previous two, but he couldn't have been more wrong. There had been an avalanche of messages and a mountain of gifts, as well as a worrying number of reports and programmes in the media.

If people had not known that Emanuel Rafael Jax Esteban was in Tarrasade they did now; Jax was looking forward to getting away on the new Willow.

Tre had arranged for the presents to be dealt with by a company that specialised in such things. They would deal with any unpleasant surprises, catalogue the remainder and send on the information for them to look through.

Kip had asked if he could use the messages as a source for his data mining, so at least some good had come of it.

Today marked the point when they stopped being cabin boys and started their lives as cats. Ean had been careful to check with each of them that they wanted a shared celebration rather than separate ones.

Jax had not hesitated and he knew that Rae hadn't either; neither of them liked the idea of leaving the other behind.

"Should go," Rae reminded him.

Jax sighed as Rae's touch softened to one last apologetic stroke.

Jax knew what to expect from when Kip's ears had been pierced. There was a small pile of gifts for Rae and another for him. Jax went first, because he had been recruited a few minutes before Rae. There was lots of discussion of where to put the holes and then Ean carefully marked the place on each earlobe before making the holes with a needle.

It hurt but not as much as Jax had expected.

In went the ears studs that Tre had given him two standards before, even though a simple earring would be more sensible while the holes were still raw. Then there was more kissing and hugging than Jax was comfortable with before it was Rae's turn.

Rae's ear studs were diamond shapes, pointed like his ears, and a glorious shade of buttery gold that matched the sunbursts in his eyes. Jax had commissioned them after finding a similarly shaped pair in silver, although he had pretended that he had merely seen them in the jeweller's catalogue and bought them.

They suited Rae as well as Jax had hoped they would.

The others watched and commented as they opened their presents, which were mostly small items chosen carefully or even made for them: a bed cover; a jacket; a small box for inside their lockboxes; a belt; a comb; a pocket multi-tool. Kip had made them each a tailored pair of his goggles and fitted earpiece.

Ean took lots of images including some of everyone together using the camera's remote control.

Then they moved their stuff into the bunkroom before having the special meal Ean had prepared for them. That was followed by games, music, dancing and singing; not that any of them would have won prizes for their singing voices.

During a lull Ean sent Jax into the kitchen to fetch another jug of fruit punch only for Tre to follow him in, sliding the door shut behind him. Jax had known that someone would speak with him but it was usually a fellow cat so he had been expecting Noe.

Not Kip; Jax smiled at the mere thought of Kip trying to give advice about such things.

"You are going with the captain," Tre told him.

That meant he would be in the relative privacy of the captain's room, which was a relief.

"Here, in Tarrasade, neither Captain Mel nor Vic needs the services of a cat," Tre reminded him.

Jax knew that both of them had arrangements with professional ladies.

"But that won't be true when we are on the new Willow, so it is important that you take this aspect of your duties seriously," Tre continued. "Remember, Captain Mel has been at this a long time. You can learn a lot from him."

Jax wondered if Ean had been worried that he would refuse and that was why he had asked Tre to speak to him. He felt a little disappointed that Ean should doubt him.

"Jax?" Tre hinted.

Jax realised he had said nothing since the door had closed. "I am fine with it," he insisted. "I always understood that it was part of a cat's duty."

He remembered the one-sided conversation with his Papá about life as a spacer. That younger Jax had been determined to fulfil his father's expectations. Now he saw those expectations differently; they had been chisels to carve him into his father's image.

Only that session had been different. When his Papá had spoken about queens and cats his voice had sounded almost wistful. For the first time Jax wondered if his father had been forced to become as he had been. Perhaps there had been generation after generation of boys like Jax who had become men like his father.

"Do you think my father was like me once?" Jax asked before he had considered the consequences of asking such a question.

Tre froze for a moment. Then he sat down at the table and signalled that Jax should sit on one of the other chairs. "Maybe," Tre admitted.

"You never say anything negative about him," Jax observed. "You never mention him at all."

"It is better that you make up your own mind," Tre replied.

Neutrality did not mean support; Jax knew that. Yet his father must have approved of Tre or he would not have chosen him to be his son's protector. Jax reluctantly admitted to himself that it might be time to begin thinking about the motivation behind some of his father's decisions. He had the means, Kip had given him access to the Navaja archive, but after finding out about his half-brothers Jax had stopped browsing the mass of information. Now he only searched for specifics or, more usually, asked Kip to do it for him.

He focused on Tre. What did Jax know about him? The answer was very little about his past other than that he was a cyborg. However Jax had learned a considerable amount about the man Tre had chosen to become and the crew he had decided to build.

"You built this crew for me," Jax pointed out. "You chose Ean."

A fleeting trace of embarrassment crossed Tre's face. "The Navaja heir always joins a Trad crew," he replied.

Jax was not fooled. Yes, the Willow was a Traditional crew but Ean ran it more like a family that specialised in raising boys who had been neglected, like Rae and Obe, or abused, like Cas and Noe, or had exceptional needs, like Kip.

Why had Tre decided that was what Jax needed?

Tre was studying him. "Jax?" he queried again.

Jax wondered whether Tre would answer his questions if he dared pose them. Not really, he decided. Tre's replies would be blocks and parries; maybe counterattacks if Jax's questions managed to hit home.

His father had intended to finish the job his genetic makeup had begun; to carve him into the archetypal Navaja clan leader. It was as if Tre was determined to do the opposite; to allow him to grow into his own shape.

But what was that? Jax realised that he had two standards to find out. Then he would be sixteen and, whether he controlled the Navaja clan or not, he would be its leader.

Each day was a step on that journey.

Each day like today.

Each experience like the one he was about to have.

He smiled at Tre. "I am fine. Today is about understanding what it is to be a spacer."

Tre laid a hand on Jax's shoulder, the gesture Jax knew Tre used to signal unequivocal approval, and nodded.

Kip watched Tre follow Jax into the kitchen and shut the door; time for The Talk. He remembered his disastrous attempt to fulfil that side of a cat's duties and shuddered.

He glanced towards Noe, wondering if he was going to talk to Rae.

Noe sidled up. "Rae would not appreciate it coming from me," he whispered, answering Kip's unspoken question. "Ean spoke with him earlier. He'll be fine as long as he keeps those teeth away from Vic's rod."

Kip still wasn't sure; he didn't want anyone going through what he had. Not that there was any reason to believe that Jax or Rae would fail. Jax was pretty, although Kip had more sense than to say it, and Rae's massages should make up for any issues associated with sharp, pointy teeth.

Noe patted Kip's arm. "Your blowjobs are more than adequate," he assured him.

Kip felt himself flushing. "Noe!" he complained, although, in truth, he was almost as pleased as he was embarrassed.

Since moving into their new accommodation in Level 2, Noe and Ean had been making him into a spacer of an acceptable standard. Just like he had to be able to get into a suit within two minutes he had to be able to fight with a knife, pilot the ship in an emergency and be comfortable with the reality that a spacer crew were intimate with each other.

It helped that he could spend most of his time on stuff that he was good at. He was still data mining across known space, using his plethora of artificial identities along with a growing number of flesh and blood people he paid as agents. The information he had found had led him to a number of intriguing inventions, like the lenses for his goggles. At the moment the most interesting one was a modular system for building spacestations.

He also continued to work on Jax's behalf; collecting intelligence, manipulating public opinion and building a war chest.

However Kip's passion was the Sphere. He delighted in each replacement component located and purchased; every tiny concession wrung from the Scavengers via Chief Nash. The

Technicians had actually started work on renovating the Inner Services and Kip was on the edge of completing the negotiation with Station Services that would mean the company he had identified could begin manufacturing the high-tech shielding he intended to have installed in the Shell.

There was a sharp pain in his ribs. Kip knew what that meant; he had zoned out and Noe had poked him.

"Sorry," he murmured automatically.

"How soon do you think you will get your knife?" Noe asked.

Kip opened his mouth to say that he wasn't good enough but shut it again. He would never be a skilled knife fighter. With Ean, Noe and Tre's help he was approaching adequate. On the other hand, he was only sixteen and that was by no means too old to be a cat; he could afford to shelter under Tre's protection for another standard without it appearing strange.

"No rush," he suggested warily, uncertain of the intent behind Noe's question.

Noe sniffed. "Good."

Kip was confused, which was nothing new when he was trying to divine Noe's motivation. He had thought that Noe wanted him to get his knife. "Why?" he queried, hesitantly.

"While you are a cat you can't meet up with Him," Noe pointed out.

'Him' was Klennethon Darrent. Noe had an unshakeable conviction that Klennethon Darrent was interested in Kip as more than a correspondent. He oscillated between casting Kip as a surrogate son or potential lover.

Kip privately agreed that Klennethon Darrent had an agenda. However, Kip was pretty sure it was about him being a typed-seven; Klennethon Darrent did not do emotions.

Whatever Klennethon Darrent's motivation, Kip wasn't sorry that he had agreed to their correspondence; exploring Klennethon Darrent's communication had become one of the highlights of his day. He began planning what he would include with his next reply; it was always a challenge to come up with something original.

There was another jab between his ribs. Kip wondered how long he had been out of it. Tre was sitting next to Ean; there was no sign of Jax and the captain or Rae and Vic.

"Sorry," Kip mumbled again.

"You are even worse than usual," Noe complained. "I asked if you were looking forward to being on the Salix."

The Salix was the cover identity for the new Willow. Apparently there had been three previous occasions in the Willow's long history when such subterfuge had been employed. It was acceptable provided it was done out of necessity and not to avoid debt or for any other dishonourable purpose.

Kip thought about Noe's question. On balance the answer was no. Even the excitement of travelling on a spacehopper ship wouldn't compensate for being away from the Sphere. Using routes without gates would only make it worse; no gates meant no light speed data relays so he would be out of touch. "It will be interesting," he replied.

"You hate the idea," Noe observed.

Kip felt himself flush. "We must become accustomed to the

new ship. Many probable future scenarios required us to be mobile at one time or another."

Noe grabbed his hand and stood up.

"Kip and I will finish up in the kitchen," he volunteered.

Ean disentangled himself from Tre. "Thank you. That would be most appreciated."

Kip watched Noe slide the door closed behind them. He wondered if that was to give them privacy in the kitchen or to make Ean and Tre or Cas and Obe more comfortable about making out on the couches of the shared area.

Not that Cas and Obe ever felt inhibited by an audience.

There wasn't much to do; most of it had been done as they went along.

"Time for a lesson in the art of petting," Noe announced as he shook out and hung up the cloth he had used to polish dry the cups. "I want you to pretend that I am a youngster that you are trying to seduce. You know; someone young, cute and naïve."

Kip knew that there was no getting out of it so he went with it. "You are young and cute," he replied.

Noe sighed. "Try again."

Kip trawled through the storyvids he had seen and the books he had read; trouble was, he had always been more interested in adventure than romance. He stepped closer to Noe. "Hold still, you have something in your hair." He gently ran a strand of Noe's hair between his index finger and thumb. "There.

Gone," he declared. He decided to risk a follow up. "You have such pretty hair."

"Better," Noe acknowledged. "Lower your voice and make it more whispery."

Kip tried again. "You have such pretty hair."

"Much better," Noe encouraged. "Your voice has an attractive tone. Let's imagine he thinks you are nice and is interested." He looked up shyly through his eyelashes and blushed. "Do you really think so?" he asked.

To Kip's surprise his rod twitched. He had not known he would find someone younger and more innocent than him attractive, especially as it was only Noe and they were just pretending.

"Stay with it, Kip," Noe ordered.

Kip managed to grasp the moment before it slipped away completely. He focused on Noe's hair. "Some of the hairs are like spun gold," he whispered.

"Are they?" Noe replied; all eyes and lips.

Kip recognised that it was an invitation but had no idea what to do.

"Hands," Noe instructed. "One either side. Start on the shoulders and begin sliding them down my back, fingertips first. Stop if I tense up."

Kip wonder when he should stop if Noe stayed relaxed but Noe went rigid as soon as Kip's leading fingertip strayed past his waist.

"Now, how are you going to get him to feel comfortable again?"

Noe asked.

Kip's mind went into overdrive; his reflex response when asked to tackle a problem. Various solutions were considered and tossed aside. Only one line of thought seemed promising; reasons for having your hands around someone's waist other than those hands being on their way to grope his butt.

He settled his hands around Noe's waist and started to hum. Then, gradually, he turned into the first step of a slow dance, drawing Noe with him.

Noe only hesitated for a brief moment and then went with it. His hands went up and rested on Kip's shoulders with his forearms against Kip's chest. "Creative," he acknowledged. "Nice. What next?"

"Play it by ear?" Kip suggested. "You are pushing me away at the moment. Does that change? Does he start joining in the humming?"

"And if he doesn't?" Noe asked.

Kip knew the answer to that. "Finish the dance, thank him for it and step away."

"And?" Noe challenged.

"Suggest we do something together than we both enjoy but doesn't involve touching?" Kip proposed.

Noe sighed. "It'll take you divs to get into his pants that way."

Kip shrugged. "Better than being where I'm not wanted."

Noe nodded but Kip was not sure if he was agreeing or merely acknowledging Kip's point of view. He decided that it did not matter, particularly as Noe started to hum. Slowly, as they danced around the kitchen, Noe's forearms moved from against Kip's chest to his upper arms, allowing Kip to gradually pull him closer.

"Next?" Noe queried.

Kip considered. He could try allowing his hands to stray downwards but it seemed too pushy.

"What might he be comfortable with?" Noe hinted.

"A kiss?" Kip suggested hesitantly. He liked most types of kissing; it was only the exchanging spit kind he wasn't sure about.

The way Noe's eyes widened and his head tipped back slightly confirmed that he was on the right track.

Kissing someone so much shorter than him could be awkward, so Kip decided to make Noe taller by boosting him up to sit on the counter.

"Lifting him up is good," Noe confirmed from his perch. "You should have picked the table."

Kip stopped on his way in to claim a small kiss. "Why?"

"Now I am taller than you, which may change the dynamic. He liked looking up to you. He might not like this as much," Noe replied.

Or he might like it just fine, Kip argued in his head but didn't say it.

"And this counter won't work as well as the table for fucking," Noe informed him. "The height's wrong for you and it's either too deep or not deep enough depending on the position."

Kip was halfway across the room by the time Noe could jump down from the counter, take a few steps and snag his shirt.

"Stop!" he ordered.

Kip reluctantly did so. "I'm not going to fuck you, Noe. Not before Ean says you are old enough."

Noe moved so he was in Kip's path. "I wasn't asking you to," he replied. "It was hypothetical."

"It's never that straightforward with you, Noe," Kip reminded him. "I may be naïve but I'm not stupid."

"You're upset," Noe observed.

All Kip wanted to do was escape into one of the simulators. Given that he couldn't do that, because he had promised Ean he would only use them during the day, he would settle for being in his bunk with his goggles and earpieces.

"Kip?" Noe pressed.

"I don't like it when you play me," Kip admitted. "It makes me think our friendship isn't real and I hate even thinking that."

Noe paled. His lips thinned and his eyes hardened. Kip's gut twisted. He wished he had kept his mouth shut. Maybe their friendship wasn't real. Kip knew how emotionally immature and needy he was; he could have imagined it.

Or it could be real to Noe as well and Kip questioning it could have hurt.

"Wondering if our friendship is real hurts because it is important to me," Kip tried. "Noe, help me out here. I am crap at this type of thing."

Noe's eyes softened. "What makes you think I understand friendship?"

Kip didn't know what to say so, instead, he stepped forward and engulfed Noe in a hug. After all, it worked for Ean.

For a moment Kip thought he had failed but then Noe relaxed and hugged back.

Rae waited until Vic stopped making appreciative murmurs and drifted off to sleep. Then he slipped away from Vic's bunk and moved silently towards the alcove where he and Jax would be living. Jax wasn't there yet; Rae would be able to hear and smell him.

He stopped and listened, trying to detect any suggestion of how Jax was doing in the captain's room. Unfortunately Cas and Obe were being particularly vocal in the shared area and when he tried to hear past that all he could find were Ean and Tre in the bathroom and Noe and Kip in the kitchen.

Rae told himself he would hear something if Jax was distressed and continued on his way.

They may no longer have a door but by tucking their bunks into an alcove, Ean had managed to come up with a way of integrating them into the crewroom without taking away their den completely. Moving all their stuff, including the mattresses, meant that it even smelt right. Rae listened for Jax again and then risked lying face down on the lower bunk, inhaling Jax's scent. He wanted to crawl under the covers and curl up but he didn't.

Jax might not like it.

Instead he changed into his sleep shorts, climbed up to his own bunk, sat cross-legged and waited.

He had been worried about being a cat, mostly because of the pointy teeth issue, but it had been easy. The massage-stuff helped, especially as Rae liked doing it almost as much as people liked him doing it to them. Giving his crewmates pleasure, feeling tense muscles relax under his hands, was nice.

Giving Jax massages was awesome.

Things had been much better since they moved from the tiny unit to the new apartment. The living accommodation in the apartment was about the same size as crewroom level on the Willow plus they had a gym and many more simulators.

The simulators were so they could pretend to be on the new Willow; the Salix. Other than Kip, who could navigate any ship, even a spacehopper, without having to think hard, everyone else had to learn lots of new skills. Rae had wondered if old people, like the captain and Vic, had enough space in their heads for lots of new skills but it hadn't been a problem. They learned a lot quicker than Obe or Cas.

Maybe that was because Cas and Obe spent so much time thinking about sex. Rae could tell from the way they smelt.

One of the new simulators was just for Rae. Kip had built two copies, one for here and one for the new ship. The novel part was the interface between Rae and the controls. Unlike simulators built for purebreds, it allowed Rae to use his phenomenally short reaction time, his speed and his strength. It was also properly adapted to how he saw and heard.

Rae wasn't sure if he liked it better when he used it to control the guns or when he piloted the ship.

His job was gunner. That was because no one could come close to his level of skill, not even Tre, while lots of people could pilot the ship just fine.

Rae liked it best when they were doing a battle sim with him on the guns and Jax piloting the ship. Jax understood best what Rae could do and never hesitated to take both the ship and Rae to their limits.

He was looking forward to trying it with the ship herself rather than a simulation.

The captain's door opened and closed; Rae picked out the soft sound of Jax's footsteps crossing the shared area and entering the crewroom. Instead of continuing towards their new den, Rae heard him detour into one of the showers.

Rae's gaze went to where Jax's washbag and robe were hanging from pegs. It wasn't like Jax to go into the shower without them;

he was fussy about stuff like that. For a moment Rae considered taking them to him but quickly decided that Jax would not like it. Instead he listened intently, straining to analyse the sound of Jax's breathing beneath that of the shower.

He didn't seem too upset.

The sound of the shower was replaced by blowers, which went on longer than usual. Once they had stopped, Rae lay back on his bunk; he didn't want it to look like he had been anxious.

Jax was wearing just a towel wrapped around his hips and his hair had dried fluffy because of the blowers. He was carrying his clothes and shoes.

Rae looked at him and twitched his whiskers.

"I'm fine," Jax whispered but he didn't look fine or sound fine or smell fine. He pulled on a clean pair of sleep shorts. Rae watched as he dug out a top to wear; another sign that he was feeling insecure. The towel was hung from a peg to dry, the clothes that needed washing were placed in the hamper and everything else was put in its proper place. "You?" Jax queried.

Rae always felt a little guilty about doing what he was about to do. He justified it by telling himself that Jax needed comfort but hated admitting it. He widened his eyes and dropped his whiskers. "Fine," he replied.

At first Rae thought it had not worked. Jax had climbed into his bunk and was closing the drapes. Having drapes was new; they hadn't needed them when they had lived in a separate room.

Rae followed Jax's example.

"You coming down then?" Jax asked.

The drapes for the top bunk were suspended from the ceiling and continued past the end of their bunks to the wall. Rae could climb down at the foot of their bunks without disturbing them.

He crouched at the end of Jax's bunk, watching for the signal that would indicate what type of contact, if any, would be happening.

Jax folded back the cover to make an opening at the wall side. Rae was quick to accept the invitation.

He loved this, being cuddled up against Jax's back with his knees tucked into the bend in Jax's legs. He preferred it if Jax was not wearing a top but he wasn't going to let a thin layer of fabric taint his enjoyment.

Later, when Jax went to sleep, he would snake an arm around Jax's waist and pull him close.

Jax liked that; Rae could tell from the little sigh he gave as his body relaxed into Rae's embrace.

20

Tre was concentrating on staying out of the way while Ean directed the packing. The trick was to look serious and occupied or Ean would focus on the fact that he was not doing anything particularly useful.

Living in two different places was new and therefore, at least for the time being, a challenge. Ean had to decide what objects would remain in the Level 2 apartment in Tarrasade or on the Salix and which would be transported from one to the other. To make it worse, they were travelling to the Salix on the Renaissance and, at least in Ean's opinion, there was a limit to the amount of luggage guests should bring with them.

It did not help that Ean was so frugal; having supplies and resources merely waiting for their return went against his grain.

If asked, Tre would have said that they were taking too much, not because the captain of the Renaissance would resent a few extra packing cases but because it would be better if both apartment and ship were set up ready for occupation. However, he had not been asked and there were, at the last count, fifteen packing cases in the shared area.

Ean was still toying with the idea of them taking them to the Renaissance themselves rather than using a courier. Even the captain had struggled to keep his mouth shut at the thought of that but somehow he had managed it.

There were some things Ean had to learn through experience.

Tre decided to drift from the crewroom to the kitchen in order to avoid the shifting focus of Ean's attention, only to be intercepted by Kip.

"There may be a problem," Kip stated.

It was not a phrase one spoke in Ean's earshot, at least not today. Tre placed a hand in the small of Kip's back, steered him through the nearest doorway, which happened to be into the bathroom, and shut the door. "What?" he asked.

"Those three Navaja ships," Kip replied. "They are definitely on their way here." He held out a pair of goggles. A cable snaked from them to an interface that Kip was carrying in one of his pockets.

Tre reluctantly took them; he much preferred using one of the 3D projectors or even a simulator. Putting them on, he was immediately confronted with one of Kip's ribbon diagrams. This one showed a topological summary of the three ships' known locations over the last three standards.

He was already familiar with most of it. Kip had an in-depth analysis of every Navaja ship. This trio, the Quetzal, the Cenzontle and the Tecolote, had a long-standing alliance. They had been avoiding contact with other Navaja crews or Navaja bases since Oro had died. The new part was them coming together in a system only two jumps away, suggesting that they were going to jump into the Tarrasade system together.

"Overlaying how the news of Jax being in Tarrasade has travelled is informative," Kip added.

It was obvious that the three ships had changed course as soon as they had confirmation of Jax's location. Tre removed the goggles and handed them back to Kip.

"If we could bring forward our departure by two days we could avoid them," Kip pointed out. "They would contact Agent Poe who would tell them that Emanuel Rafael Jax Esteban is away from Tarrasade at this time."

Tre imagined the conversation with Ean and dismissed the possibility. "It would be impolite to ask the Renaissance to alter its schedule," he replied.

"We could get Agent Poe to lie," Kip added. "He'd have no problem with that."

Tre did; Jax would need the loyalty of the Navaja crews and being deceitful was not a good way to start. "I shall propose to Jax that we should try for a carefully managed interaction scheduled for shortly before the Renaissance's departure. What can you put together about the three crews?"

Kip's gaze unfocused and refocused before he replied. "Lots. Probably too much. I need to develop and refine a profiling interface for Jax to use."

"At the moment you need to be doing whatever Ean is telling you to do," Tre reminded him. "Not a word about this until I have spoken to Jax and then to Ean."

He managed to catch Jax when he was sent to fold laundry. Tre watched, fascinated, as each garment, whatever its shape, was transformed into the same perfect rectangle.

It was not something Tre could imagine Oro doing, even as a cat. Every one of Oro's actions had been about communicating who he was and what he wanted. Perfectionism that bordered on being prissy did not fit with the image of a ruthless Navaja warrior.

Clothes-folding proved to be a useful way to monitor Jax's disquiet; when Tre told him about the ships Jax had to refold the same shirt three times and did not start on another.

"Will they want to swear to me?" he asked in a flat voice that confirmed he was anxious.

It was not the question Tre had anticipated. It made him realise that he was focused much more on Jax's survival rather than his claim to the clan leadership. "I do not know," he admitted. "They cannot swear to you until you are sixteen. They could make a public expression of intent."

"And if they do that? What do you think my uncle will do?" Jax's gaze was direct and his tone slightly more assertive; Tre braced himself for an interrogation. Jax often wanted answers Tre was either unable or unwilling to give.

The official line coming out of Kalakmul remained the same. Joaquin Oro Sebastiano Socorro had died unexpectedly, Emanuel Rafael Jax Esteban had been kidnapped and Jose Eduardo Gil Vega was interim leader. How long that situation was tenable given that Emanuel Rafael Jax Esteban was living openly in Tarrasade was questionable. Tre settled for shaking his head.

"Could they be bringing a message from my uncle?" Jax queried.

At least Tre had an answer to that. "Unlikely. Kip has been tracking them, as he has all the Navaja crews. These three have been avoiding contact with your uncle or his chains of command."

"Were they strong supporters of my father?" Jax asked.

"All Navaja crews were loyal to your father," Tre replied; Oro had made sure of that.

Jax was not content to settle for such a generic answer. Tre was not surprised when he tried again. "What types of crews are they? Did they participate in leading-edge initiatives?"

It was a good question. There were strings of systems where the Navaja clan owned all the planets and all the gates. Many, most, Navaja crews stayed in Navaja space where lower gate fees and taxes gave them an advantage over any foreign competition.

Some crews went further afield. They operated in other clans' space or the non-aligned systems between. Some were there because the risks and therefore the potential gains were greater. Others were working directly or indirectly for the clan leader, focused on expanding Navaja territory rather than acquiring wealth or merely living as spacers.

Jax's great-grandfather had coined the term 'leading edge initiative'. It was more palatable that 'anything goes as long as it isn't against a Navaja crew and isn't technically piracy'.

"Kip is preparing a briefing," Tre replied. "My recommendation based on what we know so far is that Emanuel Rafael Jax Esteban meets with the captains of the three crews here in Tarrasade and that we then leave on the Salix as planned."

Jax looked at him. "You will tell Ean."

Tre sighed. "Yes, I will tell Ean."

Tre made Ean tea. As soon as Ean saw the tray he realised something was amiss.

"What is it?" he asked, sitting down at the table.

Tre shut the door between the shared area and the kitchen. "Three Navaja ships, on their way here and due to arrive before we leave," he admitted.

For a split moment Tre thought Ean would accuse him of producing three Navaja crews just to make his life more difficult. Then Ean sighed. "They are a long way from Navaja territory. Do we have any idea of their intentions? Are you sure they aren't coming to challenge for Jax?"

"I am not sure about anything," Tre admitted. "I do know that it may be prudent to leave immediately after the meeting."

Ean frowned and then he nodded. "We will be ready."

Having another commitment, particularly one with risk associated with it, helped. Decisions that Ean would have mulled over or debated were taken quickly. Within a remarkably short time the packing was complete as far as was possible and those containers yet to be sealed had lists of what was to be added taped to their lids. Better still, the courier had been booked for the afternoon before their planned departure.

Tre had only asked Ean for Jax and Kip but Jax wanted Rae to be present and Ean did not quibble for a moment about releasing him. They used the small room that had been set aside for Jax to use for Navaja business and, as usual, Kip was there in advance to prepare.

Tre followed Jax and Rae in, wondering why he had not asked for Rae when he had known that Jax would want him there. It was probably a symptom of the age-old dilemma; caring made a person vulnerable but a person who did not care was stunted; barely human. Tre wanted Jax to be more than his father and grandfather but part of him understood why Mya and Oro had wanted him to be so hard.

Jax cared very deeply about Rae; if anything happened to Rae, Jax would be devastated.

When thinking about Rae, Tre always felt that the truth was slightly beyond his reach. He had decided to concentrate on training Rae as Jax's bodyguard. A perfect bodyguard was phenomenally skilled, completely loyal and utterly incorruptible. Rae was certainly shaping up to be all those things. On the other hand, the perfect bodyguard was disposable, which Rae was definitely not, and almost invisible.

Rae would have never faded into the background, his hybrid nature precluded that, but he was maturing into a surprisingly beautiful adolescent. Much of it was in the way he moved, which was mesmerising, but there was something about those lengthy, lithe limbs; particularly when you knew how fast they could move and the force with which they could strike. His skin looked sun-kissed and his previously mousy head fur was a fascinating mixture of gleaming autumn colours.

As for his eyes, Tre was sure they had been a uniform, velvety brown when they recruited him. Now the irises had radiating streaks of gold that almost glittered.

Then Kip projected images of the senior members of each of the three crews and all thoughts of how much Rae had changed vanished. Not only did he recognise four of them but at least two of them would recognise him.

Or rather they would see him and recognise Alejandro Reyes.

For a split moment he clung to the hope that they were not the captains but he knew how unlikely that was and Kip quickly identified Yoet Nunez as captain of the Cenzontle and Ozkr Soto as captain of the Quetzal.

Tre had known this moment was coming; it had been inevitable. He had been lucky to avoid it after his meeting with Nevin Edger.

Not for the first time, he wished that Oro had ordered his appearance changed when he had been made over into a cyborg. Of course Oro had not, because that would have lessened the message.

Joaquin Oro Sebastiano Socorro would do anything to anyone.

He waited until Kip paused for breath and turned to Jax. "I need to speak with you alone."

Jax frowned. "Is it something that Rae and Kip will have to know?" he asked.

The information would spread, as had the news of Jax's location. There was also a strong possibility that Kip knew, even if he did not understand its significance or implication. "I am giving you the option of deciding what and when to tell them."

Jax considered. "I would prefer Rae and Kip to be present, unless you strongly recommend against it."

Tre spoke slowly, choosing his words carefully and measuring their impact. "When a person joins the Navaja clan he leads the life the clan leader chooses for him. He becomes the person the clan leader decides he should be."

Kip was studying him. Rae was very still. Jax had paled.

"I have been the person I was before I joined the clan. Since then I have been three others, two sworn to Joaquin Oro Sebastiano Socorro and one, Enforcer Tre, whose loyalty is only to you." He held Jax's gaze.

Jax gave a small bow of acknowledgement.

"Two of these captains knew me as one of those other identities," Tre continued. "The first I held as a member of the Navaja clan."

"Do they know you became this other person?" Kip asked. "Or Enforcer Tre?"

"No," Tre replied. "That person, the one they knew, was declared dead."

"They will recognise you?" Jax checked.

"Nevin Edger did," Tre admitted.

"You were famous," Kip stated.

Tre had stopped asking how Kip did it. Given the correct stimulus, Kip's mind could crystallise a myriad of seemingly unrelated facts into a perfectly formed deduction.

He said it quickly before Kip could work it out. "I was Alejandro Reyes."

Jax's eyes widened and his mouth formed a near perfect circle as his jaw sagged. Then he went pink and looked excited for all of a second before the colour drained from his face and he stared at Tre in horror.

Then he ran; the door barely managed to open enough to let him leave and it sounded like he made it to the nearest head before throwing up.

It reminded Tre of Gil's reaction when Oro had ordered the cyborg to remove its mask.

Better it be now than during their meeting with the captains.

Rae was out of his chair but had yet to follow Jax; Tre could imagine him wondering if Jax would want him there or would prefer to pretend that his reaction had been less extreme. Kip looked blank, which meant the exact opposite; his mind was working so fast that there was no capacity to spare for expressions.

"Go," Tre encouraged Rae. "If you get the chance, tell him that we will reconvene as soon as he is ready."

Rae shot out the door. Before it closed, Tre saw him slow and creep along the corridor in Jax's direction.

He had decided to go and check on Ean, in case he had heard Jax throwing up, but Kip's next words stopped him.

"You are a cyborg."

Tre had thought that Kip already knew. "Yes. Have you a problem with that?"

Kip shook his head. "No. It's amazing." He hesitated and then asked. "May I have your permission to look through the medical records in the archive, the ones that relate to your conversion?"

Tre almost said no but then he remembered that he no longer had Loy. If anyone could understand what had been done to him, it would be Kip.

"Yes, but it is not a priority at this time," he replied.

"Does Ean know?" Kip asked.

Tre felt himself smile. "Yes, Ean knows. Loy told him. And Nevin Edger told Ean that I had been Alejandro Reyes. Not that the name meant anything to him."

Kip's gaze went distant and then refocused. "I don't understand why he took the risk of making you Jax's protector."

'He' was obviously Oro.

Kip was not the only one who had wondered about that. While it had got rid of Tre in a way nothing else had, not even 'converting' him into a cyborg, it had released him from his otherwise inescapable loyalty to Oro. It had opened the door to a future where Tre, where Alejandro Reyes, might turn against Joaquin Oro Sebastiano Socorro.

Tre had decided that, for once, in a rare moment of parental love, Oro had put Jax's welfare before his own. "I was, by far, the best choice," he replied.

Kip frowned and opened his mouth, obviously going to argue, when the door slid open and Jax entered with Rae behind him. If Tre had not heard him vomiting, it would have been impossible to know that his reaction had been so extreme. Tre was impressed by his recovery.

"I apologise for my weakness," Jax stated in a matter of fact tone and sat down at the table. "Kip was briefing us about the

Navaja crews."

Kip started with the Quetzal. Her crew was large, seventeen total, and Kip had images of fourteen of them; everyone except the youngest three, including the two cats.

Tre recognised three, the captain, the most senior of the three enforcers and the more senior of the two gunners. He remembered the enforcer, Carlos Perez, being a rising young star who had matured into an exceptional spacer.

He was surprised that Carlos Perez was still merely an enforcer in such a conventional crew; Tre would have expected him to be at least the captain of a crew involved in leading edge activities.

"They appear to be an exemplary crew run on Traditional lines," Kip told them. "Their rep is impeccable. Until the coup, they traded along slightly more risky routes usually within Navaja territory but occasionally going beyond. They have been operating a trio with the other two ships for over a decade."

Kip briefly displayed the other two crews, both of which were smaller than that of the Quetzal. Tre recognised the captain of the Cenzontle, Yoet Nunez, but no one else. Again, there were no images of the cats or of more junior members of the crews. Then Kip changed the display to show the ribbon diagrams he had shown Tre earlier in the day.

"They moved away from Navaja space pretty much as soon as they received news of Joaquin Oro Sebastiano Socorro's death. It looks like they have been avoiding Navaja crews ever since."

"And they turned for Tarrasade as soon as they knew I was here," Jax added.

"Yes," Kip confirmed.

They decided that Jax would need to be Emanuel Rafael Jax Esteban from the morning of the next day until shortly before they left on the Renaissance; that way he would be available to respond to any incoming communications. Then they spent the rest of the time before supper setting up a communications desk, like the one on the Renaissance.

It was something they had been planning to do but, until now, it had not been a priority. With Vic's help, Tre hung and connected a huge display frame on one of the walls while Rae assembled the desk and Kip sorted out the lighting, cameras, microphones and projector.

The idea behind the display frame was to provide a suitable background. Jax went through a number of alternatives and chose a pale green with the Navaja crest.

By suppertime they had agreed that the set up would do.

Tre noticed that Ean had been careful to make the evening as familiar as possible. The meal was made up of crew favourites and everyone, including Jax, was expected to carry out his usual duties.

After the meal, Vic and the captain went out to visit their... Tre was never quite sure what to call them. Ean called them professional ladies but in Tarrasade most people called them courtesans.

On Kalakmul a courtesan was faithful to one man and most rich men had a courtesan as well as a wife, usually some pretty girl who had been groomed for the role. In Tarrasade the courtesans, both female and male, were high-class prostitutes who controlled their own lives.

Tre shivered. He had been thinking too much about Kalakmul lately and interacting with people who had known Alejandro Reyes would not help.

Perhaps video communication with Jax would be enough and they would be able to avoid a meeting.

Once Vic and Mel had left, Cas and Obe started making out on one of the couches. Usually Ean suggested that they use the bathroom but this time he fixed Tre with a look.

"I am going to have a bath. Do you want to join me?"

Tre had not been thinking about sex, not even while watching Cas and Obe trying to lick each others' tonsils. However turning down Ean's offer would be so out of character that it would raise all manner of warning flags.

It was only when Ean had him trapped in the bath that Tre realised that those flags had already been raised. Tre was at one side of the large, circular tub and Ean was studying him from the other.

"I knew that having Navaja crews arrive would be stressful for you and for Jax," Ean began. "Even so, I didn't expect him to run out of your meeting and throw up."

Ean paused and Tre recognised the invitation to speak. Unfortunately he could not think of words to say.

"Should I speak to Jax about it?" Ean asked.

It was a challenge; almost a threat. Whichever, it was enough for Tre to find his tongue. "Some of those on the Navaja ship will recognise me as Alejandro Reyes, so I had to tell him."

Ean frowned. "And just why was that enough make him throw up?"

Tre shut his eyes. Ean was not going to let go until he had an acceptable explanation, not with Jax's welfare at stake.

"Alejandro Reyes was successful," he began cautiously. "He was held up as a role model, a hero, even though all he did was his duty. He became popular. That gave him power; power he had not sought and never wanted. It made him a potential threat to the clan leader.

"So the clan leader decided that Alejandro Reyes must cease to exist. The official line was that he had been lost while carrying out his duty. There was a memorial service. He was officially dead.

"In reality he had been converted into a cyborg. He was not the best choice. He was not the optimal age or genetic make-up. He had not tested as suitable in a psychological examination. He was chosen because of the message that choice conveyed." Tre opened his eyes; time to judge Ean's reaction.

Ean had paled but his lips had compressed into a thin, straight line; he was angry.

"So becoming a cyborg was worse than death?" he asked.

"In a way," Tre admitted. "Before me it had always been thought to be death. Cyborgs had never displayed any aspects of their previous personality and had not appeared to have any memories of their previous life. They were thought to be robots built using animated corpses."

Ean's eyes flashed. "So he wanted Alejandro Reyes' corpse walking around as a reminder of his power."

That had been one part of it. "Yes. Only it didn't work. I came through with my mind intact. I remembered being Alejandro Reyes. Unlike other cyborgs, I retained my cognitive abilities and my judgement." Tre could not help but smile. "He could not bring himself to kill me because I was the epitome of what a cyborg was meant to be but never had been before.

"So he kept me, although the fact that I had retained my identity and cognitive facilities was a closely guarded secret."

"Yet you remained loyal to him," Ean whispered. "Despite everything he had done to you."

Tre shrugged. "I had sworn an oath. Truth was, he did not know what to do with me. Then Jax was born and he had the perfect solution."

"So your loyalty transferred to Jax?" Ean asked.

Tre had not expected that particular question. "Yes, the new oath superseded the old."

"Why didn't you kill him? The clan leader?" Ean asked. "I mean, how could it be good for Jax to be raised by a man like that?"

Tre shut his eyes again. There was no simple answer to that question.

Killing Oro alone would not have been enough. Better Jax be

raised by Oro and Mya than Mya alone. A killing spree would have been best, removing Oro, Mya and the others most likely to pollute Jax's childhood. The motivation behind it might not even have been queried; cyborgs were known to be unstable and they were designed to kill.

He would have died, the clan would not have rested until the insane killer had been put down, but Tre would have made that sacrifice willingly if he could have been certain who would end up raising Jax.

Only he was not sure and he would not have been around to check.

Also a newborn was horribly vulnerable. With Oro gone, all manner of threats would crawl out of the shadows. At least Mya had been utterly focused on keeping Jax alive; he was her passport to the future she craved.

He thought back. None of that had been in his mind when he was holding a newborn baby and dedicating his life to Emanuel Rafael Jax Esteban. Tre had been in shock. Oro was Oro, the man he had served unstintingly and without reservation since the age of ten. He had felt abandoned, set adrift, yet euphoric; Oro trusted him.

That moment, when Oro had rested a hand on his shoulder and asked him to protect his son, had felt incredible.

"Tre? Are you all right?" Ean whispered.

"The risk to Jax outweighed the potential benefits," Tre replied, choosing to answer Ean's previous question rather than the one he was asking now. He held out his arms. "Come here."

Ean crossed the tub, turning so that he ended up sitting in Tre's lap. Tre wrapped his arms around him and held him close.

No, it was better this way. He was alive to protect Jax. By building this crew, by selecting Ean, he had tried to bring some balance into Jax's life. Jax coming to them at eleven, rather than fourteen, had been an unexpected bonus.

And, although he by no means deserved him, Tre had Ean.

21

Jax pulled down the hem of his jacket and made one last check in the mirror. Both Ean and Noe had worked on his outfit; a formal fitted jacket and matching pants in a rich brown that would remind a Navaja of the earth on Kalakmul, embroidered on the collar and cuffs with traditional symbols in gold and copper thread. He checked his boots. The flawless, supple leather was polished but not shiny; perfect.

He went to sit behind the desk. Off to one side he could see a small display screen. It showed Emanuel Rafael Jax Esteban with the Navaja crest displayed behind him; the symbol of the flint knife, in the colour of dried blood, against the green-blue of the Kalakmul sky.

He could not afford to be distracted. Eye contact with the person on the other end of the link was important, second only to voice and more important than body language. He sought out the small blue lights that marked where he was meant to focus his gaze.

"*Ring, Jax,*" Kip whispered into his earpiece; Kip was managing the link and monitoring the exchange from one of the simulators.

Jax had been trying to forget that he was wearing it. He changed the position of his left hand on the desk, so more of his father's ring would be visible to the camera.

"*Here it comes, Jax,*" Kip warned him. "*The link to the Quetzal.*"

A three dimensional image coalesced on the far side of the desk so that its eyes were precisely where the blue lights had been. It was not the person Jax had expected. It was Carlos Perez, the Senior Enforcer, rather than Captain Ozkr Soto.

Live, he was even more handsome than his still image; powerfully built, dark wavy hair, warm brown eyes, skin that looked tanned by a sun and a strong chin. "Enforcer Perez," Jax acknowledged.

The man seemed a little taken aback to be recognised. He bowed. "*Señor.*" His voice was a rich, musical baritone.

"How may I help you?" Jax asked.

Again, Enforcer Perez seemed surprised that Jax should have taken the initiative. This time he was quicker to recover. "*I am Senior Enforcer Carlos Perez of the Navaja ship Quetzal. I am here as instructed by your father to offer you a place in my crew.*"

This time it was Jax's turn to be surprised. He hoped it did not show on his face.

"*It could be true,*" Tre told him via the earpiece. "*There is always a backup; too much can go wrong over fourteen standards. Carlos Perez would have been a good choice.*"

"I am honoured by your offer," Jax replied. "However, I do not require a place in your crew at this time."

Carlos Perez hesitated before continuing. "*Señor, I would not be doing my duty if I did not establish that you are safe with your current crew. There have been rumours of an incident involving the Edgers."*

"I am coming in," Tre warned.

"I assure you, Enforcer Perez, that I am under the protection of the man my father selected and for whom you have provided such exemplary backup," Jax stated. This was the line they had decided to take; he was to act as if he believed what they told him. In this case it was easy; all the information they had suggested that Carlos Perez was everything a Navaja spacer should be and so many were not.

Jax watched Enforcer Perez's expression change. It went from a small frown of frustration, through preparing to speak, to shocked astonishment as Tre took up his position behind Jax's left shoulder.

They waited for him to recover.

"Colonel Reyes," he managed.

"Senior Enforcer Perez," Tre acknowledged. "I can assure you that Emanuel Rafael Jax Esteban is thriving under my protection. This is what Joaquin Oro Sebastiano Socorro wanted. However, it is good to know that an alternative crew is available should that become necessary."

Carlos Perez was over his initial shock. *"Even if my crew cannot fulfil the function for which it was built, we wish to serve, as do the crews of the Cenzontle and the Tecolote. Please allow us the privilege of being presented."*

Jax was not sure how to react. There were thirty-seven people across all three crews; far too large a number to risk.

"That is impossible at this time," Tre answered for him. "Perhaps a meeting with you, Senior Enforcer Perez, and the captains of the three crews."

There was another exchange of pleasantries before the exchange ended and Kip's voice in Jax's earpiece confirmed that the link had been cut.

Tre laid a hand on Jax's shoulder. "Well done, particularly when Enforcer Perez dropped his bombshell." He looked into the camera. "Kip, can you get confirmation that Carlos Perez was chosen as my backup?"

"Not directly," Kip admitted. *"The identity of the heir's protector appears to be one of the most highly guarded secrets. There is no mention of you fulfilling that role in the archive, never mind Carlos Perez."*

"What about my father's journal?" Jax suggested.

There was a pause. *"I am not comfortable accessing your father's journal,"* Kip confessed. *"I didn't even intend to copy it. I was looking for a way into the archive and the worm I sent mined the data crystals built into his desk. I can collect information about Carlos Perez's movements and known activities before and after your birth,"* he suggested.

"I shall look in the journal," Jax volunteered, even though he hated the idea.

Jax made himself do it straight away, only pausing to hang up his jacket before plugging into the interface built into the desk and using the goggles Kip had given him. He had opened the journal before but withdrawn after scanning a few entries. He had been hoping for some insight into his father's motivation, not a densely written, highly abbreviated record of day-to-day decisions.

At least the entries were dated. Jax zeroed in on the date of his birth, intending to try searching for key words, when his eyes were inexorably drawn to the text under the heading **23716:11:06.**

H3 finally born. Still unconvinced that M needed to go through pregnancy and labour but H3 undamaged and traditionalists impressed as M predicted.

AR problem resolved for 14 stds. Best solution available: G unaware AR alive; AR fully functional but sequestered; if H3 the one, AR unparalleled protector. Planning 3 rather than 2 backups; AR may malfunction, die or require termination. Considering CP, AA and RG: all capable but overly particular.

It took Jax a moment to realise that 'H3' was 'heir three'. Before he could stop himself he scanned forward, hoping to see 'H3' replaced with 'Jax' or even 'J' but, no, he had remained 'H3' in his father's journal until the end. Not that he was mentioned often.

He refused to dwell on it. Instead he returned to the entry corresponding to his birth. M was obviously Mya, his mother. G was his Uncle Gil. AR was Tre; Alejandro Reyes.

CP could well be Carlos Perez. By 'overly particular' Jax guessed his father meant that the three men were reluctant to bend the spacer code in pursuit of Navaja aims.

Jax closed the journal. He had what he had been seeking; some evidence that Carlos Perez was who he claimed to be. Hopefully Kip would find more because Jax wanted Carlos Perez and the crew of the Quetzal to be on his side; to be the first of his Navaja crews.

He shuddered, feeling cold, and there was an interrogative yip from the doorway; Rae.

"I must have been more worked up than I thought about speaking to a Navaja spacer," Jax suggested.

Rae's whiskers conveyed that he was less than convinced.

"I had to check something in my father's journal," Jax added.

"Kip said," Rae confirmed. He closed the gap between them. "You look tense." He lifted his hands to offer a shoulder rub.

Jax flexed his shoulders, indicating Rae's touch was welcome.

Rae's hands were warm, even through his shirt. Strong, supple fingers worked the tension from Jax's muscles. Jax shut his eyes and concentrated on the physical sensations, trying to ignore the voice inside reminding him that he had just confirmed one of his worst fears.

His father had never cared for him. Every display of interest, each scrap of praise, had been about moulding him into the perfect heir; a potential clan leader.

"Jax! Rae! Supper!" Ean called.

Rae immediately lost interest in massaging Jax's shoulders and was heading for the door, intent on food.

Jax smiled and followed.

Ean had come out of the kitchen and was waiting for him in the shared area. Jax did not even try to avoid the hug that he knew was coming.

In truth he welcomed it, although he was too proud to admit it.

"Tre said you did magnificently," Ean whispered. "He says you made a very good impression on Enforcer Perez."

Jax felt himself flush. "I only did as we had planned."

Ean kissed the top of his head before letting him go. "Tre is not one to praise unless that praise is deserved, we both know that."

Ean could feel the tension in Jax's body as he hugged him. It was the same every time Jax's disguise nanobots were switched off; Jax found being Emanuel Rafael Jax Esteban deeply stressful.

It worried Ean; being Emanuel Rafael Jax Esteban was Jax's future.

Supper, despite all Ean's efforts, felt slightly off. By the time they were halfway through, Ean had realised that it was not just Jax, who was still too tense, but the way the rest of the crew were reacting to his unfamiliar appearance.

Next time Ean would insist that Jax revert to his usual colouring, even if that meant a delay before replying to an incoming communication while the brown pigment was being cleared from Jax's system.

"So you are staying with us, not joining one of these Navaja crews?" Obe asked Jax suddenly as they were eating their apple crumble.

Ean almost retorted but the captain got there first.

"Jax is our cat and will remain so," he stated in a voice that illustrated his displeasure at the question.

Obe flushed. "Sorry," he apologised. "It's just that I don't understand how it's going to work. How many Navaja crews are going to turn up looking for him? Will they realise that Emanuel Rafael Jax Esteban and Jax our cat are the same person? What happens when Jax gets his knife? Will he leave? Will Tre go with him? What about Rae? And Kip?"

They were the same questions that ran through Ean's head every night as he lay in his bunk trying to sleep. "We have two standards before those things become an issue," Captain Mel stated firmly. "Jax cannot claim leadership of his clan until he is sixteen. I am sure that there are plans for dealing with Navaja crews who wish to align themselves with him before that time."

Obe opened his mouth to ask more questions only to close it and scowl at Cas; Ean guessed that Cas had kicked him.

Were there plans to deal with Navaja crews wanting to express their allegiance? Ean did not know.

After supper Ean made sure that Jax helped clear the table and clean the dishes before joining in with a card game in the shared area. He still went to bed unusually early but Rae went with him, so Ean decided not to worry.

Instead he concentrated on Tre, who had decided to have a late session in the gym.

Experience suggested that evening workouts meant that the day had not gone as planned.

Tre did glance at the door as he entered but continued what he was doing. Ean hopped up on a pile of mats and watched; fascinated. Most of the time, Tre was careful to behave like an unmodified purebred but, occasionally, he would move abnormally quickly or strike inhumanly hard.

Being used to Rae made it much easier to accept.

Ean found himself wondering how many times over the past twelve standards Tre had changed what he was doing because he heard Ean or another member of the crew approaching.

Finally Tre stopped, draped a towel around his neck and came over. Ean submitted to a sweaty hug; the price he had to pay for the conversation he was determined to have.

"What happened today?" he asked.

Tre hesitated but then answered. "It looks like the senior enforcer on the Quetzal, Carlos Perez, is my backup. He says he is and both Jax and Kip managed to dig up some confirmatory evidence. He has built a crew for Jax, in case something happened to me."

Ean felt as if he had received a blow to the gut. Jax belonged with them; there was no way he would accept Jax moving to another ship, even a Navaja one. "So Obe's question wasn't wide of the mark," he whispered.

Tre kissed him gently on the lips. "This is the crew Jax needs, not the Quetzal."

Ean returned the kiss but did not initiate another. "Enforcer Perez won't think that Jax would be better off on the Quetzal and challenge for him?"

Tre paused. "I do not think so. He knows who I was." He frowned. "On the other hand, he has heard about what happened with Nevin Edger, so he is within his rights to query Jax's safety. Also, he does not know what I am, so he probably believes he would win if we fought."

"But he is loyal to Jax and has his best interests at heart," Ean checked.

There was another pause. "Yes," Tre replied. "But a Navaja spacer, even a highly honourable one like Carlos Perez, might query why I chose to build a crew like the Willow's," he added. "Traditional Navaja crews are for adults and for the youngsters joining them it is about serving their apprenticeships; about maturing them into the men they were already on the verge of becoming."

Ean was offended. "We pride ourselves in turning out young men who are honourable spacers," he complained.

Tre kissed him again. "We don't merely select suitable youngsters and give them appropriate experiences," he pointed out. "We pick youngsters, boys, with great potential but considerable flaws. We..." He stopped and smiled. "You," he emphasised, "persuade them to build on their strengths and tackle their weaknesses. They don't become the men they would have been, they become better men than they would have been."

Ean flushed, recognising that Tre was paying him a huge

compliment. Tre reached for another kiss but Ean planted a hand against his chest.

"Soon," he promised. "I want to talk more first."

Tre gave a grumble of dissent. "What about if I shower and then meet you in the bathroom?"

Ean smiled. "Sounds good," he agreed.

Only Cas and Obe had claimed the bathroom and they ended up in the kitchen. Tre's expression confirmed his disappointment.

"You should have joined me in the shower," he suggested.

There would have been no conversation if they had been sharing a shower. Ean retrieved two small flasks from the back of one cupboard and two small cups from another.

Tre watched him, brows lifted, as he sat down at the table and filled one of the cups with whisky from one of the flasks.

"No, I am not going to tell you where I keep the bottle," Ean confirmed, pushing the cup across the table.

Tre sat down. "What are you drinking?"

"Cordial," Ean replied.

Tre grimaced at the thought of it, sat down and took a sip of his whisky. "What did you want to talk about?"

"Two things," Ean told him. "One is about what the captain said. What are the plans for Navaja ships turning up over the next two standards?"

Tre took another sip of whisky. "And the other?"

"Jax," Ean admitted. "He finds being Emanuel Rafael Jax Esteban highly stressful."

Tre knocked back the remaining contents of his cup. "I'd be more worried if he didn't," he replied. "He was raised by his parents to be a copy of his father. Everything I have done was designed to mitigate that; to introduce doubt. Now he is looking in the mirror and sees the outward appearance of the person his parents wanted him to be. He is wearing his father's ring. Crews who followed his father are looking at him as a future leader." He paused and considered. "Having Rae helps."

Ean almost objected. Jax did not 'have' Rae; Rae was not an item that could be owned. He stopped himself because this was not the time to argue about language. Tre was being uncharacteristically open. Ean intended to make the most of it. He filled Tre's cup from the flask.

Another refill and the flask would be empty.

"Did Enforcer Perez take the same type of vow of loyalty to Jax as you did?" Ean asked.

"If he is what he says he is," Tre replied.

Ean decided not to be distracted. "Is he as under-stretched in his role as Senior Enforcer on the Quetzal as you were as enforcer on the Willow?"

Tre smiled. "Probably."

"Then it is going to be immensely frustrating for him that he isn't going to have Jax to protect and mentor," Ean pointed out. "He's invested fourteen standards in preparing for a role he is never going to play. Maybe you should take advantage of the situation by giving him a new and challenging role, like being the intermediary between Jax and the Navaja crews."

Tre stared at him. "Ean, you are brilliant," he acknowledged. He shook his head. "You know almost nothing about Carlos Perez, the situation or the clan and yet you come up with the perfect solution. I don't know how you do it."

Ean sipped his cordial. "It's called empathy," he replied. "And I don't have to know him. I just imagined a younger, less complicated version of you."

Jax was more comfortable with the idea of meeting Carlos Perez and the captains of the Navaja crews than he had been about the video link. He wondered if it was because he felt more confident about making a good impression in person or whether his imagination had been caught by Ean's idea of Carlos Perez being his intermediary with the Navaja crews.

If Carlos Perez was to fulfil such a role he would have to be trusted with Jax's alternative identity. They would have to be absolutely certain that he was loyal. If today went as planned, they would rapidly reach the point where they were convinced or Tre killed him.

Jax found that thrilling, which made him feel slightly guilty.

They were using the secure meeting room that was officially part of Agent Poe's offices even though it had been completely rebuilt to Tre and Kip's specifications. Jax watched from the small room that contained all the monitoring equipment.

He checked the screens that showed the meeting room. The display frames on the wall had been set to show scenes of Kalakmul while the table and chairs were dressed in blue-green covers decorated with the clan symbol.

The screens that would show the anteroom and Agent Poe's outer office were blank. At first they would only be able to use the intercom microphones. Spacers expected intercoms. Use of directional microphones, cameras and other detectors required permission.

Kip had one of the speakers linked to the intercom in the anteroom where Agent Poe would welcome their guests. Jax heard doors opening and closing, as well as the voice of Agent Poe's female receptionist.

They had arrived.

"*Good morning captains, Senior Enforcer Perez.*" It was Agent Poe. "*Emanuel Rafael Jax Esteban is preparing to receive you. He asked me to request your permission for a higher level of security monitoring than would normally be the case. He does not intend to offend by making this request. He will understand and comply if you do not give your permission.*"

"*Fine by me,*" a gravelly voice replied.

"Captain Nunez," Tre mouthed.

Three other voices gave their permission, including one Jax recognised as Carlos Perez. Kip immediately activated all the scanners and detectors.

The largest of the screens showed the anteroom where Agent Poe and the four Navaja spacers were standing. Jax found the four men disconcertingly familiar. His childhood had been filled with glimpses of such men striding purposefully along corridors; powerful men in prime condition, each of whom submitted without question to his father's will.

"Well?" Tre asked.

Jax realised that Kip had been scanning for weapons or explosives.

"Nothing that can be detected," Kip confirmed. "A knife each. Not even a backup or a throwing dagger."

"Places," Tre instructed.

They left Kip in the monitoring room and walked a short length of corridor before entering the meeting room. The door they used looked like one of the other wall panels when it was closed; one of the many security measures.

The room looked even richer than Jax had expected; the covers could have been from the linen store at home. Jax resolved to thank Noe for the time he had spent hand embroidering each of the symbols.

He went to stand exactly where they had planned. Tre went to the intercom.

"Emanuel Rafael Jax Esteban is ready to receive his guests," he confirmed and then took up his position to Jax's right.

The door opened and they entered. Captain Soto was first, followed by Captain Nunez and then Captain Vega. Carlos

Perez was last and the door slid closed behind him.

Ozkr Soto and Yoet Nunez were typical Navaja spacers; dark-haired, olive-skinned and powerfully built. They, like Carlos Perez, had been born and raised on Kalakmul.

Fede Vega was different; slighter of build and paler. Jax was reminded of what he had read in the file Kip had compiled. Captain Vega was what Jax's mother would call 'mestizo'; his mother was a native of Kalakmul but his father had been a foreign spacer who had joined a Navaja crew.

It was unusual for a mestizo to become the captain of a Navaja crew; Fede Vega must have displayed exceptional qualities.

Jax seized the initiative.

"Captain Soto, Captain Nunez, Captain Vega, Senior Enforcer Perez. I welcome you. This is my Protector, Enforcer Tre."

It was obvious from Captain Soto and Captain Nunez's expressions that they recognised Tre as Alejandro Reyes. However, they did not query the introduction. Instead all bowed deeply.

"Señor, Enforcer Tre," they chorused.

Jax gestured towards the table. "Please sit, captains. Would you mind if I invited Senior Enforcer Perez and Enforcer Tre to join us?"

Captain Soto snorted. "That might be wise, particularly since either of the two of them understands far more of the situation than the three of us combined."

No one had to ask which place he should take; such conventions were ingrained. Jax was at the head of the table with Tre to his left. Captain Soto, as the senior captain present, took the place to Jax's right. Carlos Perez was left of Captain Soto and Captain Nunez next to Tre. Captain Vega, as the most junior captain present, was opposite Jax at the foot of the table.

Captain Soto seized the initiative. "Señor, may I have permission to speak freely about the current state of the clan?"

Jax nodded his consent.

"We do not know what is happening," Captain Soto admitted. "Everyone knows that General Hierra killed Joaquin Oro Sebastiano Socorro but it is never mentioned. The clan appears to be running smoothly. Crews like us, who chose to separate ourselves, have been allowed to do so. I thought an attack squad would come after us or at least we would be declared Outsiders but there have been no sanctions. Although the official line is that you have been kidnapped, Señor, there appears to be no attempt to find you."

What Captain Soto was saying was consistent with Kip's analysis; no one was sure about his uncle's intentions.

"One of the reasons we came to Tarrasade was because we felt that General Hierra would have to respond to the news that you were here," Captain Nunez added.

"Also there is the possibility that other crews will hear the news you are in Tarrasade and react to it," Captain Vega reminded them. "They might be from other clans, like the Edgers, or Navaja crews who believe that returning you to Kalakmul would curry favour with General Hierra."

"We did not want you to be exposed to such risks," Captain Soto concluded.

Jax felt warmed by their support. "Your loyalty is appreciated," he assured them. He turned to Tre. Perhaps he could use the captains' presence to extract more information than was usually the case. "Do you have any insights into my uncle's motivation?" he asked.

Three of the other four, all but Captain Vega, reacted to his question. Captain Soto grunted, Captain Nunez gasped and Carlos Perez's eyes widened in a way that was almost comical.

Jax had not expected that. These men knew that Tre had been Alejandro Reyes. What had happened between Alejandro Reyes and his Uncle Gil?

"I find it difficult to imagine your uncle wishing to harm you," Tre admitted. "However, he killed your parents, so my judgment on the matter is not to be trusted. Like Senior Enforcer Perez, I have not been on Kalakmul since your birth. People can change greatly in over a decade."

Jax nodded and moved on to the speech they had prepared. He made eye contact with each of the captains in turn. "As we are all aware, I cannot claim leadership of the clan until my sixteenth birth anniversary. The next two standards may prove challenging. We can expect other crews to seek me out. Some may be Navaja crews wishing to offer support, as you have. Others, Navaja or not, may have a confrontation in mind.

"I intend to remain with my crew, learning what it means to be a spacer," he continued. "This is the pattern my family has followed for generations and I see no reason to change it. However, you are correct. I will need a buffer between me and the crews looking for me. With this in mind, I would like to propose that Senior Enforcer Perez operates as my represent-ative, with the resources he will require to interrogate crews' intentions and react accordingly."

Jax watched Carlos Perez's expression as he made the proposal. He looked surprised but pleased.

"You could not find a better man for the job," Captain Soto agreed swiftly.

"If Senior Enforcer Perez is interested, we would welcome the opportunity to speak with him in more detail about the possibility," Tre added.

"I am interested," Carlos Perez confirmed. "I would be honoured," he added.

Jax stood, knowing that it would bring all those around the table to their feet. "I was a little too young to appreciate your oath when I last heard it," he pointed out.

The men around the table smiled or nodded. Jax guessed that some were thinking of Carlos Perez holding him as a small baby while others might be remembering that it had been Joaquin Oro Sebastiano Socorro who had placed him there.

Jax moved to stand in the open space beside the table.

This was what they had decided they must do; get Carlos Perez to speak the most solemn of the Navaja oaths in front of witnesses. Once that was done, the slightest hint of betrayal would justify death.

Carlos Perez did not hesitate for a moment; an excellent sign. Instead he knelt in front of Jax and placed his hand over his heart.

"I, Humberto Mauricio Carlos Perez, dedicate my life to serving you, Emanuel Rafael Jax Esteban of the Navaja, without reservation or limitation. I vow to protect you and your interests throughout my life and by my death. I swear, once you are an adult, to obey you."

Jax was more affected than he had expected. He had to swallow a lump in his throat before he could speak. "I, Emanuel Rafael Jax Esteban of the Navaja, am honoured by your offer of service, Humberto Mauricio Carlos Perez, and accept it."

When Carlos Perez stood up, so did everyone else and suddenly Jax felt like a child in a roomful of adults. The captains were gathered around Carlos Perez, slapping him on the back and congratulating him on the opportunity he had been offered. Jax could feel Tre just behind his right shoulder; staying close; playing the bodyguard's role.

Captain Soto and Carlos Perez changed places when they returned to the table; promoting Carlos Perez to the position of honour at Jax's right hand.

There were a few more exchanges but Jax had achieved what he had set out to do and had little to offer the captains other than to assure them that he, or Carlos Perez as his representative, would stay in contact. In their turn, the three captains seemed content to withdraw and leave Carlos Perez to discuss his new role.

Once they had left, Jax noticed that Carlos Perez looked to Tre rather than to him. Jax did not mind. It was the way things were meant to be; he was under sixteen and Tre was the man his father had selected to guide him.

"Our plan for the next two standards requires us to control the information available about Emanuel Rafael Jax Esteban's location and movements," Tre began.

Carlos Perez nodded. "That is wise," he agreed.

"However, I feel strongly that my representative should be fully informed," Jax added. "Judging the intent of incoming crews will be critical. Even those professing loyalty may have other, less honourable, intentions. His judgement must be absolutely sound and good decisions are unlikely if they are based on limited information."

"Having that type of information will make you a target," Tre warned.

"I understand that," Carlos Perez assured them. He looked to Jax. "I fully appreciate that I may end up serving you by my death."

It was the Navaja way. "I hope that will not be necessary," Jax replied. He took a deeper breath and made the offer. "The queen of my crew has suggested that you join us as clan guest for the next div. I wish to know the man who will be speaking with my voice."

Carlos Perez appeared stunned.

"Perhaps you need time to consider?" Tre suggested.

"No, by no means," Carlos Perez replied swiftly. "I am deeply honoured by the trust you are showing in me, Señor."

Carlos Perez left. The plan was that he would return the next day with his belongings, having squared matters with his crew. Jax stayed sitting at the table. Tre sat beside him.

"Kip, can you cut all audio monitoring?" Jax asked.

"*No problem*," Kip replied. "*Done in five. Five, four, three, two, one.*" The slight buzz of the carrier wave in Jax's earpiece faded away.

Tre looked towards him. His expression was blank. Jax almost backed off and did not ask but decided he must. "What was between you and my uncle? It cannot be a secret if three Navaja spacers know about it."

"We were friends," Tre admitted. "There were times when we were lovers," he added.

Jax shut his eyes. He remembered the entry in his father's journal: **G unaware AR alive**. Had his father converted Alejandro Reyes into a cyborg to punish his uncle? He imagined his Uncle Gill having to see his lover's animated body day after day, believing that he had died during the conversion process.

"Papá disapproved," Jax suggested.

"The official line was that such relationships belonged on ships," Tre replied. "They were considered an unavoidable aspect of spacing; an inevitable consequence when no women were available. So, no, he did not disapprove at first. However, he came to disapprove when the relationship persisted on Kalakmul."

"And Uncle Gil never knew you had survived?" Jax queried.

"I was ordered specifically by your father not to tell him," Tre told him. "So was Loy, who was the only other person who knew."

"Do you think that was why Uncle Gill killed them?" Jax whispered. "Because of what Papá did to you?"

Tre looked him directly in the eyes. "No. Our lives belonged to your father. It was up to him whether we lived or died. Gil understood that."

"Do you still love him?" Jax asked before he could stop himself. He was about to take the question back, to apologise for his rudeness, but Tre answered immediately.

"I do not think so. I have fond memories." Tre hesitated but continued. "Now there is Ean."

Jax was surprised but pleased by the admission; Ean deserved recognition. He decided he had pried enough into Tre's personal life. "Thank you for your candour. I apologise for the intrusion."

"Not knowing could put you at a disadvantage," Tre conceded. He paused for a moment and then changed the subject. "It went well with Carlos Perez," he observed. He laid a hand on Jax's shoulder. "Well done."

As always the praise made Jax feel warm and wanted.

Tre activated the intercom to warn Agent Poe and Kip that they were vacating the room. Kip and Tre started a conversation about the scanner settings. Jax left them to it and started making his way back to the crewroom.

He walked slowly, thinking about what he had learnt; his Uncle Gil and Tre had been lovers.

Jax had not thought much about his uncle since the day his old life had ended and the new one had begun. He had not allowed himself to do so. It was too painful.

There had been few people of significance in Jax's life up to then. Most of those did not stay long. He vaguely remembered an older and a younger woman who had looked after him when he was a small child. There had been a succession of tutors, whom he had disliked, and a variety of trainers, most of whom he had admired.

Only three people had always been there: his father, his mother and his uncle.

He had seen much more of his uncle than his father. It was rare for Jax to see his father other than at the formal evening meal, which Jax had been expected to attend once he was eight. In contrast, Uncle Gil had involved himself in Jax's education. He always knew the identity of his tutors and trainers. He asked questions that showed that he paid attention to what Jax was doing.

When Uncle Gil had asked his opinion it had felt as if his uncle was interested, not as if Jax was being tested.

Yet Uncle Gil had betrayed him. He had murdered his father and his mother. Thinking about it made Jax simultaneously sad and angry.

"Jax, are you all right?"

Jax realised that he was standing motionless in the corridor outside the kitchen. Ean was talking to him.

"I am fine," he answered.

Ean was closing for a hug. Jax knew that moving away would avoid it. Instead he stayed where he was and submitted. It felt good. Like Tre's hand on his shoulder. Like when Rae snuggled up against his back in his bunk.

Like when his Uncle Gil had smiled at him.

22

Rae took up his position at the end of the line. He could hear the stranger approaching, walking with the captain along the corridor towards the shared area where the rest of the crew were waiting.

He took a slow, deep breath. He could not smell Spacer Carlos Perez; at least not yet.

Ean was trying to catch his eye. Rae thought about pretending he had not noticed but while that would work on Vic or even Tre, fooling Ean was much harder.

He made eye contact.

"Be good," Ean mouthed.

Rae twitched his whiskers, which was more acknowledgement than acquiescence.

Ean didn't have time to follow up because the door slid open and the stranger entered, followed by the captain. He was tall, Vic's height, and between Vic and Tre in build.

Rae inhaled again, this time with his mouth slightly open to catch every nuance of the stranger's scent. Definitely purebred and with none of the weird undertones that Tre had; the ones that Rae now realised were because he was a cyborg. Rae tried to smell past a different ship and a different crew.

Carlos Perez didn't smell so bad.

The captain escorted Carlos Perez along the line, introducing them one by one; most senior to most junior. "This is our queen, Ean."

"Spacer Perez," Ean acknowledged. "Thank you for agreeing to be our crew-guest. We are honoured."

Carlos Perez bowed slightly. "The honour is mine, Spacer Ean. Thank you for inviting me."

They worked along the line: Vic, Tre, Cas, Obe, Kip and then Noe. Noe did his thing; the subtle movements of eyes, lips and body he used to suss out a target.

Rae's nose was hit, as he had expected, by a variety of aromas indicating Carlos Perez's interest.

Scent aside, Spacer Perez was skilled at not showing his attraction; Noe looked distinctly disappointed.

"These are our younger cats, Jax and Rae," Ean continued.

Rae observed Carlos Perez's reaction. Noe must have distracted him because he was late to realise that the dark-eyed lad with curly brown hair was his future clan leader.

Then, already surprised, he did not cover his dismay that there was a hybrid at the end of the row,

"Señor," Spacer Perez murmured with eyes fixed on Jax.

Rae decided to give him the benefit of the doubt; maybe he was looking at Jax rather than avoiding looking at the hybrid.

"Just Jax," Jax insisted.

Rae felt him tense and a glance sideways confirmed that Jax's eyes had narrowed and the look he was giving Spacer Perez fell far short of friendly.

To give Spacer Perez credit, he quickly realised that Jax was not pleased by his response to Rae's presence. "Jax," he acknowledged. "Rae."

It had not been a good start. Jax was annoyed. Ean was anxious. Noe was sulking. Even Tre seemed tense. Spacer Perez was on his best behaviour for the rest of Ean's tour of the apartment, accepting that he would be staying in a room other than the crewroom without question and not reacting negatively to the news that they were leaving Tarrasade the next day.

Ean left Spacer Perez with Tre and called Noe into the kitchen to finish preparing lunch. Even that wasn't a good sign; normally Ean would have stayed with their guest and left setting out the meal to the cats.

"We have fifteen minutes or so until lunch," Tre observed. "Let me show you the gym and other training facilities."

Rae exchanged glances with Jax, who gave a slight nod.

They moved to the laundry under the guise of completing some chores before lunch. The truth was that the laundry, with one door to the crewroom and another to the corridor, was the perfect position for eavesdropping on the whole apartment.

Rae perched up high, in the best place to listen, while Jax folded garments so that they would be able to point to a pile of clothes when asked what they had been doing.

Tre had not closed the door to the gym, which made it easy.

"You have reservations," Tre observed.

"I value your judgement but it is difficult not to," Spacer Perez replied. "A crew of ten with four cats, no medico, no navigator, only one enforcer and probably the youngest queen I have ever met."

"We should address the lack of a medico," Tre admitted. "May I ask you a favour, Spacer Perez?"

There was a short pause. "You used to call me Carlos," Spacer Perez replied. "I would be honoured if you would do so again."

Rae wondered when they had known each other. He wished he could smell them but they were too far away.

"Very well." Tre's tone was warmer. "May I ask you a favour, Carlos?"

"Certainly," Spacer Perez replied.

"Wait ten days before making a judgement."

There was a short silence and then Spacer Perez answered. "Ten days," he agreed.

"Good. This afternoon I will be working here, in the gym, with Rae. I would like you to join us." Spacer Perez did not speak but Rae guessed he had nodded because Tre continued. "I am sure you have realised that Rae is important to Jax."

"Many Navaja will struggle to accept a hybrid," Spacer Perez pointed out.

"Jax's father had cyborgs," Tre argued.

"There is no uncertain middle ground with cyborgs," Spacer Perez replied. "They are not people, they are weapons. Hybrids are……confusing. It is to avoid that confusion that the Navaja clan avoid them and they are banned from Kalakmul."

Rae had not known that. Did that mean he wouldn't be able to go with Jax when Jax visited his home planet? Also Spacer Perez obviously had no idea that Tre was a cyborg.

"What are they saying?" Jax whispered.

"Spacer Perez is worried that the crew isn't strong enough," Rae replied. "Tre's asked him to wait before making up his mind. He doesn't know Tre is a cyborg." Rae didn't know if he should mention hybrids. It might turn Jax even further against Spacer Perez. Luckily Tre and Spacer Perez had started a new topic of conversation, which gave Rae an excuse to gesture to Jax for silence.

"I assume your ship is in a private berth in one of the secure docks," Spacer Perez was saying.

This time it was Tre who hesitated. "We do not have a ship at the moment," he admitted.

There was a substantial pause. Rae filled in Spacer Perez's expression of disapproval.

"We will be travelling to the shipyard where she has been built," Tre added.

"Using a hired ship?" Spacer Perez suggested.

"No," Tre replied. "As passengers."

"Passengers on a non-Navaja ship?" Spacer Perez demanded. Tre must have nodded because there was a sharp intake of breath from Spacer Perez. "Colonel Reyes, please allow the Quetzal to transport you rather than trusting a foreign crew."

Rae could hear the anxiety in Spacer Perez's voice. Him being so anxious about Jax's safety made up a bit for his dislike of hybrids.

"It is out of the question," Tre replied sharply. "You will come to understand," he added in a more moderate tone. "Also Joaquin Oro Sebastiano Socorro declared Alejandro Reyes dead. Do not call me by his name."

"I apologise, Enforcer Tre," Spacer Perez replied. "I did not mean to give offence."

"Your apology is accepted," Tre assured him. "Please call me Tre. We should return to the shared area. Ean will delay the meal if he thinks we are not ready because you are a guest."

Jax was scowling at him. Rae checked that the sounds were consistent with Tre and Spacer Perez leaving the gym and walking towards the shared area.

"Tre just told Spacer Perez that we don't have a ship," Rae summarised.

Jax winced. "I am guessing he didn't take that too well."

"He wants us to travel on the Quetzal," Rae added.

"No chance of that," Jax pointed out. "It will take four divs to get to Potash on the Quetzal but only eight days on the Renaissance." He finished folding a shirt and added it to the pile. "We better go; we don't want to make things worse by being late."

Lunch settled everyone down; Ean's food had that effect on people. Noe had stopped sulking and looked smug; Rae guessed that Ean had asked if he could offer their guest Noe's services and Noe had jumped at the chance.

At least it would give Noe someone other than Kip to practise on.

After lunch, Tre had a quiet word; the faintest of whispers that only he and Rae could detect.

"I expect you heard every word of my conversation with Carlos in the gym," Tre began.

There was no safe answer to that; Rae settled for a whisker-twitch.

"I want you to fight him this afternoon only you must not hurt him. No bites. No scratches. No broken bones."

"Contact?" Rae checked.

"You can hit him but try not to leave too many bruises," Tre replied. "He might get frustrated. Be careful. I would prefer not to have to interfere."

Rae understood. Tre didn't want Spacer Perez to know he was a cyborg.

For a purebred, Spacer Perez was a superb fighter; strong, fast, accurate and always thinking. There was about a minute at the start when he thought that Rae's teeth snapping shut a finger's breadth from his throat and the edge of Rae's hand brushing his hair were misses. Then he accepted that Rae could kill him and settled for trying to land a blow.

He did, finally, manage to snag Rae's ankle as Rae jumped

over his head for the fourth time. It was one of the moves Rae had anticipated. He used the point of contact as a fulcrum, changed direction, grappled Spacer Perez's other arm, planted a foot and tossed him across the gym.

Spacer Perez still managed to fall well and roll to his feet.

"Enough!" Tre announced.

Spacer Perez stood neatly and bowed, like Jax did when a combat was over. Rae responded in kind.

"I have been training Rae since he joined the crew almost three standards ago," Tre told Spacer Perez.

"My job is to protect Jax," Rae added. He jumped up and down; it was almost impossible for him to stay still when his adrenalin levels were so high.

"Why don't you go on your treadmill?" Tre suggested.

Spacer Perez stood on the other side of the gym and watched Rae run. Tre went across and stood beside him.

"I have never seen any fighter that good," Spacer Perez admitted. "Not a cyborg, not even one of those professional hybrids who do the display fighting."

There were professional hybrid fighters? Rae had not known that.

"He isn't even fully grown," Spacer Perez added.

"He may slow down when he's full sized," Tre suggested. "But he'll be stronger."

Rae had no intention of slowing down. There was a limit on

how strong you needed to be to win at combat. If you were fast you were never too late.

"Lady Luck's teats," Spacer Perez whispered as Rae accelerated. "How does the treadmill stay in one piece?"

"It was specially built for him," Tre admitted. He raised his voice for Spacer Perez's benefit. "We will leave you to it, Rae."

Rae raised a hand in acknowledgement.

Kip had agreed wholeheartedly with Ean's suggestion that Carlos Perez should be the buffer between Jax and crews seeking him out. He had even concurred with the idea that Spacer Perez should spend some time with their crew so that Jax could get to know him.

He was less keen on one of the consequences. It had fallen to him to inform Klennethon Darrent of the situation and persuade him that he should allow a stranger to travel with them on the Renaissance.

He had been putting it off, even though they were meant to be leaving the next day. Kip couldn't escape the conviction that the later he left it the better.

Ean waited until Spacer Perez had gone with Tre and Rae to the gym before fixing him with a stare that made him squirm. "Kip, have you asked Citizen Darrent?"

"No," Kip admitted.

Ean sighed. "Kip, we are meant to be leaving on the Renaissance tomorrow. Do I have to ask the captain to do it?"

"No," Kip replied. "I have asked him for a vid link and he said he would be available this afternoon." He consulted the chronometer. "In sixteen minutes' time."

"I am sure he will agree," Ean reassured him. "Citizen Darrent understands spacer ways. Spacer Perez is a crew-guest."

Ean spoke as if that explained everything, which it probably did if you were Ean rather than an ancient security-obsessed recluse whose ambition was to control everything and everyone.

He had chosen a video link because Klennethon Darrent always suggested one and Kip usually refused; he was much more comfortable exchanging text messages.

Kip went straight to the point and made the request.

Klennethon Darrent stared at him for what had felt like minutes but was actually only eleven seconds. "You want to bring a stranger onto my ship," he stated.

"A crew-guest," Kip repeated. "Like a temporary member of the crew."

"I understand the meaning of crew-guest," Klennethon Darrent replied. "Who is this man?"

"Humberto Mauricio Carlos Perez of the Navaja, until recently Senior Enforcer on the Quetzal."

The name was familiar to Klennethon Darrent; Kip could tell. He wondered if Klennethon Darrent had been tracking the Navaja ships.

"You are certain he can be trusted?" Klennethon Darrent asked only it wasn't really a question because Klennethon Darrent didn't care about Kip's answer; he had already decided that Carlos Perez was unlikely to be a threat.

Kip replied anyway. "I am never certain. There is a high probability that he is exactly what he says he is and that therefore he can be trusted."

Klennethon Darrent smiled. Kip never liked it when Klennethon Darrent smiled; it meant he was up to something. "Then all that matters is what I want in return for letting him travel with your crew on the Renaissance."

Kip opened his mouth to object but had shut it again. Such negotiations went better if he waited until Klennethon Darrent made the first move.

"Two things. The first is that you spend a hundred minutes with me, face-to-face, playing board games on each of the six days we are underway," Klennethon Darrent proposed.

As far as Kip knew, Klennethon Darrent had not been planning to be with them on the Renaissance. There was no point because Ean refused to allow Kip to spend time with him; Kip was a cat and cats did not speak face-to-face to outsiders, not even Klennethon Darrent. Even allowing them to have daily contact was a massive concession.

"I can't even take that proposal to Ean unless it's going to be in a shared area with other members of the crew present," Kip pointed out.

Klennethon Darrent frowned slightly. "In the viewing lounge

and other members of the crew are welcome to be present."

"I can take that to Ean," Kip had agreed. "What's the second thing?"

"A promise from you that once you have your knife you will call me Klenn."

Kip felt himself blushing.

"That's non-negotiable," Klennethon Darrent warned him.

At least he didn't have to mention it to Ean. "If that is what you want, Citizen Darrent," he conceded. "I promise to call you Klenn once I have my knife."

"Good," Klennethon Darrent acknowledged. "Now take my proposal to Spacer Ean."

Kip closed the link and went to find Ean. He was in the kitchen looking over the duty rosters for the Salix.

"What is it Kip?" Ean asked once he had realised that Kip was lurking.

"I did it. I asked," Kip replied.

Ean stiffened. "Please don't tell me he said no. We'll end up on the Quetzal."

"We won't," Kip insisted. "I could arrange for the Salix to be delivered here. It's just a better option for us to go to Potash to pick her up."

"So he said no then?" Ean checked.

"No, he said yes," Kip replied. "Only he had a condition." He explained what Klennethon Darrent wanted.

Ean frowned. "I didn't think Citizen Darrent was planning on being on the Renaissance."

Kip decided not to point out that Klennethon Darrent had changed his plans purely to spend time with him. Instead he shrugged.

Ean studied him. "You are all right with it?"

"It will be fun," Kip admitted. "He can beat me at both chess and Go and face-to-face is more exciting."

Ean sighed. "Very well. Klennethon Darrent is a very dangerous man, Kip. Never forget that."

Kip settled for a nod and escaped, muttering that he needed to send a message confirming that Ean had agreed.

Once he was in his favourite simulator he sent a text message to Klennethon Darrent before sorting through the data that had arrived recently.

Most of it was automatically incorporated into his various models and simulations but there were always titbits that were worthy of his personal attention. After he had finished perusing them, he started looking through the updated models, beginning with those that had been prioritised for his attention.

He had finished with the boring task of buying or selling things to generate credit and was about to start researching an interesting new sensor when Tre pinged him with a text message from Simulator 5.

I would like you to give Carlos an intelligence briefing, concentrating on ship movements using

data obtained from open or purchased sources.

Kip started filtering his ribbon models to remove the deductions based on hacked data that could not be obtained in other ways. **In the projector room?**

No, he is in Simulator 4. Kip, humour me by sticking to text rather than opening a verbal link.

Kip did wonder why Tre had chosen to use the simulators and only text but that thought was swiftly sidelined as he decided what to include and in which order.

One of the best things about being a member of a team was the challenge of explaining what he did in terms others could understand and appreciate.

He sent a text message to Simulator 4, copying it to Simulator 5 for Tre's benefit. **Please signal blue when you are ready to proceed, red if you wish to pause and amber if you require further clarification. Feel free to ask questions at any time.**

There was a blue signal from Simulator 4.

Carlos Perez was no slouch in the thinking department; he rarely asked for clarification and the battery of insightful questions showed that he was spotting implications as well as keeping up. Kip even had to include extra material. He was impressed.

In the end it was Tre who brought the briefing to a close by signalling red and telling Kip to meet them in the projector room after five minutes.

The door was open as Kip approached; Carlos Perez sounded quite excited.

"I've never seen an intelligence system like it. How did you develop the technology? Is it commercial or did you commission it? How long did it take to develop? How do you collect the information? Where is the team of analysts? Are they based here in Tarrasade? Can it be made mobile?"

"Come in, Kip," Tre called.

Kip entered reluctantly.

Tre turned to Carlos Perez. "Meet the inventor of the system, the collector of the information and the team of analysts."

Carlos Perez stared at him, stranded in shocked incomprehension. Kip felt himself flushing a deep crimson.

"How?" Carlos Perez finally managed.

"I like data mining and I'm good at mathematics," Kip replied. "Jax asked me to help so I did," he added.

Carlos Perez went pale. He turned to Tre.

"There is no level of commitment beyond 'helping'?" he queried.

Tre glanced at Kip. "Kip, do you have somewhere else you can be?"

Kip nodded and sauntered out the door, which closed behind him.

He hurried back to Simulator 2, stripped off and climbed in. As he did so, he reminded himself that what he was about to do was wrong. No one he respected would say otherwise.

He still did it. He activated one of the microphones in the projector room.

"*...dangerous it is to have an outsider with this level of knowledge,*" Carlos Perez was saying.

"*All the information is in the open domain or can be obtained from data brokers,*" Tre replied. "*Kip could produce an equivalent analysis of another clan, or any other organisation. He chooses to do it for Jax because Jax is his friend.*"

"*But...*" Carlos Perez began.

Tre cut him off. "*It is the way it is, Carlos. Hopefully, by the end of the ten days of open-minded reflection you promised me, you will have a better understanding of the situation.*"

Different parts of Kip's mind raced off in different directions. Listening to Tre talking to Carlos Perez reminded Kip of the way Tre spoke to Jax; Kip wondered if there had been a time when Carlos had been a youngster under Alejandro Reyes' command.

Carlos Perez's reaction to Tre's revelation had been worrying; all Carlos had been able to think of was tying Kip to the Navaja. Kip had no intention of being under anyone's control; he hadn't spent his life avoiding Centre only to end up owned by a spacer clan.

Or by Klennethon Darrent; Kip kept returning to his promise to call Citizen Darrent 'Klenn'. Maybe Noe was correct and Klennethon Darrent wanted to be his lover. Kip shuddered; Klennethon Darrent was old enough to be his Grandpappy's Pa.

Was that ageist of him? In a world of extended lifespan and age-retard did age matter? There had to be a considerable age gap between Tre and Ean, probably over twenty-five standards, but that felt just fine.

There was a century between him and Klennethon Darrent.

The soft ping of an alert distracted him. It was a message he had been waiting for, confirming availability of a component he was hoping to use in the Sphere. All other lines of thought were diverted into the lower layers of his mind as Kip began negotiating a bulk buy at a fair price.

He loved working on the Sphere; it reminded him of being in his Grandpappy's workshop building models.

Jax had mixed feelings about Carlos Perez. The man was bursting with excellent qualities but he was Navaja through and through. Spending time with him made Jax think about how he was going to win the loyalty of the Navaja crews and, even more difficult, that of the people of Kalakmul.

At least his attitude to Rae had changed. That was hopeful because it suggested that practicality could trump prejudice. Once it had been established that Rae was the best bodyguard available, it no longer mattered that he was a hybrid.

Jax's gaze went to where Rae was making last minute additions to his backpack. He had known that Rae was a skilled fighter but not that he was without peer; Carlos had been adamant about that.

Rae pulled the fastenings on his backpack shut and gave the whisker-twitch that asked if Jax was ready. Jax nodded and they joined the others in the shared area.

The packing cases had gone; couriered to Klennethon Darrent's private docking bay in Prime the afternoon before.

"Can I ask about the route through the station?" Carlos asked. Jax could hear in his voice that he was struggling with Tre's refusal to share the detail of their plans.

Jax sympathised; although it was acceptable to limit information given to a crew-guest, every time Tre or Jax chose not to trust him must feel like an insult.

"We are heading for Prime," the captain told him. "Our lift is in a private dock there."

It was the easiest of journeys; up by one private elevator car to the Outer Residential Ring and then by another to Prime. They were met by Garner Parrad.

"Captain Mel, Spacer Ean, it is good to see you and the crew again," he greeted them. "Spacer Perez, it is an honour."

Ean stepped forward to complete the introduction. "Carlos, this is Citizen Garner Parrad. Will you be with us for the journey, Citizen Parrad?"

"The majority of it, Spacer Ean," Garner Parrad confirmed. "If you do not mind, we will go directly to the ship. The packing cases you sent ahead are already aboard."

Watching Carlos' face when he saw the Renaissance was fun. Jax was impressed that he managed to stop himself asking questions until they were in their usual quarters.

"Is the ship owned by an organisation?" he asked.

Jax glanced at Tre, who gave a tiny nod.

"The Renaissance is owned by Klennethon Darrent," Jax admitted. "We are his guests."

Carlos swallowed. "You have an alliance with Klennethon Darrent?"

"No," Jax replied. He looked to Kip but Kip was off in his head somewhere.

Ean chose to step into the gap. "Citizen Darrent has identified Kip as a youngster with potential who can benefit from his support. I think he remembers how difficult life can be for a very clever youngster. He occasionally helps us because we are Kip's crew."

Jax marvelled, not for the first time, at Ean's ability to make the extraordinary seem normal.

The largest room in the guest quarters was either still as they had left it or had been set up as before. Ean frowned slightly to see that Jax and Rae's den remained separate.

Jax held his breath. Would Ean make them move into the main crewroom when it was only seven nights? He watched Ean looking about the room, deciding how much work it would involve.

"I expect you to leave the door open," he decided. "It will be an alcove, like in Tarrasade."

Tre suggested that Carlos might enjoy seeing Tarrasade from the viewing galleries so they grabbed a quick lunch as the ship undocked and left the unpacking for later.

Cas and Obe decided to stay in the crewroom but everyone else accompanied Carlos. Jax wondered if they, like him, wanted to see Carlos' face when he saw the amazing hall with its sweeping stairs and the two end-to-end viewing ports along the mezzanine levels.

Jax was not disappointed.

They sat on the side of the ship closest to Tarrasade as the ship moved away from the station. Jax chose to sit next to Carlos; after all the whole point of having him as a crew-guest was to get to know him.

"Klennethon Darrent owns Prime," Jax told him. From this distance and position they could see the top four tiers, each larger in diameter than the one above. They couldn't see the Sphere yet, it was obscured by the main disc. He laughed. "It turned out I own the Sphere. One of my ancestors won it in a game of cards."

Carlos managed not to grimace. "Is there anything in the Sphere worth having, Señor?"

"Jax," Jax reminded him. "Owning the Sphere gives me or my representative a place on the Committee. Also Kip has taken an interest in the Sphere; renovating it is the type of project that interests him."

"But you own it," Carlos checked.

"Yes, I own it," Jax confirmed, "but I couldn't afford the debt associated with its maintenance costs, never mind the credit to renovate it. Kip is paying for it. In return he has my word that I will never sell it to anyone else and that I will leave it to him in my will."

"Kip is young to have access to such funds," Carlos stated.

Jax imagined the questions Carlos would be asking if he was not stopped from doing so by the spacer code. He was probably wondering whether Kip was from a rich family or maybe even if he was Klennethon Darrent's son. "Yes," Jax answered, which he realised would be frustratingly lacking in detail. "Kip is very generous," he added.

Carlos would have probably plied Jax for more information but, at that moment, Klennethon Darrent arrived, accompanied by Garner Parrad. The captain introduced Carlos to Klennethon Darrent, who was polite but obviously totally uninterested.

He settled at one of the tables to play chess with Kip.

"We could play," Carlos suggested.

Jax knew that Carlos wanted to talk. So did he, but only if it was all right with Rae. He checked and Rae's whisker-twitch confirmed that he was fine on his own for a while; Jax guessed he would watch the stars for a bit and then, given that they didn't have access to simulators, go to the gym.

"Enforcer Tre was correct," Carlos began as they set up the board. "My viewpoint needed adjustment. I was being far too parochial."

So things had not gone as smoothly between Tre and Carlos as Tre had suggested. Jax was not surprised. The Salix would seem relaxed and disorganised compared with a well run Navaja ship.

"As clan leader you will need to look beyond the clan," Carlos continued. "Your father, for all his qualities, did not make the most of alliances between the Navaja clan and others."

It was a massive understatement. While he had never actually broken an agreement, Joaquin Oro Sebastiano Socorro had been infamous for exploiting loopholes and activating exit clauses in unanticipated ways.

Jax now knew how far his father would go; not hesitating to kill his own son so that Navaja could end an alliance without having to pay compensation.

He took two pawns from the board, put them into his clenched hands behind his back and held them out.

Carlos chose white.

Jax knew he should say something. Carlos' statement had been a criticism, however mild, of Joaquin Oro Sebastiano Socorro's leadership style. He would not have made it unless Tre had been encouraging him in that direction.

Or maybe merely being on the Salix, observing the crew Tre had built, had been enough.

Jax decided to be bold. "I am not my father or my grandfather," he stated as Carlos made his first move; the pawn in front of his queen.

Carlos was prudently silent.

Jax mirrored his move. "Also, I do not have an over-inflated idea of my importance," he added, watching Carlos carefully to monitor his reaction. "I am heir because I was conceived for that purpose. In many ways I am no different to Rae; genetically engineered for the role I am expected to fulfil."

He saw Carlos stiffen slightly. Then he forced himself to relax and jumped his king's side knight towards the centre of the board.

Jax briefly wondered if Carlos was using one of the standard strategies. Not that winning the game mattered; it was the conversation that counted. "I do not rail against that destiny," Jax continued, again mirroring Carlos' move. "I am a symbol. The clan will unite behind me."

Carlos did not comment. He moved his queen's side bishop, forcing Jax to be defensive.

Jax moved a pawn to release his queen. "That symbol of unity is replaceable," he pointed out. "Over the last five generations there have been thirteen 'heirs', only four of whom became clan leader."

This was obviously not news to Carlos, who said nothing and moved a pawn, releasing his queen as Jax had done.

"If I die another genetically tailored individual could be conceived and raised," Jax reminded him as he moved his queen to cover Carlos' most likely next move. "Indeed this may be what my uncle is doing."

Carlos still did not react. He mirrored Jax's move with his queen, creating a standoff between the two pieces.

Jax was becoming impatient. Was there nothing he could say that would shake Carlo's composure? He was determined to find some of Carlos' limits. "Or the clan could go back to the old ways," he suggested.

Carlos lost interest in the board. Jax found himself facing intense, passionate eyes.

"Old ways that wasted all the clan's resources fighting over who should lead," Carlos retorted. "The clan was close to oblivion time after time." He was on the edge of saying something else but stopped.

"I would like to hear your thoughts," Jax encouraged.

"I was going to point out that a leader who can unite the clan, however ruthless or cruel, is better than that."

It explained why the Navaja clan tolerated its leaders' excesses; much was sacrificed on the altar of unity. "I have no intention of allowing the clan to revert to the old ways," Jax assured him. "Let's play," he added, making his next move.

Jax won, which surprised him. Given that he did not think Carlos had thrown the game, the result suggested that Jax had learnt far more than he had thought during two standards of losing to Kip.

Or maybe Noe's occasional forays into Carlos's field of view had distracted him. As they put the pieces away, Jax decided Carlos deserved a heads-up while Noe was out of earshot.

"Rae and Kip are superb at what they do," he pointed out.

Carlos frowned at him, puzzled.

"Noe is also more than he seems," Jax warned him.

Carlos' gaze went to Noe, who knew immediately that his target's eyes were on him. He offered Carlos his best smile and, as if unable to do otherwise, Carlos responded in kind.

Jax sighed; at least he had no reason to believe that Noe had any aims other than refining his skills while giving Carlos pleasure.

After supper, when Noe had vanished with Carlos, Rae brought Kip into their den. Jax wasn't surprised that Rae should invite Kip, only that he had done it without asking.

Rae must have thought he would say no but that Kip's need for company outweighed Jax's preference. Why was Rae worried about Kip? Did Kip have feelings for Noe? Was he upset by Noe's enthusiasm for Carlos' company? Or was it something to do with Klennethon Darrent?

Maybe Kip just smelt sad.

They piled onto Jax's bunk. Kip connected up a small speaker and played some of the music he had processed so it suited Rae's hearing as well as a purebred's. Rae brought out some nut clusters; Jax and Kip had one each, even though they weren't hungry, so that Rae had permission to polish off the rest of the bag.

They talked mostly about Carlos. The general opinion was that he was impressive, both as an individual and a spacer.

"I wish more Navaja spacers were as honourable as Carlos," Jax admitted.

Rae twitched his whiskers. "Why aren't they?" he asked.

Jax was about to say that not everyone had Carlos Perez's qualities when Kip spoke.

"Who set the standard?" he asked. "And what made Carlos

Perez rise above it?"

Jax found himself thinking about the entry in his father's journal; 'capable but overly particular'. The problem was that the standard had been set by his grandfather and then his father.

"I need to raise the standard," Jax acknowledged. He sighed. "I don't know why Carlos' personal standards are higher." He wondered if it was something to do with Carols' family or the crew he had joined when he had been a cat. He sighed. "It's not like I can ask."

"You can look up where he is from and the ships he has been on in the Navaja clan records," Kip suggested.

Was that against the spacer code? Jax guessed not; Carlos was sworn to him. "Can you get his record up for me?"

Rae gave a soft yip that reminded him that they were hanging out and that it could wait until the next day but Jax ignored it. Within a minute he had his goggles on and was looking through the first part of Carlos' record; from when he had joined the clan at fourteen to when he had been sworn in as Tre's backup at the age of twenty-three.

He was from one of the old Navaja families; the second youngest of six sons. He had four sisters. Jax tried to imagine growing up with nine siblings and failed miserably.

Carlos had been the brightest and best of them. As such, it was expected that he would be offered by the family directly to the clan leader rather than placed with a Navaja crew.

The offering had happened when Carlos was approaching his fourteenth birth anniversary. That was unusual. Families usually offered their sons early, hoping to attract the clan leader's attention and garner favour.

Jax began his list: big family; not given away too young.

Then there was Carlos' first crew. It was Trad but large and there was a familiar name associated with it. It had been Colonel Alejandro Reyes' crew; the one had he travelled with when he was not on Kalakmul and which he had taken with him into combat.

A crew that Alejandro Reyes, Tre, had handpicked.

Jax took off his goggles. Rae and Kip were off the bunk, dancing to the music. Dancing with Ean for exercise had improved Kip's movement enormously.

As for Rae, well, Jax told himself that anyone would find that lithe, fluid body attractive. It was only natural.

After Kip left, Jax had a shower. When he emerged, Rae was curled up in his own bunk. Jax put on sleep shorts and climbed into bed.

Rae wasn't asleep yet; Jax could tell from his breathing. He was probably waiting for Jax to invite him down only there weren't any drapes and people might see Jax's bunk through the open doorway.

Jax told himself that he did not want to be seen cuddling Rae because it was private and personal; the last thing he wanted was Obe teasing them about it in front of the others.

He pulled up the covers and shut his eyes, hoping that sleep came quickly.

23

Tre was delighted with the Salix. She was perfect because she looked utterly ordinary and was extraordinary in almost every way.

She reminded him of Ean.

The ship had two modes. She could be flown conventionally from the control room or she could be operated from interfaces that took full advantage of the simulators' capacities.

Given that Kip had designed the simulators, those capacities were astonishing.

There were fifteen simulators, each of which could double as an acceleration chair as well as being a control interface. Three were located in the control room, one in the main gunnery tower, two in the engine room, three in dedicated simulator rooms, two in a backup location on the hydroponics level and the other four in another room on the crewroom level. They were hardwired into the ship's network, which had inbuilt redundancy, and there were two emergency power systems in case main power failed.

After an uneventful trip on the Renaissance they had jumped

into Potash, taken possession of the ship, picked up a ridiculous number of crates and jumped through an ungated hole to a little-used system. There they had spent the next six days installing all the specialist equipment Kip had ordered, including the simulators, and begun testing.

Obe, to everyone's surprise, was turning into a talented technician. In one of the crates had been five sets of mobile micro-manipulation equipment consisting of gloves, goggles, compact power pack and belt-mounted control system. As soon as Obe had used one he had been hooked. As he had explained to Ean, using the equipment cut out any frustration; you wanted to do something, you did it and it was done.

Vic could not stop smiling.

Tre knew how he felt. Today they had run the first set of drills, finishing up with Carlos as battle commander, Jax as pilot and Rae controlling all the guns.

As Ean had observed, it was a good thing everyone else was in the equivalent of an acceleration chair because when Jax said he was taking things to their limits he meant it.

Tre made sure he intercepted Carlos on his way to the debriefing session. The way Carlos' eyes were shining reminded Tre of the youngster he had known.

"You are right," he acknowledged. "Any fraction, however small, of Kip is worth having. He is like a sun. You appreciate and take advantage of the sunlight but no sane person tries to control a sun."

Tre remembered the young Carlos having a liking for grand analogies.

"And the young señor shows such promise. There is nothing a Navaja admires more than a leader who takes them to their limits without exposing them to the fear of failure. The way he utilised Rae's phenomenal skills without subjecting the ship or the crew to excessive stresses was incredible." His face suddenly fell.

"What is it, Carlos?" Tre asked.

"I do not want to leave after a div. I shall, because it is my duty, but I want to stay with you and the young señor as you plan for the future."

Carlos' words released a surge of hope that left Tre feeling slightly dizzy. If Carlos felt like this, so would others.

"I am sure that Jax will wish to have you beside him as soon as that is possible," he replied. Tre decided to have another word with Kip about trying to identify 'AA' and 'RG'. Perhaps it was time to consider approaching selected Navaja crews rather than waiting for them to come to Jax.

The debriefing, which was held in the dedicated meetings room, went well. Everyone but Kip was effusive about the ship, the new equipment and how smoothly the new systems were running. Kip was quiet, taking note of what people were saying but not contributing.

Tre hung around when the others left, knowing that Kip would be closing down his interfaces and the projector.

"What's wrong?" he asked, deciding to take advantage of Kip's tendency to focus on the question asked.

"I hate being isolated from the data streams," Kip admitted. "Seven days is too long."

"What if we popped back through the hole to Potash?" Tre suggested. One of the Potash gates had a light speed data relay.

Kip smiled, which was good to see. "That would be nice," he admitted.

"Anything else?" Tre asked.

"Carlos talks about every Navaja ship having at least some of the systems I have developed for the Salix," Kip replied. "But I worry about giving one clan that level of advantage. I mean..." He trailed off.

"You think you trust Jax but you can't help imagining that he might turn into his father or his grandfather," Tre suggested.

Kip flushed.

It was a legitimate concern and one that Tre knew was dangerous not to address head on.

"Show Carlos the true cost of the Salix," he suggested.

Kip's gaze went distant for a moment. "All of it? Even the development costs?"

"Yes," Tre confirmed. "Have you ever considered setting up companies to produce and sell some of your inventions?" He watched Kip's reaction; the way his gaze slid away and the flush that appeared at the top of his cheeks and across the bridge of his nose. He sighed. He was always way behind as far as Kip was concerned. "How many?" he asked.

"They aren't all mine," Kip qualified. "At the moment I only own forty-six of them outright."

"And the ones you have an interest in?" Tre asked.

"All of them, even the ones where I am just an investor?" Kip checked.

Tre nodded and braced himself.

"Seven hundred and thirteen," Kip replied. "I think. A few of them may have gone under in the last seven days. Sometimes even a good product cannot find a buyer." He brought out his goggles. "The company that makes the lenses in these was one of the first ones I funded."

Tre was beyond surprise. "And you were how old?" he asked.

"Nine," Kip admitted.

Tre's understanding of Kip shifted, as it did periodically. Suddenly he appreciated why Kip hated being separated from the data streams so much. Not only was he tracking ships, overseeing the renovation of the Sphere and playing stock markets across Known Space, he was involved with seven hundred and fifty-nine companies. Then there was the data mining; Tre knew that was as much a part of Kip as breathing.

"We'll start heading back to the hole," Tre promised. "As soon as we are there we will jump through."

Kip smiled at him. "Thank you."

Kip was surprised but pleased when Tre suggested that they jump back into the Potash system just so that he could access the data streams. It confirmed that having the Salix had shifted the situation in the direction that Kip had hoped; Tre was more confident that they could deal with unexpected confrontations and less obsessed with staying hidden.

Maybe he should have mentioned the companies earlier. It had never occurred to him that Tre had not guessed at least some of it.

They walked together to the closer of the two shafts and went down a level to where the crewroom and galley were located. Fitting the Salix with customised gravitational field generators had allowed Kip to give them an additional habitable level above and below the array while preserving the illusion that the ship was a standard 14-hex-eight-6.

Also having adjustable gravitational field generators gave them more options during manoeuvres.

Tre suggested during lunch that they begin heading back to the hole and the captain picked up on it immediately. They had a quick vote: ten in favour; none against.

"Are we going to do any more dedicated testing?" Vic asked. "Wouldn't it be better to head somewhere and test on the way?"

"If we are going to head somewhere we could pick up a load first," Ean pointed out immediately. "There are a wide variety of loads to be had in Potash."

Kip liked the idea of trading, even if any profit they would make wouldn't scratch the surface of what the Salix had cost.

"Maybe we combine a trading run with checking up on the Petunia Mae," Tre added. "Do you know where she is, Kip?"

"The Ennui system," Kip replied. Thoughts went off in two different directions. One was speculating which load available in Potash would generate the most profit in the Ennui system. The other was analysing why Tre was interested in the Petunia Mae.

He wasn't the only one to be surprised. Ean was frowning at Tre.

"I thought about finding out about Medico Kem's plans," Tre admitted.

"You think he would leave the Petunia Mae?" Vic queried. "He seemed pretty settled there and the minkies think highly of him."

"Minkies?" Carlos queried.

"The Petunia Mae is a salvage ship," Jax explained. "It's a three way partnership between a family called the Tuckers, the crew and a group of mink–human hybrids. Medico Kem is a member of the crew."

"I could recommend some medicos to approach," Carlos volunteered. "Or you could consider Luis Delgado, who is medico on the Quetzal."

There was a momentary silence before Jax responded. "I like Medico Kem. He is remarkably……resilient."

There were nods from other members of the crew and a whisker-twitch from Rae. Kip agreed with them. There was something reassuring about Medico Kem. Also, he had been the minkies' medico, which probably meant he was the best person to care for Rae.

"If he is not interested or not available a list of other medicos to approach would be very useful," Ean added. "Thank you, Carlos."

After lunch Kip managed to slip into Simulator 2 before his training session, taking advantage of Ean's belief that food should be allowed to settle before taking exercise. He mapped the Salix's path to the hole. They were scheduled to jump through just after ship's midnight, so if he stayed awake afterwards he could hack the light speed data relay and initiate his usual searches as well as checking his account at the Stellar Exchange. That way he would have lots of information to analyse by morning.

Luckily he had set his alarm to warn him about his upcoming training session because he had become distracted researching what the Petunia Mae had been up to over the last eight divs. He had just enough time to change and be on time for his session with Ean.

Dancing as a form of exercise had caught on. Noe, Cas and Obe usually joined Kip and Ean for the first part of the session; even Rae had been known to turn up.

Kip hurried through the open doorway, intent on not being late, only to stop abruptly when he was faced with a magnificent body clad in skintight shorts and a sleeveless vest.

He had flushed crimson before even realising it was Carlos. Kip looked away and scuttled to his usual place at the front, facing Ean, grateful that everyone else, including Carlos, was behind him.

He settled quickly into the pace and rhythm Ean was setting, helped by the music. Unfortunately, the second part of the routine involved turns and Kip discovered that Carlos was directly in front of him.

During the first three turns, Kip's gaze was drawn inexorably to Carlos' butt. Then, on the fourth, he realised that Noe was turning behind the music and, on the fifth, their eyes met for a moment before Noe turned.

It was enough for Kip to be certain that Noe was up to something.

As he turned back to face front, Kip suddenly realised that Carlos was probably studying his butt too.

"Kip!" Ean warned as he lost his place. "Concentrate!"

Kip partitioned off the part of his mind thinking about Carlos, leaving the surface of his mind, the part best connected to his body, following Ean's instructions.

Surely Carlos wouldn't be interested in his skinny butt, even if it wasn't covered in baggy shorts.

Once the dancing was over the others usually left, leaving Kip to practise his knife fighting with Ean. As Kip went over to pick out two practice knives, he could hear Carlos speaking to Ean.

"Would it be possible for me to stay and assist?" he asked.

Kip hoped desperately that Ean would refuse.

"Thank you for offering, Carlos, but it will be better if Kip and I stick to our usual routine," Ean replied.

"I understand," Carlos acknowledged. "Perhaps another time." He raised his voice. "I shall see you later, Kip."

Kip felt himself flushing again. He raised a hand, not trusting himself to speak without squeaking.

With Carlos gone it was easier to concentrate on his lesson with Ean. It proved to be one of his better sessions; Ean was always encouraging but this time Kip knew he had earned the praise he received.

At the end, once they had completed their usual cooling down exercises, Ean told Kip to sit down and began rubbing liniment into his leg muscles.

"Carlos is a very handsome man," Ean observed.

Kip felt himself reddening.

"And I think he finds you attractive," Ean added.

"Why?" Kip squeaked.

Ean looked up and smiled. "There are two answers to that, Kip. The first is that there is very little rhyme or reason to why one person finds another attractive. The other second is that you are growing into a fine looking man, Kip, like your father and your grandfather."

Kip guessed his Pa and his Grandpappy weren't bad to look at; he had never thought about it.

"You are over sixteen. That means it is up to you and you are free to be intimate with any member of the crew, including a crew-guest," Ean reminded him. "I think you can trust Carlos to treat you well," Ean reassured him. "If that is what you decide."

Kip realised that Ean was suggesting Carlos might want to fuck him. Unexpectedly, he found the idea of it exciting. "What about Noe?" he asked.

Ean laughed. "I think we both know that Noe has probably done everything short of stripping the two of you naked and shoving you into a room together."

Until today, during the dance routine, Kip hadn't realised anything of the sort. However he trusted Ean's judgement.

Ean reached up and pushed a strand of hair back from Kip's face. "If you are interested, it might be best if I have a word with him. He needs to know that your experience is limited and that you don't find it easy to speak about such things."

Kip found himself nodding.

❃ ❃ ❃

Ean had quickly realised that Carlos found Kip intriguing. Carlos' interest had started when Tre had given him a glimpse of what Kip could do and had escalated when he had become aware of Kip's connection to Klennethon Darrent.

Carlos had watched Kip and Klennethon Darrent playing chess on the Renaissance. Meanwhile Ean had studied Carlos. He had seen the moment when Carlos' attention had shifted from the interaction between Kip and Klennethon Darrent to Kip himself. It had been when Kip had stretched, drawing Carlos' eyes to his long, slim, pale neck.

Ean had checked the others, to see if anyone else had noticed. His eyes had locked with Noe's, who was doing likewise. They agreed; Carlos found Kip attractive.

Since then Noe had given Ean a running commentary on Carlos' character. It had not taken much: a comment here; a look there. Between them, without ever needing a discussion, they had decided that Carlos would be very suitable as Kip's first.

Kip needed a good experience. Being found attractive by a fine specimen like Carlos would be a bonus. It would do wonders for Kip's confidence.

So it had not been much of a surprise when Noe delivered Carlos to the exercise session and, by the Lady, Carlos had looked good in his stretchy shorts and top; Obe's eyes had almost popped out of his head.

It had been enough. Kip had noticed and, to both Ean and Noe's delight, responded.

Having checked that Kip was definitely interested, Ean sent Kip off for a shower and went to find Tre. As always, a sweaty Ean reminded Tre of another type of workout. Ean accepted a kiss but then slipped out of his grasp and batted his hands away.

"Carlos is interested in Kip," he began.

It took Tre a moment to realise that Ean meant interested in a sexual way. Once he had, his surprise was evident. "He is?" he queried.

"He is," Ean replied with confidence. "And Kip is interested in Carlos."

Tre frowned slightly. "You want me to warn him off?" he asked.

"No!" Ean sometimes wondered if Tre had the slightest clue about relationships. "Carlos is exactly what Kip needs. If Carlos comes to you for advice, or to ask permission, the message is that Kip is immature and inexperienced but available and interested."

Tre shook his head. "As long as you are sure. Carlos won't ask me. He's a stickler for doing things properly. He'll ask you. You're queen."

"He may come to you for advice," Ean insisted. "If he does, tell him to take it slowly and be careful."

Tre was right; once he had showered and redressed, Ean found Carlos lurking as he headed for the galley. They entered together. Jax and Rae were there preparing the ingredients for supper. Ean handed them a tablet listing everything that was needed from the storeroom or hydroponics and told them to shut the door on their way out.

Then he gestured that Carlos should sit at the table and started making tea.

"It's about Kip," Carlos began. "I would like to be sexually intimate with him and wish to confirm that I have your approval."

Ean liked Carlos' direct approach but could not resist a quick tease. "Do you have reason to believe that Kip is interested?"

Carlos' expression was a picture. It had obviously not occurred to him that Kip might not find him attractive. "In the gym…" he began and then trailed off. He flushed slightly before pulling himself together. "Perhaps you could confirm that for me, Ean."

Ean took pity on him. "I believe you may be correct and that Kip is interested," he replied as he filled the teapot and brought the tray over to the table.

It wasn't a difficult conversation. Noe had briefed Carlos thoroughly. Carlos knew how Ean ran the crew, including that cats on the Willow, or the Salix, had more say in who fucked them than was usually the case.

He also was aware of Kip's fragility; something he obviously found attractive.

"Hurt him and you will regret it," Ean finished up.

Carlos took the warning well. "It is a mark of an honourable spacer that former crewmates have fond memories of him," he replied. Then he looked into Ean's eyes. "You can trust me with him, Ean. I know how special he is."

Ean did trust him, even if Carlos had no concept of how special Kip actually was.

Supper was fun because the crew was divided into three. There were those who knew for definite that something was happening, namely Tre, Ean, Carlos and Kip himself. Then there were those who were almost certain; Noe, who had been encouraging things along, and Rae, whose nose was never wrong about such things. Everyone else was at a different point on the path between suspecting something was up and realising that the something was between Carlos and Kip.

There was a wonderful moment when Obe caught on. His eyes widened and his gaze went from Kip to Carlos and then back to Kip. His mouth opened and Ean braced himself for some misjudged comment that would send Kip scuttling for Simulator 2. However, before he could speak, Obe's expression had crumpled with pain as someone, Ean suspected Noe but did not know how he had managed it from where he was sitting, kicked or jabbed him.

Then he turned wounded eyes on Cas, who could not understand why he was being blamed.

Ean had wondered if Carlos would push things along quickly with Kip but instead he suggested they play games to while away the evening before the jump, which was scheduled to happen shortly after midnight.

They began with a game of sticks. Long coloured sticks were allowed to fall into a disorganised heap on the table and then everyone tried to extract one in turn without moving the others.

It was the equivalent for Rae as cards were for Kip, so it was a matter of who would come second.

Ean wondered if Tre would be able to compete with Rae if he used his cyborg abilities. Not that he would, because he would consider it cheating.

Then they played a ridiculous game where everyone had the name of a famous person stuck to their forehead and had to ask yes/no questions until they guessed who it was. The game had never worked well until Kip had suggested having a set list of famous people, which was an excellent idea because it encouraged the younger members of the crew to learn some history and a bit about current affairs.

After that they had a singsong. Carlos not only played the guitar but he had a fantastic voice, an impressive repertoire and could deliver a comic song in a way that had all of them in stitches.

They finished up with Carlos singing a romantic ballad that was definitely directed at Kip. Better still, Kip realised because he went a delightful shade of pink.

Their new procedure for jump required Jax, Rae and Kip, so Ean would have been happier if they had jumped next morning rather than at midnight. However Tre had wanted them to jump as soon as they reached the hole and Ean had acquiesced.

He sighed as he stripped off and climbed into one of the simulators on the crewroom level. Gone were the days when they took jumps sitting on the couch in the shared area; now each one was treated as if it was a potential conflict.

Given what had happened when they jumped into the Verdant system, Ean had reluctantly accepted the new reality.

Nothing happened, which was hardly surprising given that they were using an ungated hole well away from the shipping lanes that crossed the Potash system.

Ean guessed that someone could have tracked them jumping through the hole eight days ago and decided to wait around in case they decided to return. Not that it seemed very likely.

He waited for the captain to give the all clear and was about to open the simulator when Kip's voice came over the speaker.

"Ean?"

It was a simulator-to-simulator link rather than an open channel. Ean wondered if Kip wanted to discuss the situation with Carlos. He activated his microphone and opened his end of the channel. "Yes, Kip?"

"I've been in contact with the Stellar Exchange. There is a message for you. I thought it might be urgent. Shall I forward it?"

"Yes," Ean replied. His mind went immediately to Ben but he dismissed that possibility; Ben had made it clear that he and Art were intent on a clean break. It was not from Kip's parents because Kip would have said. Maybe one of the ladies he had met on the Stellar Rover?

It was from the account Ean had opened in Ben's name, using the balance he had funded. Ean's hand was trembling as he decompressed and opened the video message.

Ben looked dreadful. He was too thin, his hair was straggly and Ean was almost certain his face was painted. Ben only ever painted his face when he was trying to cover bruises.

Ean had an overpowering desire to bury his knife in Art's gut.

"By the Lady, Ean, I hope you get this soon. It's all gone. Every credit. His and mine. He owes. For all I know, I owe

too."

Ean shuddered. Art wouldn't think twice about using Ben's name. At least Ben would have never allowed his fingerprint or retina pattern to be used on a loan agreement.

"We're in a system called Logan's Star on a spacestation called Logan 2. I finally got him to consider looking for a crew but we have nothing to buy in with and you know Art, he wants an advantage. Well he's only got one left, me. He's been telling crews what a good fuck I am."

A knife in the gut was too good for him.

"I only know because one of the men had a speck of decency in him and told me," Ben continued. *"Of course Art said he didn't say it and, once he admitted it, he said he didn't mean it. Only I know it'll happen, just like everything else has."* He looked directly into the camera. *"I walked away this morning and I'm not going back. I'll find some work. Anything that will pay enough for a safe place to sleep and three meal bars a day. Anywhere he won't think of looking.*

"Trouble is, there's only one small Stellar Exchange here so, once he realises I'm gone, all he has to do is watch it. It won't be worth the risk of checking every day. I've asked and this message will be compressed and fed into a priority stream to Tarrasade so it will take six days to get there and at least another six for a reply to arrive. I know you'll reply immediately if you're there so I'll wait thirteen days from today and then I'll check. Hopefully he will have given up by then."

Ean's gaze darted to the date in the upper right hand corner. Tomorrow, no today, was the eleventh day. Was it possible to get a message there within a day or maybe two? How much would a one-off light speed message cost?

Much more than Ean could afford.

"*Ean?*"

It was Kip. Ean did not want to talk to Kip. He needed to speak with Tre or perhaps the captain; yes, the captain.

"*I can make a message accessible from the Stellar Exchange in Logan 2, within one point two days.*"

Ean froze. Was that possible? How much would it cost? If Ean said yes now, the message would make it in time. If he hesitated it would be too late.

"*Is it Ben?*" Kip asked tentatively.

"Yes," Ean whispered.

"*I can open a bank account in his name,*" Kip replied immediately. "*Ben will be able to realise the balance as credit tokens.*"

Kip sounded so certain, as if opening bank accounts systems away in other people's names was something he did every day.

"*Will credit be enough?*" Kip asked. He hesitated but then asked. "*Is he in trouble?*"

"He's trying to avoid Art," Ean admitted. "He thinks Art may be watching the Stellar Exchange." He took a deep breath. "Ben said he would wait thirteen days and then check the account again. I don't know if he means tomorrow or the day after."

"*I'm on it,*" Kip assured him. "*You concentrate on recording some vid for the message. I'll activate the desk.*"

Kip was talking about the desk in what they called the office. Ean closed the channel, climbed out of the simulator and dressed. The office was one level up.

He walked towards the ladder that they rarely used, telling himself that he wasn't avoiding Tre or the captain; it was merely a matter of saving time.

He could not bear the thought of Ben checking and there being no reply; of him letting Ben down.

He settled at the desk, which was activated as Kip had said it would be. As soon as he sat down, Kip's voice came from one of the speakers.

"Ready when you are, Ean. Just talk and we can cut out any bits you don't want to send."

Ean took a deep breath. "Ben, you did the right thing. What matters now is getting you off that station, away from Art. We arranged for some credit tokens. Details are at the end of this message." Then he remembered all the times Art had wheedled his way back out of trouble; back into Ben's affections. "This isn't your credit, Ben, so you do not have the right to share it with Art. It is for you, to get away. Get passage anywhere, as long as it has a Stellar Exchange. Once there, you can send me another message. I'll make sure there is enough credit in the account." He looked directly down the camera lens. "I love you, Ben. Best friends forever. Stay safe."

There was nothing else to say so he stopped the recorder and sat back.

"Do you want to check the message?" Kip's voice asked from the speaker.

Ean nodded before remembering that Kip could not see him. "Yes," he confirmed.

It would do; Ean did not think he could do any better if he tried again. At the end of the video he had recorded were the details of the bank account Kip was setting up and three suggested destinations.

"*I don't have enough real time information about the Logan's Star system to know what transport is available*," Kip admitted. "*Is the message good to go?*"

"Yes," Ean replied. "Thank you, Kip."

"*No problem*," Kip replied.

Ean sat at the desk, thinking about what he had done. How much credit was Kip spending sending light speed messages? It would be far more that Ean could ever hope to repay. Then there was the credit Kip was putting into the bank account for Ben.

"Ean?"

It was Tre; the door had opened without Ean noticing.

"What's wrong?" Tre asked.

Ean's throat threatened to close but he forced himself to speak. "It's Ben. He's in trouble. Kip helped me send a message." He swallowed. "Only it had to be light speed, because Ben is relying on me and we've been out of contact eight days, so it was almost too late when Kip spotted it." He fixed his gaze on the surface of the desk. "I let him send it even though I know I can't pay him back. All I could think of was not letting Ben down."

Tre was there beside him, turning the chair and gathering him into a hug.

"Kip sends light speed messages all the time," Tre assured him.

Being hugged felt so good that it took a moment to focus on what Tre had said. "How does he pay for them?" Ean demanded.

Tre hugged him again. "Lady knows. Maybe he doesn't."

Kip was sending messages without paying for them? Was that even possible? If it was, it was stealing. Ean knew he should have asked more questions but all he had cared about was helping Ben.

Tre must have felt him stiffen. "Or maybe he does," he added hastily. "Kip can afford Mulligan drives. What are a few light speed messages compared to that?"

Ean wasn't convinced; Tre had said Kip sent them all the time.

Tre kissed his forehead. "Tell me about Ben."

It did not help because talking about Ben and watching Tre's reaction just made Ean feel a bit sick. What if the crew voted against taking Ben back? Ben had walked away from them twice. He had preferred to believe Art rather than accept the evidence that Art was a traitor. Other than Ean, who would want him back, never mind trust him?

Tre did not mention what might happen next. Instead he reassured Ean that he had done the right thing and suggested that they go to bed.

It was late. Ean concurred.

Only he couldn't sleep. He oscillated between worrying about Ben, imagining what might be happening to him, and worrying about Kip's poorly developed sense of right and wrong.

In the end he slipped out from between Tre and the wall. Given how late they had gone to bed, it was only a hundred minutes short of ship's dawn. He would sit in the galley until it wasn't too early to run one of the showers; he didn't want to wake anyone.

Then he realised that Kip's bunk was empty. It didn't look as if it had been slept in. The drapes were pulled back and the bedcover was smooth.

Could he be with Carlos? Ean dismissed the possibility; Carlos obviously meant to take things slowly.

Could he have fallen asleep in the simulator? Ean pulled on some clothes and headed for Simulator 2, which was one of the four on the crewroom level.

As he approached he could hear someone. He slid the door open. Kip was shutting down the simulator and pulling on his clothes.

"Kip?" Ean queried.

Kip jumped and turned to face him. He looked tired.

"Did you fall asleep in the simulator?" Ean asked.

"No," Kip replied. "Setting things up for Ben took longer than I expected. Don't worry though. I got the message off as soon as you had finished it."

Ean felt guilty. He had not thought to ask how long it would take Kip to set up the bank account. He should have checked that Kip had finished and gone to bed. "Kip, thank you for your help but I really will need to pay you for the light speed messages you sent, even if it is in instalments."

Kip shook his head. "No need. I didn't pay for them." He did not look even the slightest bit guilty.

Ean braced himself. "Kip, they may only be messages but it isn't fair if you get them free while other people have to pay so much for them. Taking something and not paying for it is stealing, even if it's only a message."

Kip smiled. "I knew you'd say that, it was just a matter of when. So I came up with a solution. It's the same one Citizen Darrent uses. If you own one-tenth of the Stellar Exchange you get free messages, even light speed ones."

It took a moment for Ean to realise that Kip meant the Stellar Exchange across the whole of The Fringe.

"You could afford that?" Ean asked. Even to his own ears, his voice seemed faint.

This time Kip flushed. "I started really trying to accumulate credit when we needed the drive for this ship. Then I thought Jax might need to pay the whole debt associated with the Sphere, so I worked a bit harder at it. Now it's really easy. The more you have the easier it is to get even more. So I started a shopping list and one-tenth of the Stellar Exchange was at the top because I knew you would want me to pay for my messages."

Ean could not resist asking. "What else is on the list?"

Kip's gaze slipped away. "You know. Spacer stuff. Ships. Spacestations. More Mulligan drives. Gates. Planets."

Ean found himself thinking of a boy with a galactic scale construction set. "People live on ships and in spacestations and on planets, Kip," he reminded him.

"I know," Kip assured him. "Like in the Sphere."

Ean had to admit that Kip's plans for the Sphere had been sympathetic to everyone involved, particularly the Scavengers. He might have asked more but, at that moment, Kip gave an enormous yawn. "Off to bed," Ean ordered. "I expect you to sleep in."

Kip smiled. "No problem with that." He closed the simulator and sauntered off in the direction of the crewroom.

Ean watched him go. Kip was sixteen. He could live until he was Klennethon Darrent's age. Ean could not help but wonder if Known Space would look the same once Kip had finished with it.

Maybe it would look better; it was a nice thought.

He checked the chronometer. A few cups of tea and he would be able to run the shower. He headed for the galley. To his surprise Tre was sitting at the table nursing a cup of coffee.

"You weren't there," Tre explained. "I thought I'd check on you. Then I heard you with Kip and didn't want to interrupt."

Ean was touched; Tre hated getting up early. "Did you hear what he said?"

Tre shook his head. "I'm not like Rae. I have to make a conscious decision to augment my hearing."

"He didn't pay for the light speed messages because he doesn't have to. Apparently if you own one-tenth of the Stellar Exchange they are free," Ean explained.

Tre's face was a picture. Ean had never seen him looked so stunned. The word flabbergasted came to mind.

Ean poured him another cup of coffee while he recovered.

"Centre locks up all the typed-geniuses it can find," Tre pointed out once he was over the worst of the shock. "When I first found that out I was disgusted. I thought that it was another aspect of their obsession with control."

"Now you wonder," Ean suggested.

Tre shook his head slightly. "Now I imagine someone with Kip's abilities but not his character and I understand perfectly."

24

Tre had known that Carlos would be horrified by the crew's decision to retrieve Ben and offer to take him back. Carlos found out immediately after the Meeting where they had decided. Tre could see him biting his tongue, fighting the urge to comment on something that, as crew-guest, was none of his business.

Instead he made the Navaja hand signal requesting an urgent conference.

Once they were on the other side of the gravity generators, out of earshot of even Rae, Carlos could not hold it in any longer.

"This Ben has displayed his lack of loyalty on more than one occasion," he began. "He has a close association with this other man, Art, who is a traitor. Ben, knowing or unknowing, could be the bait in a trap. It is possible that he has been in enemy hands during the last seven divs. His mind could have been worked over. He could be a plant. Within seven divs he could have been made into an assassin."

Tre had considered every one of the options Carlos was raising. "What is worse than a known risk, Carlos?" he asked.

Carlos considered and then deflated with a sigh. "An unknown risk."

"We are going to convert an unknown risk into a known risk," Tre assured him. "If we were in a different situation we would have a specialist team who would pick up Ben and make an assessment. However, we do not, so we will proceed with caution."

Carlos hesitated but then nodded. "I do not wish to intrude but would it be possible to know a little more about Ben?"

Tre paused for a moment, deciding how much he could say without breaking the code. He would concentrate on the events that could be found in the crew's public record and only comment on aspects of people's personalities with which Carlos was already familiar.

"Ben was cat when I found the crew," Tre began. "I had picked the Willow because it had the perfect history and Mel was, is, an exemplary captain. I quickly decided that I was only interested in keeping three of the existing crew; Mel himself, Vic and Ben. All three were sound personalities, had generous natures and no ties to anyone outside the crew."

Tre thought back. It had been between the Willow and another Trad crew. Vic had tipped the balance. The big man radiated reliability and kindness, reminding Tre of the men who had helped him when he had been torn away from his home and everyone he had cared for.

"So I worked on getting the others to move on and recruiting suitable replacements," he continued. "Finding appropriate adults proved difficult. I decided that as I had twelve standards, I should not worry if some of the ones I wanted to get rid of hung around for a few extra standards or if all I could find were youngsters who needed training.

"Ean was first. Vic spotted him. He was fourteen, Ben was sixteen and they bonded, like youngsters often do. Ben cushioned Ean's transition into spacer life and the two of them developed together. I knew I wanted them as the backbone of the crew I was building for Jax.

"It had been going well enough. Ben and Ean had their knives and were shaping up well. We had recruited another cat, Hal, but by the time he was heading for his knife I could see he wouldn't do. He obviously saw himself as a future queen. Luckily he was shrewd enough to see that Ean would become queen, not him.

"So I made sure the profit margin increased. Sure enough, as soon as the cat had his knife he bought out. We took on Cas to replace him."

Tre did not go into details. Ean had spotted Cas catting for the type of crew who broke boys rather than cared for them. He had obviously not been with them long; there had still been some life in his eyes.

There had been this moment when Ean had looked at Tre with utter trust in his eyes. Before then it had not even occurred to Tre that they should challenge. They were not a crew that challenged; whenever Tre had fought it had been because a crew had wanted their cat, not the other way around.

Only Tre needed Ean to trust him; letting Ean down at that stage in their relationship had been a worse idea than challenging for a pretty boy who was obviously too young and probably too damaged to save.

Luckily Cas had worked out just fine. Or rather, in retrospect,

Tre had experienced Ean's amazing instinct for spotting a boy with potential for the first time.

"I think I became complacent," Tre admitted. "I had it all mapped out. In my plan Lou, our queen, would stay long enough to train Ean and retire two or three standards before Jax joined the crew. Ben had the potential to be a talented pilot. We would look for more lads with high potential while I kept my eyes open for any qualified spacers who made the grade, as unlikely as that seemed. There were still five crew members who had to be moved on but three were heading for retirement, the fourth was looking over other crews every time we docked and I could not see the fifth giving me too much trouble.

"Then it slipped away from me. It started when Lou died in his sleep." Tre still thought it had been suicide but it could have been an accidental overdose. "Ean was too young, barely twenty, but I knew by then that he was the queen I needed and there was enough support, just, to get him voted in.

"Only it precipitated a series of changes. San and Rex retired and Eli, our nav, bought out rather than recognise Ean's authority. It left us short-handed.

"Anyway, we were clubbing and this navigator from another crew, Art, danced with Ben. Next thing I knew he wanted to buy in and I couldn't come up with enough valid reasons to get the others to oppose it."

Tre recalled trying to make Ean vote against. Ean had not wanted Art in the crew but Ben, his best friend, had asked him to vote for. Tre had pushed hard, reducing Ean to a sobbing wreck, but in the end Ean had sided with his best friend rather than his lover.

Carlos was studying him. Tre could tell he wanted to ask something. He gestured that a question would be appropriate.

"They did not trust your opinion?" he queried. "About Art?"

Tre understood that for Carlos, who had grown up on Kalakmul and always spaced as part of a clan crew, it would seem strange. "They listened," he replied. "But in a non-aligned Trad crew I have no authority. There is the captain, there is the queen and then there are the others. Art looked good and talked better. He was a fully qualified nav. He could buy a respectable number of shares. Worse, he was obviously besotted with Ben and Ben felt the same about him." He offered the smallest of smiles. "Spacers are romantics."

He received a similar smile in return.

"I recognised that Art joining was a setback," Tre continued. "Also, if Ben did not see sense then he would leave with Art and that would be a loss. What I did not appreciate was that Art had a gambler's nose for an opportunity. He sensed that the crew was doing well and would do better. He dug in, intending to be along for the ride, and I decided to bide my time. I thought I had six standards to get rid of him.

"Only I didn't. The call came three standards early and Art was still there. One look at Jax, disguised or not, and he knew something was up." Tre thought back. "I think everyone did but the others were trustworthy. Jax was crew. They would never betray him."

"Including Ben," Carlos queried.

"Including Ben," Tre confirmed. "Anyway, in the end it was not Art who betrayed us. It was Medico Loy, whom I brought into the crew after we recruited Jax and Rae."

Carlos was silent for a moment. "I would have judged Medico

Loy to be trustworthy," he admitted.

Tre appreciated the support. "It taught me a lesson. You need to judge the person in front of you, not the person you remember."

"Which also applies to Ben," Carlos observed.

It was an excellent point.

Having calmed Carlos down and got him thinking, Tre invited him to the briefing that Kip had prepared on the risks associated with taking Ben back.

Jax and Rae were also there, even though Tre was sure that Rae couldn't follow a tenth of it.

Tre himself was soon struggling.

"I've already taken some steps to reduce some of the risks and mitigate others," Kip admitted.

The multicoloured diagram changed four times. Each time there was less red and more blue, which Tre appreciated meant significantly less risk overall. "Without checking?" he queried.

Kip flushed. "The opportunities to act were time limited," he replied.

"What did you do?" Jax asked.

Tre did not miss the way Kip's gaze slid sideways to Carlos, which Tre interrupted to mean that he did not want Carlos knowing the length of his reach.

"Concentrate on the major outcomes," Tre suggested.

Kip considered. "We got enough credit to Ben so that he could buy a pod-passage. I also managed to find out a little about Art's actions. I know he tried to find out the destination of Ben's pod-passage and I know he has sent messages from the Stellar Exchange. I have assumed that he is trying to sell Ben's where-abouts as a way of finding Jax. I have changed the destination of Ben's passage. This reduces the danger to Jax and means Art will have sold inaccurate information."

Tre blinked; what had Kip been up to if those were the things he was willing to admit? He could see Carlos frowning, trying to work out how Kip had arranged credit for Ben or find out what Art had been doing.

"Good work, Kip," Jax acknowledged.

Rae smiled, baring his teeth. "When Ben doesn't turn up where Art said, the buyer will kill him."

Tre watched Carlos' reaction to Rae's comment; he approved greatly. It also distracted him from thinking about what Kip had been doing, which was a relief.

Kip swapped the diagram for another. This time there was some grey, illustrating the aspects of the situation about which Kip had insufficient information to make a judgement.

"It is much more difficult when we take Art out of the equation and concentrate solely on Ben," he admitted. "There are three possibilities. The first is that Ben is as straightforward, honest, trustworthy and loyal as we believe him to be. The second is that he has changed and intends to betray us. The third, the tricky one, is that he thinks he is still the person we know and trust but someone has fiddled with his head, or his body. You know the type of thing: implanted bomb; tracking transponder; alternative personality who is an assassin." Kip gestured that he could think of many more.

"Of course we have the same problem with anyone we meet," Kip continued. "But it is more significant with Ben because his association with us makes him a target for manipulation."

"I believe we will be able to rule out the second possibility quickly," Jax proposed. "Ean's instincts and Rae's nose will detect Ben's conscious intentions."

"I agree," Kip responded. "The great thing about Rae's sense of smell is that most purebreds don't even know they broadcast information that way."

To Tre's surprise, Carlos accepted what Jax and Kip were saying. Instead of discussing the second possibility further he focused on the third. "So we must develop a way of screening people," he pointed out. "What do you already do?"

Kip was struggling. He hoped he was hiding it, at least from everyone other than Rae. Whenever he saw Carlos, which was unavoidable during a meeting like the one they were in, all he could think of was how it had felt to be kissed, fondled and fucked.

The fucking was a recent development; last night had been Kip's first time. Being fucked had been even better than Carlos using his hands or his mouth; not that either of those alternatives was to be passed up when offered. Carlos was, as Noe had warned him, extremely skilled and very solicitous of his partner's pleasure.

Kip wondered if he would end up addicted to sex. Noe's blowjobs were fun; bursts of pleasure like firecrackers going off in his brain. With Carlos it was much more intense; like the biggest, most amazing firework display.

During orgasm there were no thoughts, only a wonderful, cleansing wave of pleasure. Carlos could build that wave into a tsunami, soaring ever higher before it crashed through layer after layer of Kip's mind.

He wasn't even sore; he had followed Noe's instructions to the letter so he had been properly prepared. If there was any damage, which he doubted given how careful Carlos had been, using the e-machine afterwards had sorted it.

Carlos had asked a question and all Kip could think was how sexy Carlos' voice was and what those lips could do when they weren't talking.

"Kip?" Jax queried.

For once even Jax's voice wasn't enough to make him focus. He searched his mind; no, he had no memory of Carlos' question.

"Carlos asked how we screen people," Rae informed him with a whisker-twitch that confirmed he knew exactly what Kip had been thinking.

Kip thrust all thoughts of Carlos' other skills into a corner of his mind and slammed down a partition. Then he pretended that Carlos-with-clothes was an entirely different person from Carlos-without-clothes.

It was a stretch but Carlos helped by behaving as if Kip-without-clothes did not even exist.

They came up with a series of tests that they would try out on Ben. Both Carlos and Tre were satisfied that what they were proposing was at least as effective as the Navaja clan's security screening, probably better.

"We have to get Ben to agree to the tests," Tre pointed out.

There was a short silence. Ben had to comply or they couldn't risk bringing him onto the ship. The obvious person to persuade him was Ean but even Kip could see that Tre asking Ean was a really bad idea.

Ean still hadn't got over Tre stuffing Ben into a pod and leaving him there for a standard. The truth was, and they all knew it, if Loy hadn't told Ean, Ben would still be podded and hidden on Mercy Station.

"I shall go to Ean and ask his advice," Jax decided.

Jax went off to speak to Ean. Rae followed. Tre looked from Carlos to Kip and then back to Carlos. Kip could feel himself beginning to blush.

"We'll speak later, Kip," Tre declared and left. He even shut the door behind him.

Kip started to close all his models and shut down the equipment, as he would have done if Carlos hadn't been sitting there observing him with what Noe called 'those dark, sultry, suggestive eyes'.

The partition Kip had put up was feeling decidedly shaky.

As soon as the last display had been deactivated, Carlos caught his hand and, with a practised tug, landed Kip in his lap. Kip might have objected but a kiss put paid to that.

By the time the kiss finished he was half naked and Carlos was lifting him up and putting his butt on the table.

Nine-tenths of him wanted it. The other one-tenth hated the idea of someone coming in and seeing them.

The one-tenth won and Carlos detected his reluctance immediately. He gave a low growl of disappointment but followed up with a soft kiss on the lips as he pulled away.

"You have no idea how sexy you are," Carlos complained. "Every diagram, every deduction, every suggestion; it makes me want you more."

Kip would have never guessed; Carlos had appeared completely professional throughout the meeting. Maybe it was just pillow talk. He hopped down from the table and did up his clothes.

Carlos smiled. "I shall have to wait until tonight."

Kip shivered at the thought of it.

"Perhaps I should come to your training session this afternoon," he suggested.

"No!" Kip objected before he could censor his reaction. He flushed. "I can't concentrate when you are there." He could see that Carlos did not see anything wrong with that. "Ean expects me to concentrate," he added. "He's worked so hard getting me fit and teaching me knife-fighting. I hate letting him down."

Carlos' teasing smile faded into a more understanding expression. He reached out a hand and caressed Kip's cheek.

"Ean means a great deal to you youngsters," he observed.

"To everyone," Kip insisted. "You admire Tre. Ask yourself why he values Ean so highly."

"Ean is Tre's lover," Carlos replied.

Kip could see that Carlos did not understand but decided that it was not the type of argument you won with words. Carlos would learn to appreciate Ean. "Time to go," he announced. "I have duties."

Duties turned out to be nursing along the young plants in hydroponics while Noe interrogated him about Carlos. Kip was soon wishing that Jax and Rae were there; Noe was suggestive rather than blatant when Jax was about.

Eventually he had given enough detail to satisfy Noe's curiosity. Noe sighed.

"You're so lucky," he said with something close to wistfulness in his voice.

Kip was confused. "You gave him to me, Noe," he pointed out. "You could have worked the situation so that he never even glanced at me."

"Not Carlos," Noe replied. "Carlos is good looking and nice but he's just a man. You. Your reaction to sex. It's so simple. It isn't muddled up with any other stuff."

Kip wasn't sure that was true. Before Noe he had thought he was too ugly and weird for anyone to find him attractive.

On the other hand, he had been pretty much a virgin before Carlos. Noe's first experiences had been when he was so young that Kip hated thinking about it.

Surely there was someone somewhere who could understand

what Noe had been through and help him. "Maybe one day…" he began.

"Forget it, Kip," Noe ordered. "Done is done. Gone is gone. We each live with our own past."

They finished tending the plants and then Kip harvested as many fruits as he could, a small basket of tomatoes and another of strawberries, while Noe picked the herbs and greens that Ean needed.

Ean was alone when they delivered them to the galley, which Kip did not register as suspicious until Ean sent Noe away and asked him to shut the door behind him. Then he told Kip to sit down at the table.

Kip belatedly realised what was coming and felt himself turning crimson.

"How are things between you and Carlos?" Ean asked, sitting down beside him.

"Fine," Kip assured him. "Better than fine." If he kept talking Ean might not ask too many embarrassing questions. "It's fun. He's been very kind and gentle. Noe made sure I knew what to do."

"So there are no problems with the physical side of things?" Ean checked.

Kip had not thought that he could go any redder but he could. "None," he replied, trying to sound firm rather than squeaky.

"He is only going to be with us for a short time," Ean reminded him. "Perhaps I should have considered that before giving him permission to be intimate with you."

Kip was lost.

Ean smiled. "I don't want you to have your heart broken," he added gently.

Kip had never even thought of that. Was he in any danger of falling in love with Carlos? He didn't think so. Carlos was... ...Carlos.

Ean was studying him; waiting for a reply.

"It's just a crewmate thing," Kip assured him. "He's enjoying teaching me about fucking and I'm enjoying learning." He took in Ean's shocked expression. "I know that doesn't sound very romantic."

Ean shook his head and smiled. "It is exactly how it should be, Kip. It is just that I have never heard it put quite like that. I am very glad that it is working well for both of you."

Ean turned away and began to get up, signalling that the conversation was over. Kip was relieved. It could have been worse. Then, unexpectedly, he remembered Noe's wistful expression.

"Ean, have you any ideas how we can help Noe?" he asked.

Ean sank back into the chair. "Noe needs help?"

"About sex," Kip clarified.

"Noe needs help about sex?" Ean asked disbelievingly.

"He said that I was lucky because my reaction to sex was so simple rather than being muddled up with other stuff."

Ean eyes widened and he paled slightly. "Thank you, Kip."

Kip was lost again.

"Thank you for telling me," Ean clarified. "To be honest, Kip, I do not know if Noe will ever let me, or anyone, help him."

Kip knew that Ean was wrong about that. "You've helped him every day since that moment you refused to let Tre get rid of him," he pointed out. "Not only is he a thousand times better off with us than with a crew like the Saber's or with a man like Scar but we trust him and he really appreciates it."

Ean's colour returned with a little extra. "And you are a good friend to him, Kip. Let me think about it. Maybe he won't let me help him but perhaps I can think of ways to make it more likely that he will learn to help himself."

Kip liked the sound of that; Noe was happier believing he was self-sufficient, even if he wasn't.

✳ ✳ ✳

Not even worrying about Ben could stop Ean thinking about what Kip had said about Noe.

Ean knew that his relationship with Noe was different from with the other youngsters. It was difficult to treat him like an ordinary adolescent. Knowing he was a ruthless, manipulative killer who would do anything to survive got in the way.

Taking on a semi-feral boy like Rae had been risky. Allowing Noe onto the crew, code or no code, had been foolhardy. Tre had been correct. Ean had been naïve.

And yet, amazingly, it had proved to be the right thing to do. Noe had chosen to limit his behaviour so that he could stay in the crew. He followed most of Ean's rules. He had made many positive contributions. He helped Kip cope with everyday life. Kip regarded him as a friend and, maybe, Noe saw Kip in the same way.

Most importantly, he had helped Jax escape from the Talon and reunited him with Tre.

The evidence suggested that Noe was loyal. Astonishingly, given his history, he appeared sane. He was even capable of small acts of kindness without expecting anything in return.

So it was time Ean stepped up and did his job as queen.

Ean imagined what would happen if he suggested that Noe should seek psychiatric help and shuddered. It was out of the question; he doubted that Noe would ever forgive him. Instead Noe had to be persuaded to help himself and Ean knew that the best way to do that was through a shared activity.

Like getting Kip fit via the communal dance sessions.

The more he thought about it, the more positive Ean became. Noe was not the only one who could benefit from learning about what lay behind people's motivation and behaviours.

There was no time like the present. Ean decided to use the slice of time between lunch and his training session with Kip. During lunch he suggested that Noe help him unpack the fabrics, which were still in packing cases, and begin the process of organising their storage.

Noe had helped design the new fabric storage cupboard. It was five times the size on the one on the Willow. Noe wanted the fabrics arranged by weight and by colour. The heaviest gauge fabrics, mostly wools, would be on the lowest shelf while the finest silks were on the highest. Colour, according the spectrum would go left to right with reds at the left and violets to the right.

The section to the far right had been set aside for patterns.

Ean decided to jump straight in and see how it went.

"It's a relief to be on a ship again," he admitted as they sorted the silks from the other fabrics and began grading them. "I understand about being queen on a Trad ship. In Tarrasade, I was constantly having to deal with unfamiliar situations, like trying to get what we needed out of Agent Poe and negotiating with the Committee."

Noe did not comment although Ean knew he was listening; Noe always listened intently.

"I only have experience of two situations, living in a whore-house and being a member of a Trad crew." He had caught Noe's interest; Ean could tell from the way Noe's movements had slowed. "Having Jax in the crew, I think the unfamiliar situations will keep coming," he added. "I want to be able to make sound deductions about strangers' motivations and intentions. I believe I have good instincts but I want more expertise to draw on." He stopped and waited but Noe did not contribute. Ean thought about asking for his opinion but decided against it.

"I am going to put together a learning programme for myself," he continued. "I thought I would start with human psychology and behaviour. I expect I'll find it tough, because I never had much formal education." He paused but Noe still did not speak.

"I was wondering if you would be interested in being my study partner. I find it much easier to learn if I can talk about the ideas with someone else."

There was silence. Ean began wondering what he would do if Noe did not reply. He knew he should give Noe longer but the urge to end the silence was building.

"I would like that," Noe admitted just before Ean could not stand it any longer.

Ean managed not to sigh with relief. "Good. Maybe we can set aside a regular time."

"What about Ben?" Noe asked.

Ean had not expected that. What did Noe mean? Was he worried that Ean would want to study with Ben rather than him?

"Ben may choose not to rejoin the crew," he pointed out. "And, even if he does, Ben is a pilot. I imagine he will be much more interested in learning about the Salix's piloting interface than in studying psychology or behaviour."

Noe stroked the fabric he was holding. "What is he like?"

It was an acceptable question; Noe was asking about character rather that background. What was Ben like? Ean had to think. To him Ben was Ben. "Easy to live with. Always does his share and a bit more. Observant." He considered. "Intelligent. Not clever like Kip. More like the captain or maybe Jax. Good with numbers and technical stuff like Vic." He remembered larking about with Ben in the tail-end levels of the Willow. "He has a good sense of humour and can be a bit of a tease."

"But he fell for a bad one like Art," Noe pointed out.

"Everyone has their faults," Ean replied but he knew that was more of a platitude than an explanation. "Ben's include allowing his feelings for people to cloud his judgement. At first he liked Art, so he gave him the benefit of the doubt. Later he loved him, which made it even worse.

"As for Art, he has his qualities. It's easy for your eye to be caught by them. They distract you from his faults. And he did, maybe does, love Ben."

Noe sniffed. "Love is overrated. People in love do stupid things. Like telling the people they love that they will love them no matter how they behave and then being surprised when they behave badly."

Ean was impressed by Noe's insight. He wondered, not for the first time, about his life before the slavers had raided his planet. Noe never mentioned it. Ean only knew about the slavers because of Kip's research. "Setting high standards for those you love and then sticking to them is hard," Ean agreed. "You create exceptions. You want to give in. You forgive too easily."

Noe finally took his eyes off the fabric and looked at him. "You don't," he observed.

Ean held his gaze. "I spent my childhood seeing the damage caused by making too many allowances," he confided.

Noe looked away again before responding. "Was it your mother?" he whispered.

Such a question was unforgivably personal but Ean managed

to swallow the reprimand before it passed his lips. For the first time in almost two standards Noe had opened up.

It hurt to think about it: the beautiful young woman whom everyone had adored; the mother he had idolised; the girl no one ever said no to, even as her addictions killed her.

Standing on a stool to reach the bottle of laudanum that had been placed beyond her reach.

"Yes," he replied. "Love, or what people thought of as love, killed her."

Noe took a deep breath and exhaled slowly. "My mother thought that loving someone meant you never said no. No matter how crazy his religion. No matter how many times he wanted sex. No matter how many children he expected her to bear and raise. No matter if he beat her for being too exhausted to perform her wifely duties."

Ean wondered if Noe had killed him.

"I know what you are thinking," Noe acknowledged. "This Noe would. I would not hesitate for a heartbeat. I would poison him, pretend to cry at his funeral and build my family a better life without him. That Noe was too sweet, too gullible, too naïve." He looked again at Ean. This time his eyes were hard; like stone. "The slavers changed that. Watching them kill everyone too old, too young or too pregnant to take changed that."

Ean's blood ran cold. The hair on his neck stood up and he could feel sweat trickling down the small of his back. He knew he should say something but the words stuck in his throat.

"They took their time." Noe's voice was flat; emotionless. "The leader said it was an object lesson, so the rest of us would behave. It wasn't. It was his men's payment. Those men lived for those moments: to torture; to rape; to kill.

"I couldn't watch. I turned away and, unlike the adults and older children, they let me. That was when I saw him. I could see what he was thinking. He believed he did not belong with those monsters.

"Of course he did, he was one of their crew, but that did not matter. What mattered was that he thought he was better than them. I walked up to him and I put my hand in his and I looked up at him. I looked at him like my mother looked at my father. That mindless, unconditional trust.

"And it worked. He asked for me as part of his payment. The leader made him pay the market rate and he did. When he left the crew, at the next port, he took me with him."

"What happened to him?" Ean asked because that was the easiest of the questions in his head and, perhaps, answering it would distract Noe from thinking about what had happened to his family.

Noe shrugged. "He was killed in a fight. Only by then I was part of a spacer crew. Not a good crew but a crew. It was better than being a slave." His chin came up. "And now I am here, with you."

Ean rallied. "Where you belong," he stated firmly. "At the beginning of a promising future that you deserve."

Noe laughed. It was not a nice laugh. "Thank you. I know you believe that."

"So will you," Ean replied.

It was a promise Ean was determined to keep.

25

Ean forced himself to relax. Spacers could not afford to appear nervous. Avoiding challenge was all about appearing confident and self-assured.

Inside the passenger terminus in Carruthers Station 2, Ben was being unpodded. Hopefully he would be handed the message informing him he was somewhere completely different from where he had expected and asking him to meet old friends outside.

Ean had the captain, Vic and Rae with him. They were accompanied by Carlos for added protection. Not Tre; Ean had insisted on that.

Carlos' stay with the crew had extended; picking up Ben and then intercepting Medico Kem meant that they would be away from Tarrasade for four divs.

Every time the outer doors opened Ean caught a tantalising glimpse of the corridor beyond but there was no sign of Ben. Ean began thinking of all the ways Kip's plan could have gone wrong. He imagined Ben languishing in an unlabelled pod in some storage facility or on his way to a system in the Far Fringe.

Finally, twenty minutes after the scheduled unpodding time, he spotted Ben at the far end of the corridor. What felt like minutes later, but was probably less than thirty seconds, the doors slid open and Ben emerged.

He looked better than he had in the vid. Ean's heart began thumping even harder. He wanted this so much.

Then Ben's arms were around him. It had been so long; close to two standards. Ean hugged back.

"Who is the hunk?" Ben whispered.

"Carlos," Ean replied in a low voice. "Crew-guest. He's an enforcer." He pulled away, allowing Vic and then the captain to greet Ben. Rae was acknowledged with a gesture, as was appropriate for a cat. Rae responded with a whisker-twitch.

"We've picked out a bar to talk in," the captain explained once Ben and Carlos had been introduced.

They moved as a crew with Vic watching the front and Carlos at the rear. Once they reached the bar they settled at one of the tables and the captain ordered two pitchers; one of beer and the other of fruit punch.

"I have three things I would like to say," Ben announced as the rest of them were sampling their drinks.

The captain gestured that he should continue.

"Firstly I don't want to go over what I discussed with Captain Mel last time. I will never agree with what Tre did but I understand why he did it. He believed that the alternatives were worse. Given what happened to the Willow, he was correct about the level of risk even if he was wrong about the leak."

Ean managed to keep his mouth shut; it did not matter if Ben believed Art was a traitor or not.

"Secondly what was between Art and me is over. I never want to see him again. He is addicted to gambling and, like all addicts, he lies to himself and to everyone around him. He is never going to change.

"Thirdly and most importantly, thank you for helping me." He looked directly at Ean. "I will pay you back."

Ean was about to say that it was not necessary but the captain had already started to speak.

"That is clear, Ben, thank you. We agree that it is better to concentrate on the present and the future rather than the past. Unfortunately we are still trapped in the quandary in which Tre found himself. We care about you. Once others, outsiders, realise this, they may use you as leverage. Whatever you, whatever we, decide has to protect you and us."

Ben did not reply immediately. Instead he drank some of his beer, which Ean recognised as one of Ben's ways of buying time to think. After what felt like too long he put his mug down and replied. "Like waking up and finding out that I am somewhere completely different to where I expected," he observed.

"Like that," the captain confirmed. "Ben, if you don't want any more to do with us, we can arrange for you to get a fresh start far enough away that there can be little risk."

"At the other end of a journey that will take a decade in stasis," Ben suggested.

Knowing Tre and Kip it would be more like three. Ean would never see Ben again. The thought of it hurt even more than he had expected.

"You said that was the option if I didn't want anything more to do with you," Ben hinted.

Ean's heart leapt.

"We want you back on the crew," the captain told him.

Ben wanted that too; Ean could tell from his eyes.

"But we have to be sure it is safe," the captain continued. "There will be tests. If you pass, you can rejoin the crew and we will be able to explain why we are being so cautious. If you fail, the best we can do for you is that pod passage to a far flung sector."

"You voted to take me back?" Ben queried.

"Ten for, none against," Vic confirmed. "Even Noe, who has never met you, voted for."

Ben's gaze went to Ean. Ean could tell what he was thinking; the crew had voted in favour because Ean wanted it so much.

"I have missed you, Ben," Vic said gruffly. "I was pleased to see the back of Art but I really missed you."

"We believe you belong with us," the captain added. "We wanted Art to step up rather than letting the gambling and his greed get the better of him. If that had happened the two of you would still be with us. When Art decided to leave we wished you the best but we never wanted you to go."

Ben flushed. "Thank you," he whispered. He flexed his shoulders, took a deep breath and exhaled. "I would be honoured to rejoin the crew and I am willing to go through any test in order to do so."

First stop was the medical centre. Kip had booked time on three different scanners and briefed Vic on what was needed. The rest of them were offered the options of leaving or waiting in the designated area.

There was no question of leaving; they would wait. They walked through the indicated opening and found themselves in a room along with far too many other people. Ean looked for a second exit, there was one in the opposite wall, before checking out the other occupants.

There were two other crews there. Each had taken one of the corners and the rest of the room's occupants were keeping at least two paces away from them. Ean paused just inside the doorway. The other crews stayed where they were but everyone else moved up so that another corner became available.

Ean led the way to the vacated corner. As neither of the other crews was sitting they, too, stood.

Ean assessed the other crews without looking at them directly. One was a little down at heel with a queen who looked like he spent too much time tripping on stuff. They were obviously standing because of the other crew; the fragile queen looked like he should be sitting down.

The other crew reminded Ean of the Saber's only they were better dressed and they didn't have an underage cat with them. There were five of them, all about Carlos' size but nowhere near as good looking, ranging in age from about twenty to about forty. The oldest had a captain's badge pinned to his collar.

They were eyeing Rae.

It wasn't overt. If it hadn't been for Rae's reaction Ean might have missed it. Rae's head fur was standing up, especially at the back, and his whiskers were arched.

Unfortunately it just made him more attractive.

Then one of the bolder ones made eye contact and Rae snarled. At least he didn't growl or not loudly enough for a purebred to hear.

"Rae," the captain warned quietly.

Carlos began squaring up and Ean could feel the situation escalating. So could the others in the room. The crew with the fragile queen withdrew further into their corner while the singletons and pairs risked entering each other's personal space rather than be involved in the incipient conflict.

Then a beautiful, willowy man swept into the room with a youngster beside him and an enforcer behind. He had one look at Rae and then turned to the other crew.

"Behave yourselves," he chided.

Ean relaxed. His whole view of the other crew changed. Instead of a group of men looking for a youngster to fuck, they were a proper crew, some of whom had a wandering eye.

The willowy man looked them over, nodded to Captain Mel and then made eye contact with Ean.

"I am Dee, queen of the Halberd."

"Ean, queen of the Salix," Ean replied.

"I recommend Joe's in the market for fruit and vegetables, Lee's Kitchen for meals and The Circle for dancing," Dee told him. "Good to meet you, Ean."

Ean nodded. "Likewise. Thank you for your recommendations."

The crew of the Halberd left, the big men obediently following in Dee's wake. Ean had another look at the queen in the other corner and decided to sit down. A faint sigh of relief travelled around the room and the fragile queen sank gratefully into one of the chairs that lined the walls.

The scans took the rest of the morning. By the time Ben and Vic rejoined them the others had left and various people had come and gone.

"We had to pay extra and wait longer to have the scanners set up the way we wanted," Vic explained as they exited the medical centre.

"Vic is going to take the scan results to the ship," the captain informed Ben. "The rest of us will have lunch and do some shopping."

The plan was for Kip and Tre to go over the scan results. If there was nothing amiss they would take Ben back to the ship for questioning.

It was tempting to lunch at Lee's Kitchen but Ean did not need Carlos to tell him that they could not risk following a stranger's recommendation. Instead they picked another place that Rae assured them smelt good.

The food was tasty but different; Ean picked up some of the

spice mix they sold at the counter.

Then they went shopping. As Dee had said, Joe's stall was by far the best. Ean decided to ignore the risk; he wasn't going to buy second rate.

A quick stop at one of the Stellar Exchange booths allowed the captain to confirm that there was nothing unexpected on the scans so they could head back to the ship.

"What's next?" Ben asked as they made their way towards the secure berth they had rented.

"Tre will wire you up to a brain scanner and question you," Ean admitted.

Ben sighed. "Tell me he is being paranoid."

Ean shook his head. "He isn't. You'll understand when we are free to explain."

Tre watched them approaching using the feed from the cameras in the secure berth; Kip's ability to reroute data had a multitude of uses.

Vic had reported that both Rae and Ean were convinced that Ben was not lying. There was nothing of note on the scans. Tre did not expect to find anything during the interrogation.

No, what concerned him was the effect that reintroducing Ben would have on the crew; specifically on Ean. Ean still had not forgiven him for rendering Ben unconscious and putting him in a pod. Unless Tre could move the situation on, Ben's presence would be a constant reminder of the rift between them.

On the other hand, Ean looked happy. Being with Ben had that effect on him. Tre briefly, uncharacteristically, allowed himself to think about the future. He would be by Jax's side or dead. Either way, Ean would need other people.

He opened the outer door of the airlock as they approached.

"Ben," he acknowledged.

"Tre," Ben replied. He sounded wary, which was hardly surprising.

"If you would follow me," Tre stated, framing it as a request although they both knew it was not.

Kip had adapted one of the two simulators on the hydroponics level, so they would be climbing down rather than up. Tre watched Ben catch Ean's eye and nod reassuringly as he stepped onto the ladder.

"I can't believe you lost the Willow," he said once they were walking towards the simulator room on the hydroponics level.

Tre refused to rise. "It taught me to check before trusting anyone," he replied. "Even an old companion." He decided to push on. "I do trust you, Ben. I believe you would never act against our interests. This is merely a precaution."

"I had no doubts about Loy," Ben admitted, "so I cannot tell you to go with your instincts and forgo the precautions."

It was an excellent point. "I am glad you are back, Ben," Tre added. "This crew is better with you in it. Also Ean missed you greatly."

"There still isn't a ring on his finger," Ben observed.

"A ring would represent a commitment I am in no position to give," Tre volunteered. "If you make it through this examination, which I am sure you will, we will be able to tell you more and you will understand."

Ben's expression confirmed he was unconvinced. "Let's get on with it then."

They tried every trick Tre or Kip had been able to come up with and, as expected, found nothing. By the time they were finished it was obvious from the data that Ben was exhausted so Tre was not surprised that he could barely drag himself out of the simulator.

Tre decided not to mention it or offer to help.

"I expect you would like some sleep," he suggested.

Ben shook his head. "Sleep can wait. If I've passed, I want to know what the big secret is."

Art had not told him but Tre knew he believed that Jax was from a family that was important enough to make him worth kidnapping. "You passed," Tre confirmed. "I'll call a Meeting."

Watching Ben's reaction to the others was entertaining. Even seeing Rae had not prepared him for the change in Obe and Tre did not miss how his eyes kept returning to Kip.

Had Kip changed that much? Tre tried to be objective. At fourteen Kip had managed to be both skinny and plump; an unfortunate combination of underdeveloped muscles and puppy fat. Now he was slender; bordering on lean. His skin, hair and nails were in much better condition; the whole crew had been witnesses to Noe badgering him to look after them properly. He was nowhere near as attractive as Cas or Jax or Rae but his looks were more than acceptable.

Carlos certainly thought so and there was no doubt that Carlos' attention had affected the way Kip carried himself.

The captain opened the Meeting by welcoming Ben back to the crew.

"You know everyone other than Noe," he added. "Noe has been with us since soon after you left."

Noe was regarding Ben with what Tre recognised as a typical Noe expression; suspicious disguised as neutral.

"After you left, Tre decided to confirm our suspicions," the captain continued. "Jax was from a prominent spacer family and Tre was, is, his protector. He had selected the Willow's as a suitable Traditional crew for Jax to learn about spacer life."

Ben nodded. "I guessed as much."

"Since then events have occurred that have revealed Jax's identity to the crew," the captain explained. He looked to Jax.

Tre fixed his gaze on Ben.

"I am Emanuel Rafael Jax Esteban, son of Joaquin Oro Sebastiano Socorro of the Navaja," Jax told him.

Ben's eyes widened and his jaw went slack but he pulled himself together remarkably quickly.

"That explains a great deal," he replied in a voice that was almost, but not quite, normal. Then he looked over to Ean, caught his eye and smiled. "An adventure."

Tre remembered the two of them as adolescents. Ben's dreams had always been fanciful with much excitement, while Ean's had been about home and family.

Ean smiled back. "On occasion it has proved to be a little too dangerous for my liking."

By suppertime Tre was ready to admit that it had gone well. Ben fitted in so well that it was obvious that there had still been a Ben-shaped hole in the crew.

It was good to see Ean so happy.

Over supper and afterwards everyone vied to tell Ben about what had happened since he left. Tre's gaze strayed to Carlos, who was having the sense to stay quiet so that he could listen and learn.

There were certain things that everyone chose not to mention, like Noe killing Scar and Kip's capabilities.

Ben did his bit. Tre had forgotten what a great listener he was, responding to every twist or turn in the story, and how entertaining his comments could be.

The evening was winding down. Ean had sent Jax and Rae off to bed. Carlos carried Kip off into the guest cabin. The captain had retired and Noe had vanished soon afterwards; a sure sign that he was going to make sure Mel slept well.

When Cas and Obe began making out on the couch, Ben put an arm around Ean's waist and steered him into the galley, calling out for Vic and Tre to follow.

"Shut the door, Vic," he ordered. "Come on, Ean, where's the whisky?" he demanded.

Ean brought out four of the flasks; three of whisky and one of cordial.

Ben shook his head. "Ean, you've got worse rather than better. No one could get drunk on that amount, not even you." He sat down. "Carlos and Kip?" he queried.

"Not serious," Ean assured him. "The way Kip puts it is that Carlos enjoys teaching and Kip enjoys learning."

Tre was not sure Carlos saw it that way. Carlos had always been attracted to the special or unique.

Ben filled his small cup with whisky. "Four cats? How can we go clubbing with four cats?"

"We don't," Vic admitted.

"No clubbing?" Ben queried. "No one mentioned that. I might have reconsidered my decision." He smiled to confirm that he was joking. "Seriously, how old is Kip? Has he made no progress towards getting his knife?"

"Ean's been training him," Tre replied. "He's well up to standard."

Ben raised an eyebrow.

"We could promote both Kip and Noe," Ean admitted.

"Noe looks young," Ben observed.

"Noe hasn't been young for a long time," Ean replied. "And he is lethal with a knife."

Tre was surprised; Ean had resisted the notion of promoting Noe because it would mean losing what little control he had over Noe's behaviour.

"You must think this spacestation is safe," Ben pointed out. "Otherwise you wouldn't have chosen to divert my pod to it. We could promote Kip and Noe, go dancing and then come back here for a party."

Despite being sure that Ben was sound and the station was safe, Tre still hesitated; his mind was full of scenarios where Kip was challenged or Jax stolen.

"Or look for another station where that would be possible," Ben suggested. "Tre, do you want Jax to experience spacer life or not?"

"Ben has a point," Vic added. "And people are much less likely to make the connection between the crew of the Salix and Emanuel Rafael Jax Esteban out here than back in Tarrasade. Also Kip may say he's in no rush but he does want his knife. He wants to be able to tell his grandfather that he's made it as a spacer."

"You've done well with him, Ean," Ben praised.

"He's a very special young man," Ean replied.

Ean's reply was probably the understatement of the millennium, Tre mused as he emptied his cup for the second time.

He poured a third; the advantage of the flask was that Ean would still allow him into his bed after the four small whiskies it contained.

Of course Ean might be planning on spending the night with Ben; before Art the two of them had often slept together. Tre stared into his cup. He knew the rule; no ring, no say in whom Ean chose to invite into his bed.

In truth, Ean would be better off with Ben than with him.

"Tre, are you listening?" Ean asked.

"No, I was thinking," Tre admitted.

"I said that perhaps you, Carlos and Kip could do a risk assessment tomorrow morning and I'll check if we can extend the option on the secure berth past noon if we decide that is desirable."

"Good ideas," Tre acknowledged.

Ben laid a hand on Ean's arm. "Ean, I would like to have a private word with Tre." He glanced at Vic. "I hope you don't mind, Vic."

Vic knocked back his fourth whisky and stood up. "Not at all. Good to have you back, Ben."

"Good to be back," Ben replied. "Ean?" he hinted.

Ean looked warily from Ben to Tre and then back to Ben.

"You promise to play nice?" he asked.

"No," Ben answered. "Ean, putting it off won't help. Go with Vic."

Tre knocked back his third whisky rather than watch Ean leave. Someone, probably Vic, closed the door behind them.

"This is nothing to do with Art," Ben began. "Art is in the past. Gone. I want to talk about Ean."

Tre poured his fourth, his last, whisky.

"Persuade me that you aren't bad for him," Ben challenged.

Tre swirled the amber liquid around the cup. Maybe, this time, he should not evade.

"I can't because I am," he admitted. He looked up and saw Ben's surprise at his admission. "Ben, if I were free I would make Ean the centre of my world. He is extraordinary, amazing, and I…" He hesitated and then decided to commit. "I adore him."

Ben's surprise melted into something Tre suspected was sympathy.

Tre looked away; back to his whisky. "Only I am not free," he continued. "I have not been free since I was ten and my family sent me into the service of Joaquin Oro Sebastiano Socorro. Even Oro's death did not free me because fourteen standards ago he put his newborn son into my arms and I swore the most solemn of oaths. I will live and die for Jax.

"Even if there was a way out of the oath I would not take it. My planet, my clan, deserves the type of leader Jax could be. Not ruthless and cruel like his father. Not a monster like his grandfather. Not a megalomaniac like his great-grandfather. They deserve a leader who is capable of compassion.

"This crew was, is, key. I chose you and Vic and Mel. Then we recruited Ean. I wanted to build a family that could teach

Jax how to be a man. It seemed to be working. Cas and Obe, even Hal, changed from boys with problems that could have destroyed them into promising youngsters.

"And so far so good." Tre downed his last whisky. "I have had some luck. Jax was only eleven when we picked him up at Carrefour so there was a greater chance of him being young enough to influence. Then there was Rae. Even from their first meeting, Jax cared for Rae, which gave me hope. Since then he has accepted Kip as an equal and he has connected with Ean's version of morality. After the Willow was destroyed, he insisted that we rescue everyone when his father, even at Jax's age, would have calculated each person's strategic worth and decided that most were expendable."

He looked at Ben again and, this time, held his gaze.

"So, if you were to ask me where I see us in twenty standards' time, my answer is that I will probably be dead. Jax will be clan leader or still fighting to become clan leader. Ean will hopefully have half his life ahead of him and the thought he might spend it with you will make me sleep more easily every night from this day forward."

This time it was Ben who looked away and drained his cup.

"Trust you to turn out to be the genuine article," he replied. "A tragic hero. No wonder Ean is so in love with you."

"I am not a hero," Tre objected. "I do my duty and keep my word."

"Is Jax worth it?" Ben asked.

Tre froze. "He has to be." He made himself relax. "Ean will bring out the best in him. Rae will trust him. Kip will challenge the way he has been taught to think. Men like Carlos will follow him."

"And you?" Ben queried.

Tre knew the answer to that. "I shall stand in his father's place until his sixteenth birth anniversary. After that I will obey him."

"No matter what the order?" Ben challenged. "What if he ordered you to kill Ean?"

Tre imagined it. After serving Oro it was not difficult. "I would not obey. I would be forsworn. I would take my own life."

Ben shuddered. "So much for an adventure," he muttered.

He stood up and gathered the cups and flasks. He placed the flasks on the counter for refilling and began washing the cups.

"Thank you for explaining," he told Tre. "It helps. Knowing you love him, ring or no ring, is a relief. Yes, I intend to be there for Ean when he needs me, like he was for me." He looked over. "Go to him. I shall finish up here."

Tre hesitated.

"Go," Ben insisted.

Tre crept into the crewroom. Ean was sitting in the corner of his bunk with his knees pulled up, like he had as a youngster. It was a sure sign that he was anxious.

A deliberate scuff of sole against floor ensured his attention. Tre watched him uncurl.

"Well?" he asked as Tre came close.

"We cleared the air," Tre replied. "Being able to talk freely made it easier." He sat down on the edge of the bunk. "I think things will be good between us." Tre could see Ean beginning to analyse the situation so he leaned into the bunk and kissed him gently on the lips. "I told him that I loved you," he added as he pulled away.

Ean's eyes were large and young. "You did?"

"I did," Tre confirmed. "Because I do and I am proud to do so."

Ean put his arms around Tre's neck and drew him close.

✻ ✻ ✻

Kip managed to slide out of the foot of Carlos' bed without waking him, which was a first. He briefly considered using the head attached to the guest room but quickly decided against it; Carlos would wake up and that would mean more fucking.

More fucking would be enjoyable but would leave him useless for the rest of the morning.

He gathered his clothes, picked up his shoes and crept out of the room, intending to put on at least his underpants once he had a closed door between him and Carlos.

"Had a good night, Kip?" a loud voice asked.

Kip was caught between sliding the door shut, hanging onto his things and shushing Obe. His shoes and underpants lost out and ended up on the floor but at least the door was closed and he didn't think Carlos had woken up.

Obe crouched down, picked up Kip's underpants gingerly between his forefinger and thumb and held them out.

Kip had to reorganise the way he was holding his other clothes to take them.

"You didn't answer my question," Obe reminded him; thankfully at a lower volume.

Kip felt himself flush. "Very good, thank you," he replied, trying to work out how to crouch down and pick up his shoes without dropping anything else.

Obe took pity on him and retrieved the shoes. "Carlos is one fine specimen of manhood," he observed, handing them over.

"That doesn't matter," Kip objected but then he blushed again. Was that true? He did find Carlos physically attractive. "It wouldn't be enough," he amended. "Carlos is really nice."

Obe smirked. "And having that package we all spotted under his exercise shorts doesn't hurt."

Kip did not have to reply because Ean materialised in one of the doorways a little way along the corridor.

"Obe, we are not a crew that speculates or asks personal questions about our guests."

Obe jumped and turned. "Yes, Ean."

"Kip, when you are dressed, I would like a word."

"Yes, Ean," Kip replied, wondering what he had done.

"No rush," Ean assured him.

Ean was sitting at the table drinking tea. No one else was about and Kip realised that it was still early. Ean looked up and smiled as Kip came through the doorway. Then he poured a second cup and placed it in front of the adjacent chair.

Normally Kip would sit further away but he took the indicated place.

"Ben thinks we should promote you," Ean began.

Kip was surprised. He had thought that the decision had been made to wait. "I am only just seventeen," he pointed out.

"It isn't about age, Kip," Ean replied. "You've been with the crew over two standards. You have all the necessary skills, including being able to handle yourself in a knife fight. You already make an adult's contribution to the crew." He smiled. "I am very proud of you, Kip. You have made magnificent progress."

Kip felt his cheeks turning red for the third time that morning.

"Is there any reason we should not promote you?" Ean asked.

Kip's mind went into overdrive. The most obvious reason was that once he had his knife he would be open to personal challenge. On the other hand, a spacer within a crew was rarely challenged in such a way as it was invariably followed up, or even pre-empted, by a crew-to-crew challenge. The only other reason against it was that Kip didn't want Ean to stop looking after him. However, he was reassured by the fact that Ean still looked after Obe and Cas, even though they had their knives.

Inverting the question led to more productive lines of reasoning. A crew with four cats was unusual and would attract attention they could do without. Kip himself looked old enough, and mature enough, that an outsider would wonder why he was still a cat.

Interestingly, the same argument applied to Rae; like many hybrids he was maturing much more quickly than a purebred adolescent. The thought sparked off many others, reminding Kip how little they knew about Rae and his future.

They really needed a medico.

"If we aren't going to contact Medico Kem we should consider the medicos Carlos recommended," he told Ean.

Ean laughed. "How is that an answer to my question, Kip?"

"Sorry," Kip acknowledged. "The risks associated with promoting me are outweighed by the risks of delaying," he replied. He hesitated and then continued. "If promotion is based on skill level and physical maturity, Rae would also qualify."

Ean looked taken aback.

"We don't know Rae's true age," Kip reminded him. "Nor anything about how he was designed to mature."

"I realise that," Ean murmured. He frowned, obviously considering the issue. "He's still within his growth spurt." He sighed. "I am not certain how Jax would react to Rae being promoted before him."

Kip did; badly.

After breakfast Tre asked Kip to assess the risk associated with staying in the station a few more days and then present his findings to both Tre and Carlos. Kip settled quickly into the task; it was merely an extension of the work he had done when selecting Carruthers 2 as the destination for Ben's pod.

He soon decided that the risk would only increase if one or more of four events occurred.

The first was that they were recognised. This seemed unlikely. Even if it happened, the Carruthers system did not have a light speed data relay. The information would spread slowly; at a ship's velocity rather than the speed of light.

The second was that someone had tracked Ben. A truly persistent investigator could have followed the pod, although he or she would have had to realise that its electronic identity had been swapped on three separate occasions. It was much more likely any tracker was still patiently waiting for Ben's pod to arrive at Palasque Four.

The third was that someone was following them. That someone would have to have a Mulligan drive, be staying at least one system behind so Kip never detected them and never be fooled by Kip's methods of disguising what hole they used when leaving a system.

The fourth was that there were tracking and reporting devices attached to the Salix. These devices would have to be sophisticated enough that Kip could not detect them. Even if they did exist, Kip could not think of a way of them reporting the Salix's location in a system without any gates and they had passed through five of those on the way to Carruthers.

The worst scenario was if both the third and the fourth possibilities happened simultaneously. They could be in trouble if there were tracking and reporting devices attached to the Salix and a spacehopper ship was following them using the information generated by those tracking devices. However, the probability of that happening was the same wherever they were.

On balance, extra time in Carruthers 2 made no difference provided they left within five days of their arrival, which was before the earliest possible time that news of their location could enter the data streams.

It was a challenge to present his findings in a way that meant that Carlos could understand the outcomes but did not pick up on things Kip did not want him to know. By the time they were done the morning was half over.

Tre kept smiling; amused by the way Kip wriggled out of telling Carlos what he could do.

Kip wondered if Tre realised that there was another whole set of activities that Kip kept hidden from everyone, including Tre.

"We will tell the others at the Meeting that staying here is no more risky than moving somewhere else," Tre summarised. He checked the chronometer. "The Meeting is in the galley in ten minutes' time. We will tell you anything relevant afterwards, Carlos." He looked meaningfully at Kip. "Don't be late, Kip."

Kip was still wondering what the look was for when Tre had left, the door had shut and Carlos' arms were around him.

"You were gone when I woke," Carlos reminded him reproachfully and then followed up with a kiss that Kip felt all the way to his toes.

By the time the kiss was finished, Kip had forgotten how he

had intended to respond. It was all he could do to remember that he had a Meeting to go to.

Carlos smiled and pulled away. "Later," he promised.

Kip managed a nod before retreating to a safe distance and scuttling out the door.

At the Meeting, Ben proposed that Kip was promoted and Ean must have discussed it with everyone else during the morning because it was passed eleven to zero.

Kip was pleased. Becoming a competent knife-fighter had been difficult and being promoted ahead of schedule felt like a reward for working so hard.

"Noe and I have discussed the possibility of him being promoted at the same time," Ean informed them after the vote. "Noe has said that he would prefer to remain as cat a little longer."

Kip was surprised; Noe had always given the impression that he was desperate to get out from under Ean's thumb.

Ean smiled at him. "Kip, Tre and Carlos have been assessing the risk of staying here a few days longer and us going on the razzle to celebrate Kip's promotion. I am proposing that we give Kip his knife tomorrow, have a celebratory lunch and go out in the evening."

The vote was unanimously in favour.

26

Rae made himself sit still while Noe brushed the dye onto the tips of his eyelashes. It smelt horrid.

He often wondered how Noe got him to agree to stuff like this. It usually happened when he was trying to avoid lots of other suggestions that had sounded worse but probably weren't.

At least he had one of Ean's best lunches inside him; the captain had given Kip his knife and then they had turned their attention to a table laden with all their favourite foods.

"Two minutes and I will take it off," Noe promised. "Then you need to go have your shower and come back while your head fur is still damp so I can style it."

Rae was about to open his mouth and say that he didn't want his head fur styled when Noe followed up.

"If it's been styled Ean will be less likely to brush it," Noe reminded him.

Ean was probably anxious about going clubbing and he did like brushing Rae's head fur when he was worried. Rae still remembered when his fur had stood on end because of the static Ean had managed to get into it.

"And you ought to want to look your best," Noe added. "Jax will expect it."

Rae did want Jax to be proud of him.

"Shouldn't you be concentrating on Kip?" Rae asked.

"Kip is with Ean," Noe replied. "I'll be joining them to do his hair later."

Looking in the mirror once Noe had finished with him confirmed that all the effort had made a difference. Having darker eyelashes drew attention to his eyes while the plaits and ornaments woven into his head fur made it seem like a special occasion.

Jax came up behind him. "Nice," he confirmed.

Rae turned and tried not to stare. He wasn't sure what Jax had done but every bit of him looked and smelt even better than usual.

"Cas did my hair and painted my face," Jax admitted, smelling a little embarrassed.

"It looks great," Rae assured him.

Jax sounded and smelt relieved. "Better get dressed then," he pointed out, looking over at where their clothes were hanging.

Rae watched Jax dressing out of the corner of his eye. Noe had made what he called their razzle pants out of stretchy fabric and Ean had insisted that he remake Jax's because they were unacceptably tight.

Even so, the pair Jax was pulling on still outlined every one of the lines and curves with which Rae was so familiar.

Vic, Tre, Carlos and the captain were already waiting in the shared area; Rae guessed that Ean had invited the captain into the crewroom.

Both Tre and Carlos stared at Jax. Tre sighed. "Well he looks nothing like his father."

Carlos swallowed. "But…"

Tre slapped him on the back. "You worry too much. Anyone trying to steal Jax will get the shock of his life, won't he Rae?"

The thought of it was enough to bring Rae up on his toes; whiskers arched, hackles raised and lip curled.

Carlos relaxed. "True. You looked so good there, Rae, that I forgot you were our secret weapon."

Rae decided that was two compliments rolled into one and smiled. He liked Carlos. Not only did he treat Kip well but he always was generous with his praise.

Obe and Cas appeared next. Cas looked amazing and Rae did not miss how Jax's eyes followed him.

He wished he could look more like Cas but head fur was not hair and there was nothing he could do if Jax liked rounder eyes and ears.

Then Ben towed Ean out of Ean's corner of the crewroom and into the shared area. Ean was objecting.

"It's too much," he complained.

"Rubbish," Ben retorted, not stopping until he had Ean directly in front of Tre.

Ean looked really nice. His hair was loose and someone, probably Ben or Noe, had painted the outer corners of his eyes with an intricate pattern. There were other things too, the kind of stuff Rae could never pick out but added up to make a big difference.

Tre pulled him close and kissed him gently on the lips. "You look beautiful," he murmured in a voice that was too low for the other purebreds to hear.

Ean flushed, which made him looked even better, and stopped complaining.

Ben smiled.

Noe and Kip soon joined them. Noe was Noe; all eyelashes and cuteness. Rae approved. The problem with being a hybrid is that people expected you to be dangerous. Noe looked harmless but nothing could be further from the truth.

Kip didn't look beautiful like Cas or cute like Noe or handsome like Carlos. Rae decided that he still looked like Kip but better; like when the artists in the market in Carrefour would draw people and sell them the picture.

Around his right thigh was the scabbard for the knife the captain had given him that morning. Rae could see the knife's leather-bound hilt and gleaming pommel.

Rae wanted his knife. Once he had his knife he could defend Jax properly.

The captain smiled and announced, "We walk."

Tre led and Carlos was at the rear. Rae's job was to stick close to Jax, which suited him just fine. As Ean always said, their crew walked proud but did not strut.

They left the docks where the secure berth was located and headed through the spacer quarter towards the market Ean had picked out. Once they were there, Rae could understand why Ean had selected it. It was an afternoon and evening market; with entertainers weaving their way between stalls that were selling luxuries rather than food or essential supplies.

Everyone's attention was on them. At first Rae found it unsettling but he soon realised that the glances and comments displayed admiration tinged only slightly with envy. He couldn't hear or smell anything that suggested aggression.

They had browsed a number of stalls before stopping at one specialising in jewellery. Rae kept his attention firmly fixed on those around them while Carlos tried to get Kip interested in any of the jewellery on offer.

Kip, being Kip, had yet to realise that Carlos wanted to buy him something.

The cloths draped over an adjacent stall moved, attracting Rae's attention. He watched. Sure enough they moved again; something was under the table.

Noe was helping Carlos out by drawing Kip's attention to some hinged rings for putting long hair into a tail.

The cloths parted momentarily and Rae got a glimpse of a person looking out. It was a child; Rae wasn't sure how old. He relaxed slightly. A child was unlikely to represent a danger.

Kip was admiring the hinge and clasp mechanism on one of the hair rings while Carlos pointed out another with a more intricate pattern worked into the metal.

A hand snaked out from between the cloths and snagged one of the objects piled into a basket close to the edge; so the child was a thief.

Rae knew what Ean thought of thieves. He also knew what it was to be hungry. The child's wrist had looked very thin.

"What are you looking at?" Jax asked.

"Nothing," Rae replied; he did not want to get the child into trouble.

Carlos had given up on trying to get Kip to consider a fancier hair ring and was about to settle for the one with the mechanism Kip liked when the stallholder realised that she was going to miss out on a better sale and brought out a tray covered in hair rings of that type.

One of the hanging cloths moved very slowly to make a narrow gap through which Rae could see an eye. It was blue, which was unusual.

The child had realised that Rae had seen him.

Rae stared back and twitched his whiskers.

"Is there a problem?" Tre asked.

"No," Rae assured him. When he looked back the gap had closed and there was no sign of the child.

Kip insisted on a hair ring made from a hard alloy so the mechanism would not wear and then Carlos picked out three for Kip to choose from. To Rae's surprise Kip selected one with an engraved pattern rather than the plainest.

Finally Carlos had paid and they could move on.

Ean decided they should have some refreshments and Tre chose a table adjacent to a wall with clear lines of sight. They had a pitcher of punch and a large plate of snacks. They were good; not as nice as the ones Ean made but tasty.

Rae kept his eyes open and his ears pricked for trouble while thinking about the briefing Ean had given them about the Carruthers system. There were meant to be no permanent residents in Carruthers 2, just visitors, transients and workers who commuted there on a daily basis. Most people lived on the one habitable planet and the other spacestation, Carruthers 1, had a small residential sector.

What was a child doing in Carruthers 2? Certainly Rae hadn't seen any others.

Rae vaguely remembered Kip saying something about couples in the Carruthers system having to buy a licence before they had a child.

He decided he needed to check if he had things straight.

"No children," he observed as an opener.

Ean frowned slightly. "No. All the families live on the planet." He looked at Kip. "I don't believe local children are allowed on either of the spacestations until they are over fourteen."

Kip looked distant for a moment, like he always did when he was trawling stuff out of his memory. "A trip to Carruthers 1 is included as a field trip in the standard school curriculum. Otherwise the only children would be with people passing through."

Maybe the child had been left behind by mistake. Or perhaps there was a population of feral children that no one mentioned in the official records.

"No feral children?" he checked.

Kip frowned. "I didn't find any mention of them."

"Have you seen a child, Rae?" Jax asked.

Rae flushed; he should have guessed that Jax would see straight through him.

"When we were in the market," he admitted. "Just for a moment. He was hiding." Rae was pretty sure it was a boy although he knew he could be wrong.

Ean looked anxious. "Maybe we should report it."

"Maybe we should mind our own business and leave it to the locals," Ben retorted.

"Can you see him now, Rae?" the captain asked.

Rae checked. "No," he replied.

"Then I think Ben is correct and we should not interfere," the captain decided. "Ean?"

Ean sighed. "I suppose that would be for the best." He finished his cup of punch. "Drink up and we'll check out the other side of the market before hitting our first club."

Jax liked Carruthers 2. It felt much less civilised than the other spacestations he had visited. As there weren't any families or children everyone was assumed to be able to look after themselves. Station Security were thin on the ground and the few Jax had spotted were heavily armed. Jax guessed they only got involved when matters got seriously out of hand.

He had known that Rae had seen something in the market but he hadn't known what until Rae had started to ask about children.

It was a relief that Ben and the captain stopped Ean investigating; they were there to walk the station and enjoy themselves.

The club was exciting. The lights were low and the music pulsating. It was early; there was only one other crew there when they arrived. Ean led the way to other corners and they had barely decided who would sit where when Cas was on his way to the large, central dance floor with Obe close behind.

Jax stayed at the table and watched Cas, who was well worth watching. He wanted to be more familiar with his surroundings before risking the dance floor. After about fifteen minutes three other crews had arrived and Jax had a better grasp of how clubbing worked. Two of Tre, Carlos, the captain and Vic always stayed at the table. Cats did not go up to the bar. No one went to the toilets alone and if one of the cats needed to pee one of the enforcers went with them.

Rae was itching to move; Jax knew that sitting at the table without anything to do was difficult for him. Even so, Jax was not ready to dance; not yet.

"Go," he encouraged.

Rae twitched his whiskers.

"Go," Tre added. "I'll stay with him until you get back."

So Rae joined Cas, Obe, Ben, Vic and Noe on the dance floor. As soon as he started to move Jax was transfixed. It was as if Rae was in vivid colour and everyone else had faded into the background.

"By the Lady, that is worth watching," Carlos declared. "He dances almost as well as he fights."

Ean sighed. "He looks so grown up."

"Hybrids mature quickly," the captain pointed out. "Looking at him, you'd think he's about Kip's age or even older." He frowned. "Ean, what do you think about his mental maturity? Is Rae ready for his knife?"

Jax didn't like the sound of that one little bit. The plan was that he would receive his knife on his sixteenth birth anniversary, in accordance with clan tradition. That was twenty-two divs away and the thought of Rae being a full member of the crew without him for all that time left a sour taste in his mouth.

"I'm not sure," Ean admitted. "I think it would be a little too soon."

Jax agreed; far too soon.

"Let's dance," Tre suggested, standing up. "Come on, Ean. You too, Jax. Dancing in a club is a gap in your experience that needs to be filled."

It was fun; more so that Jax had anticipated. It helped that Rae danced with him, matching his steps and, every time the music suggested it, offering him a hand for a spin or grasping him around the waist for a lift.

Being lifted focused Jax on Rae's strength. Knowing how strong he was, even watching him toss Carlos across the gym, was different from experiencing it firsthand.

Every time his feet left the floor Jax felt a weird sensation that started in his core and travelled outwards until it rippled across his skin, raising every hair.

"Enough," he declared during the fifth or sixth lift.

Rae put him down immediately; his whiskers drooping slightly.

Jax tried for a reassuring smile. "I need a rest. You continue dancing. I like watching you."

Rae would have insisted on escorting Jax back to the table but Ean also wanted a break, so Tre was leaving the floor. Jax settled down in the same place as he had occupied before.

Noe, who Jax had thought was still on the floor, sidled up beside him.

"You and Rae dance together well," Noe observed, stirring his drink with a straw.

"Rae could dance with anyone," Jax replied.

"But he doesn't," Noe pointed out.

Jax watched for a moment. It was true. Rae did not touch anyone else. When Jax was not there, he danced alone.

"He adores you," Noe said quietly.

It was not a word Jax was comfortable with. "We are best friends," he acknowledged.

Noe snorted and sucked some liquid up his straw.

"Why did you tell Ean you didn't want your knife?" Jax asked, keen to change the subject.

"The captain," Noe admitted. "Rae can't give blow jobs and you only go with him because it is your duty. He deserves better than that."

Jax felt himself flush; he had not thought of that. When they were in Tarrasade it did not matter because the captain visited a courtesan but they had already been travelling for over two divs.

On Traditional ships, captains had their own cabins, only came into the crewroom when invited to do so by the crew's queen and did not have intimate relationships with crew members who had gained their knives. The rules were meant to preserve some distance, so the captain could make hard decisions during emergencies.

"I offer," Jax complained. "He always says no and we play chess instead."

Noe looked at him. "You were raised to be selfish. Considering that, you don't do too badly."

Jax was still trying to work out if that was an insult or a compliment when the music changed to a slower, more romantic tempo. Rae was sitting beside him before the beginning of the fourth bar.

Then the three of them enjoyed the spectacle of Carlos trying to persuade Kip onto the floor. By the time he succeeded the music had sped up again but at least he had managed to get Kip dancing.

A little longer and Ean decided they should move clubs.

The corridors had transformed; filled with crews on the razzle. Jax recognised the danger; when crews were high on alcohol, dancing or stuff, it was easy for them to lose their judgement and cause or take offence without considering the consequences.

Hopefully with Tre leading other crews would be intimidated into remembering proper behaviour.

Jax walked between Rae and Noe with Cas and Obe in front of him and Ben and Ean behind.

In Carruthers 2, like most stations, some of the junctions between the main corridors were enlarged to create plazas; the market they had visited had been in one of these and there appeared to be another up ahead.

Whatever was happening there was loud; Jax could hear music and what felt like the stamping of many feet.

Tre slowed and then diverted them into a bar. Three crews were already there; hot and sweaty as if they had been dancing.

They took the fourth corner while the captain and Vic ordered drinks they did not really need so that they could talk to the bartender.

"Apparently they convert the big plaza at the next junction into a giant club three nights out of five," the captain told them as Vic placed the tray of drinks on the table. "It's called The Circle."

"The queen of the crew we met at the medical centre mentioned The Circle," Ean volunteered. "I thought he was referring to an ordinary club."

"The less wild crews use the bars that are close by, ones like this one, like tables in ordinary clubs," Vic added, indicating the bartender with his chin. "Abe warned us that the drinks you get in The Circle are often spiked and that the toilets are places better avoided."

Ean frowned. "Maybe we should find another club. The last one was fine."

Ben groaned. "It was just ordinary. The Circle sounds exciting. How much does Abe want to reserve this table for us?"

Approaching The Circle fuelled Jax's anticipation. Music pulsed from the plaza ahead and the corridor was illuminated by coloured lights that changed in keeping with the beat. The air felt moist.

About ten paces from the end there was a table at which sat a woman. Behind her were two heavyset men.

"You are new here," she suggested.

Tre nodded.

"We have rules," she told him. "You need to give the name of your ship. No challenges are to be resolved in The Circle. You can settle your business at the Killing Square once station night is over. If one of your crew steps too far out of line, the whole crew leaves. Ten credits a head but fifty for a crew like yours. We like Trad crews here. Everyone will need the back of his hand stamped but we don't expect you to let us touch your cats; you can stamp them. The ink of the stamp fades in a day but it'll get you in and out for tonight." She studied Jax and Noe in a way no spacer would risk. "You might be best off using a bar for cooling off rather than one of the tables inside."

"We have that in hand," the captain replied. He looked to Ean, who nodded. "We are the Salix," he added, pushing a fifty credit token into the reader.

The woman stamped Ean's hand and then handed him the stamp and watched him stamp everyone else. As Ean stamped Rae, she smiled.

"I'm afraid hybrids can't enter tonight's dancing competition. Last club night of each div we have a special competition for hybrids."

"Thank you," Ean replied. "You have been very helpful."

They walked the last ten paces into the plaza and Jax's senses overloaded. It was so vast, so loud, so crowded with sweating, writhing men.

Ten seconds passed and his mind began to cope. The plaza was enormous; four times bigger than the largest in Tarrasade and twice the height of a normal level. Jax guessed it had been enlarged into the service levels above and below.

Their corridor opened onto a mezzanine. Around the walls, at the level they were on, there were tables. To his right Jax could see a rough-looking crew on the first table and, beyond that, at the next table, he was pretty sure there were two men fucking.

To their left were other crews; each at a table. Most were drinking or sniffing stuff. Some were singing. A few were playing cards or dice. Between the tables wove waitresses and waiters wearing high heels, a thong and nothing else other than a credit token reader.

"I think this was a bad idea," Ean began.

"We are here now," Ben insisted. He pointed to the next level in, another seven steps down. "There are the crews like ours."

It was true. The next level in was a ring-shaped dance floor, about twenty paces wide and divided into quarters by the four stairways leading from the corridors into the centre of the plaza.

There was space between each dancing crew, like in a normal club. Jax remembered what the woman at the entrance had said. The people who ran The Circle liked Trad crews and that part of the club had obviously been designed with Trad crews in mind.

"We can't stand on the stairs," Tre reminded them and led the way down the steps.

Other crews moved to make them space and Jax began dancing because there didn't seem to be another option.

Wherever he looked there was something unexpected and new. The next level in was what the announcer, or master of ceremonies, or whoever he was, called the pit. It was over a man's height lower than the level they were on and it was a solid mass of dancers; shirtless, streaming with sweat and moving to the music.

Luckily there was a balustrade between the two levels. Jax imagined falling into the crowd; he doubted that even Tre or Rae would be able to get him out again.

At the centre of the pit was a two level circular stage. On the lower level was what Jax guessed was the dance competition. Above, on a central dais, were six cat–human hybrid dancers who were obviously professionals.

They moved almost as well as Rae.

After a while Jax began to grasp how it worked. There was a bar in each quarter of the upper, outer levels. One bartender at each served the Traditional crews while three others dealt with the orders brought by the waiters and waitresses from the tables above. Some of the crews at the tables came down to their level to dance. Others risked the pit.

Crews like theirs, who did not intend to use a table, rested by leaning on the balustrade.

Once he felt more comfortable, Jax began to pick out more detail: a tall, thin dancer initiating an outbreak of pogoing in the pit; a waitress getting her breasts and buttocks groped as she unloaded her tray at one of the tables; a crew taking it in turns to fuck their underage cat.

His gaze kept going back to that until Rae moved to block his line of sight. Rae leaned in close so that his whiskers brushed against Jax's cheek, bringing his mouth close to Jax's ear. "We are better than that," he assured him before grasping his hand and pulling him into a dance move.

Jax was distracted by the realisation that the weird sensation, the one that started deep inside and ended up rippling across his skin, wasn't just when Rae lifted him; any pull or push while they were dancing had the same effect.

The more he felt it the more Jax liked the sensation. Only he wasn't sure that he should because it was triggered by Rae being strong and in control, which meant that he was weak and was allowing Rae to control him.

The Navaja clan leader could not afford to be weak. He could not allow another man to control him.

But there was no table to escape to and it felt so good.

Finally, thankfully, Rae stopped dancing and Jax realised that Ean had been approached by another crew.

Whiskers tickled his ear. "It's the crew of the Halberd," Rae told him. "We met them at the medical centre."

They leaned on the balustrade while Ean attempted to converse with the queen of the other crew. Jax could see that it was hopeless; the music was too loud. He was wondering when Ean would give up when a hand grasped his ankle.

At first he thought it had to be Rae but Rae was standing beside him. He tried pulling back but the grasp was firm. There was a yank. His foot left the ground and he stumbled, catching himself on the balustrade.

It was someone reaching up from the pit. Jax refused to panic. What was his attacker trying to do? Pull him through the uprights? The gap was far too small.

Jax twisted, trying to look down, while seeing if he could get his foot out of his boot.

What he saw changed everything. Men were climbing up, using others' cupped hands and shoulders as footholds. They were going to grab him and pull him over the balustrade.

Jax was about to call for help when the lead climber sailed backwards and vanished into the crowd; Rae had aimed a punch between the uprights. Next the grip on Jax's ankle loosened and Jax caught a glimpse of a ruined face falling away. Given the blood on the toe of Rae's boot, it had been a kick. Rae straightened up, reached down over the balustrade, grabbed one of the climbers and tossed him across the heads of the dancers in the pit.

The man almost reached the stage before landing in the crowd, taking down three of the dancers who, given the adverse reaction of those around them, were part of a crew.

The other climbers dropped down and vanished.

It was over almost before it had begun.

Tre's hand grasped his upper arm.

"I'm fine," Jax assured him, knowing that Tre's enhanced hearing could filter his voice out from the noise. "Rae dealt with it."

Tre looked tense but then nodded. He turned to Rae. "Are you all right?"

Rae gave a reassuring whisker-twitch. He looked pumped but otherwise fine.

The others were beginning to realise what had happened. Ean paled. Carlos was looking about for any sign that it was an organised attack rather than just an opportunist crew trying to steal a cat they fancied. The Halberd's enforcer said something in his queen's ear.

The queen smiled. "Some people have no manners," he said, forming each syllable carefully so that even a novice could read his lips.

Even through the adrenalin high caused by the attack, Jax could recognise that the tall, beautiful man had style.

Had the Halberd's crew had a role to play in the abduction attempt? Was the distraction they had provided planned?

Kip was giving one of the hand signals he had worked out with Tre. Jax didn't manage to catch its meaning but given Tre's reaction he assumed Kip was suggesting that the Halberd's crew was not involved.

Jax was relieved that Ean insisted on a timeout at Abe's. Not that he was shaken, he was determined not to be, but he was thirsty and he expected the others were too.

Their table at Abe's was unoccupied. The younger members of the crew, including Jax and Rae, piled onto the fixed seating in the corner while the captain, Ean, Tre, Vic and Ben sat on chairs or stools. Carlos went up to the bar and ordered three pitchers: one of beer, one of fruit punch and one of water.

Jax noticed that Cas and Noe made sure that Kip was on one end of the long, curved seat so that when Carlos brought the tray to the table he could ask them up to move up and sit beside him.

Jax watched Carlos put an arm around Kip's shoulders.

Did he want Rae to do that? At the moment it would be nice, like it had been nice to sit down.

❋ ❋ ❋

Rae had wanted to grab every one of the climbers and toss them across the pit. He hadn't because that would have meant leaving Jax's side.

It wasn't about punishing the men. It was about protecting Jax.

At least he had kicked the one who had dared touch Jax. Rae had felt something beyond the man's nose give; there was a good chance the man was seriously injured, even dead.

It would serve him right.

Ean had been right to suggest a timeout at Abe's. Rae hoped they decided not to go back. The dancing had been great but The Circle wasn't the type of place you took a cat like Jax. Everyone had wanted him and too many of the crews had left their judgement at the door.

At least Jax was safe now, sat at their table at Abe's, sandwiched between him and Noe. Rae took advantage of their closeness to assess Jax's scent. Jax had been scared by the attack but he had stayed calm and now was recovering.

If they had been alone, Rae would have put an arm around Jax's waist and hugged him close. As it was, he made sure they were pressed close together: leg against leg, shoulder against shoulder and hip against hip.

They drank their drinks and visited the toilets in relay. No one mentioned returning to The Circle.

"Are we going back?" Vic asked as he finished his beer. "It was interesting but I don't think it was our type of place."

"We'll vote on it," the captain proposed.

No one voted in favour, so they set off for the secure bay.

Ben did suggest they could visit another club on the way back. No one disagreed but no one agreed either; Rae was pretty sure they would end up going straight home.

They set off. Rae realised that Jax was limping slightly; his leg must have been injured when the man had pulled it. Rae hoped that the man wasn't dead; just in lots and lots of pain.

They were into the stretch of corridor that led to the market when Rae heard it; a high pitched squeal and then another.

"What is it?" Tre asked immediately. Rae could imagine him augmenting his hearing and focusing in on what had alerted Rae. He tensed and then relaxed. "Nothing to do with us," he stated.

Rae wished he could dismiss it so easily. The voice was high pitched; it could be a woman's but it sounded like a boy's to him.

As far as he knew there was only one boy; the one under the

table in the market.

Then he saw something up ahead; a crew. One of them was dangling a small figure upside down by an ankle.

The boy had stopped squealing, so only Tre had any idea of what was happening. Rae glanced sideways at him. His attention was on Ean; probably deciding how Ean would react.

The boy suddenly flailed about and managed to attack the man holding him.

The man dropped him. "He bit me," he complained.

The boy was up and running towards the market. Unfortunately the crew weren't slow to pursue. He wasn't going to make it. Perhaps he could have normally but he was injured.

Rae was off before he had thought about the consequences.

"Rae! Come back!" Tre ordered but Rae was already at full speed. He shot past the other crew, grabbed the boy as gently as he could and kept running.

He heard and felt the breath being knocked out of the boy by the impact. At least it meant that he did not struggle or call out.

Rae slowed down once they were in the market and found a hiding place between a canvas screen and the wall. He put the boy down and pressed a finger to his lips. He also kept a firm hold on his captive; Rae remembered how slippery he had been when people caught him.

The boy was bleeding from a cut on his lip and over his eye. Even so, he seemed quick to realise that Rae had saved him.

"I saw you earlier," the boy whispered.

Rae hushed him. He needed to listen for pursuers. It wasn't easy; there were several voices mixed in with many other sounds.

Then he heard it; the patient, measured tone of Ean's voice. Rae moved his head and ears to the best possible position.

"One of your crew took him," a voice complained. "Give him back."

"You have admitted that the boy is not your cat," Ean pointed out. "Therefore we do not have to give him back."

There was angry muttering.

"The boy stole something," the man replied. "We want it returned."

Rae turned to the boy and held out the hand that was not holding him.

The boy scowled at him.

"You'll need to give it back or they won't give up," Rae whispered. He hoped the boy hadn't been foolish enough to swallow it; the crew would probably want to cut him open to get it back.

The boy reluctantly produced a silver bracelet.

"If we get it back, will you let us deal with the boy?" Ean asked.

There was a pause. "What about reparations?" the other man demanded. "We could take the boy to the authorities. There would be a reward. They don't tolerate thieves here."

"Or we could sell him to a crew who like them young," another voice added.

Any sympathy Rae had for the other crew vanished.

Ean's voice when he replied had a sharper edge.

"How much would the station authorities give you if you handed him in?" he asked.

There was a pause. Rae could imagine the man working out how much Ean would pay.

"Five hundred," he stated, which was ridiculously high but probably only a quarter of what a bad crew would give for an opportunity to have their fun without facing any consequences.

"Done," Ean stated. He raised his voice. "Bring him here. Now."

The boy must have heard because he began wriggling in Rae's grasp. Rae shook him; not too hard but enough to shock him.

"Stop it," he ordered. "I'm not going to let go and even if I did there is no way you could get away from me."

The boy stared at him with his strange blue eyes.

"My crew have negotiated a deal," Rae explained. "You give back the bracelet and they will let us deal with you."

"Why?" the boy asked.

Rae scowled at him. "Be thankful anyone is willing to help you."

It was only when he rejoined the others that Rae began to realise how badly he had screwed up. Tre's expression and body language was hard and unforgiving. The captain and Carlos looked disappointed. Even Ean seemed exasperated.

Jax would not look at him.

Ean finished the negotiation and they continued to the secure berth. No one spoke until they were through the market and walking down the corridor beyond.

"What's going to happen to me?" the boy asked. "Can I be your cat?"

"No," Ean answered. "We do not have thieves in our crew. We will treat your wounds and then pod you. When we dock somewhere with an orphanage that will take you, we will hand you over."

The boy began struggling again but Rae had no intention of letting go. "I don't want to go to an orphanage," he complained.

"You don't have the choice," Ean told him. "Does anyone know what they do to thieves here?"

"I think they chop off a hand for the first offence," Vic replied.

Rae wondered if that was true. True or not, the boy stopped struggling.

When they got inside the secure berth Ean took the boy's hand and told Rae to let go. Rae watched them walking towards the ship, which Vic was unlocking.

He looked at Tre, whiskers drooping and ears back.

"I am ashamed of you," Tre stated. "We will talk in the

morning." He turned away and followed Ean.

Rae watched the other walk towards the ship. Jax walked next to Kip. He did not look back at Rae.

The captain stepped up and laid a hand on Rae's shoulder. "We all mess up occasionally, especially when we are young. You did well at the club. Tre is right. Better we talk it through in the morning."

He guided Rae along the gangplank into the ship. Rae climbed the ladder and crept into the crewroom. Jax was already in their alcove; Rae could hear him and smell him.

Rae didn't know what to do so he waited until Jax went into the shower. Then they swapped places. Jax was still acting as if Rae wasn't there.

When he came out of the shower Jax was lying facing the wall.

Rae hung up his clothes on a hook, pulled on sleep shorts and climbed up into his bunk.

They both lay there, silent, in their separate bunks, Jax facing the wall and Rae the ceiling. To Rae the dancing and the high of saving Jax seemed an age ago.

He heard Jax's intake of breath; he was going to speak. Rae desperately hoped it wouldn't be too bad.

"You left me," Jax told him. "You abandoned me in favour of a total stranger. I cannot rely on you."

Rae's world cracked and splintered. He whimpered. He desperately wanted to go to Jax: to push his head into his hand and beg forgiveness.

He did not dare. He would not be able to bear it if Jax pushed him away.

27

Even watching Rae eat made Kip sad. Rae had always relished eating. His eyes had lit up when he saw the food and he had obviously enjoyed every mouthful. Now he merely chewed and swallowed. If it wasn't for Ean badgering him, he wouldn't be eating enough to maintain his body condition.

It had been going on for almost a div, ever since the evening in Carruthers 2 when Rae had rescued the boy. It should have been over long ago. Rae had talked it through with the captain, with Ean and with Tre. He had admitted his mistake, apologised and promised never to do something so foolish again.

Only Jax would not forgive him.

Kip wished someone could get Jax to see how unreasonable he was being.

He sought out Noe and found him in the laundry. Noe looked at him in surprise.

"I am going to talk to him," Kip announced.

Noe raised a brow.

"Jax," Kip clarified. "About Rae."

Noe sniffed. "It won't do any good."

"I've got to try," Kip insisted.

Noe studied him. "What makes you think you will succeed where both Ean and Tre have failed?" he asked.

Kip recognised the truth in that. For a moment he considered giving up but even the thought of it felt wrong. "I must."

Noe sighed. "Sit down," he ordered.

Kip reluctantly sat on one of the hampers. "You won't persuade me out of it," he insisted.

"I am not going to try," Noe assured him. "I am going to give you some ammunition."

By the time Noe had finished briefing him, Kip had a newfound respect for Noe's understanding of what made people tick. Every time Noe had explained one of the building blocks of Jax's motivation, it had resonated with facts Kip had known.

Kip was convinced that Noe was right. Now he had to make Jax see it.

He picked a time when Rae was training. Jax was tidying his bunk and locker. He did a lot of tidying and cleaning these days, which probably meant he was as miserable as Rae but better at hiding it.

Kip stood in the opening between the alcove and the rest of the crewroom. He pointed at the bottom bunk.

"Sit down," he ordered.

Jax glanced at him, scowled and carried on sorting his clothes.

Noe had been clear; Jax might have to be shocked into listening. Kip tried again. "I am a full member of the crew. You are a cat. This is an order. Sit down."

Jax sat. Noe had been correct. He looked a bit stunned rather than cross or resentful.

"You are going to listen," Kip told him. "Then you are going to think about my questions and answer them truthfully." He did not wait for a response. "Rae saw himself in the boy. He remembered what it was like to be feral. For a moment, he allowed his empathy to override his judgement. Are you capable of appreciating that?" He waited for an answer.

Jax looked away.

"Answer me!" Kip demanded.

"Yes, I can appreciate that," Jax admitted.

It was a start; step one accomplished.

"You were not especially at risk when he went to help the boy," Kip pointed out. "You had both Tre and Carlos to protect you. The main danger when walking a corridor is a challenge. Can Rae respond to a challenge?" Again he waited.

"No," Jax admitted.

"Describe the situations in which Rae is meant to protect you," Kip ordered.

Jax hesitated but Kip waited him out. "Non-challenge situations. Abductions. Attempted assassinations," Jax admitted.

"Situations like at The Circle," Kip suggested.

Jax looked daggers at him but nodded.

"Or on the Petunia Mae," Kip reminded him. "Where he took incredible risks to make sure he was on the Talon with you. He was with me, did you know that? We were in the ducts with the commander and his men standing on the floor above us. I was terrified. Then I looked around and he had gone. After you. Without a word."

Jax did not look the slightest bit guilty. It was like Noe had said. To Jax, Rae's phenomenal loyalty was normal.

"Rae has never let you down," Kip stated. "Not on the Petunia Mae or the Talon or Verdant or Carruthers 2."

Jax opened his mouth and shut it again.

"Did Rae let you down in Carruthers 2?" Kip demanded. "I want an answer. Yes or no."

"No," Jax admitted reluctantly.

Step two finished; Kip pressed on.

"So why are you punishing him?" Kip asked.

This time Jax looked guilty. "I'm not," he complained.

"Torture doesn't have to be physical. Emotional torture works just fine." He paused to let that sink in. "You are his best friend," Kip reminded him. "He has never had a father or a mother or anyone to care for him. You have spent the last three standards building and reinforcing his ties to you. You have made yourself by far the most important person in his world."

"He has Ean. And you. And Tre," Jax objected.

"Any of whom he would abandon in a heartbeat if you needed him," Kip pointed out. "Is that it? Were you jealous of the boy? Should Rae only protect you? Only care about you?"

Jax stared at him with surprisingly vulnerable eyes. "I wasn't jealous," he managed.

There was something in that response that Kip did not understand. He would think about it later. "So why are you punishing him?" he repeated.

"I'm not!" Jax retorted.

Kip wasn't certain he had fulfilled step three but he decided to push on.

"Then why are you pushing him away?" Kip asked.

Jax was silent. His gaze was fixed on the wall behind Kip.

"I can think of some possibilities," Kip continued. "You could be terrified of him abandoning you so you have decided to abandon him first. Is that it?"

Jax flushed. "Rae would never abandon me," he admitted.

Kip took a deep breath. He really hoped that Noe was right. "Or you could be scared of what you feel for him. Pushing him away could be less scary than what you felt when he danced with you."

Jax did not know what to say. He had managed to get through conversations with Ean and even Tre. Nothing they had said had reached him. Now Kip, of all people, had put a crowbar into each crack in turn and levered him open.

Had what he had been feeling when he was dancing been so obvious that even Kip could see it?

"You have to think about Rae's feelings as well as your own," Kip told him. "He is miserable. He doesn't even want to eat."

Ean had told Jax that Rae was pining. Jax had refused to listen. Rae wasn't like some dog that pined for his master.

Kip was looking at him, waiting for some response. When he didn't get one he pushed again.

"You have to sort this out, Jax. It should have been over the day after he mucked up. You have made it a thousand times worse by torturing him for most of the last div. What are you going to do about it?"

"I have not been torturing him," Jax objected.

Kip just looked at him and Jax felt himself flush.

"What are you going to do?" Kip repeated.

"I'll think about it," Jax conceded.

Kip scowled at him. "Not good enough."

"I need to think," Jax objected.

"You need to act," Kip insisted.

Then Kip suddenly went quiet. All colour drained from his face. Jax was wondering what was wrong but then he heard it; the growl.

It was Rae: standing behind Kip; out of Jax's line of sight; growling.

Jax sprang off his bunk and hurried over. By the time he was halfway across the alcove he could see Rae. Rae's fur was bristling and he was snarling. "Stop it, Rae," Jax ordered. "Kip and I were arguing but it was only between friends."

The snarl vanished and the growl ceased. "He upset you," Rae objected.

Jax was overcome with shame. Rae was angry because Kip had upset him. He had been upsetting Rae for almost a div and Rae had just accepted it, getting more and more miserable.

He reached past Kip and grabbed Rae's hand.

Rae looked down at their clasped hands and then at Jax's face. The golden rays in his eyes bloomed, turning his eyes from brown to gold.

Jax realised they had not touched since they were in Abe's.

"Come here," he insisted, pulling him into the alcove and towards his bunk. "You too, Kip."

Kip hesitated. "You sure?"

Jax didn't know if the question was directed at him or Rae but he answered it anyway. "Yes."

They sat on Jax's bunk. Kip kept looking towards the rest of the crewroom as if he would like to escape.

Jax took a deep breath and began. "Rae, I am sorry. I'm not sure why I reacted so badly to what happened in Carruthers 2. That was what Kip and I were arguing about. Whatever, I shouldn't have been so mean to you."

"You weren't mean," Rae insisted.

"Yes I was. As Kip pointed out to me, I have been pushing you away. I am not sure why." It wasn't really a lie. Jax did not understand why he felt the way he did. "The three of us are friends. Kip was being your friend when he told me off. You shouldn't get cross with him for being your friend. You scared him."

Rae's whiskers drooped and his ears dipped. "Sorry, Kip."

"It's fine, Rae," Kip replied. "I scare easily, you know that. I did upset Jax. I wanted to make him see that he was hurting you." He put his right hand palm down on the mattress. "Friends," he proposed.

Jax put his hand on top. "Friends," he agreed. He guessed that was one of the things friends did; tell you truths you did not want to hear.

Rae's long-fingered hand came down on top. "Friends," he echoed.

Kip pulled his hand from under Jax's.

"I am going now." He looked at Jax. "Even if you can't explain to Rae why you acted the way you did, you could apologise for it and stop doing it." He stood up and walked away.

Jax watched him leave. Rae did not remove his hand. It was still over Jax's. Jax thought of pulling his hand away but he didn't. Rae might interpret it as more rejection.

"I am sorry, Rae," he whispered. "I'm not sure why I reacted so badly to what happened in Carruthers 2 but I should have listened to everyone telling me how unfair I was being."

"I left you," Rae replied as if that justified everything Jax had done.

"Only for a few minutes," Jax admitted. "I wasn't in any danger. They might have killed the boy or given him to a crew who would have done unspeakable things to him. I understand why you wanted to stop that." He took a deep breath. "It might not have been that. It might have been what happened at the club." He risked glancing at Rae's face.

Rae twitched his whiskers. "The attack?" he queried.

Jax almost said no. He almost admitted to what he had felt when they danced. Only he didn't because that would mean sorting out whether he wanted it or not.

"Yes," he lied.

Rae leaned closer. "I would never let anyone take you."

A delicious shiver passed over Jax's skin. His body knew what it wanted. It wanted Rae to protect him. "I know that," he replied. He looked into Rae's eyes. "Best friends."

"Best friends," Rae agreed.

❊ ❊ ❊

Ean knew he should have gone into the galley and shut the door. With the door closed he wouldn't be able to eavesdrop on Kip telling Jax off.

It had never occurred to him that Kip could or would do such a thing. Even more astonishing, he was being surprisingly effective.

It might work; Ean hoped so. Nothing else had.

Then he spotted Noe listening from the laundry. He kept nodding his head and, as Ean watched, he held his breath and mouthed, "Good."

Ean realised that Noe had told Kip how to get through to Jax.

Then Rae turned up and there was an awful moment when Ean feared Kip's intervention would make the situation worse rather than better. Luckily Jax stepped in and defused the situation, which was a relief.

Ean decided he had listened for too long already. He stepped forward into Noe's line of sight and beckoned him over. Noe came reluctantly but Ean was insistent. When he was close enough, Ean put a hand in the middle of his back, guided him into the galley and shut the door.

"Well done," he acknowledged.

It took a moment for Noe to realise that Ean knew. "It had to be Kip," he explained. "Jax sees Kip as his equal."

Ean shivered, thinking about what that implied about how Jax saw everyone else. "Let's hope it works. Tea?"

They sat together drinking tea and discussing their latest psychology assignment, which was due by the end of the div. A few minutes in, Ean declared that they were actually studying and set the timer.

After an initial spell when they had studied informally, they had decided to sign up for a course offered by The College for Self Improvement in Tarrasade. Ean had made the down payment and they had been sent an evaluation exercise that they both had done well enough to be allowed to study Psychology 1.

Studying with Noe was interesting. Ean was beginning to suspect that Noe wasn't just shrewd and manipulative; he was clever. Ean wasn't sure exactly how clever: more so than Ben or the captain; maybe more so than Jax or Tre; nowhere near Kip but that was to be expected.

They had decided to study in twenty minute bursts because the evaluation exercise had established that Noe could concentrate effectively for seventeen minutes while Ean could manage twenty-eight. The timer had reached eighteen minutes when the door slid open and Ben entered.

"Sorry," he acknowledged. "I didn't think this was one of your study times."

"It isn't," Ean replied. He smiled at Noe. "We started talking and it seemed right."

Ben turned to leave. "I'll leave you to it."

"No need," Noe insisted, standing up and putting their cups onto the tea tray. "We were finishing, weren't we, Ean?"

Ean checked the timer and deactivated it. "Yes, nineteen minutes is close enough. I'll log the time in our study report."

He looked across to where Noe was carrying the tray to the side counter. "Are you going to check on Kip?"

"If he hasn't escaped into his simulator," Noe confirmed.

Ben put the kettle on and waited for Noe to leave.

"Kip needs checking on?" he queried, sitting down at the table.

"He decided to have it out with Jax about Rae," Ean admitted. He almost mentioned Noe's role but decided against it; Noe would not like it.

"And that will work?" The scepticism was clear in Ben's voice.

"Kip is Jax's friend," Ean replied. "And Rae's."

Ben frowned slightly. "I thought it was Kip and Noe who were tight." He smiled. "Who would have thought Kip would end up being so social? He was such a loner when he joined."

"Kip has a good heart to go with his big brain," Ean pointed out. "Once he had settled, he was fine."

Ben leaned back. "One day I'll work out who Kip is and how a youngster of seventeen can get a Mulligan drive. Clever trick, using someone as prominent as Jax as camouflage for someone even more important."

Ean felt his cheeks reddening.

"It's fine, Ean," Ben assured him. "I don't expect you to tell me. It's all part of the adventure and having a spacehopper ship is beyond awesome. It's incredible that we can get from Carruthers to Ennui in under a div."

The Ennui system was where the Petunia Mae was working.

There had been a huge space battle there centuries ago and the locals had finally recovered enough to want the debris cleared.

"I still get a thrill every time we jump through an ungated hole," Ben admitted.

Ean preferred gates even though, as Tre had explained, any added risk associated with using an ungated hole was far outweighed by the chances of being attacked at a gate.

At least they only used mapped holes, so there was little chance of emerging too close to a star or other hazard.

Ean made the tea and brought the tray back to the table. As he did so he tried to spot Kip, Noe, Jax or Rae through the open doors. It looked like Jax and Rae were still in their alcove, which was hopeful, but there was no sign of Kip or Noe.

"Tell me about Medico Kem," Ben encouraged.

Ean tried to find the right words as he poured the tea. "He's one of those people who looks ordinary but isn't. He's been through terrible times and still managed to keep his integrity."

Ben nodded. "So he meets your standards, which I agree is saying something, but why do we want him rather than another medico on the crew?"

"He might not agree to join us," Ean admitted before turning his attention to Ben's question. "He's worked with hybrids, so he will not be put off by having to treat Rae. I don't think we could put him in a situation that was worse than one of the ones he has been in, so he's not going to be a weak point in a crisis." He considered again. "He isn't arrogant like many medicos are and he listens. I like him. We all do, even Jax." He paused and then said it. "After Loy, we are more comfortable with someone we already trust."

Ben seemed content to leave it there; Ean wasn't sure if he was convinced or not. Knowing Ben, he would want to meet Medico Kem before making up his mind.

"You haven't told me about Loy," Ben pointed out. "I had to hear it from Vic that you were Loy's price for betraying his crew."

Ean felt himself flush. "It wasn't like that. They had got to Loy before Tre contacted him. He needed credit to pay off debts and maintain his age retard."

"But he insisted on taking you with him," Ben pointed out.

Ean did not like thinking about it. He still struggled to understand how someone so pleasant on the surface could have such murky and twisted depths. "He wanted me because I was Tre's. It was as simple as that."

Ben smiled. "I doubt that." Then he changed the subject. "So what are you going to do about the boy in the pod? Surely you aren't going to turn him over to an orphanage without even giving him a chance. What was his name? I bet you managed to get it out of him before you podded him."

"It's Geo," Ean admitted. "He claims to be twelve. I was going to suggest unpodding him ten days out of Tarrasade and seeing if he's a runner. I don't know if the others will vote for it though."

Ben smiled. "It doesn't seem like our crew without a boy or two. Also, it would do Jax good to have younger ones about."

Tre had spent most of the day, like he had most of the last div, trying to work out what he was going to do about Jax and Rae. He had begun to think that the situation was irredeemable. Jax was doing a horribly accurate imitation of his father; when Oro had made a decision he never reversed it, no matter the consequences. As for Rae, it was likely that he was on the slippery slope that headed through depression towards suicidal despair.

Now, suddenly, they were best friends again.

He watched them throughout supper. Rae had seconds and then thirds, followed by two huge helpings of apple crumble. Jax was less tense and his skin was a better colour. When they were clearing and cleaning the galley, while the rest of the crew had coffee and conversation, Rae teased Jax and Jax bopped him on the head with a spoon.

Tre caught Ean's eye and raised his eyebrows. Ean mouthed, "Later."

Later was in the bathroom, which suited Tre just fine. Tre thoroughly enjoyed soaking in a hot tub with Ean. Sometimes they talked. Usually they fucked. Occasionally they just relaxed together.

This time Ean talked and he listened.

"Kip and Noe," he checked when Ean had finished.

"Yes," Ean confirmed. "Apparently Jax will listen to Kip when he won't to anyone else. Noe says it's because Jax sees him as his equal. Of course Kip wouldn't have had a clue what to say, just like he hasn't for the last div, but Noe told him how to approach it."

Tre was fascinated. "Tell me you eavesdropped. Please."

Ean flushed slightly. "I may have heard some of it."

"Thank the Lady for that," Tre confirmed. "What in Known Space did Kip say to make Jax change his mind?"

"I am not sure Jax had made a decision to reject Rae," Ean told him. He was silent for a moment; obviously thinking through what he had heard. "I think what it boiled down to was that Jax had just realised that he had feelings for Rae. He did not know how to deal with them so he used the incident with Geo as an excuse to push Rae away."

Tre had not expected that. His mind went back to the two of them dancing together in the first club they had visited and then at The Circle. Then there had been the way that Rae had dealt with the would-be abductors. Tre could see Jax finding that attractive.

At least it explained why he had been so ineffective at getting through to Jax; he had been on completely the wrong track.

"Does Rae know?" he asked.

Ean considered. "Rae was convinced that Jax was rejecting him because he had failed as his bodyguard."

"That was true before," Tre pointed out. "Did he overhear any of the conversation between Jax and Kip?"

"Some of it," Ean admitted. He thought a little longer. "I don't know if he heard that bit. He turned up when Kip and Jax started arguing, which was after that. Then I stopped listening."

No one eavesdropped on Rae because Rae would know. Tre decided that he would observe Jax and Rae together before deciding what to think. His initial reaction was that a sexual relationship with Rae, who was utterly loyal and completely committed to Jax's welfare, was much better than with a stranger.

Then something Ean had said sank in. "Geo?"

Ean turned pink. "I got his name before putting him in the pod. Ben thinks we should give him a trial as we head in for Tarrasade. He thinks that having cabin boys would be good for Jax."

That was true; in Tre's original plan Jax had joined as a cat and there had been cabin boys so he would not be the baby of the crew. "Boys?" Tre queried.

Somehow Ean managed to go even pinker. "Wes will turn twelve soon. Or we could recruit another boy from one of the orphanages."

It would make more sense to recruit Wes; they had been investing in his education. Tre, as the person paying Wes' fees, had received regular reports. Each one had included a handwritten note from Wes describing what he had been doing. Based on the two sources of evidence, he appeared to be shaping up well.

Tre reached out, pulled Ean towards him and laid back. Ean settled into his usual position against Tre's chest.

"I am glad Ben is back," Ean admitted.

"So am I," Tre acknowledged. "And after today I am considerably fonder of Noe. All we have to do is recruit a medico, find someone to fulfil the intermediary role so Carlos can stay with us and acquire a couple of cabin boys. Then the crew will be just about perfect."

Rae had started to feel better as soon as Jax had taken his hand and pulled him to their alcove. His anger towards Kip, which had appeared scarily quickly, had vanished and, when it did, he felt right inside rather than wrong.

Jax had apologised for being mean and then, after Kip had left, he had explained that he had been more upset by the attack at The Circle than Rae leaving him to rescue the boy. Rae wasn't sure that was true, Jax had not smelt right when he said it, but maybe Jax was trying to make Rae feel better about mucking up.

Rae decided it did not matter. What counted was that Jax was letting him close. They were back to being best friends.

Or were they? It had felt good earlier but now, as they changed into their sleep shorts before climbing into their bunks, it didn't feel right. When Jax put on a shirt to sleep in Rae was sure there was something wrong.

Jax had even picked out the softest of his sleep shirts; the one he only wore when he was feeling bad. Rae tried to think it through and kept coming back to the lie Jax had told; when he had said it had been the attack that had upset him.

Should he leave it? Rae remembered how he had felt since Carruthers. No, he couldn't risk going back to that. They had to clear it up.

"You're sleeping in that shirt," he pointed out.

Jax looked down and stroked the front of the shirt, as if seeing it for the first time. "So?"

"You only do that when you are unhappy," Rae told him.

Jax sat down on his bunk. Rae stood a few paces away and waited. He had a squirmy feeling deep inside. This could turn out well or badly.

"I liked dancing with you," Jax admitted.

Rae was overcome with relief. That was it? He grinned. "It was fun." He thought back. "I wasn't sure if you liked it." He watched the colour changes in Jax's skin, listened to his breathing and checked the way his scent was changing.

What about the dancing had worried him so much?

"Do you think we touch too much?" Jax asked.

"No," Rae responded immediately. He did not have to even think about it. He only touched Jax when either Jax wanted to be touched or he wanted to touch Jax and Jax did not mind. He crouched down at Jax's feet and looked up into his eyes. "I will never touch you when you don't want me to."

Jax gave a little sigh that ended in a weak laugh. "I know you won't. That's part of the problem."

Jax's reply made no sense to Rae. It had to be some weird, purebred thing. Or maybe it was a weird, Jax thing.

"Maybe we should cut out the touching," Jax proposed.

Rae didn't like the sound of that one little bit. "There are times when I need to touch or to be touched. Do you want me to go to someone else?"

"No!" Jax retorted.

Rae realised he was onto something. "Do you want to touch someone other than me?"

Jax looked away. "No," he admitted.

"Do you want to be touched by anyone other than me?" Rae asked softly.

Jax looked at him and their eyes locked. "No."

"I promise…" Rae paused, reaching for the right words. "I promise never to touch you when you don't want to be touched. I promise to stop touching you whenever you say."

Jax uttered a tiny sound that made Rae want to touch him very badly. He put out a hand but stopped before reaching Jax's face.

Sure enough Jax leaned in to the touch.

Rae cradled Jax's chin in his palm and rubbed the pad of his thumb across Jax's cheek. He avoided Jax's lips, even though he yearned to feel their soft fullness.

Jax wasn't ready for that. Rae could and would wait. Given the way his breathing was catching, Jax liked being touched very much indeed. Maybe the wait would not be so long.

And if it was, even if Jax decided that best friends didn't do stuff like that, Rae would live with that decision.

He would do anything to avoid being pushed away.

www.ingramcontent.com/pod-product-compliance
Lightning Source LLC
Chambersburg PA
CBHW030535020726
47494CB00005B/1377